C000120270

Born in Scotland, made **MISTRY's** life. Over thi from a small village in W(her teaching degree. Once here, Liz fell in love with three things: curries, the rich cultural diversity of the city… and her Indian husband (not necessarily in this order). Now thirty years, three children, Scumpy, the cat, and a huge extended family later, Liz uses her experiences of living and working in the inner city to flavour her writing. Her gritty crime fiction police procedural novels set in Bradford embrace the city she describes as 'Warm, Rich and Fearless', whilst exploring the darkness that lurks beneath.

Having struggled with severe clinical depression and anxiety for many years, Liz often includes mental health themes in her writing. She credits the MA in Creative Writing she took at Leeds Trinity University with helping her find a way of using her writing to navigate her ongoing mental health struggles. Liz's PhD research contributes significantly to debates concerning issues of inclusion and diversity of representation within the most socially engaged genre of contemporary crime fiction Being a debut novelist in her fifties was something Liz had only dreamed of and she counts herself lucky, whilst pinching herself regularly to make sure it's all real.

You can contact Liz

Website: https://www.lizmistry.com/

FB: @LizMistryBooks

Twitter: @LizMistryAuthor

Unjust Bias

LIZ MISTRY

Being different could cost you your life.

DI Gus McGuire Book 8

Published by

Murder Books Publications

PUBLICATIONS

Copyright © Liz Mistry

Liz Mistry has asserted her right under the Copyright Designs
and Patents Act 1988 to be identified as the author of this
work.

This book is a work of fiction and any resemblance to actual
person living or dead, is purely co-incidental.

A CIP Catalogue Record for this book is available from the
British Library

Apart from any use permitted under UK copyright law, this
publication may only be reproduced, stored or transmitted, in
any form, or by any means, with prior permission in writing
of the publisher or, in the case of reprographic production, in
accordance with the terms of licences issued by the
Copyright Licensing Agency

PRINT ISBN: 978-1-8381821-1-3

DEDICATION

FOR MY FAMILY WHO ALWAYS OFFER
UNCONDITIONAL LOVE, SUPPORT AND
ENCOURAGEMENT
AND
IN SUPPORT OF THE LGBTQ+ COMMUNITY

PROLOGUE

Heart hammering, she wandered round the living space, her eyes flitting everywhere, scrutinising each item on display, logging each photograph. Iris paused at the doorway of her son's room, breathing in his essence as her gaze rested on his favourite teddy. The one he pretended, at 11, to be too old for, but still kept on his pillow and cuddled every night. His trainers, the new ones she'd bought for his birthday last week, neatly placed on the floor by his desk. The tablet his dad had given him and that had made his cheeks glow as he worked out how to use it, lay off-centre before his laptop. With a sigh, she allowed her fingers to trail over the tabletop as she soaked up every photo on his windowsill, every Post-it on his cork board before resting on his iPhone.

She moved to the baby's room – all pink and fluffy, filled with teddies and smelling of baby lotion. Her heart stuttered as she closed the wardrobe, hefted the changing bag onto her shoulder, and fastened the carrier across her chest, her hand floating over the red fuzz on her baby's head.

She paused by the door, cradling the baby in its sling, and took a last look around. Had she ever been happy here? She tried to grasp the fleeting memories of laughter and joy that circled the external edges of her memory and then gave up. Would she miss this flat? It was everything she'd wanted; modern, filled with mod

1

cons — luxurious by anyone's standards – yet she wouldn't miss it. Not one bit. Not the pain. Not the judgement. Not the suffering and mental torture. None of that.

With a critical eye, she scrutinised the room, looking for mistakes, telltale signs that would give her intentions away. She could see none. Still, that knowledge didn't ease the hawk-like claws that gripped her stomach. The sound of the elevator arriving stirred her and as the doors swished open, revealing her 'minder', she schooled her face into its usual smile. Not too friendly, but not remote enough to cause comment. 'Almost ready, Gabe. Lock up for me, will you?'

Gabe, the strong silent type, in his fifties, raked his eyes over her following instruction number one as issued by her husband – 'make sure she's not dressed like a slut'. As she walked into the lift and waited for him to enter and press the button for the ground floor, she pretended not to notice. Her jeans, T-shirt, and jacket did not differ from those she wore any other day, so would provoke no warning signals. She prepared for Gabe to follow instruction number two, which would occur as soon as the elevator doors closed. Without him asking, she looked straight ahead, and she spread her arms out wide to her sides, her fingers almost skimming each side of the lift's walls and moved her legs akimbo. She'd long since become used to this indignity, and so had Gabe. His face an inscrutable mask, Gabe knelt and skimmed his shovel sized palms up her calves and thighs, progressing to her body and over each arm. The faint smell of his Invictus aftershave tickled her nostrils, but she didn't react, for they were both well aware they were on camera. Their every move recorded so her husband could check at a whim that neither she nor Gabe had behaved inappropriately.

Gabe's voice, ruggedly familiar, filled the small space. 'Need to check the baby carrier too, Mrs M.'

Iris swallowed, but kept her arms stretched, allowing him access to the baby sling. This violation hurt her more than the ones inflicted on her personally. It was like her baby was being invaded by his prying hands. As if sensing her discomfort, Gabe's fingers hesitated as he skimmed the inner fabric of the carrier. But neither of them betrayed this by word or deed. It was more than Gabe's job was worth, and Iris knew better than to resist.

Today, though, she had another reason to worry, for inside the nappy, Iris had concealed a plastic bag containing all the money she'd siphoned off over the past few months. Everything hinged on it not being found. Her life and that of her children depended on this. For if her carefully orchestrated plan failed, there would be no other chance for her. It had to work.

As the lift came to rest on the ground floor, Gabe turned and positioned himself next to her, hands linked in front of his crotch – a bodyguard rather than a prison guard to any casual observers. Iris breathed easier but schooled her face to reflect nothing except the cool disinterest she'd learnt was the only acceptable expression by her husband's standards.

Escorted to the limo, Iris transferred her daughter into the car seat, accepted the mobile phone Gabe handed her, and slipped it into her pocket without checking it. She never had notifications. Its only purpose was to call Gabe when she was ready to be collected – and for her husband to track her whereabouts.

Gabe's eyes met hers through the rear-view mirror. 'School play, is it, Mrs M?'

Aware that, even here in the limo, he monitored her actions, her every expression, every response, Iris allowed her lips to flick into a polite smile. 'Yes. Jacob's singing. Afterwards, there's a parent/teacher coffee afternoon. I'll be done in two hours.

Gabe nodded. He knew all this already. Her husband had already logged it into Gabe's work list and had confirmed it with the school. This was her only window of opportunity, and Iris was determined to use it.

When they pulled up in the car park, the security gates swished closed behind them. Gabe assisted her out of the car and helped her reposition the baby carrier around her. Frowning, he looked at the changing bag and Iris handed it over. He shuffled his hands through it before returning it to her shoulder.

Iris, griping pains gnawing at her insides, walked up the steps to the entrance. Once inside, she'd be able to breathe easier. As she continued, she expected Gabe to call her back, or her phone to ring and her husband demand that she return home.

Please let me get inside. Please let me get inside.

The door opened and Iris entered, almost collapsing in relief as they too swished closed behind her.

'Mum?'

Jacob was there right in front of her, hopping from foot to foot. This was the trickiest part where she relied on her 11-year-old son to have set everything up.

'Come on.' He gripped her hand and dragged her through corridors, smiling at teachers and friends as they moved. He stopped near the entrance to the hall and, lowering his voice to a whisper, said, 'Phone.'

Iris took her mobile from her pocket and stuffed it into the depths of the bin. Their eyes met and Jacob, looking so much older than his age, gripped her hand once more and pulled her along. 'Amar's going to cover for me. He'll put on my costume. Nobody will notice.'

Iris, glancing behind her, half expecting Gabe to be towering over her, nodded and began to jog in order to keep up with her son. 'Ms Turner left the exit unlocked and her boyfriend's car's three streets over. We can do this, Mum.'

Wishing she was as sure of their success as her child, Iris followed him and when he pushed open a fire exit at the other side of the building and it made no noise, she began to hope they could escape. The car was where Jacob's teacher had promised it would be, with the key stuck under the rear bumper and a package of money and burner phones on the front seat. It had been years since she'd driven, but she couldn't think about that. Not now.

Following her contact's directions to keep two degrees of separation from each of her contacts, Iris drove out of Newcastle and put distance between her and her abusive husband. When they reached Manchester, she phoned the number her contact at the Protected Person's Service had given her. Two hours later, he arrived. She handed him the detailed evidence about her husband's criminal activities that she had hidden alongside her money in the baby's nappy, and he handed her their new identifications. Iris considered it a fair exchange. After issuing strict instructions about contacting no one from her old life, he transported her and her small family to Bradford with unfamiliar names and a different identity. This would be the start of their new lives together.

PART ONE

SIX YEARS LATER

OCTOBER

CHAPTER 1

Angel

I sidle in and take my usual seat at the back of Manningham All Saints Church. I'm glad to be out of the October wind and rain. Nobody pays me any attention as I settle in, allowing the incense and soft lull of prayer to wash over me like a familiar lover. I ease myself forward on the pew, so my back doesn't rest against the wooden frame. My shirt sticks to the still oozing welts, and I roll my shoulders in a vain attempt to pull the fabric away from my wounds. Good job it's too damn cold to take off my coat. I smile, imagining their faces if they saw the bloody strips down the back of my otherwise pristine shirt. But that's my secret to keep. My secret shared only with my God.

The prayers end and an expectant hush descends over the congregants as they await the sermon. I flinch as the female minister rises from her place in the pulpit. It goes against the grain to see a woman preacher offering solace and guidance anyway, but as if to flaunt her liberal beliefs, this particular one celebrates her son's presence with his boyfriend in the front pew. It is this aberration that sticks in my craw. This trend towards 'wokeness' that inflames my ire. Instead of studying her as she spouts forth her unholy lesson, I concentrate on the congregation. Over the weeks since I joined this church, I've identified the congregants who are uneasy with her presence as their spiritual leader. Those who look askance when she speaks. Those who have voiced their objections to the same sex weddings she prioritises over other legitimate ones. She is not universally loved, and that knowledge keeps me coming back, for I know I can find likeminded people within these worshippers. People who will help me achieve my aims to re-instil the sanctity of God's holy wishes into those sinners who struggle with depraved thoughts and deeds.

My gaze drifts to the older couple sitting one pew down and to the right. They sit apart from the others – alone and lonely. I know all their secrets, for in the past weeks I have made it my business to find out everything about them. With a smile, I note the foot and a half distance between them. I watch as Claude slides closer and attempts to take her hand. I almost snort my appreciation when *she* responds by snatching it away and extending the chasm between them. They will be my priority.

It's easy to discover who will be next, for it's there, ever-present in his slumped shoulders, the permanent pained expression on his face, and the way his body angles away from his family. This is an emasculated man. One whose wife holds his balls in a vice and I suspect that she's the reason he spends more time in the Cock and Bottle than he does at home. My shoulders tense in sympathy with him. He's being cuckolded, but not by another man.

My final target is already in the bag. I was reluctant to recruit him at first because underneath his pleasant demeanour runs a core of unbridled darkness – a darkness that I will need to work hard to keep under control. As the sermon ends, I realise I haven't absorbed a single word of her toxic smiling affability and it doesn't bother me at all, for my aim to subvert and realign the moral compass of this parish is taking fruit. Soon, my pact with God will redeem those suffering from clouded thoughts and evil deeds. Soon, Pure Life will be born, and our beliefs brought into practice.

JANUARY

CHAPTER 2

Detective Inspector Gus McGuire stood behind the glass window of the observation room and watched his father, Dr Fergus McGuire, conduct the post-mortem on the 17-year-old rough sleeper. The sterile environment of his present resting place, a stark contrast to where they found him just a few hours earlier.

Two 13-year-old kids trying to sneak a fly ciggie before heading down to Bradford Grammar had discovered the boy, now identified as Zac Ibrahim and, judging by their pallor and tear-streaked cheeks, neither of them would do that again anytime soon. Zac had been wedged behind some skips owned by shops on Oak Lane in Manningham at some point overnight. With it being so early, the greengrocers and the halal supermarket responsible for the skips hadn't yet had cause to visit them, having discarded their rubbish before closing up the previous evening.

The stench of rotting vegetation, with an underlying tang of ammonia, had greeted Gus when the CSIs cleared him to view the body in situ. His initial thoughts had been that the boy was much younger, but a driving licence ID gave Zac's correct age. He lay flat on his back, eyes closed, and hands crossed over his stomach. He could almost have been sleeping if it wasn't for the remains of the preceding night's drizzle on soaking clothes and the blueish tinge to his lips. He was fully clothed, although each garment was mucky and tattered

– not the designer wear Gus often saw on youngsters these days. Hissing Sid, the crime scene manager, had turned the boy's wrists so Gus could see the underside. Faded scars spoke of a history of self-harm and possible suicide attempts, while more recent angry marks indicated the use of restraints of some description. It had been one of the local special police constables who'd added the information that Zac was homeless and that, although he was mostly in Bradford city centre, he was often to be seen in this area, trying to reconnect with his family and friends.

Zac looked peaceful in death – in direct contrast to the marks on his arms which told of a tortured life. He'd been a kid – so defenceless, his death so unnecessary and anger barrelled through Gus, stunning him with its unexpected ferocity. Zac had been denied the chance to grow up, to make something of himself, to enjoy life. Gus had witnessed scenes like this before, so why was this one different?

It had been a while since Gus attended a post-mortem and, as the familiar nauseating unease settled in his stomach and the strange, yet distinctive dizziness threatened, he remembered why he had, in recent times, delegated this responsibility to his DC, Talvinder 'Taffy' Bhandir. Taffy had been all too keen to attend PMs. The youthful officer found them fascinating and always came back with detailed reports. However, something about the tragedy of this young boy's death had grabbed Gus by the throat.

Even after years as a major crime detective, investigating more murders than he could count, it affected Gus when the victim was young and he'd investigated too many teen deaths, and each one took a bit more of his soul. That Zac Ibrahim was a known rough sleeper made it much more poignant. His parents weren't any more interested in their son now he was dead, than they had been when he was alive and Gus hated their pious self-righteous excuses that revolved around the fact that the youngster was gay and therefore a sinner and, by extension, in their minds, deserved to die.

So, Gus had come to the PM. He couldn't let Zac go through this on his own and although there was no pathologist more respectful than his own dad, a nagging tattoo hammered in his head telling him he had to attend. He was aware that this was illogical. Whether it was he or Taffy who attended the PM, Zac Ibrahim wouldn't be alone. When he'd tried to explain his compulsion to his lodger, Detective Sergeant Alice Cooper, she'd teased him and told him he was 'going soft' because of his newfound fatherhood. Perhaps she was right. Finding out about his own three-year-old son had changed him, made him more introspective, and had altered the projection he'd had for his future. A series of disastrous relationships had left him feeling that he would saunter into middle age alone and unencumbered. Now, finding out about Billy, he no longer considered the aging process so clear cut. For the rest of his thirties and into his forties, he would focus on Billy's needs. He smiled, because that made him happy. Despite the physical distance between him and his son, Gus was doing all he could to make up for the years he'd missed from Billy's life.

Glad that his dad seemed to be done with the drilling and squishy part of the PM, Gus breathed easier. In spite of the sterile environment and the fact that none of the PM smells could infiltrate the viewing room, Gus still imagined they were there.

Dr McGuire glanced up at him and Gus registered the concern in his father's eyes, despite the mask that covered his lower face.

'You all right there, Angus?'

'Yeah, fine, Dad. You done?'

'Aye, give me ten minutes, and I'll talk you through it.'

After a final glance at Zac, Gus left the cool suite with relief and wandered along to his dad's office. This was a familiar room to Gus, but he hadn't visited it for a while — not since Taffy took over PM duty. With a smile, he studied the various photos his dad had on his desk. There was one of Gus and Katie, his sister, when they were kids at a petting zoo. One of his parents gazing adoringly into each other's eyes as if they were still in the throes of first love. Gus envied them that. They were such a devoted couple and despite the grey in their hair and the wrinkles on their skin, their eyes shone with love and vitality. Moving on, there was a photo of Gus and Billy next to one of Katie and her partner, Gus's ex-wife, Gaby, with their newborn baby. Gus's eyes lingered on that one for a second. Katie had been poorly and was recovering from cancer and it pleased him to see her pixie haircut was growing in well after all her treatments. Katie's smiling face as she looked at her baby brought a pang of guilt. They'd asked Gus to be their sperm donor and Gus had refused. There was still an atmosphere between them when they met, but Gus, in his less emotional moments, was convinced he'd made the sensible decision. Who in their right minds could expect him to donate sperm for his ex, who was now married to his sister?

The door opened and his dad, wheezing, lumbered in and shuffled round to fall into the seat behind his desk.

'Surprised to see you at the PM, Angus. Taffy not free today?'

Gus shrugged and lowered himself into the seat opposite. There was no point in trying to bluff his dad, for he'd see straight through any subterfuge, so Gus went with the truth. 'Couldn't stand the thought of not being here. Felt I owed it to the boy with him being all alone and all that.'

Fergus nodded. 'Aye. I understand that. Being a da' changes things, doesn't it? Took me a while tae get used to doing PMs on kids after we had our own. Still gets to me sometimes.'

He cast his gaze over the family photos adorning his desk and his smile widened. 'Well, we'll dae right by Zac, Angus. You an' me, we'll dae right by the laddie.'

He leant forward, resting his enormous arms on the desk and exhaling. 'So, I'll get on wi' the basics and you can get my report later on, OK?'

When Gus nodded, he got straight to the point.

'Someone manually strangled the victim. I say manually, because there were faint markings indicating thumb prints across the front of his neck and fingerprints towards the back. And petechiae around the constriction site, as well as ecchymosis and swelling on his eyelids. His hyoid bone was broken.' As Fergus shook his head, his frown deepening over his brow, Gus prepared himself for worse to come.

'So, moving onto his general condition. The poor laddie was malnourished – emaciated, I'd say, but no visual evidence of drug use – track marks, dental indications, or the like. Of course, the tox labs aren't in yet, so that's just an impression that the results will confirm or disprove.' The doc paused, his fingers drumming on the desk as if he was playing an instrument, and Gus waited for his dad's insights.

Shaking his huge, tumshie heid, Dr McGuire exhaled. 'There's an abundance of evidence of – to quote the bard – *Man's inhumanity to man.*'

His smile when he glanced at his son was self-conscious, as if he'd been caught out in an indulgence. Gus smiled back, uncertain if that was an apt response. Over the past few months, his dad had become more and more fascinated with Rabbie Burns, both his works and his life. An atheist, Dr McGuire had no time for organised religion, and yet, these frequent Burn's quotes seemed like a man reflecting on his life. A worm of anxiety wriggled across Gus's neck, making the hairs stand up. But then his dad was talking again, and the moment passed.

'Over the past few months, poor Zac has been subjected to numerous assaults, both sexual and physical. This is evidenced by the presence of bruises, at different stages of healing, covering his torso, legs, and arms, and anal lesions – possibly indicating non-consensual sex – and a recently broken rib. My report details each of them. However, none of these are recent and therefore not a contributing factor to his death. Marks around his wrists and ankles show he was restrained prior to death – this could have been some sort of sex game gone wrong – I'll leave you to work that one out. I suggest you look for proper metal shackles rather than fabric or cable ties – the lab may offer more information on that. Time of death? Hmm, I'd say two days before he was found, and this is interesting.' He scraped his fingers through his greying stubble. 'Lividity indicates they moved the body post-mortem. From the patterning on his buttocks, lower arms, and soles of his feet, he was sitting upright – perhaps on a chair – much like you are now, Angus, for at least a couple of hours before being moved. I've sent various samples off to be tested, but I'm thinking a wooden chair – judging by the splinters under his fingernails. However, of course, he could have gathered the splinters elsewhere. Questions?'

'Defence wounds?'

'Hmm.' Dr McGuire tilted his head to one side. 'I couldn't identify any defence wounds. The only marks round the neck came from fingers showing manual strangulation. Those, by the way, are smooth – so no chance of IDing the killer through fingerprints. So, in summary, no signs of a struggle or sign of a fight. Of course, the killer could be responsible for the previous injuries. It's your job to work out all the finer details. You'll have to wait for the results.'

Keen to get back to the incident room, Gus stood. 'Thanks, Dad, appreciate this.'

He hesitated a moment and then continued. 'When does the new pathologist arrive?'

His dad grinned and hefted himself to his feet, moved round the desk, and slapped his massive arm around his son's shoulders. Gus loved the weight of it on him. It reminded him of many childhood memories with his dad wrapping his huge arms round Gus and hugging him so tightly he thought he might never breathe again. This proximity brought with it the familiar smell of this old man's pipe tobacco and tweedy perfume. Hearing the wheeze in his dad's chest and noticing how, despite his girth, he seemed frailer, Gus was glad he'd at last agreed to go part time.

'Aw, she's due in a couple of weeks, but laddie, don't expect her to be as up front with her suspicions as me. Some of these new pathologists want their T's crossed and I's dotted before they commit to having a shite, never mind sharing provisional information with the police.'

Gus had worked with other pathologists and knew his dad's warning was fair. Still, he'd rather have a jobsworth pathologist than a dead dad, so he was OK with that. 'See you for lunch on Sunday, Dad. Billy's coming, so best make sure you have ice cream in – he's addicted to the stuff.'

His dad tightened his hug and then saluted as Gus opened the door. 'Already on that. Your mum will spoil him, no doubt.'

Gus hesitated and turned back. 'She's not baking, is she?'

Shit, the last thing he needed was his mum poisoning her grandson with some well-meaning inedible 'delicacy'. Fergus winked.

'Nope. I've convinced her that ice cream will be enough. Instead, she's knitting him a cardigan.'

'Whaaat?' In all his life, Gus had never seen his mother knit.

His dad shrugged, and his grin widened. 'New hobby. I think her less than elegant knitting is the lesser of the two evils, don't you?'

Gus laughed and waved. 'Thanks for that, Dad. I owe you one.'

He was almost out the door when he paused. 'Hey, Dad. It could be worse, you know. She could've taken up life drawing again.'

Fergus McGuire snorted. 'Aw no! There's no way I could stomach any more of that. I think I'll encourage the knitting.'

Despite the despondency he carried with him on entering the mortuary, Gus left with a smile on his lips.

CHAPTER 3

'I'll not tell you again – get away from my parents. This is police harassment.' From his florid face to his pugnacious, feet-widened stance and clenched fists, Nasir Ibrahim looked set to pop a blood vessel.

To diffuse the tension, Gus splayed his hands towards the man in a placating gesture. 'We're only here to ask you and your parents a few questions about your brother. You want to find his killer, don't you?'

However sincere Gus's intentions had been, they were way off the mark, as his words elicited a surge of toxic rage. 'How dare you call that abomination my brother? He was scum. You hear me? Scum and he's where he deserves to be – in a gutter – dead because that's where he lived his life.'

Behind Nasir, his parents stood on the steps of their terraced house. Mrs Ibrahim cowered beside her husband, tears streaming down her face as she clutched her scarf round her head. Mr Ibrahim, stony faced, glared at Gus, but did nothing to contradict his elder son's words. What a damn farce this was. With their teenage son murdered and dumped behind a skip, not a stone's throw from their home, Gus had expected more grief than anger from the boy's family. Councillor Nasir Ibrahim's words had floored Gus. How could anyone on hearing of their sibling's death behave so outrageously? How could he subject his parents to this despicable hatred? Nasir Ibrahim, as well as being a Conservative councillor for the area, was also a solicitor with his business based on Oak Lane. He knew the law and, despite his irrational outburst indicating to the contrary, the man was aware Gus was within his rights as an officer of the law to interview the Ibrahims.

Although reluctant to go in heavy-handed, especially when grieving parents were involved, Gus could see no alternative. Whatever anger was fuelling Nasir's rage didn't look like it was about to abate soon. 'Look, Mr Ibrahim. This is a murder investigation. If you don't allow me to interview yourself and your parents, we'll have to take it down to the station.'

'Oh, adding police brutality to your repertoire now, are you? I'll have you—'

'Oh, for god's sake shut up, you stupid, insensitive, trumped-up little excuse for a solicitor and let us do our damn jobs.' DS Alice Cooper had stepped forward and now stood nose to nose with Nasir, hands on hips and dark eyes flashing.

For a second, her outburst silenced even the gathering crowd of neighbours. Gus swallowed and then opened his mouth to try to de-escalate the situation, but no words sprung to mind. Thankfully, Mr Ibrahim senior stepped into the breach.

'Let's get it over with.' He gestured for Gus to follow him indoors and then sent a warning glance to his son, who had the grace to bow his head and remain quiet.

Under his breath, Gus said, 'God's sake, Al, what was that?'

She shrugged and grinned. 'Worked didn't it?'

Gus rolled his eyes. He couldn't argue with her, for it had worked – just not quite how he'd hoped the start of his interview with bereaved parents would go.

In silence, they trooped after Mr Ibrahim senior up the steps, along the hallway, and into a stuffy living room which smelt of incense and spicy tea. Mr Ibrahim positioned himself before a gas fire, hands behind his back, and glared at Gus. Mrs Ibrahim, still sobbing, perched on the edge of an old-fashioned sofa and Nasir Ibrahim flanked his dad. Neither man offered Mrs Ibrahim so much as a supportive glance, so Alice, perching next to her, smiled. The older woman glanced at her husband, her eyes wide and panicked, before pulling away from Alice and standing up. Without another word, she took up position by her husband's side. The message was loud and clear. This family was offering a united front against the police. The question was, why? Was it only because they disapproved of their younger son's lifestyle or something more than that?

With the need for platitudes redundant after the earlier encounter, Gus dived straight into the questions. 'When did you last see Zac?'

'Months ago.' Mr Ibrahim refused to look at Gus and instead focussed on something over his left shoulder.

Annoyed that he could appear so dispassionate when they were here to investigate his son's murder, Gus stood so the older man was forced to meet his gaze. The resultant flash of anger in the older man's eyes and the flare of nostrils made Gus's pleasant smile widen. Though, when he spoke, there was nothing but politeness in his tone. 'Could you be more specific than that?'

The older man crossed his arms across his chest and continued to match Gus's gaze. 'No.'

This was going nowhere. The Ibrahim's were uncooperative and Gus suspected nothing would change that, so he turned to Mrs Ibrahim. 'When did you last see or hear from Zac?'

Her eyes flicked to her husband, but he continued to stare ahead. 'Same time as my husband. Months ago.'

Gus turned to Nasir Ibrahim, whose florid colour had abated from beetroot to tomato red. 'And you, Mr Ibrahim?'

Nasir's mouth moved, as if considering whether to reply. At last, he sighed. 'To speak to months ago, but I saw him at Manningham All Saints Church where I do my surgeries. He'd wangled his way onto some outreach programme.'

'Did you speak with your brother?' Alice asked from her seat on the couch.

Refusing to look at Alice, Nasir shook his head, his lips curved in a snarl. 'He's no longer my brother, and no, I didn't speak to him. We all cut him from our lives when he chose to get into bed with the devil.'

The sanctimonious way the other man raised his chin made Gus's skin crawl. He'd come across people like the Ibrahims before and it was as if he sold a bit of his soul every time he swallowed down his disgust at their attitude. Still, it wasn't up to him to police their attitudes. It was his job to catch a killer.

'Can you account for your whereabouts from Monday afternoon through till this morning at around 7 a.m.?'

'Now you're accusing my parents of having something to do with his death?' Nasir's colour escalated from tomato to beetroot once more and his body swelled with full-on aggression.

Gus smirked. 'I thought you were a lawyer, Mr Ibrahim? You must be aware of the difference between a question and an accusation. But to be clear – I'm making no accusations. On the contrary, I'm offering you and your parents an opportunity to exclude yourselves from our list of suspects by providing alibis. Standard police procedure, as you well know.'

A half hour later, the Ibrahim family's alibis noted, Gus and Alice inhaled the sharp winter air as if cleansing themselves of the toxicity emanating from the Ibrahim home.

'A-holes – the lot of them. Bloody a-holes.'

Gus could only agree with Alice. The Ibrahim family were indeed a-holes. 'Yes, but if these alibis pan out, they're not murderers. Let's go to this church Nasir mentioned.'

CHAPTER 4

When Gus had phoned the vicar from Manningham All Saints' Church – a Reverend Anne Summerscale – she'd offered to round up everyone who had been involved with Zac as part of the outreach programme. So, he and Alice, holding steaming coffee mugs, sat in a circle with a huddle of parishioners. The enthusiastic vicar had informed them that these people had known Zac 'to one degree or another'.

Under cover of enjoying his drink and the home-baked cookie that accompanied it, Gus observed them. The vicar's energy wasn't replicated by those sitting in the circle and judging by the studious way they avoided meeting Gus's eye, neither was her desire to 'help catch whoever did this atrocious thing to Zac'. Even her husband, Graham, seemed reluctant to be drawn into this little group activity. Despite all the chairs being near equidistant from each other, somehow, the vicar's husband had manoeuvred himself away from the others. His entire body language shouted, 'pretend I'm not here' and Gus sympathised with him. While Anne was friendly enough, she was also somewhat overpowering and how she shuffled the flock of people together, overriding their objections and concerns, spoke of a woman to whom obstacles existed to be swept aside. According to his notes, Graham had been Zac's point of contact for the homeless outreach project. It was Graham who arranged a timetable of support for Zac which included allocating personal hygiene time, life skills lessons – like computer skills and setting up a bank account using the programme's address so he could claim benefits.

An older couple – Gus glanced at his notebook: Ada and Claude Douglas – sat side on to each other, their rigid backs and equally rigid smiles giving off vibes of an unresolved marital argument interrupted by this impromptu meeting – one they were desperate to get back to, but only in the privacy of their own home. Ada and Claude's contact with Zac had been minimal, involving serving food to him and other homeless people on the three days in which the programme offered free meals to rough sleepers. While appreciative of the minister's intentions, by the end of the hour-long session, Gus had added names to his list but felt that somehow, the most likely suspects seemed to be either Zac's family or perhaps someone he'd come across while sleeping rough.

Afterwards, they'd chatted with the small group of Zac's acquaintances who hung out at the Forster Square arches. However, no matter who they spoke to, they drew a blank and were struggling to find witnesses, much less potential suspects. Nobody had a clue how Zac had ended up murdered and bundled behind a skip in Manningham.

With an uneasy pressure in his gut, Gus and Alice returned to Lilycroft Police Station, the building the local community referred to, not so affectionately as, The Fort. Only to be met with more negatives – no CCTV footage of Zac with anyone who hadn't already provided an alibi, no suspects raising their ugly heads, no tips from anonymous sources, no motives that could be substantiated. Gus slumped into his chair and looked at the murder board, the weight in his gut expanding as he considered the sparse information surrounding the image of Zac Ibrahim in death. Gus liked to juxtapose the photo of the victim with one of them alive and doing something they enjoyed. It forced the team to consider them as vibrant living beings and showed more effectively just what their killer had taken from them. Here, there was no corresponding snap of a smiling Zac – his parents refused to provide one and their uncaring attitude had sent rockets of molten anger up Gus's spine. The bastards had cancelled their son – but no matter what they might do, Gus was determined that he would not allow Zac Ibrahim to be cancelled.

CHAPTER 5

Angel

I savour the rivulets of sweat pouring down my torso and seeping into each fresh wound, intensifying the pain and making me writhe in blissful rapture. It is this that brings me closer to my God. It's almost an out-of-body experience. Like I'm on another plane – a higher plane. Can my frame survive any more? In my reflection, as I stand between my two mirrors, I watch, fascinated, as my blood and perspiration mingle and undulate in pink streams over my scarred back. With one decisive effort, I inhale deep into my lungs and then release a bellow as I lift my whip one more time and deliver a final lash across my shoulders.

Did I pass out? I'm not sure, but when I return to normality, breathing fast and hard, but more in control, I'm on my bed, traces of ejaculate sticking my now flaccid penis to the duvet – another one of my bodily fluids to add to the potent mix soaking into the fabric. I remain where I am, absorbing the throbs that still wrack over my skin. The events of the past couple of days were unexpected. A learning curve to be improved upon. We can't afford to have any more dead bodies. That's never been my aim. Redemption and realignment are the goal. But Zac was a liability – of course that wasn't his fault. Yes, he was more difficult to realign than expected, but we could have persevered with the intensive therapy.

What we hadn't accounted for was his obstinacy, and that was his downfall.

As I roll onto my back, my penis peels itself away from the sheet and lies subdued atop my testicles, my mind still on the sinner. Zac was no loss – even his family disliked his life choices – and his links to us are tenuous, so I'm not concerned with the police presence. Nobody knows about Pure Life because we operate on a need-to-know basis. But, today, in the aftermath of my self-flagellation – my offering to God – I can admit it gave me a thrill almost as acute as that experienced earlier. However, it is my duty to the others, to the group, to withstand my own demons and lead by example. I will not allow the death of a worthless sinner to lie on my conscience, however, I will learn from this slight error of judgement.

PART TWO

APRIL

TUESDAY

CHAPTER 6

What a fuck of a day – too many ass wipes acting like he owed them something. Now, Carl Morris was looking forward to vegging out and scrolling the internet with a glass of beer and a ready meal. By the door, he kicked off his Dior Oxford shoes, loosened his Gucci silk tie, and shrugged off his Ralph Lauren jacket, allowing it to pool on the carpet as if he'd melted like an overweight snowman. He smiled as the image ran through his mind and he tugged his fingers through his cropped hair, ignoring the dandruff that flaked onto his Armani shirt. That he itemised his clothes by their designer status spoke volumes about the contrast between his humble upbringing in a cramped terraced house in Killarney with his abusive dad and his useless alcoholic mum and his current wealth. He was self-aware enough to realise that counting what he owned in terms of their monetary value stemmed from his determination to never be vulnerable to another human being again.

It was all part of his need to control everything around him and that included all his things, be it his staff, the wenches he had occasional liaisons with, or the expensive inanimate objects and luxurious possessions he surrounded himself with. Was it crass? Probably. Was it unnecessary? Definitely, but the truth of the matter was, Carl didn't care. He'd earnt the right to own these things – worked hard for it – and he revelled in dominating those he came in contact with.

With a sigh, he rolled his shoulders, first one, then the other, trying to release the stiffness that would lead to one of his tension headaches if he didn't get rid of it now. He should have gone to the gym and followed up with a sauna and massage. But he was too knackered even for that. His cheek muscles were in rigour from smiling and pretending he didn't want to slam his fist into the face of the superior-looking arsehole he was broaching a deal with. It was a lucrative business opportunity and although it would have many benefits for him; he was tired of acting like he didn't care that they couldn't get over his Irish brogue. Snobby bastards! You'd think after all these years and all the money his business acumen had earned them, they'd fawn over him. But, with their Eton vowels, and horsey laughs, they still looked down their noses at him even though he could buy and sell them a hundred times over.

He shrugged and flung himself onto his sofa. He was being unfair. Tiredness always made him resent the silver spoons that had allowed his business partners to adorn themselves in shit that smelt of roses, while he remained on edge about using the right cutlery, or saying the right thing, or laughing at the right jokes. No amount of money and skill made him less of an imposter in the eyes of those tossers. The only thing that pacified him was the knowledge that he had access to proof of every one of their many indiscretions. He had the power to yank those spoons from their mouths and stick it up their moneyed arses.

Still rolling his shoulder, he prodded his fingers deep into the knot, groaning at the painful pleasure that elicited as the clump lessened. What he needed was some down time. Time to unwind and throw off the tension that had steadily built across his shoulders all day.

This was always a difficult day for him. The anniversary – the day his life stopped. The day his world altered beyond all recognition. The day he'd been betrayed. Six years ago, he'd lost everything – well, everything that mattered to him. Everything that he'd fought so hard to protect. His most valued possessions – his status symbols. The shame of losing them was too much for him. He'd heard the whispers, sensed the muffled giggles behind his back, witnessed first-hand the disgust and pity of his peers. Oh, he'd paid them back. Of course, he had. That was his way – the fighting way – and it was the only one he knew. If he hadn't got to them physically, he'd hit them where it hurt more – in their bank accounts. But despite all his efforts, the person he actually wanted to punish, the one he craved to pay back, had evaded him. Yes, he'd managed some minor revenge – those who'd been part of his downfall and those who'd been lulled into taking their eye off the ball – yes, he'd got them – ended them. Still, it wasn't enough. Beneath his massaging fingers, he felt the tension seep back into his shoulders. His heartbeat picked up a notch, hammering against the tightness in his chest, forcing him to pant like a fucking dog to get a breath.

He exhaled, squashing the anger out thorough his mouth, and then forced himself to his feet. His legs were heavy – as if he'd run a marathon – and all he wanted to do was to remain where he was and allow his rage to consume him. Experience had taught him how destructive *that* could be, and there was no way he'd allow that bitch to control him like that – not again. *Never* again.

At the time, he'd vented his rage on everyone he'd found who'd helped her. Every one of them got their punishment. It rankled that she was still free after all these years.

In the kitchen, he opened the pristine fridge, grabbed a beer, and scowled at his reflection in the gleaming appliances. Bitch had never once had to use them, but he'd still supplied them. Top of the range and yet she'd turned her back on them – spurned his generosity, like he hadn't dragged her from the dirt and made her into someone other women envied and men desired.

The migraine tugging at his temple and shooting across his forehead weighed heavily on his head. He leant his forehead on the fridge, savouring its coolness. Then, after tapping it three times on the sleek surface, he pushed himself upright, slammed his fist into it, denting the surface and yanked it open again, grabbing another three bottles from inside. He knew what would make him forget.

Slouched in front of his laptop, he glugged a mouthful of frothy beer and powered up the machine. *This* would pass the next few hours in mind numbing activity.

As dusk fell behind him, both the Tyne and Millennium Bridge, with the Baltic Centre for Contemporary Art curled underneath, watched over him as he wound himself deeper and deeper into the depravity of the dark web. This was his distraction of choice. Deeper and deeper he delved, seeking depravity and horror, not because he wanted to participate in it, but because it was the only thing that could reach him now. The only thing that alleviated the anger.

Whirling images of the worst things humans could inflict on others sped across his retinas, none registering, none eliciting the horror they once would have. He needed something, anything, to pierce his shell of nothingness. Then…

Fuck! It hit him between the eyes. Still, it took seconds to register, and he had to backtrack. He homed in on the image – zoomed in, tracing the contours of the face that stared from the screen. He flicked to the next image, and that one snatched his breath away. Same location, different subject, and as he looked at it, his heart broke, while a spiralling cobra, ready to pounce, sidled through his body – insidious, determined and oh so deadly.

Good things came to those who waited, and Carl Morris had waited way too long.

CHAPTER 7

Gus lived for the times when he could see his son, Billy, and he'd never been so appreciative of the Easter holidays before. As an adult, they'd drifted past him, but now, as a parent, holidays like these signposted dedicated time to spend with his lad. Each time he saw the boy, he noticed the changes even a few weeks apart had brought, and his heart broke a little. Every second counted as Gus attempted to snatch back those missed opportunities that three years of ignorance had wrought. Now, with Bingo dancing at his feet, he opened the door to welcome his son and the boy's mum, Sadia, conscious that his smile was forced and all too aware of the increase in his heart rate and the bundle of maggots roiling in his gut. A combination of bittersweet emotions; heart-wrenching love and the squirming angry maggots reminding him of all he'd missed tinged these meetings. The strain of remaining civil to Sadia for depriving him of his son left him deflated and angry. He was aware that he had to find a way to deal with it or risk losing his son altogether. But what was worse was the pity he felt for her. He'd loved her more than he'd ever thought possible, and it had taken a lot for him to move on from the relationship when she left. She'd had her own demons to exercise and Gus knew all about those. Even allowing for her demons and the trauma of her father's suicide and revelations about her dearly beloved mum, Gus couldn't bring himself to forgive her for denying him that time with his son.

His lodger and detective sergeant, Alice Cooper, lurked by the kitchen door, her arms folded across her middle and tutted, before issuing a strident hiss along the hallway. 'For god's sake, Gus, loosen up. Billy's gonna think you're going to eat him if you don't.'

Gus snorted and rather than look at her, flipped his middle finger up at her behind his back as he stepped forward when the tornado that was Billy launched himself into his arms, with Bingo barking and jumping, his moist tongue licking the boy's bare legs.

'Daddy, Daddy, I got a treat for Bingo. Let me down.'

Billy's lilting Scottish lilt made Gus smile. Despite Sadia keeping her Bradford accent and Billy not being in school yet, he'd still absorbed the lilt from his nursery playmates. The boy's curls were reminiscent of Gus's own dreads and when he smiled into his dad's face, the eyes that looked back at Gus were near identical to his own – a startling blue with a darker outline round the iris making them shimmer. There had been no need for a DNA test.

As Gus ruffled his son's hair and allowed him to slip down to feed Bingo the dog treat he held in his chubby hands, Gus braced himself to greet Sadia. No matter how hard he tried, his shoulders tensed and the genuine smile he'd given his son became brittle on his lips.

'Hi, Sadia. Drive down OK, was it?'

Sadia, hesitating at the bottom of the stairs, Billy's bag at her feet, nodded. Rather than meet Gus's eye, she focussed on the sight of her son and Bingo rolling about on the hallway floor, Billy giggling and Bingo, pleased to have a playmate with as much energy as he, prancing and licking the boy. When the silence between them lengthened, Sadia flicked her hair back from her face and glanced up at Gus, a fleeting, uncertain smile darting across her face as she bit her lip.

Something fluttered in Gus's chest – a mixture of frustration and anger? It couldn't be anything more. Not after the hurt she'd caused him. He cleared his throat and grabbed Billy, hefting him onto his shoulders and stepped away from the door with a, 'Kettle's on. You better come in.'

As he walked along the hallway, tickling Billy as they went, Sadia lifted her son's bag and trailed behind him. Placing Billy on his feet in the kitchen so he could greet Alice, Gus ignored the tight-lipped scowl she sent in his direction over the boy's head.

'Auntie Alice, have you got tuna? Can I have a tuna and sweetcorn sandwich?'

Alice grinned and turned to a plate of sandwiches wrapped in cling film that sat on the table. 'Ta da – tuna for his lordship, with sweetcorn, I hasten to add.'

Gus grinned and directed Billy over to the sink to wash his hands. Alice had introduced the boy to the filling on his last visit and, according to text messages from Sadia, it was the only sandwich he'd eat.

'Hi, Sadia. Grab a pew and sit down. Ignore His Mardiness – he's got no manners, but I have.'

Chairs were scraped back, and Alice and Sadia sat down at the dinner table with Billy between Gus and the boy's mum. He focussed on Billy, while Sadia and Alice's conversation flowed around him. The way Alice smoothed things over with Sadia irked him. She was right to do so. It was just, for him, the effort was too much. He was relieved that Sadia had insisted on staying with Shahid, Imti, and Serafina at The Delius on Barkerend Road for their flying two-day visit. It meant he could focus on being with Billy and not have to confront his muddled feelings for her.

'Is your work OK, Sad?' Alice had spent a few minutes filling Sadia in on a series of machete attacks in Bradford city centre which they'd just solved and had now thrown the ball back in Sadia's court. Thankfully, she hadn't dragged up the awful, stilted investigation into Zac Ibrahim's death. That was still too raw for the officers.

'Em, well...I'm considering a move – not sure it'll pan out, but...' She shrugged and lifted her mug to her lips, as if doing so would offer some sort of protection.

Gus's eyes flew to Sadia. *Moving*? Where the hell is she moving to now? The Outer Hebrides, The Orkney Islands...Anywhere to make it harder for him to build a relationship with Billy. His heart sped up, and it was only when Alice kicked his shin that he realised he was glaring at Sadia.

He swallowed and cleared his throat, hoping his voice didn't betray his concern. 'Where you thinking of moving to?'

But Sadia just shrugged again as she lowered her mug to the table. 'Nothing's certain yet, Gus. It might never happen.'

She got to her feet and dropped a kiss on Billy's head. 'Now you be a good boy for your daddy. I'll come and pick you up on Thursday, OK?'

But Billy was too busy dropping bits of tuna on the floor for Bingo to answer. Sadia gave a half laugh and turned to Gus. 'Looks like he won't miss me one bit. His bag's by the door. Have fun.'

Before Gus or Alice could reply, she was along the hallway and out the door.

Alice looked at Gus. 'God's sake, Gus, think you could have made her any less welcome? '

But Gus wasn't concerned with that. He was thinking about the shimmer of tears he'd spotted in

Sadia's eye and the way his stomach plummeted at the thought that he'd upset her. Why was all this so hard?

Thrusting these troublesome thoughts to the back of his mind, he focussed on his son, determined to enjoy the short time they had together, well aware that his trip to Scotland at the end of the month depended on their being no major incidents in Bradford. He exhaled and looked at Alice, who was making silly faces at Billy, reducing him to fits of giggles. How the hell was she going to react when he told her he'd applied for a transfer to Scotland?

CHAPTER 8

Flynn

I'd agreed to come. To do this for the group. Anything to keep the peace – that's me. No – it was more than keeping the peace. It's about doing what's right. Helping my community, making things better for my friends – or trying to. I know that, even so, it's getting old now. Old and a bit creepy, if I'm honest – maybe a little *threatening*? *Worrying*? I balk at using the word dangerous, but it echoes at the back of my mind. At the beginning, I could just bite my tongue and go along with it, but the last couple of sessions had become worse. More threatening and I was finding it more difficult to keep my true feelings under wraps. When I was with my mates online, I was still full of attitude and bravado, but that was wearing thin. I wondered if all of them felt the same way deep down inside. If they were all conflicted, weary, angry, confused?

I rest my head on the bus window, letting the images flash by me in a whirl as I consider what lies ahead for me and try to ignore the dicks at the back who're whispering about me in voices intended to carry.

Wankers!

Cradling my rucksack filled with a change of clothes, I wish I was going to my best mate Carrie's house instead of putting myself through this crap. A sleepover, *they* said, but I know it's just an excuse for an extended version of their course. Carrie's OK with covering for me, but she's worried about me. The way she gripped my forearm, her purple lips all pinched and how her green eyes seemed duller than usual as she begged me not to go, says it all.

'Don't go, Flynn. You don't have to. It's not your battle. If they're your friends, they'll get it, won't they?'

The 'It's not your battle' echoes like shards of ice in my head, giving me brain freeze. She's wrong, is Carrie. It *is* my battle. It's OK for her to wash her hands of it all. She doesn't get how bad things are for kids like me. How could she? Besides, I don't see many others battling by my side. Too many of them debating toilet issues and not enough of them getting down to deeper, more real issues about keeping us safe and about our rights – we are humans, after all.

As I approach my stop, my chest sort of clams up, like *it's* telling me not to go too. I realise my fingers are gripping my backpack way too tight and I release them a little, wishing my palms weren't so clammy.

Don't get me wrong, I'm not confused about me. No, I'm all right with who I am. It's just some arseholes have issues with it, but day to day I cope with that – the jibes, the sarccy comments, the weird looks. 'Fuck them all' is my motto and most of the time it works 'cause I've got so many folks in my life who aren't dicks.

This stuff is so next level though. I get what we're trying to do with all this undercover, illicit *James Bond* crap, but I'm not sure I'm cut out for much more of it. Some of the group are sooo strong – so determined – that I feel guilty when I'm online with them and I can't bring myself to confide my worries. I don't want to seem weak and needy. God, some of the stories they've told me make me want to reach through the ether and hug them. In comparison, I've had it easy – they're the real survivors and I'm like a tagalong. Not that they see it like that. I've been up front with them about how supportive my sister and mum have been. It's only my mum that's given me any grief. Dad says she'll come round, but I'm not so sure. Will she? Some of my online mates got chucked out of their homes and ended up homeless. There's nowhere safe for the likes of us on the streets and nowhere safe in the shelters, either. Fucked if I know how they've survived. How they keep smiling. How, after all they've been through, they channel their anger into this. Into something so positive, so worthwhile. It's this that keeps me going. It's this knowledge that makes me stand up and ring the bell.

As per my instructions, I get off two stops early and instead of sticking to the main road, I dodge down a side road that leads to an alley adjoining the hall. Adds ten minutes onto the journey, but I gotta do it. They check. I know they do because they challenged that skinny lad last week and had him in tears because he didn't stick to the rules. I wonder why they're so adamant we 'take precautions'? I guess it's to avoid the cameras and the busy roads and that worries me. Why would we need to avoid cameras?

Thankfully, the whispering dicks don't get off the bus at my stop and I allow myself to relax. Last thing I want is them hassling me. Not tonight. Not when I'm already feeling so crap.

As I approach my destination, my steps slow. The clamp in my gut tightens, and for a second, I think I might soil myself. But the sensation fades a little and I keep going. This session promises to be worse than any of the others. Yet in this session, I have to find an ally. The very thought of it tightens the vice again and I bend over, arms wrapped round my belly. I have my target in mind. A kid about my age. She's so timid and keeps her head bowed all the time. I've seen her leg jiggling up and down, getting faster at some of the worst parts of the sessions. I suspect that they've forced her to attend, yet everything about her, other than the juddering leg, speaks of compliance. Still, I don't think I'm wrong. I hope not anyway, because as I see the building loom in front of me, the lights dim behind curtained windows, I vow that this will be the last time I come here. But even though I whisper the words beneath my breath, they don't carry the conviction they should. I know I'll be back to the second session of the week on Friday. Just as I know Carrie, despite her misgivings, will cover for me and my parents would trust me to be at Carrie's. After all, it's not like I have friends to hang out with. Most dumped me like I'd asked them to eat shit after the 'big announcement' – the one me and Carrie call *Flynngate*. The one that changed my life forever and signalled the start of my new life – my real life – the one *I* want to live – the one I'm entitled to live.

CHAPTER 9

Angel

As I cast my eyes over them, they lower their heads one by one, each of them unable to withstand the censure I inject into my silent stare. They look like a sea of daffodils bowing their heads in sleep as the light fades to darkness. I've perfected this in front of my bathroom mirror at every opportunity over the past few months – this look of disdain, where I tilt my head back, chin up, eyes narrowed. It's imperative to maintain my authority, and this is only one way in which I do this. When I'm satisfied that each of them sits, cowed and nervous, I allow my stern gaze to soften.

Carrot and stick, Angel, carrot and stick.

Their continued supplication allows me to assess them at ease. To monitor them against the backdrop of our new surroundings. The harsh lighting provided by the floodlights blazing down on them sets them on edge. An inspired idea methinks – to replicate an interrogation setting. The all-encompassing cold of the bare sandstone walls seeps right into their marrow, despite the slight heat that reaches them from the lights. They're all shivering, their bodies craving warmth. I've made them remove their outer garments and socks and now they sit before me divested of not only warmth but also dignity. Not that they have that, anyway. Their animalistic cravings negate any semblance of dignity, not just in the minds of righteousness, but in the eyes of God. Of course, *we're* warm enough. Under our special tunics and hoods, we're wrapped up with thermals and jumpers. No point in our suffering – after all, we've done nothing wrong. They're the ones on trial here, not us.

There are eight of them – each of them deviants, each of them afflicted by their own individual disease, each of them despite their aberrant thoughts, desperate to be shown the light, to atone for their transgressions. To be led away from the temptations of the flesh – from their bizarre and repugnant sicknesses, promiscuities, and disgusting behaviour – and into the light of goodness and normality, of morality and sanctity, of chastity and purity.

Each one of them has become part of my flock. Lambs to be nurtured in justness and right. I smile as my gaze rests on a balding and greying bowed head, observing how, with his eyes closed and his hands clasped to his chin, his lips move in desperate prayer. This one is more mutton than lamb, yet the need for redemption is imperative. His sins have been part of his being for much longer than the others. His sins are more ingrained and the devious manner in which he hid those disgusting thoughts and actions makes him the worst sinner of the lot and he will suffer for it in order to repent.

My eyes glide along the line to the girl sitting next to him. She is problematic, I note. We've never had one like her before and she will be a challenge to break – but break her we must. Her eyes trouble me, the way they're always the last to lower, the looks she casts around the others – probing and unfathomable. What is she thinking? Instead of casting her head downwards to the floor in meditation like the others, hers flit around the group and there's something in her demeanour that makes me pause. By now, in our last week she should be acquiescent yet still her hands bunch into fists and – I sigh – those furtive glances towards the others worry me. Although, she does try to take part in the discussions and has never complained or been anything other than compliant. Perhaps I am misreading her. Perhaps she is filled with confusion. Experience has taught me that confusion can be a dangerous thing. The marks on my back tell me that, but self-flagellation is something I yearn for. It's not for everyone to attain the heights of pain that transcend sin. Her head dips lower and her fists are no longer clenched against the chair. There is hope for her, and I smile. Wouldn't bringing her to atonement be an achievement greater than all the others?

I decide to do the only thing I can do. I'll extend her therapy, allow her the chance to sublimate her behaviour. Another round of sessions should suffice. We were aware when she approached us that her deviance would be more difficult to correct than the others and perhaps we'll need to create an individual programme for her. I make a mental note to discuss it with See later on. See is very adept at drawing up workable strategies, so I'm convinced we'll succeed. If not, well – there's always Plan B.

Moving on, I skim over the two timid kids, then I frown. Surreptitious looks are passing between them, and I observe the flush blooming in Ali's cheeks and the trace of a smile on Bailey's lips. My gut clenches and an image of my fist slamming into each of their faces in turn flashes before me. The urge to act is so strong. I step forward, fists clenched and heart hammering, my face flushed as beads of sweat speckle my upper lip. My breath comes in harsh pants that scrape through the urge and I can barely control myself, knowing that the whip will punish any excesses I succumb to. Then See's fingers come to rest on my arm, squeezing gently, her smile beneficent, her eyes flashing a warning, while her fingers loosen on my arm. I pull myself together. Shrugging her hands away, I step backwards and angle my body away from the group.

Aware of the whispered conversations behind me and the dizzying buzz of energy circulating the room, I inhale deep calming breaths and focus on releasing the tension in my hands and shoulders.

This is not the time to lose control. Not at this stage. Not today. Come on, Angel. You can control this. You've controlled it before and you will do it now. These things are sent to try us.

My acolytes, Hear, See, and Speak, move forward, their bodies shielding me as I manage my anger. Their individual stares, although not as effective as mine, when combined, bring order to the group.

Berating myself for my lack of restraint, I promise myself a session with the repentance whip later. I take one final breath, force 'the look' back on my face and turn round. Sweeping my attendants aside, my energy concentrated on handling the sinners, I step forward, eyes blazing. I raise one hand, my finger extended and home in on Ali, a smile twitches my lips as he squirms on the wooden seat. His brow furrows and his lips quiver as he realises I've caught him in salacious thoughts. I could blast him with the power of my wrath, but instead I lower my voice to a whisper that makes each of them lean forward, their gaping eyes fixated on me as they strive to hear my words. In little more than a whisper, I put an end to their uncertainty. 'Hear, See, move Ali to the front.'

The sinners collapse back against their chairs, involuntary gasps escaping their lips as Hear and See both grab the boy under his arms. He tries to resist, but they persist and half drag, half march him before me.

'Knees.' The single word fired at Ali with long, slow, quiet velocity is enough to bring tears to his eyes.

'No, no please, Angel. I'm sorry.'

Electric frissons spread up my spine and a satisfying tingle spreads in my crotch – a feeling which the repentance whip will satiate later. I lower my voice even more and bend over close to the boy. I can smell his fear – his sweat like strawberries and cream to my desirous nose. I celebrate the terror in the pallor of his face, his dilated pupils, the globules of sweat across his lips.

'*Knees.*' I hiss the word, like some Voldemort character, and that thought draws a snarl of humour from my mouth, which bends him to my will.

He slips to the damp concrete floor, head bowed, shoulders slumped and without me having to remind him, he leans back and grips his ankles with his hands. It won't be long before his shoulders feel like they're being yanked from the sockets and his kneecaps feel on fire. I look at Bailey, who averts his eyes, waiting to hear his fate. He doesn't get it – that his punishment is to witness Ali's suffering. My smile widens as I address the group in conversational tones, all trace of menace dissipated although it hangs like a cloud over them ready to fall if the need arises. 'Mindfulness video for half an hour.'

I signal for Speak to dim the lights and start the video and the corrective sounds and images of natural sexual pleasure blare and flash over the screens. Myself and my aides prowl among them, forcing them with encouraging prods between the shoulder blades to look when they try to avert their gazes. Ali, rigid, facing the front, weeps in silence. His poor body protesting at the pressure on his upper body and his knees, but he knows that this punishment is justified. This 'normalisation therapy' is an integral part of the process.

CHAPTER 10

Flynn

'Come on, come on.' My leg jiggles up and down. I'm wearing my Beats and have my laptop positioned so anyone entering my bedroom can't see the screen.

I'm the only one in the Zoom meeting so far, but I'm torn between being desperate to see the others and wanting to throw my headphones on my bed and take off – maybe to Carrie's. It's the first time since I've been in the group – well after the first one, when I was so nervous, I almost crapped myself anyway – that I'm tempted to just skip it. But I can't. I can't let them down. Besides, we've agreed – no matter what, you either attend the meeting or let someone know you can't and why and you have to use the safe word. It's our way of looking out for each other. Keeping ourselves and each other safe. Nobody knows better than us how fragile a person's hold on life can be. How even the little things can twist your mind and send you diving for the pills or the razor blades.

I crick my neck, pissed off at being so early. I'm early for everything. Ever since I was little, my mum says, I was always first out the door, dragging her and Millie behind. Always eager to get going, and this desire for punctuality had lasted into my teenage years. OK, maybe not the whole 'eager' to get everywhere early thing. No, the haters beat some of that eagerness out of me over the past few years. Despite all that crap, I still can't break the habit.

The screen flickers and I grin as a smiling face appears on the screen.

Lucy! That's no surprise, Lucy's never far behind me. Although, I suspect that for her it's not so much an eagerness to be early for everything, but more of a need to connect with us. In so many ways, we are her lifeboat – her one link to keeping afloat. God, what a state of affairs if she has to rely on us to keep her afloat. Lucy's attendance is sporadic, though, and that's all down to whether she can find a safe laptop to access. But tonight, she's managed as, judging by her backdrop, she's in someone's living room, rather than a dodgy internet café.

'Hey, Flynnsy, how's it holding? You look awesooooome!'

Lucy speaks in a Brummie accent. Her upbeat voice and the way she makes rabbit ears with her hands and sticks her tongue out at me, lifts my spirits. As my dad would say, Lucy is a trooper. Homeless, apart from the odd time couch surfing or…well…whatever – I've only ever seen her with a smile on her face.

'Hey, Luce. You all right? See you've found somewhere to kip. You safe?'

The sparkle in Lucy's eyes fades as she looks off screen and shrugs, but seconds later she's pouting at me, her familiar grin once more on her lips.

'I'm awesome, Flynnsy. No need to worry about me. This queen can look after herself.' She winks, her impossibly long lashes sweeping the tops of her cheeks for a second before she diverts me from asking more about the house she's in. 'You? How's the 007 stuff coming on?'

Despite the wideness of her smile and her teasing tone, I notice the shadow lurking in her eyes and something grips my heart and squeezes. Lucy's not all right. She hasn't said so, but I can tell. I open my mouth to press her for more information about where she is and why she's there, but before I can respond, three more faces pop onto the screen and the square boxes framing each face adjust to accommodate the new entrants. Despite my misgivings about Lucy and about my 007 stuff, seeing my friends makes me smile. These people are like me. They have personal experiences to share, they get what I've been through, and they support me. They listen and nothing I reveal shocks them. My nervous leg jiggle stills and my concerns about Lucy fade as the chatter bounces around the screen as we chat about music recommendations, make jokes, and tease each other. Just doing the stuff other teens take for granted. Chatting about stuff folk like us rarely have the chance to because being a 'normal teen' is never top of the agenda for us.

It's Lincoln who, after a while, brings the meeting round to more serious matters – the group's activism. Lincoln, twenty-one going on sixty, is the self-appointed daddy of the group. And it was he who brought us together. From London, Lincoln is more worldly wise than we are. He'd been homeless for a long time in his mid-teens but had turned his life around with the support of new foster parents. He took his responsibilities to the rest of us seriously and at every meeting he includes a – what he dubbed – 'Trigger Shout Out'. It's important for us and Linc expects each of the six members, including himself, to talk about our mental health status. It gives us the opportunity to discuss the highs and lows of the past week. Gives us the chance to help each other and learn from our friend's experiences.

'OK, Bev's texted to say she's got Parents Over Shoulder so she can't get on tonight. She's used the safe word, so we assume that things are no worse than normal for her, so…' He paused, smiled, and splayed his hands before him, before putting on a TV presenter voice and singing, 'Trigger Shout Out. Who's going first tonight then?'

Lucy, normally the first to jump in to update her status, becomes absorbed in picking flaking nail varnish off her nails and remains silent. Again, that gripping sensation at my heart as we exchange glances. I want to say something, but I don't know what. I'm reluctant to land Lucy in it and she clearly doesn't want to say owt. By the time I decide to push her a little, Lincoln has shrugged and moved on. 'Flynn?'

As the newest group member, it had taken me time to confide all my thoughts and anxieties in this forum. But over the months, the others' honesty and kindness had encouraged me and usually I'd be pleased to share. However, today reluctance weighs heavily on my shoulders, and I find myself torn between worrying about Lucy, who just isn't herself, and anxiety about my crap. Only two of the group are doing the '007' crap – me and Bev. But Bev's not here tonight, and that makes me feel pressurised. I know her family situation is sooo much worse than mine and yet she's logging everything. Writing down all the actions her religious community is taking against her. She's so brave and here I am being a wuss about summat and nowt. I'm well aware of how much the others rely on mine and Bev's work. The more we comply, the more political pressure we can bring to bear. Each of us has, over the past year, recorded our experiences, whether at homeless centres, in our own homes, or in situations like the ones Bev and I are involved with. Unlike me, Bev lives in the Scottish isles and her experiences differ vastly from mine. I could have done with her presence to calm my hammering heart, but there is nothing else for it.

With my head bowed, choosing my words with care, I begin.

'It's hard. You know? I hate every meeting I go to. I want to yell and scream and act out, but I know I shouldn't. They've changed the venue again, and that makes me wary. It's like they're gearing up for something and whatever it is, it won't be good. That Angel's a fucking fascist.'

I rub the back of my hand over my mouth and risk a glance at the others. All of them – Lincoln, Davy, Anita, except Lucy – are staring at me, slight frowns meandering across their foreheads as they absorb every word. Lucy's looking off centre, and I'm sure there's a shimmer of tears in her eyes. I inhale and offer a tentative smile.

'Tonight, Angel went batshit crazy. Grabbed one lad and forced him to kneel on the concrete slabs for half an hour while those fucking videos played out on the screen. He kept increasing the volume, till all we could hear were humping sounds – fucking gross – like that's gonna work.'

It's only when I stop speaking that I realise I'm crying.

'Fuck.'

I spit the word out and drag my sleeve over my eyes. *Come on Flynn, get a bloody grip, eh*?

'Aw, crap, Flynn. I'm sorry you're finding this hard.' Biting his lip, Lincoln pauses as if considering his next words. 'You can pull out, Flynn. You don't have to do it anymore. You've got a shed load of evidence from Pure Life. It's time to withdraw.'

I straighten my shoulders and glare at the screen. 'No fucking chance, Linc. I've got to keep going. If I leave, what'll happen to the others? They've nobody but me on their side.'

Davy, a round faced Mancunian, moves closer to the screen, his eyes filled with worry. 'Aw, Flynn. You can't be responsible for them. Think about yourself. You've logged it all in your diary?'

I nod. 'Course. First thing I did when I got home. Look, I'm sorry for being a moan. You've all been through so much and I've had it easy by comparison. I can do this.'

For the first time since the others joined the meeting, Lucy speaks. 'Get out, Flynny. Just don't go back. You need to leave and keep yourself safe.'

Before anyone can respond to her words, there's the sound of something crashing to the floor from Lucy's screen. Then she's on her feet, things clattering behind her. All we can see is her torso as she speaks to someone off screen – her voice all weird and shaky.

'I'm sorry, Nigel. I'm sorry. It's just some friends. I…'

But then a tattooed arm passes in front of the screen and a massive fist lands on Lucy's belly. She bends over crying while the man she's with – this Nigel – punches her again and again. The sound of each hit thuds through the speakers. 'You whore, you fucking poofter, whore…'

Then Lucy's screen goes blank. For long seconds, we stare in silence at the spot where Lucy's image was moments before. Lincoln, muttering under his breath, starts tapping away on another screen just out of sight. 'Where are you, Luce? Where are you?'

As we wait for Linc to find Lucy's location, I grip the edge of my chair so hard my fingers cramp. Leaning forward, my heart almost bursting it's gripped so tight, I lean in, and exchange glances with Davy and Anita. We all know what Linc's doing. He'd set this up for just this sort of scenario. Each of us has trackers on our phones so Linc could monitor our safety and respond quickly should any of us implement the safe word. He's breathing hard and droplets of sweat speckle his forehead as he works. My heart's thudding in my chest and I begin a silent chant inside my head, faster and faster, in time with my heartbeat.

'Be OK, Luce. Be OK, be OK, be OK, be OK, be OK, be OK.'

After what seems an age, but is barely half a minute, Linc punches the air. 'Got it.' And my silent chants slow down as I listen to Linc phoning 999. 'Domestic abuse situation at 33 Garrett Street, Solihull. My friend was FaceTiming me when I saw her boyfriend punching her and dragging her by the hair to the ground.'

We all know that he isn't Lucy's boyfriend. This isn't the first time Linc's had to call in the police because Lucy's taken a risk too far. We also know that they will file no charges against Lucy's abuser. But right now, the only important thing is that Lucy, in all her awesomeness, is safe.

Lincoln turns to us, his face pale as he switches to speaker phone so we can all hear.

'Officers are en route. Can we take your details?' The tinny voice comes over the airwaves and as Linc gave his details, Davy, Anita, and me exhale. Now, all we can do is wait till Lucy calls us back. Wait to find out how badly she's been injured this time.

We wait long into the night, our bedrooms growing darker behind us, none of us willing to leave our screens even for a moment to switch on a light. We try to keep each other's spirits up with empty promises of Lucy being fine. And as we worry about the fate of our friend, I make a decision. Because this sort of crap still happens,

I have to continue going to Pure Life. For Lucy and others like me who get this crap every day. I have to do my bit to gain data about our lives – about the stuff we go through just to be who we are. I owe it to myself, but more than that, I owe it to my friends and especially Lucy.

When the call comes through to Lincoln, it's gone midnight and it's not Lucy's voice we hear. It's the police.

'You are cited as Lucas Smith's next of kin. I am sorry to inform you that we found Lucas Smith, bleeding from multiple stab wounds to the upper body. He was transported to Birmingham City Hospital but was pronounced dead on arrival.'

Lincoln, tears streaming down his face, shakes his head, but all he can say is, 'She was Lucy. Lucy Smith.' Before he hangs up.

CHAPTER 11

After two magical days with his son, Gus was back at work. Time spent with Billy didn't compensate for the fact that, after months, they had made no progress on Zac Ibrahim's murder. The absence of his son's energy and humour made it sadder and even more poignant. Here was Gus, desperate to snatch any time he could with Billy and Zac Ibrahim's parents couldn't even be arsed to give their son a decent burial. Gus's friend Mo had convinced a sympathetic imam to perform Zac's burial rites and Gus and his team, with the help of Mo's mosque, had financed the funeral. Gus was glad the boy now rested in peace in the Muslim section of the Cemetery Road Graveyard.

Still, Gus's overpowering sense of responsibility for the boy dragged him down. He'd pleaded with his boss, DCI Nancy Chalmers, to allow his team more time, but as lead after lead dried up, the resources allocated to the investigation into Zac's death were trimmed. What irked Gus most was the suspicion that, had Zac's relatives hounded the police, the case would have remained open. As it was, with nobody mourning the dead lad and his parents eager to sweep his death under the carpet combined with no other body and no viable leads, the investigation was being wound down.

Now, studying the crime board for a final time before Taffy disassembled it and filed it in the *unresolved recent crime archive*, Gus, coffee cup in hand

– the one with the slogan *World's Best Dad* in large red balloon letters on the front; a gift for last year's father's day from Billy – wracked his brain to see what else they could have done. What other avenues they might have explored?

Alice joined him and sighed. 'This sucks. It really sucks. I hate that we couldn't get justice for him. Hate that whoever did this got away with it.'

Gus offered a half smile and continued his perusal. That was the narrative he'd conjured up in his head too – the idea of some gleeful murderer out there living their life to the full while Zac's body rotted away to nothing, his young life snuffed out. However, another narrative also lingered in his mind – one where whoever had robbed Zac Ibrahim of his life, was disintegrating with remorse – unable to function, falling into a guilt induced swamp that might – if they were lucky – result in that person coming forth, holding their hands up and giving closure and justice to the dead boy. Even though the chances of that were slim, he still had hope. 'I can't see a single gap in the investigation, Al. You?'

'Nope.' Counting off each strategy on her fingers, Alice listed them as if repeating this process for the umpteenth time might shake a lead out. 'One – no CCTV near the skips or in the alleyways behind them. No CCTV from the surrounding terraced houses. The last sighting was at the Keighley Road entrance to Lister Park at 6 p.m. where he was on his own. We checked the Cartwright Hall cameras and those at the Boathouse – but got zilch. Of course, that doesn't mean he wasn't in the park – just that he wasn't near those cameras between then and when his body was discovered.'

Gus took up the narrative. 'Two. His mates from town – if you can call acquaintances who are drugged out junkies mates – couldn't give us a sodding thing.'

Gus exhaled. They'd interviewed the addicts and the rough sleepers Zac spent time with, but they had nothing to offer other than unsubstantiated lies and half-baked truths in their attempts to squeeze some money from the interviewing officers. None of them bore fruit.

'Three.' Alice took over again. 'The couple of rough sleepers he spent most time with — Liza and Danny. They said that Zac had told him he was taking steps to work his way back into his parents' lives. Working on making them proud of him again.'

Giving up on the counting, Alice snorted. 'Bloody makes me mad, how they treated him. They would never let him into their lives – no damn way.'

'Yeah, we wasted a lot of time checking them out, as they seemed to be the obvious contenders, didn't they? But cast-iron alibis to go with their dubious morals.'

Gus cricked his neck. 'Lack of evidence of recent sexual activity, although the PM report detailed evidence of old anal lesions, seems to rule out a sexual predator or a sex act gone wrong.' With a sigh, he placed his treasured mug on his desk, rolled his shoulders to release the remaining knots, and said, 'We need to box it up. We'll keep it on a back burner in case something comes up. But for now, it looks like we have to admit defeat.'

With her lips pursed up, Alice snorted. 'Yeah, because questioning a woman who stabbed her husband after years of abuse is soooo much more worthwhile than investigating the bastard who murdered a 17-year-old.'

Gus couldn't disagree with Alice – not really. However, their hands were tied. A man was dead and regardless of their personal opinions on the matter, his death needed investigating and Nancy had allocated the investigation to his team. 'Part of the job, Al. You know that.'

Alice's eyes darkened, and he suspected she was thinking about a dingy building where she'd once had to make her own life or death decision. He swung his arm round her shoulder and squeezed. 'Come on, mardi arse, let's get to it.'

CHAPTER 12

DC John Compton's fingers flew across his keyboard, his eyes flitting over the three screens semi enclosing him at his home workstation. As soon as the notification had come in, his stomach sunk to the ground like a ship's anchor dragging him spiralling downwards as momentary dizziness clouded his vision. It was *that* notification – a red alert he'd set up months ago and had hoped he'd never hear that sound.

But today he had.

Every one of his various devices had emitted the warning, and now he had to deal with it. He threw his headphones onto the busy desk, knocking over a half filled can of Red Bull, and the strains of 'Bohemian Rhapsody' filtered eerily into the silence. Compo was no longer concerned with singing each Queen member's role in turn and brandishing his air guitar around his miniscule flat. This notification had ruined his rare day off. Almost before he'd settled behind his multi screens, he'd implemented various illegal strategies to unfurl encryptions, trace links, and access data on the deep web in order to quell the flood of depravity that was about to be let loose. Not that he could stop it – hell no – it was already out there in the ether and any hacker worth their salt could access the very stuff Compo wanted to keep hidden should they choose to. Compo's triggers were placed so deep into the dark web he knew that when they alerted him, things were bad. This wasn't the pop up crap he'd dealt with over the past months with ease. This was more insidious, more depraved, and a real threat to those he loved. As he worked to bring it down, he muttered under his breath, 'Oh no, oh no. Please, not this. Oh no.'

He located the site of the alert and froze, his entire body, normally in perpetual motion, froze and all colour leached from his round face. Beads of sweat popped across his forehead and his underarms became moist.

This is bad. Really bad.

Reaching for his mobile phone Compo took a few deep breaths to ground himself. He had to alert the team about this pronto, but before he could speed dial his boss, DI Gus McGuire, his doorbell rang. Compo swallowed, wondering for a moment if someone had detected his presence on that awful site. Surely not. After a mental run through of all the strategies he'd implemented, he dismissed that possibility. He exhaled and then swallowed as the ringing doorbell continued, the harsh sound challenging Freddie Mercury to *let me in* rather than *let me go*. Hands over his ears, Compo, beanie hat covering his curly brown hair, swung away from the screen.

Why am I being such an idiot? No geek or hacker could find me that fast.

Yet the strident buzzer sounded and was now accompanied by frantic hammering.

'Let me in, Compo. I know you're in there. You gotta let me in. It's important.'

Compo relaxed. Visions of a faceless enemy standing on his doorstep wielding some sort of torture weapon or other dissipated. He jumped up to let his visitor in, then his gaze returned to the screens and the horrid, close-up images there. He dipped back, set the computer to standby, and glanced round his small, crowded living room for anything else he might not want his uninvited guest to see. Satisfied that nothing was immediately obvious, he walked through the gallery of dead pop and rock stars that lined his short hallway and approached the door.

When he flung it open, Jo Jo almost fell into the flat. So intent was he on gaining access he hadn't heard Compo's approach and was now hammering with all his might. Sweat flew from the lad's brow as he pummelled, and his eyes were wide and frenzied. Seeing his young friend in such a state, Compo groaned and stepped forward, enveloping the lad in his chubby arms and, despite Jo Jo being almost a foot taller than Compo, he cradled the distraught boy's head against his chest. And held on until his shuddering sobs abated. Jo Jo was Zarqa – Gus's goddaughter's best friend. Compo had become acquainted with them during an investigation the previous year. Social services had separated Jo Jo and his little sister, Jessie, for a short time after losing their mother to cancer, but they were now resettled together in a foster home on Quarry Street and were thriving. Both Compo and Taffy had adopted the lad as a little brother – Taffy because he'd been with Jo Jo when his mum died and Compo through their shared interest in techie stuff.

The lad must have implemented similar alerts to Compo and had discovered what Compo had unravelled not an hour earlier. Why that surprised Compo, he didn't know because Jo Jo was almost as adept with digital technology as Compo was himself. In fact, he'd been mentoring the lad since his mum's death and often after a session, Taffy would join them, and the three of them would game for hours on end.

At last, Jo Jo pushed himself away from Compo, dragged the back of his hand across his face, and marched down the hall into Compo's living room where he stood before the blank screens, his eyes flashing, his jaw taut, and his fists clenched by his side.

'You seen it, Comps? You seen what they're doing to Jessie?'

CHAPTER 13

Flynn

'You know this is stupid, don't you Flynn? I mean, those Pure Life folk aren't just sick, they're dangerous too.'

I sigh. We're in Carrie's room and I'm narrowly avoiding getting a headache with all the glittery pink crap she has stuck all over the walls by lying back on her bed and closing my eyes. Carrie's got a point, but *she* didn't see what happened to Lucy.

Shit, Lucy. Can't believe she's gone. Can't believe that happened right in front of us. I want to confide in Carrie. Tell her all about it – about Lucy, about my online friends, but I keep what I tell her to a minimum. Not because I don't trust her, but because she'll worry. She's the best mate I've ever had. My lips curl up and I snort. Who am I kidding? She's the only mate I've got. The only one of the bitches that stuck with me after Flynngate. I know she gets hassled for staying friends with me. I've seen the looks some of the others send her at school and I've heard the whispered crap and the taunts directed at her. It maddens me, but I don't know what to do about it and there are only a couple of teachers who're OK with me – only two that I trust – two that have our backs and call the tossers out for bullying us. But Carrie gives as good as she gets. She's always been tough like that. Even in nursery she didn't stand for any crap from the bigger kids. She's been my rock for years and I don't tell her how much I love her often enough. I really should. I sit up, punching one of her fluffy pink cushions and wedge it behind my neck, and force Lucy and what happened to her to the back of my mind. I squint over at Carrie, giving my vision time to adjust to the overpowering pink eye ache. She's sitting next to me on the bed, mirror in hand and applying neon pink lipstick in between having a go at me.

'Hey, Carrie?'

When she looks up, I grin. 'Love you, you know?'

She smacks her lips together before prodding me with her finger and laughing, all trace of her earlier worry gone from her face. 'Love you too, Flynnster, but I'm *not* letting you change the subject.'

Her brow furrows, and she slips her hand into mine. 'It's not safe, Flynn. You know it's not safe? Those reactionary assholes are weird. And…' She squeezes my hand right tight, like she wants to break my fingers. 'You're taking stupid risks for a bunch of folk you barely know and have never met.'

I don't correct her because she wouldn't get it. Carrie thinks she's the only one who understands me, because she's been with me every step of my journey and I can't hurt her by telling her that Linc and Lucy and the others get me in a way that she can't. That they give me a purpose. They show me that I don't have to be passive about who I am. That I can be proactive. Carrie thinks I should keep my head down and avoid conflict and before I met the group, I thought the same. My family thinks that way too. But now, having seen what others have gone through, learnt how the real world is, I'm different. I realise it's more than just *my* narrow, cushioned world with Carrie and my family and a few other protectors in my corner against a load of idiots who think they're funny when they write crap on my locker or call me names in school. It's about more than the folk who don't have the guts to do owt else to me – who moan and whine and revel in making my cloistered little world uncomfortable. There's more at stake. *Much more*. Through my online friends, I've learnt about real trauma. About abuse and victimisation, about loneliness and fear and last night – I saw how far people will go to hurt people like me. Besides, Carrie only wants to protect me, take the sting out of things for me, help me navigate past the obstacles I'll face, but sometimes it's suffocating. Maybe I don't want to always sidestep the challenges. Maybe that's the problem. Maybe too many people avoid facing stuff and calling out crap. I want to chisel away the barriers. Make them smaller, less scary, and I can't do that by not facing them.

'I…' But the words won't come, so instead, I force a grin to my lips and shrug, letting my eyes do the pleading for me.

She lets my hand go and sits up, leaning against the headboard of her bed, her gaze holding mine in that penetrating glare she reserves for other folk and I flinch, half expecting a tirade. But when she speaks, it's in a whisper and I have to move my head closer to her to hear her. 'You've been through sooo much, Flynn. It's time for you to let someone else stick their neck out. I'm worried about you. *Really* worried.'

My resolve wavers and I almost smile and tell her I won't attend tomorrow's meeting. But then Lucy flashes into my mind again – beautiful, upbeat, flamboyant Lucy. Lucy, who always had time for me. Lucy who never let the knocks bring her down – fucking dead Lucy. DEAD Lucy. And despite my hammering heart and the gnawing fear in my gut, I shake my head and say, 'Sorry, Carr. I gotta go.'

Her shoulders slump and a whoosh of air leaves her lips as she taps the back of her head against the wall. 'Aw, Flynn.'

I grab her fingers again and this time it's me who squeezes tight, as if I'll never let them go. I promise tomorrow will be the last one.

Using a tissue to wipe the pink from her mouth, Carrie glowers. 'Yeah right.'

I nudge her. 'Come on, Carr, don't be mad at me.'

As she exhales, her lips twitch, and I can tell by the spark in her eyes that she's forgiven me. 'OK, Flynn. I'll cover for you, but this better be the last time or I'll bloody kill you, right?'

CHAPTER 14

'Right, eyes this way, folks.' Gus observed the team he'd gathered in the incident room after hours. After what Compo and Jo Jo had brought to him only an hour ago, Gus had known he'd have to call them back in on this one. He had no other choice. This was too close to home and although they would hand the information to cybercrime, there was no way his team, with their personal connection to the victims, could let it go. He knew there were images of Jo Jo out there on the dark web. He also knew they could rear their ugly head at any time. No matter how often cybercrime or Compo took them down the risk of some arse uploading them again was a constant worry. He just hadn't expected it to pop up today. He cast a glance towards Jo Jo, who, despite his ashen face, seemed to be holding things together for now. If he had asked his team to investigate officially, he'd have had no option but to exclude Jo Jo from the mix, but as he was going off books, he reckoned Jo Jo's expertise would be beneficial.

He'd already outlined Compo's findings to Alice, but Taffy had only just arrived, out of breath and with the remnants of a lipstick kiss on his cheek showing that he'd cut short a date to be part of this. Gus nodded at Taff, vowing to take the team out when this was all over.

'Thanks for coming. I know, unlike Al and I, you have a life outside these four walls, but—'

'Speak for yourself, Gusset No Mates.' Alice's tone was light, her smile wild as she teased Gus, referring to the way Jo Jo's sister insisted on calling him Gussy, which Alice, much to Gus's annoyance, had changed to Gusset.

As the others tittered, Gus shook his head. All humour would evaporate after Compo revealed his and Jo Jo's findings, so Gus would give them this small reprieve at his expense. Even Jo Jo's lips twitched in response to Taffy's. 'Would have thought you more of a boxer shorts than a thong man, Gusset.'

'OK, OK, joke's on me, but that's your lot. What Comps is going to share is difficult to hear.' Gus looked at his IT expert and, with a wave of the hand, opened the floor to his officer. 'Comps?'

In a pair of baggy joggers, Compo, beanie hat still covering his curls, stepped forward. He cleared his throat and swallowed. One hand plucked at the hem of his well-loved, but ragged 10cc 'Are You Normal' T-shirt, pulling it off his shoulder and distorting the writing on the front. A splodge of ketchup trailed like blood splatter from the 'L'. His other hand held a control which activated the large screen in front of which they all sat. 'Em, well, em.'

He snuck a look at his colleagues and then at Jo Jo, who stood apart from Gus, Alice, and Taffy. Taffy grinned at him.

'It's OK, Comps. It's only us lot and you're way smarter with geekie stuff than any of us. Just spit it out, bruv.'

Taffy's encouragement seemed to do the trick for after an audible inhale of breath, followed by an even louder exhale, which sent a waft of onion breath over the waiting officers, Compo straightened his back, turned, and pressed the control to bring an image onto the screen. For a second, the only sound in the room was the whirr of air conditioning and electronic noises from Compo's PC system.

Then Alice's, 'Fuck, fuck, and fuckity, fuck, fuck,' broke the silence.

Followed by Taffy's, 'Sugary shite dumplings, that's grim.'

Gus, aware of the sensitive nature of the picture on the screen, glanced at Jo Jo. The teenager, eyes averted, now gnawed on his lip. His fingers clamped together so tight his knuckles had turned white. When Gus had first seen the image of Jessie in her too short pyjamas, her My Little Pony toy tucked under her arm with a butt plug in one hand and nipple clamps in the other, it had been on Compo's PC. Now, seeing the image blasted onto the oversized screen, and knowing that it was discovered on a seedy dark website catering for depraved minds, it was uglier – more insidious.

They grabbed illegally captured photographs through hacking personal computers and sold them in auction lots to the highest bidder without the victim's knowledge. They called them 'slaves' and those who bought the stills or videos owned these unsuspecting people. The mere thought of how many images of unwary victims were in circulation, sent cold rage up Gus's spine.

In the one they looked at now, Jessie's eyes were wide, her pupils dilated as if wary. She gazed off the screen at a shadowy figure. Although the auction hadn't ended, the site's owner had paused the flashing 'BIDDING' sign below Jessie's image. To the side, an active chat was playing out online. It was the content of this chat which made the scenario so much worse.

Compo, nodded towards Jo Jo. 'Me and Jo Jo both got separate alerts directing us to this site earlier on this evening and despite my best efforts I couldn't shut it down, nor could I obtain a genuine lead to the origins of the site. The encryptions are sophisticated and although we – I – alerted cybercrimes and they're working on this too, we're being bounced around the world like bloody Phileas Fogg.'

Taffy frowned. 'I don't get this, Comps. What the hell's going on? What's the site all about?'

Before Compo could reply, Jo Jo leant forward. 'The bastards are selling images. It's an online auction. They scoop up images through hacking people's webcams and then sell them to the highest bidder.'

'But…' Taffy threw his hands in the air and slumped back in his chair. 'I don't see the point.'

Jo Jo snorted. 'They're collectors. Sick fuckers who collect all sorts of illegally obtained images. What they're doing is creating 'slaves'. It's a different kind of trafficking and half the people being bought and sold know nowt about it.

'So.' Alice, voice matter of fact, nodded. 'Some sick fucker hacked your web cam, because that image is of your old bedroom.'

A flush flared across Jo Jo's cheeks. It was no secret that Jo Jo had once earnt money to keep his little family afloat by performing sex acts via webcam for money. Nor was it a secret that images from that time were circulating on the dark web. Periodically, Compo's detailed monitoring system elicited alerts, and he took them down. However, this was the first time they'd featured Jessie. Gus was all too aware of the guilt someone with Jo Jo's moral compass would carry, so he walked over to him, and placed his hand on Jo Jo's shoulder. 'None of this is your fault, Jo Jo. It's those sickos who are to blame. Not you.'

Jo Jo swept his arm across his mouth, straightened his shoulders and met Gus's eyes. 'I disagree, Gus. This is *all* my fault. I brought those predators into our house and I'm the one who forgot to lock my door, which is why Jessie's standing there holding fucking sex toys with those fucking sickos bidding on her.'

Gus tightened his grip on the boy's shoulder, then turned to his team. 'The thing is, from' – he glanced at the clock which showed when the bidding had been paused and frozen at £4000 – 'five past eight, this lot has become much more sinister. Comps, talk us through the chat box at the side.'

Compo stepped forward again. 'At 20:02 some sick fucker threw a spanner in the works.'

Compo directed their attention to a highlighted chat communication from a punter calling themselves *DarkNight123*. 'This *DarkNight123* has bypassed the bidding for this lot – Jessie's image – by offering half a million for her location and an additional half mill for delivery of Jessie to him.'

Compo's voice wobbled on the last sentence as he sent a sideways glance towards Jo Jo, whose body was so rigid Gus worried he might break in half.

Taffy's mouth fell open. 'What the actual f—'

'Me, the cyber team and Jo Jo are trying to track down this *DarkNight123*, but so far, no luck. The main issue is—'

Alice snapped her fingers. 'I got it. Because he's announced his desire to buy Jessie, every bastard accessing this auction now has a million quid incentive to find her. What can we do? How can we make sure we find them before they locate her?'

Gus stepped up. 'We've put a Family Liaison Officer in with Jessie and Jo Jo's foster parents and the cybercrime unit are footing the bill for a protective detail for both Jessie and Jo Jo, which is outside their home as we speak. However, although we're not officially linked to this, we can't turn our back, so we'll wind up our current investigation without Compo's help – we're nearly done with it anyway – and Compo will be free to pursue this in his own time. He needs us to sift through any generated data. Jo Jo here' – he smiled at him– 'is seconded to the team. This will be run from Compo's flat as we mustn't let Nancy get wind we're working on this under the radar. She wouldn't be happy to have us working on such a personal case. Besides which,' He paused and dragged his fingers through his loose dreads before continuing.

'We need to make sure Jessie's safe. I won't order you, Alice and Taffy to do—'

'Don't you dare, Gus McGuire. Don't you damn well dare. We're in. You know we're in. No way can we trust this to cyber squad – sometimes I think they're about as effective as ghostbusters. No, we're in. That right, Taff?'

'Too right it is, Al. We're in.'

CHAPTER 15

Carl Morris had spent the last few days in the company of a deep and all-consuming anger. With every passing hour, it had grown in ferocity, his only respite in the gym provided by his top of the range apartment building, pounding the punch bag as if he believed he could grind it to a powder of leather and stuffing on the floor. The target of each punch existed only in his memory. Her smile stripped away to reveal a mocking smirk that should have alerted him to her deceitful nature. With every punch, he splattered her face into a pulp of blood and sinew until even in his mind's eye, she was unrecognisable. He looked forward to playing out this fantasy for real and was using every advantage his money could buy to locate her.

It wasn't only her betrayal in leaving him that fed his voracious anger, it was the consequences of her actions that he'd witnessed only the other week. Her inability to recognise the depths to which she would descend in her attempts to hide herself and what was his from him was inexcusable – unforgivable. He slammed his gloved fist against the bag – *left, left, left, right, left,* then again, *right, right, right, left right.* – feeling the burn in his arms and shoulders as droplets flicked from his sweat sleeked hair and rolled down his brow, stinging his eyes. He would punish her. That wasn't in doubt. However, he had to find her first. Beside him, his new phone – an untraceable burner – buzzed, signalling an incoming call. There was no rush to answer. They'd call back in five minutes – that was the rule. So, he completed a last frenzied cycle of punches – *left, left, left, right, left*, then again, *right, right, right, left right*. When he was done, bent over, fists on his knees, he caught his breath before dragging the gloves off. Heart rate slowing, he grabbed his water bottle and slurped half of it before tipping the rest of it over his head. With a nod at his bodyguard pounding the treadmill nearby, he walked into the changing room and after locking the door behind him he switched the shower on. No point in taking chances, was there? Not that he didn't trust his bodyguard – he paid him enough after all – but caution was in Carl's nature, so he took no chances.

The phone rang again. 'Yep?'

'Got a lead, boss man. A location like. Closest we've got so far.'

Carl's lips tightened; his eye twitched. Was this tosser playing with him – dragging it out for extra bucks? If so, he'd be sorry. Carl had already waited too long. It was time for action and if these low lives didn't understand what he was capable of, then perhaps it was time to show them. 'I want an address by tonight. If not? Well, let's just say, you'll wake up tomorrow missing some body parts.'

The other man's laugh was self-assured, as if he knew Carl couldn't get to him. Carl smiled. Let him think what he liked. He knew exactly how to reach this so-called cyber expert and, more importantly, he had the money to ensure his threat wasn't an idle one – no matter that the man thought being in St Petersburg made him out of Carl's reach. Dealing with oligarchs had its bonuses, after all.

'Tonight, or else. You can't say I didn't warn you now, can you, Ivanov? I look forward to your call.'

Carl hung up, the smile fading from his face to be replaced by a scowl. He didn't know if the man had picked up on Carl's implied threat when he used his name, but he hoped so. Give him something to chew over. An incentive to come up with the goods pronto.

CHAPTER 16

Flynn

Even after being with Carrie, I don't feel better. How can I? Lucy's dead – fucking dead and it's crap and – I punch my pillow, wishing it was a wall. Wishing it was that bloke Nigel's damn head. The police told Linc that they've charged him with her murder, like that's supposed to make us feel better. Nothing's gonna do that. Nothing's gonna bring her back.

I roll onto my back and stare up at my bedroom ceiling and wonder if this hollow clawing wound in my gut will ever mend. I can't eat, can't sleep. Should've told Carrie the truth. Should've told her about Lucy and what happened to her. But she'd just tell me to give up the 007 stuff, and it's even more important that I do something now.

I lean over the edge of the bed and stretch my arm under the mattress until it touches my book and I pull it out. Linc told us what to do. I'll write down what happened to Lucy and why it happened to her in my diary. Documenting this stuff gives us evidence. Evidence we can use to make them listen. Evidence about how we're being failed at every fucking turn. Adults make laws and rules about us, but not a single one of them *gets it*. Not really. Not unless they've been through it. They need to know that we need protection – legal protection – that's what Linc says, and I agree.

Lucy's death was so needless. So fucking unnecessary. If they'd just got her into a hostel. Seen her as worthy. As the wonderful person she was.

I grab my special purple pen from the drawer of my bedside cabinet and open my book on the next clean page. I want to write about Lucy, but not only her death – her *murder*. I want to capture the essence of her. Her beauty, her strength. How she brought light to the world – like a star.

I can barely see the page as I write, for tears keep trickling out of my eyes and no matter how hard I rub them away they're never-ending.

Lucy Smith was my friend. She was a star that shone so brightly that she eclipsed the darkness. She wasn't always called Lucy, and she told us that when she wasn't Lucy, she was sad and shrouded in darkness. It was only as Lucy that she shone. So vibrant, so strong, so full of life.

Then, she was MURDERED!

But I won't talk about that yet. For now, I'm going to talk about everything that Lucy was. She loved nail varnish, did Luce. The brighter, the better, and if it was glittery, then that was even more awesome. Awesome was Lucy's favourite word, and she used it a lot. Sometimes I wondered what she found in her world that was awesome, for Luce didn't have it easy. Her family chucked her out at thirteen, and for all that time she survived with her nail varnish and her awesomeness right up until she didn't…

I can't write any more. Can't think about what we saw last night on our Zoom chat. I'm not ready for that yet, so I put my purple pen back into the drawer, close my diary, and shove it back into its hiding place. Then I have an idea. Something I can do in honour of Lucy's awesomeness. I creep through to Millie's room. She's gone off shopping with her mates, so she won't catch me. Her room's a tip: clothes strewn all over, not one of her dirty garments hit the hamper. I tiptoe over to her dressing table and sift through her stuff until I find what I want.

Sitting on her bed, I open the bottle and sniff in its acetone smell, wishing it would give me a high and make me forget. But it won't. It's not strong enough. I pull the brush out and watch the gloopy neon purple glittery syrup drip back into the bottle and I smile. This is exactly awesome enough. It's exactly Lucy enough. With my right hand, I take the varnish and paint the nails on my left hand – in memory of my friend, the most awesome Lucy Smith.

CHAPTER 17

By the time Artemy Ivanov phones back, it's late and Carl's almost on the point of making the phone call he threatened to make earlier. But, depending on what information his Russian contact offers, Carl might still give the order. After all, the greedy Russian tried to give him the run around.

Despite his cool voice when he answers, Carl's heart pounds as if trying to escape from his chest. He's so close now. So close he can almost smell her perfume – that sweet scent he used to find so alluring, so tantalising, but now the very thought of it makes him want to throw up. For weeks – months even – after she left, he'd catch wafts of it as he moved around the penthouse. Once, he'd been in a lift and one of the women wore the same scent. It had been too much for him, so he'd barged through to the door and left the elevator two floors early. But that was in the early days – the days when his grief and anger vied for dominance in his psyche. Now there was no such conflict. Grief no longer played a part in his decision-making processes. Now every move was fuelled by his thirst for revenge.

'Tell me you've got the location.'

Ivanov's voice, thick with phlegm and rough with too much smoking, grated over the line. 'You are too impatient, sir. I have narrowed her location down to a city in your piddling little country, but I need more time to pinpoint a more precise locality. She has been careful, and her lack of online presence has been—'

'No excuses.' Carl barked the words down the line, interrupting the other man's whining. He smiled as the silence between them deepened and darkened. Artemy had expected his jibe at the size of the UK compared to his monolithic country to irk him. He didn't understand that Carl was no patriot. What had this country ever done for him? He'd got where he was now, despite this 'piddling' country. However, the jibe was an ill-informed move by his Russian expert, for it gave him another excuse to hurt the man. Not through any sense of loyalty, but because he hated to be poked fun at. Gone were the days when he would take such paltry jibes lying down. But that would have to wait.

'I gave you the deadline and, what do you know, the little hand's just clicked past midnight, so you're late.'

'Aw, sir.' A bout of hacking coughing which turned Carl's stomach interrupted Ivanov's conciliatory speech. The Russian was disgusting.

'I said…' Still recovering, Artemy spluttered, the words rushing into one another, his thick accent making it almost impossible to make out what he was saying. 'By tomorrow. I'll have the information by tomorrow. I promise. You've got to understand, it's complicated, no? There is someone trying to hack the site, and I am forced to take diversionary precautions to secure my anonymity. But they are insistent. Insistent and devious. You don't want anyone knowing why we've set the auction to pause, do we? Don't want to draw attention to us, do we?'

This was new – additional information Carl had hitherto been unaware of. Was this so far unidentified hacker going to prove problematic for him? Was he a competitor? Did they have skin in the game, or were they just intrigued by his offer of a substantial reward? Perhaps, in hindsight, that had been a mistake. Perhaps such a sizeable amount had drawn the cockroaches from the woodwork. He thought about it, sizing up the implications of Ivanov's information. He was paying Ivanov well because his specific skill set had come to Carl highly recommended. He'd been told the Russian could deal with these sorts of obstacles in his sleep, so he suspected the man was inflating the complexity of the issue to negotiate more payment. Well, that wasn't likely to work. Not on Carl anyway, not on someone whose ruthlessness had brought him to where he was today.

Carl allowed the silence to gather weight and close in on them before replying, each word delivered with a staccato edge. 'Noon tomorrow, and not a second later.'

He disconnected the call and threw the burner phone onto the couch beside him. Ivanov had let him down, but not only that, he'd tried to trick him into paying more. Perhaps the disgusting, wheezing computer geek had underestimated Carl's reach in his country and that would never do. He thought about it and then picked up another burner phone from the coffee table before him and dialled the single number saved. After two rings his contact answered, and Carl made his request.

'I have a target for you– Artemy Ivanov, hacker from St Petersburg.'

The distorted voice echoed down the line. 'Primary or secondary target?'

Carl thought about that for a second. His initial intention had been to eliminate his contact, now he reconsidered. His heart rate slowed down and a warm glow took up residence in his chest. What could be more of a punishment for Ivanov than letting him live to see the consequences of his cheek and greed? 'I think we'll go for a secondary target. Whoever will cause him the most lasting and painful grief – his mother – partner – hell, his pet dog if necessary. Locate and capture the target but hold off despatching them until I give the order. I want to make sure I've got every piece of information from him before he becomes incapacitated by his loss. Oh, and I require proof prior to payment. Understood?'

The indistinct voice laughed. 'But of course. I know your tastes by now. I'll upload proof to the usual place.'

FRIDAY

CHAPTER 18

It had been after midnight before Compo had bundled Jo Jo into one of Bradford's Elvis taxis. After a day fraught with frustration, the lad had been wiped out. Still, he dug his heels in. Compo, backed up by Taffy, had insisted that Jo Jo needed to go home, catch up with his foster mum and his sister and have some downtime before returning. Not that Jo Jo hadn't been helpful – he had. More so than Taffy, who was about as computer literate as a prawn. Still, Taffy had his uses; when presented with a screen filled with data, he patiently sifted through it and slowly they were building up a profile of their opponents.

At around one-thirty, Taffy had succumbed to the lethargy that had been building all evening. Slow progress was draining and now, with Taffy slumped on the couch, snoring and mumbling indistinct conversations with one of his sisters, Compo exhaled. Compo wasn't used to having other people in his flat when he worked and it affected him – slowed him down, although he wouldn't hurt their feelings by telling them that. In The Fort, he'd created a workstation that barricaded him in, and he'd grown adept at blocking out the activity going on around him. Here, in his small flat, he found it harder to cope with distractions. It was partly because in this particular job, Gus had given him carte blanche to bring into play all his skills, regardless of the legality of the programmes he was running. That wasn't an issue for Compo – they were working off grid and he was skilled enough to feed key information anonymously to the official police cyber team working on the website. It was that he didn't like change. This was his space and how he operated in the seclusion of his small flat was private. With Taffy around, he was a little off centre. Jo Jo was OK, because he and Compo worked seamlessly together, with Jo Jo often able to anticipate what Compo was doing. Jo Jo, without being instructed, had taken it upon himself to distract Taffy when Compo was flying near the edge. Compo smiled at this – there was no way that Taffy could detect any illegal activity anyway, besides which, his friend, in these circumstances and with their boss's backing, would turn a blind eye.

However, with Jo Jo gone and Taffy asleep, it was Compo's time – time to get serious and bring the fuckers down.

So, to prepare for the all-nighter ahead, Compo went about reclaiming his space as much as he could and getting his mind in the game. First, he walked into his small hallway and looked at the series of framed pictures of musicians that adorned his walls – Freddie Mercury, Jimi Hendrix, David Bowie, Jim Morrison…there were too many to mention, but each of them held a special place in his heart. Taffy thought it was morbid and had expressed concern over Compo's mental health in the past, but Compo had just shaken his head and smiled.

'It's an homage, Taff. My celebration of what they've achieved and the joy they brought to the world despite dying too soon. It's not morbid. How can it be? Each of them left something magical behind. How great is that?'

Taffy's smile hadn't reached his eyes and Comp knew he was worried about him, but what more could he tell his friend? Music and computers were Compo's world. They were the two things that had helped him through the darkest times of his childhood. Of course, he'd considered ending his life. It had been hard being the geeky kid with no friends and a series of foster families more concerned with cashing the cheques than looking out for him. The older foster kids had bullied and abused him, and his last foster father had whipped him with a leather belt. These experiences had driven him very near the edge. It was escaping into the world of computers with music his only company that had allowed him to hold off till he could escape. Now, he'd added another category to his life raft – his friends.

Since joining Gus's team, Compo had become part of a family that looked out for him, valued him, nurtured him and, while the music and cyber stuff made him happy, it was his friends who grounded him, who gave him the sense of belonging that made him happy for the first time in his life.

Fortified by an overwhelming sense of positivity, Compo's face broke into a huge grin as he winked at the Jimi Hendrix picture before moving back into his small living area. As he went, he threw a blanket on Taffy's sleeping form, grabbed the remaining half full pizza box and put off all the lights until the only illumination was the area around his workstation. After depositing the pizza within easy reach, he sat back down behind the panels of screens and keyboards, pulled his headphones over his ears, switched the volume up, and selected the Hendrix version of *All Along the Watchtower*. Like a gladiator preparing for battle, Compo took a moment to prepare himself, allowing the music to wash over him with his eyes shut before exhaling.

'I'm coming for you bitches.'

His fingers flew over the keyboard and for the first time that night, his head was crystal clear. He had three jobs to do tonight – first to break the firewalls and encryptions put in place by the site's admin, reveal their identity, and locate their current position. Second, repeat the process with the mysterious bidder who'd caused the auction to pause and taken its threat level to a much higher level. And third to locate the hacker who'd intervened and who, earlier searches had revealed, appeared to work for the mysterious bidder.

When he'd done that, the rest would be up to Gus and the team, although he would do a deep dive to get as much information on these three key players as possible.

Writing code and running undetectable programs was a special skill set of Compo's and as his fingers flew, all their earlier prep work gave results. Engaged in the battle with the anonymous predators who posed a threat to his friends, Compo pulled in favours, swatted away counter measures, dissolved firewalls, and diluted encryptions, each step taking him just that bit closer to his ultimate aim of revealing who was behind the threats to Jessie and Jo Jo. Once he'd done his bit, he was confident that Gus and the rest of the team would carry the battle forward to a satisfactory end.

With Jimi Hendrix still blaring through his headphones, Compo, for the first time since he'd seen Jo Jo and Jessie on the slave auction, felt he might get somewhere. His blurred vision was a minor inconvenience and his ongoing reliance on Red Bull and pizza focussed his mind. Another piece of information landed on his screen, and he punched the air and flung his headphones onto the desk. 'Yes!'

Behind him, Taffy mumbled a response, pulled the cover over his chest, and began to snore again. Compo grinned and punched the air again but lowering his voice as he repeated his earlier exclamation. 'Yes!'

Finding the location of the guy who'd set up 'Slave Site' had been fairly easy – well, for Compo, anyway. The guy had thought he was being savvy by obtaining a

VPN address to hide his IP. However, Compo had located the site creator at an address barely spitting distance from Compo's flat in Bradford city centre – *who says the world's a big place*? Pushing further, Compo stared at the ID that appeared on his screen and frowned. A flash of white rage seared through him, making him want to punch the wall. He'd come across this name before and so had the team. It would give Gus great satisfaction to follow up on that in the morning.

However, that was only one part of the jigsaw, and Compo still had work to do. He linked his fingers and, extending his arms away from his body, stretched till they cracked. He was ready to take on the might of the real hacker. The bidder had been no more competent than the site admin, however, he or she had employed an expert hacker to cover their tracks. Compo had only followed the haphazardly encrypted IP locations until the hacker stepped in and blocked up all the holes in the anonymous bidder's armoury. This was a worthy opponent – someone who knew how to keep their identity hidden.

'Let the battle commence.'

Compo grinned as he weaved and ducked through encryptions, cursing when his attempts to detect back doors through which he could enter and drop his own back door were thwarted. Slugging energy drinks and scoffing chocolate were par for the course as Compo bounced on his chair, swinging it round to view other screens, immersed in his job and grinning when he thwarted his opponent's attempts to create back doors which would lead them to Compo.

'Oh, no you don't, my friend. Not on my watch.' With that, he grabbed his headphones, slammed them back on his head and, fingers flying over his keyboard, he used a strategy he'd used before – deflection. In haste, he implemented an attack which would keep his adversary occupied in one area, while Compo attempted to gain access under the radar using another programme created for such stealth operations.

Speed was Compo's friend and after an hour with various programmes designed to hide his actual intention running in the background, he was satisfied. The misdirects were complicated and threatening enough that his opponent would be obliged to counteract them, he finally hit pay dirt and quick as a flash, before his adversary realised what he was up to, he ducked in, dropped his back door in an elusive area and dropped right back out again before his opponent could detect him.

Sweat poured from his face as he slumped in his chair, grinning and panting. Now they could monitor the broker's activity, which could lead them to the bidder – Compo leant forward, set up a few alerts, and then studied the screen. It was too early to ascertain if he'd got away with it, but he was hopeful. However, regardless of whether his activity would remain undetected, he'd got a location for the broker – St Petersburg.

Tiredness made his shoulders ache, and he was aware of his heart hammering in his chest – a side effect of too much caffeine. His eyes were gritty, and he longed to slump off to bed, but his job wasn't done yet. If he wanted to keep the broker blindsided, he'd need to make sure his focus was elsewhere. He sifted through his music and changed the track: 'Back in the USSR' by The Beatles. His back twanged and his arms were leaden as he pulled himself forward and set the final part of his plan in motion. Scrunching his eyes open and shut a few times, he allowed a small smile to spread across his lips.

The broker would be busy for the next few hours combatting the arsenal Compo had released on them.

Job done, he jumped to his feet, threw the headphones down, stretched his arms up and to the side rotating his shoulders as he moved, and then began a sort of uncoordinated jog on the spot which progressed into a circuit of his small living room come office. The only problem was Taffy half sprawled across the sofa. With his feet dangling over the edge and his size 11 boots discarded on the floor, the area was like an obstacle course to be manoeuvred over. Unfortunately for both Taffy and Compo, Compo wasn't the most coordinated of men and combined with the aching tiredness in his limbs, inevitably, disaster would ensue. Within moments of starting his wake-up exercise, Compo had crashed against Taffy's legs, tripped over his boots, and landed on top of his snoring colleague. Winded, he lay with his face centimetres from Taffy's face, while Taffy, in his half sleepy state and assuming he was under attack, punched him in the ribs as he tried to push himself into a sitting position.

'Ouch, Taff. No need for that.' Compo rolled off his colleague's frame, rubbing his ribs as he did so, and cracked his head on the edge of the coffee table while sweeping a half full can off the table and onto his own lap.

'Awww.' Compo attempting to rub both his head and his ribs simultaneously groaned and let his head fall onto the carpet where he lay with his eyes closed.

'What the heck, Comps. What was all that about?'

Still recovering, Compo wafted a hand in the air and groaned some more as the liquid from the energy drink can seeped further into his khaki cargo pants, spreading in a stain that resembled a drunk caught short before he reached the urinal. 'Awwww!'

Now that Compo's had removed his bulk from Taffy's skinny frame, Taffy swung his legs round and sat up, grimacing when he caught a bag of popcorn with his foot sending a cascade of yellow sticky kernels onto his friend. 'Aw crap, Comps. Sorry.'

Compo's groans intensified. 'Awwwwwww!' But now he opened one eye and glared at Taffy. 'Think you nearly killed me, Taff.'

But Taffy was looking round the room, his face scrunched up like a determined two-year-old on a nappy filling mission. 'You hear that?'

'Awwwwwww!'

'I'm serious, Comps. Do you hear that? Sounds like – sounds like…' He prowled round the room, collecting a fluff of popcorn on his socks as he went. 'The Beatles!' He turned a triumphant grin towards Compo. 'You got your tune for this case, bro, which means you've found something. Tell me what it is.'

Pulling himself to his feet, Compo studied his wet pants with a frown and then cast his eyes around the bomb site that was his small flat. 'Yep, I found something. We need to get the boss and Alice over here. However, you're gonna clean up this mess while I have a shower. No way I want them seeing me or the flat in this state. It looks like I've wee'd myself.' He grabbed a tissue and began rubbing at the wet patch on the front of his trousers, before giving up with a sigh when he only added white blobs of tissue to the fabric.

As he headed to the small bathroom, Taffy grabbed a plastic bag and began tossing empty biscuit and sweet wrappers and crisp bags into it while grabbing a huge Raja's Pizza box in the other hand and transporting the lot through to the kitchen. Compo was just about to slam the bathroom door shut when the doorbell went.

Shit! Looks like Gus and Al are here already.

Giving up on his plan of showering, Compo redirected himself to his bedroom, grabbed an almost identical pair of cargo pants from a pile which may or may not have been of clean clothes, and swapped his trousers. At least he wouldn't look like he'd pissed himself. However, on his return to the living room, rather than his boss and colleague, Jo Jo, plastic bag in hand, was helping Taffy gather up the remnants of their all-night work session.

'Thought I told you we'd got this, Jo Jo. It's not even eight o'clock and you should be in…'

'Easter hols, Comp,' said Taffy and Jo Jo together before the younger man, in a quiet voice, added, 'Besides, I can't sleep. Not with all that out there. Not when Jessie might be under threat.'

Compo studied Jo Jo for a moment. True to his word, the dark circles under Jo Jo's eyes spoke of a sleepless night and combined with the frown that puckered his brow and had taken up permanent residence there since the other night, Compo hadn't the heart to send him away. Besides, Jo Jo was almost as good as Compo with digital stuff, and he was a lot more competent than Taffy. 'Hoover's over there. I'm going for my shower.' But before he could, the doorbell rang and Gus and Alice trooped in. Alice flung herself onto the couch, snatched a stray piece of popcorn from the coffee table, and threw it into the air before catching it in her mouth. 'Nobody believe in home security, these days? Not like we're five-o or anything, is it?'

Compo glared at Taffy until the smell of the bacon butties Gus had brought with him distracted him. Resigned to the delay in his shower plans, Compo grabbed two of the rolls and between mouthfuls explained what he'd found and how that could help them if the hacks he'd put in place remained undetected.

'For now, though, if I were you I'd focus on this Bradford location and this scrote who's behind the slave scam.'

He turned to his screen and brought up an image. 'That's the Slave Site owner.'

Four pairs of stunned eyes took in the image Compo had pulled up. They all knew him – had all had interactions with him over the years – Razor McCarthy – one of the gang leaders on Jo Jo and Jessie's old estate.

Jo Jo gasped and took a step closer, fists clenched by his sides and his eyes flashing. 'Really? Really? That tosser. I knew he was after summat. I damn well knew it. But this? Why would the sick bastard do this to Jessie?'

Gus placed a hand on the lad's shoulder and squeezed. 'Don't worry, Jo Jo. Razor McCarthy's going nowhere. We know where the scrote is and he'll get what he deserves. I promise.'

As Gus moved away from Jo Jo, Compo went over and engulfed him in a hug. 'We'll sort this, Jo Jo. Don't worry, it'll all be over soon. Gus and the guys will bring him in while the cyber team takes control of the website. It'll give us valuable insight into what's going on.'

Jo Jo, placing his palms on Compo's chest, pushed himself away from the computer nerd. 'I don't care about who controls the damn site. I don't give a toss if you get valuable fucking insight. This is Jessie we're talking about. My sister. Hasn't she been through enough?'

For long moments, the only sounds in the room were Jo Jo's laboured breathing and the faint burr of Compo's PCs doing their thing in the background. The adults looked at each other, none of them knowing what to do. Compo wanted to scream at his boss, '*You sort it Gus. Get this sorted now. Help the kids*.' But deep down inside, he knew Gus couldn't make Jo Jo feel better. How could he? None of them could guarantee that they could obliterate those images. They could only take down the site and charge the owner for illegal website activity.

Jo Jo turned accusing eyes on Compo, anger making each of his words feel like a slap. 'You know Razor couldn't do this – not on his own. He couldn't have set this up. He's too bloody thick.'

This was true. Compo had already considered this but had planned to mention this possibility to Gus in private. As he'd dug further back, he found that the initial administrator of the site had relinquished it to Razor over a year ago, and Razor had taken over the ongoing updates and new auctions. Clearly McCarthy considered this a lucrative trade with little risk and had been reaping the benefits for the past few months. That was going to stop now, though. Hopefully he'd realise his back was to the wall and reveal the person who'd offloaded the site to him. If not, Compo could eventually work it out. For now, though, that wasn't his primary focus because McCarthy and his mysterious benefactor weren't the only threat to Jo Jo and Jessie.

This hacker – the broker – and the anonymous bidder's request to locate Jessie's current whereabouts had serious implications. Compo ran through everything he'd put in place, searching for a glimmer of inspiration that would make the entire process of identifying the more threatening figures quicker, but deep down he knew he'd done his absolute best. It was all a waiting game as far as those two were concerned, and Compo was certain the measures he'd set in place would pay dividends.

Compo yawned, and as a red bloom flushed his cheeks, he offered a half-hearted shrug. 'Oops, sorry. I'm knackered, boss. I need to shower and have a kip. If Jo Jo's all right with it, he can monitor activity and waken me up if there are complications.'

Dragging his feet, Compo shuffled over to the bedroom, deciding sleep was a greater priority than showering. It was only as he pushed the door open that he realised he'd delivered his entire findings while looking like he'd peed himself. If he hadn't been so tired, he'd have explained what happened, but all he could manage was, 'By the way I've not wee'd myself – ask Taffy.' Before slouching into his bedroom, leaving his guests to sort themselves out.

CHAPTER 19

'See? I told you I'd get the goods to you on time, didn't I?'

Carl Morris's mouth turned down at the cocksure bravado coming down the line at him. Even with his accented English, Ivanov sounded like a right wanker and Morris was pleased he'd already decided to extinguish the Russian's cocky light. Only what he deserved, after all. With his fingers tightening on the burner phone, Morris kept his tone friendly. 'You ever heard that old English saying about pride coming before a fall?'

As expected, the obscure reference was lost on the Russian whose only response was a baffled, 'Eh?' followed by, 'I'm Russian, you understand? We have many sayings here also, but none about pride. Is that to do with gays?'

Philistine! Morris grunted and was about to snap at the man, but before he could, Artemy spoke. 'I know the site owner's location. Not that he has created this on his own. He's too much of a – I think you call it – waster, to be the brains behind it. But finding out additional information is your job, I believe.'

Ivanov's inflection rose in the last word of his sentence, making it sound more like a challenge than a statement. Morris's fingers tightened even more on the phone and although the other man couldn't see him, his eyes narrowed, his lips tightening as he scowled at the phone. 'Just spill the information I've paid you for. I've no time for your stupid insinuations.'

'Ah, that's just it, boss man. Things have changed a little and I've had to take additional, shall we say, unexpected precautions to protect my interests.'

Morris inhaled and began walking round his penthouse. He'd hoped the other man had taken his threats seriously, but it appeared he hadn't. The man's analytical powers clearly did not stretch beyond his cyber work, and self-preservation was a skill he had yet to hone. 'I already told you not to mess with me. I don't suffer fools well and your incessant petty manoeuvrings really piss me off. I warned you about trying to extort more money from me. It is unprofessional and I will not tolerate it. '

'Ach, no, my friend. You misunderstand. I'm not trying to extricate more money from you. No, that is not my intent. What I am trying to do is to warn you…'

Ivanov's attempts to backtrack sent a spasm of anger up Morris's spine and if he hadn't also been amused by the slight panic to the man's tone, he would have scalded him with his tongue. Instead, he tutted. 'Tt tt ttt.' And in a singsong tone which got louder every time he repeated the sentence, said, 'You're warning me? You're warning me? You're warning me?' Until he ended on a near bellow which reverberated around the flat before silence prevailed.

'No, no. I'm sorry. I haven't been clear. I must tell you what happened last night. Someone, a hacker perhaps, has—'

'No! I won't listen to any more of your crap. Give me the locations and then your obligation will be over.' For long moments, all Morris heard was elevated breathing from the other end of the line. He wondered if he'd have to tighten the thumbscrews with a more explicit threat. He was reluctant to do that. He always derived more enjoyment when his punishments were delivered unexpectedly, so he didn't want to reignite any sense of doom in Artemy's mind.

When Artemy spoke, his voice was quiet – almost a whisper. Yet his tone was urgent, his words rushing over themselves as if he expected Morris to shut him down again. 'Someone's onto the site owner, boss man. I'm trying to locate who. I do this for free. I don't want no money for it. It's free, for you.'

For a moment Morris hesitated. Was the Russian playing him? He sounded petrified, but it might all be an act. Morris tapped the edge of the phone with his index finger as he weighed up the odds. Did it matter to him if some hacker was sniffing around the Slave Auction site? Not really. As soon as he got the owner's details, then he'd move quickly. Still, it wouldn't do any harm to keep the Russian dangling – get his money's worth from the hacker and then he could act. 'You owe me, Artemy. Find out what you can about this mysterious hacker, but in the meantime, I want the information you have on the site's owner.'

'OK, OK.' Artemy's tone though still a little elevated didn't carry the same tinge of panic as earlier. Morris grinned. That was all to the good. Artemy thought he'd dodged a bullet, and that served Morris well. The Russian wouldn't know what had hit him.

'Boss man, I'll text you the details. I'll do it right now and when I locate the other hacker, then we are even, no?'

Morris paused in front of the large mirror that hung above the lounge fire; his face breaking into a wide smile. This was precisely what he wanted. 'Deal.'

Seconds later, his phone notified him of a text. He opened it and saw the name and address of the slimy little scrote who had angered him so – well – the other slimy little scrote who had angered him. Nodding, he spun on his heel and lifted a second burner phone from the coffee table before auto dialling the single number saved to the device. When it was answered, his instructions were simple. 'Punish Artemy Ivanov soon. I'll await confirmation on the site.'

About to hang up, a thought occurred to him. 'Take your time with it. I'll pay extra and there's no rush to make him aware of his punishment. He still owes me some info. I'll let you know when to tell him.'

Although the person on the other end of the call remained silent, Morris could hear their breathing and knew they had received his message. He flung himself on the sofa, poured a large drink, and savouring the fiery liquid as it trickled down his throat, he glanced at the family photo positioned in pride of place right next to him on the coffee table. He tipped his glass towards it, his index finger pointing at the figures in the image and 'You, my dear, are about to regret betraying me, big fucking time.'

Still grinning, he downed the rest of the glass, undid his top button and slumping back on the sofa he pulled a blanket over his body. Perhaps now he'd be able to grab some much needed sleep.

CHAPTER 20

'Can't believe that little shit Razor McCarthy's behind this, can you?' Alice, nipping in and out of the traffic in her little Mini, glanced at Gus who was seated in the passenger seat. 'Gus, you listening? I said—'

'Yeah, Al. I heard you. Just give me a minute, huh? Give me a chance to think through everything Compo told us.' He scowled out the window at City Park, as they drove up Godwin Street and onto Prince's Way toward Manchester Road, oblivious to the way the sun caught the mirror pool casting sparkles through the water. Something niggled him, but he couldn't quite put his finger on it. All he knew was that whatever it was, it churned his stomach.

He'd not seen Razor McCarthy for months, nor had he heard word that he'd been brought in for any misdemeanours. That wasn't necessarily surprising. Razor was careful. He was the brains on the Belle Hill Estate and, unlike his rival gangster, Hamid Farooqi, otherwise known as Hammerhead, Razor was smart and ran a tight ship. Last time Gus had encountered Razor was after a knife attack on the estate. He'd been sure Razor had instigated it, but of course the shit didn't stick. Razor McCarthy and his henchmen, – Arthur Goyle – nicknamed Goyley and Holden Powell – known as HP to his friends and enemies alike – had got off with it.

Now having him in the frame for this set his teeth on edge. Razor might be bright, but as Compo rightly pointed out, he wasn't a bloody genius. He wouldn't have been able to set up this sort of dark web slave auction scam without a lot of help, and it was that thought that sent shivers up Gus's spine. He half-turned in his seat as Alice pulled up at the traffic lights. 'You know what I think, Al?'

'Mmm, let me think.' She tapped her fingers on the steering wheel and grinned at him. 'That I'm due a pay rise?'

Despite his worries, a smile flashed across Gus's lips, only to disappear seconds later. 'Yeah, you'd have to put the effort in for that. I don't know about you, but I'm thinking…' He paused and shook his head.

Alice tutted as she moved into gear and moved off. 'For God's sake, spit it out, will you? We're almost there, and I want to know where you're coming from before we bring Razor in.'

'Zodiac.'

Alice glanced at him, her eyes wide and her mouth a perfect 'O'. Before she responded the learner driver in front of her stalled and she had to brake hard. 'Shit, crap, and smelly doody doo doos.' As she waited for the car in front to set off again, she turned to Gus. 'You serious?'

Still hesitant to put his thoughts into words, Gus shrugged. He had no proof that Zodiac was behind the Slave Auction, but his gut told him she was. His lips twitched – like that would stand up in a court of law. He gave Alice a gentle nudge.

'Smelly doody doo doos? Really? No, don't answer that. To be honest, I've no idea if I'm right about Zodiac, but it sort of makes sense, doesn't it? We're all agreed that, smart though he is, Razor is no cybercrime expert. No way could he do this without help and—'

'That serial killing scumbag had it in for Jo Jo and—'

'Compo found evidence that someone had hacked his PC.'

Alice had followed Gus's thought process, and that gave Gus's suspicions more gravitas. Alice was no fool and if she'd joined the same dots he had, then maybe they were onto something. At least if Zodiac was behind the website, then there'd one less criminal to catch, for the serial killer was already incarcerated. As silence reigned in the car, Gus glared out the window, his mind working overtime as he tried to make sense of it. 'If Compo hadn't been up all night, I'd have him working on this already. If anyone can either eliminate or confirm this, it's him. Damn! He needs his rest – needs to recharge his batteries – he looked knackered, didn't he?'

'Jo Jo? He's got the skills…' Alice's words tailed off by the end of the sentence. 'No, not Jo Jo. He's too close to all this. Not sure he'd be able to focus, anyway.'

'Agreed. We'll wait for Comps and in the meantime, we'll bring Razor in, see if we can rattle something loose.'

As they continued to drive, Gus studied Alice's profile. Had that frown and the tightness around her lips always been there or was it a direct result of the reference to Zodiac? Alice and his boss, DCI Nancy Chalmers, had shouldered the brunt of the interviews with the killer and it had taken its toll on both of them. He didn't want to risk setting Alice back again if they had to re-interview Zodiac and there was no way they could indulge the prisoner's fantasies by allowing Gus anywhere near the interrogation. He sighed. Perhaps it wouldn't come to that. Maybe he'd got it wrong, and Zodiac was nothing to do with this. Perhaps Razor would come clean and tell them everything they needed to know. Yeah, right. There was more chance of Alice's Mini developing some extended leg room.

CHAPTER 21

Flynn

'Like your nails, Flynn.' Carrie flings herself on the wooden bench beside me and grabs my hand, examining the bright purple varnish with a critical eye. 'You could've at least trimmed your cuticles first, you wazzock, and you've smudged too.'

I grab my hand back, wishing I hadn't agreed to meet Carrie for a Starbucks in City Park. She's too damn observant by half, and the last thing I need is to have to lie to her. Not that I can help it. I can't tell her about what happened to Lucy. Well, not yet, anyway. Not till after tonight's meeting. I scowl down at my trainers and sit on my hands, hoping that she'll lay off me about the nail varnish if she can't see it. Not such bloody luck. She's like a Rottweiler with a bone when she sets her mind to it. I sense her eyes on me, but I don't look up. Instead, I move my feet around, as if I'm shuffling some imaginary stone or summat about. Maybe she'll take the hint and just chill.

She stretches her feet out in front of her and I smile when I see that she's painted her toenails rainbow colours. She wiggles her toes, wanting me to comment on her artistry, but I'm too pissed off about her noticing my feeble attempts to honour Lucy to oblige – not right now, anyway. Then she slides closer to me and links her arm through mine before resting her head on my shoulder. 'What did your mum say about your nails, Flynn? Did she think it was a good sign?'

The way she exaggerates the words *good sign* makes me giggle and I forgive her for going on about my nails.

'You got it. She was all smiles and jokes while she pretended not to notice. Imagine what she'd have been like if I'd chosen pink? Kept glancing at them, though. Like a bit of bloody purple glitter on my nails changes owt. I reckon she'll be off to Primark next stocking up on the bras and dresses again.'

My voice hitches on the last sentence, and Carrie squeezes my arm tighter. I sooo wish I could tell her everything – about Lucy – about the group. What we've all been through. How we just want the crap to stop. If anyone would get it, it's Carrie. But I bite my tongue and put on a smile as I jump to my feet, dragging Carrie with me. 'Come on rainbow girl with the stunning rainbow toenails' '

Extending her leg and tilting one foot back and forth she squeals like a toddler. 'You like them, Flynny? You really like them?'

I roll my eyes, aware that Carrie's excitement has drawn eyes from nearby on us and jump right into our routine. 'I don't like them, I—'

'Love them!' Carrie, clapping her hands, dances on the spot, and suddenly the world seems nicer – funny what a set of rainbow nails can do.

'Come on, show off rainbow nails, coffee's on me.'

CHAPTER 22

'What the actual fuu…' Razor McCarthy was chilling at his mate HP's house when the weird text came in.

'You seen this, HP? What's this all about?' Razor turned his screen towards his mate slumped on a bean bag, spliff between his fingers, a Heineken can and a line of ready cut coke on the table beside him.

HP peered through the smoke fuzz, eyes scrunched up as he tried to read the text, and then collapsed in a fit of high-pitched giggles, before trying to pull himself upright. The only trouble was, the bean bag seemed to have sprouted arms that wrapped round the idiot's torso, pulling him backwards to sprawl, legs akimbo half off the seat. His antics nudged the table, which knocked his lager over, where it soaked in a frothing mess into the coke.

Razor glared at his giggling mate and stood up, kicking him on the shin as he passed. He walked through the house and out into the back garden. HP was a right slob. His gaff was minging and the only reason Razor had deigned to visit today was because he figured HP was becoming a liability. Too much product sampling and not enough keeping his head in the game. Razor wanted to tell the fucker to pull his act together. With HP so fucking out of it, it was time to cut his once trusty henchman loose. He'd get Goyley on the case – get him to pay some of the neighbourhood scrotes to douse his house or summat. Razor appreciated a clean break and

HP would be no great loss. He smirked and took the roll-up from behind his ear, flicked his Clipper, and lit up. Besides, making Goyley deal with the 'clean up HP op' served two very distinct purposes – one, it offered Razor plausible deniability if the crap hit the fan and two, it was a timely reminder to Goyley that no one was indispensable.

Dodging the burst bin bags and crap that covered HP's back yard, Razor scowled. His own garden was a mess – but that was a deliberate ploy to make sure his gaff didn't stand out in the neighbourhood. Last thing he wanted was the kids on the block realising how well off he was. He'd considered moving out, leaving Goyley and HP to protect his assets on the estate. But HP's addiction put paid to that idea. He'd have to train a new lad to help Goyley, and that would take time. He inhaled deeply, savouring the bitter taste of the smoke as it hit the back of his throat. *Might get a better gaff – a detached house in a posh area.* Hell, maybe he'd settle down with that bint he was screwing. She'd told him she was up the duff. Well, maybe it was time to give a more 'family man' persona. Besides, Angela was all right in the sack. Not opposed to a bit of arse action and didn't expect loads of apologies and crap if he got too rough. And the bitch could cook, too. Yep, maybe that's what he'd do. Settle down with Angela and pretend to be respectable and leave Belle Hill Estate behind to rot while he reaped the benefits of their lack of ambition. Sometimes Razor wondered what these people got out of life. They all seemed content to live in misery, copulating, taking the produce he supplied, and sinking deeper into squalor. Yep, maybe it was time to move on – to move up.

What the hell was that mysterious text about? He flicked his fag end into the accumulated pile of rancid rubbish and brought the message up again.

Unknown number: Dude, you need to get out. That mad fucker with the money from the Slave Auction site has located you. He's got connections. You're not safe!

Not safe? Razor had seen the action on the site and was happy to pause the action on Lots 57 and 58. No skin off his nose and they'd promised him a big payout. When he found out where those two scummy slaves were, he'd be able to afford a fucking mansion in Ilkley, never mind a detached house in Bradford. But what if this text was the real deal? What if that fucker had broken through the encryptions? Fuck, Zodiac. That psycho could have set him up – could've given his location to the big bidder – could've worked a scam or summat. Razor exhaled and leant back on the pebble-dashed wall. Nah. Zodiac couldn't be behind this. No way – that fucker was locked up in La La Land on 24/7 watch. He grinned. Still, how had this fucker got his number? This was his business burner, and he'd only started using it last week. He had rules, had Razor. Don't use a burner for longer than a fortnight.

Head bowed, he allowed the cogs to turn in his brain. He needed a strategy. Needed to keep himself safe till he worked out who this mysterious sender was. He pushed himself off the wall and re-entered HP's house. Before he left, he had things to do. He needed to do them damn fast. He marched along the hallway and up the stairs, breathing through his mouth so that the overwhelming stench of weed combined with body odour wouldn't make him gip. He knew where HP kept his supply of burner phones, so avoiding HPs double bedroom, he entered the single room next to it and headed past the bundles of less than fresh clothes scattered over the bare floorboards and to the single bed with its soiled sheets bundled up in the middle of the mattress. With his nose scrunched up, he bit the bullet and thrust his arm between the mattress and the bed frame and rummaged around until he located a box covered in plastic and pulled it out. He repeated the process twice more until he had three burner phones still in their unopened packaging. Grabbing a Tesco carrier bag, he thrust them inside and rolled his shoulders. A strange prickling sensation niggled at the back of his neck as if someone was watching him. He thrust that thought aside as he loped downstairs and out into the garden again.

Once in the open air, his breathing eased, and he gulped in great breaths, preferring the stench of rotting vegetables and dog turds to the claustrophobic marijuana and BO from indoors. He paused, glanced round to make sure he was unobserved, and then took both the burner phone with the strange warning on it and the phone he used to contact his family from his pocket. On the back of a cornflake packet, he jotted down his family's numbers and Goyley's most up-to-date burner before taking the SIMs out of both phones, snapping them in two and thrusting them into a pile of rubbish spewing over the concrete yard. He then dropped the phones themselves onto the ground and with his heel stamped on them till they were in smithereens, then swept the sole of his trainer over them to disperse them throughout the garden.

Satisfied that he'd broken the link between his phone and his current location, Razor pulled his hood up over his hair and sloped out of the garden. He knew this estate like the back of his hand, so it was easy to navigate his way out by the least populated areas. Once out of the estate, he broke into a run and jogged down Manchester Road till he reached the Interchange. He had no clear idea where he'd go yet, but before he decided that, he had calls to make, so keeping his head down and his head averted from any cameras, he sloped into the Greggs café, ordered a coffee and a sausage roll, and slinked off into a corner booth which afforded a little privacy. With the plastic bag on the table next to his takeaway cup, Razor opened one of the burner phones and activated it. His first call was to Goyley, which was answered straight away.

Goyley was used to Razor calling on unknown numbers, so, although cautious, he always picked up. ''Lo.'

'It's me.'

'OK…Whassup?'

Razor smiled. Goyley knew to be cautious even on the burners. 'Summat's come up. I might be compromised. Need you to get to my gaff, grab me all my bucks, and bring it to me at the usual place.'

'OK. On it, boss.'

'Hey, be careful and ditch the phone pronto, OK?'

'Copy that.'

'Just one more thing.'

'Yeah, anything, boss. You name it and it's done.'

'HP's compromising our operation, mate. He's an addict. He needs to go. You got me?'

Goyley didn't reply immediately, and Razor could almost hear the wheels turning in his mate's mind. Goyley wasn't the brightest cabbage on the allotment, but he was obedient – well, usually. What Razor was asking could be a step too far. Even for someone as loyal as Goyley.

'You want me to tell him to go? To like, well, leave Bradford or summat?'

Razor let the silence lengthen. It would be better if Goyle came to the realisation himself that Razor wanted something a lot more permanent. A sort of half laugh drifted down the line and Razor knew Goyley had caught on.

'You want me to – what? Off him? Like stab him or summat?'

This was Razor's cue to reassure his mate – get him onside. 'No, what are you like? No way I'd expect *you* to do that.'

A more convincing laugh from the phone made Razor smile as he cast his final hook. 'You're too important to get your hands dirty. You're my right-hand man, get me? I rely on you too much, don't I?'

'Yeah, yeah, that's true, boss. You and me go way back. I've always been your main man, right?'

'Right, Goyley. You're a trooper, you are. But, like I said, HP's gonna bring us all down. The Five-O have already been sniffing around him.'

OK, that wasn't entirely true, but Goyley didn't need to know that.

'He's so fucking doped up that he'll spill everything to them. We'll end up doing 25 years in Armley or Wakefield. But that's not gonna happen. Not if we sort it, yeah?'

'Fuck, 25 years for a bit of dealing and that?' Goyley's voice wavered, and Razor imagined him chewing his lip like he did every time Razor told him off.

'You gotta factor in the other crap, mate. The whores, the online stuff, the stabbings – it'll all stack up against us. It's bad news for us if he snitches – and he will. You know how the junkies are. They'd sell their granny for a sniff of coke.'

This time when he spoke, Goyley's voice was firmer. 'OK, OK, I'll sort it. What do you want me to do?'

Razor's grin widened. *Gottcha*! 'You need to bung him some coke and wait till he's out of his skin. Then pay some lads on the estate to torch his house.'

'You want to burn him alive?'

'Course I don't *want* to do that – it's a necessity, innit? There's too much DNA and crap linking back to us in his gaff. It's the only way.' Now for the final thrust – the deal clincher. 'Course, if you're not up for it, I can get someone else in. I'll be needing a new man anyway to replace HP—'

'No, no. I'll do it. I'll get it done today.'

'Good man. Knew I could rely on you. Now chop chop. You've a busy day ahead of you.'

Confident that Goyley would get the money to him and deal with the HP problem, Razor took a swig of his coffee and stuffed the sausage roll into his mouth. Shit, he was starving. As he chewed, acrid wafts of adrenalin fuelled perspiration fugged over him. Alongside that, the lingering stink of marijuana from HP's gaff clung to him. He scowled. When Goyley met him with his money, he'd find out if he'd got the take down on HP sorted. Man was a fucking animal and HP deserved all he got.

Phone in hand, he hesitated, then fired off a text to his mum. She owed him big time, and she'd be too scared not to carry out his orders.

Burner phone: Mum, get yourself to my house and dump all my electronic equipment and my stash before the pigs get there. You better fucking do it, or else. Remember who pays your bills.

That should do it. Razor left the café and headed for the men's toilets. He found an empty cubicle, so he went inside, repeated his earlier process with the SIM from the burner phone he'd just left and flushed the pieces. Lifting the cistern, he tossed the phone inside, leaving the water to do its job in hiding it. Next stop was Lister Park, where he'd meet Goyley, and then after that he'd catch a train from Foster Square to Shipley and then catch a train to Carlisle where he could lie low till he worked out just how serious this threat against him was.

CHAPTER 23

As they drove onto the Belle Hill Estate, Gus kept a lookout for Razor or his thuggish friends. With such nice weather, it wouldn't surprise him if they were out and about, spreading their own special brand of misery on the estate. As usual, when entering the poorer estates in Bradford, the contrast between the area in which he lived and worked, and these ex-Metro estates struck Gus. Manningham might have its problems with drug usage and gang affiliation, but, except for the few poor, ghettoised pockets, there was a sense of being able to breathe – to live. Here on the ex-Metro housing estate that was Belle Hill, the overpowering aura was of decay. Most gardens were overflowing with broken furniture, overflowing bags of rubbish, and crap. Those with any greenery were overgrown and tawdry looking. At least fifty per cent of the houses had boarded-up windows and, with it being the school holidays, the streets were filled with kids in ill-fitting dirty clothes staring at them as they drove past. Gus acknowledged that their presence on the estate might be the extent of their Easter holiday's excitement.

Cars dotted along the streets that made up the estate were either built up on bricks with various parts missing or were upmarket vehicles without number plates. Gus understood how hard it was to police this particular estate. It was renowned for its lawlessness, which was why the likes of Razor McCarthy and Hammerhead plied their trade. The few families that held down jobs ultimately escaped and didn't look back. Gus was amazed that Jo Jo's small family had survived here for so long and he acknowledged that their survival had been in no short measure down to Jo Jo. Circumstances had forced the lad to do whatever he could to protect his sister and his mum. How many Jo Jo's on this estate were forced to do stuff they shouldn't have to? Gus shuddered.

'No sign of him, Al. Turn right here and we're on his street.'

Razor's street was no different from the others they'd driven through, and Alice pulled to a halt just outside his gate. Razor's records revealed that, after his dad was beaten to a pulp and left the city, he'd lived here with only his mum and sisters for five years. He'd refused to name his attacker, but everybody knew that it was Razor who'd left his dad minus a spleen. That had been the first documented incident of Razor's violence, and it had showed him as someone not to be meddled with. It wasn't long before he became one of the two gangsters ruling the estate. Nobody in their right mind would dob Razor in because, as well as having his history of violence behind him, Razor also had well-paid, well-motivated thugs to do his bidding.

The McCarthy residence seemed as poorly maintained as the others in the street. The gate hung off its hinges and cat shit dotted the concreted front garden space. A couple of old sofas with their arses hanging out sat with an upturned box in front of them. Scattered around them on the concrete were lager cans and fag ends. The windows were mucky, but behind the dirt, Gus recognised curtains similar to the ones he had in his own front room. He had bought his after advice from his last girlfriend, Patti, and he knew they cost an arm and a leg. He suspected that concealing his wealth behind mucky windows was Razor's way of blending in – pretending to be one of the lads while in secret living in luxury. No 'making do' for Razor McCarthy and his family. Unlike the poor blighters who got hooked on his drugs or fell under his control.

He got out of the car and waited for Alice to lock it before together they squeezed past the broken gate and, dodging the cat poo, approached Razor's home. While Alice scanned the front of the house for movement, Gus hammered on the door. After a couple of seconds with no sounds from inside, Gus repeated the knock, accompanied by, 'Come on, Razor. You might as well come out. We only want to talk.'

Still nothing, but from the corner of his eye, he saw movement on the street. He swung round, already moving towards the figure that was walking down the road – Goyley.

At the same time as Gus identified the lad, got out his warrant card and identified himself, Goyley's head jerked up and met his eyes. 'Aw shit.' He walked backwards at speed for a few steps, before spinning round and taking off.

Idiot! Gus shrugged and rolled his eyes at Alice. 'You stay here, Al. I'll go get the little tosser.'

Repeating his earlier statement, Gus took off after the lad. 'Police, stop. We need to talk to you, Arthur Goyle.'

'No' – wheeze – 'fucking' – wheeze – 'chance, porky pig pie.'

When Gus arrived at the end of the street, where Goyley had taken an abrupt right, he'd already gained on the lad.

Goyley's laboured breaths floated backwards through the still air, and Gus grinned. Arthur Goyle might be able to down more pints than him and be a dab hand at menacing young kids, but he was no match for Gus in the running stakes. Increasing his pace, Gus got within arm's length of him and that's when Goyle made the mistake of glancing round. Startled by Gus's proximity, he tried to speed up, but Gus surged forward and hooked a leg round Goyley's ankles. In what seemed like slow motion, Gus watched Goyley's hands flapping in the air as his body folded forward like a lanky cartoon character and he landed flat on his face, bursting his nose open. Hands cupping his bloody nose, he rolled onto his back, glaring up at Gus. 'Pweece Bwudality, that's what dis is.'

Gus's grin widened. 'Really, *Arthur*? You're gonna go down the police brutality route, are you?'

Struggling to sit up, Goyle, blood dripping between his fingers and landing on his designer jeans, scowled at Gus. 'You punched me. My lawyer will have you bang to rights.'

Alice strolled over, her hand extended, holding her mobile, recording everything. 'Bang to rights?' Alice's wide grin matched her amused tone. 'You think this is the bloody *Sweeney*, *Arthur*?'

'Eh? Tweeny?'

Shaking her head, Alice winked at Gus. 'Yeah, *Arthur*, you're defo more *Tweenie* than *Sweeney*.'

'He swalted me. Look. Mah dose is bust.'

'Not what the video evidence will show, *Arthur*, sweetie. It'll show you ignoring a reasonable request from an officer of the law to stop.'

Although Gus was enjoying the interaction between Alice and Goyle, he needed to find out where Razor was and the fact that his henchman had run indicated he knew something. It also gave Gus the means to apply a bit of pressure, so he handed a bunch of tissues to Goyle and helped him to his feet, ignoring the small gathering of foul-mouthed kids who'd appeared from the dark recesses of the estate.

'Hey, Goyley, you let the plods catch you? Wait till Razor hears, eh?'

'Hey, Pigman, let him go. We'll back him up. We saw you punching him.'

'Yeah, our word against yours, Piggo.'

'Hey, bitch, you fancy some of this?'

A boy, who'd only recently reached double figures, clutched his crotch as he thrust in Alice's direction. Alice swung her phone round to record the faces in the crowd and as expected they dispersed faster than they'd arrived, with a few of the braver toerags, whooping and catcalling as they left and a few of the more stupid ones taking time to pick up bits of junk from a nearby garden to hurl in their direction.

'Tossers,' said Alice under her breath as she sidestepped a half full can off Stella that frothed out over the road on landing.

'Thing is, Arthur. The fact you ran means you've given us probable cause for a stop and search.'

Now he'd mopped up most of the blood and was pinching the bridge of his nose. Goyle's words were clearer though still nasally. 'I dow my rights, you know. You failed to identify yourself as a porky pig pie. Dat's why I ran.'

Alice smiled and shook her head from side to side. 'Aw, Arthur, Arthur, Arthur. I know Razor's the brains of the outfit, but come on – duh? Here I am – recording you – video evidence doesn't lie, now does it.'

'So, Arthur.' Gus stepped forward. 'I am about to conduct a stop and search, which will require you to allow me access to your pockets. The reason for this search is that you failed to stop when asked by a police officer. You can see how that might raise suspicions that you may be carrying an illegal weapon or drugs.'

Goyle's face paled as he glanced to the side, considering his options. Gus could almost hear the cogs in the boy's brain moving. *Should I run or face the music?* With the absence of his support network, Goyle's shoulders slumped and, taking the cue, Gus stepped forward.

'You got anything in your pockets that might harm me, Arthur? You know anything sharp: needles, knives, or anything. If you have and you failed to inform me, any charges against you will include assaulting a police officer.'

Head bowed, Goyle shook his head. Less than a minute later, Gus and Alice studied the bags lined up on the wall of the nearest garden – two of a white powder, presumably cocaine, three containing various pills, and six bags of weed.

'Well, well, well, Arthur. Looks like you've got enough there to justify a trip to The Fort in what I've heard your friends call a pig truck. Course, we might be prepared to help you out if you tell us where your mate is.'

Goyle exhaled, and biting his lip, glanced round as if checking that none of his fans had returned before speaking. 'Dun't know where he is. Got a text this AM saying he was splitting, and I'd to do these – eh – I mean a few jobs for him, like,'

'You mean deliver these drugs?'

'Never said that, like.' He shrugged. 'No. It were some other jobs, like. Housework and that.'

Alice's laugh rung out clear and loud. 'Didn't have you down as an au pair, Arthur.'

'A pair of what?'

Gus smirked. 'Never mind. So, why's he gone? Razor, I mean?'

Goyle shrugged, looking anywhere but at Gus. 'No idea. He just upped and left. Said I'd to move some stuff for him.'

'From his house? His PC and stuff or drugs and stuff?'

The lad's Adam's apple bobbed up and down as he struggled to find a plausible denial. 'No, no, nowt like that.'

Gus turned to Alice. 'Get a warrant to search Razor McCarthy's house. Cite that Arthur Goyle stated Razor instructed him to remove items from the premises. Also, add the info Compo's uncovered as probable cause.' He grinned. 'While you're at it, put out a BOLO for McCarthy and get some officers to transport this toerag to the Fort. I think I'm due an uncomfortable conversation with Nancy to explain what we've been up to. God knows how she'll react to being kept out of the loop on this.'

CHAPTER 24

Still reeling from Nancy's telling off, Gus reflected that rather than going completely off piste, he and the team should have at least run it by Nancy. She might have been reluctant to go through official channels, but he should have realised that she'd have pulled in some favours from her contacts in cybercrimes. She'd have known that expecting his team to back away from this would be futile. Now he'd pissed her off.

She'd insisted he get Compo to send his findings to the cybercrime team so they could legitimise it and add their weight to Gus's warrant request to search Razor's home. However, in the end, the warrant had been unnecessary because, while Gus was trying to build bridges with Nancy over the phone outside Razor's home, a silver Porsche drew into the street and pulled up right outside his house.

'Nance, let me call you back. Someone's just pulled up outside Razor's house in a ten-year-old, but nonetheless very expensive, Porsche.'

'Don't you dare hang up, Angus McGuire. Don't you—'

But Gus silenced her protestations by flipping his phone shut and pushing himself off his perch on the next-door neighbour's wall. He exchanged a glance with Alice, before stepping forward to meet the woman who was stepping from her car. She took one look at them and pushed her sunglasses up her nose, pursed her lips, and uttered a single word. 'Police?'

Gus got his warrant card out and introduced himself and Alice. 'And you are?'

The woman scrutinised the warrant card before smiling, her straight teeth gleaming in the late morning sunlight. 'I'm Gemma, Razor's sister. I presume the little turd's got himself into some bother or other.' With an exaggerated sigh, she leant back against her car, folded her arms across her middle, and smirked.

Gus studied the tall slender woman, wondering at the contrast between her elegant, almost model-like stature and that of her brother whom she would tower over by at least a foot and a half. Choosing to ignore her implied question, Gus smiled. 'Any idea where he is?'

She pushed herself away from her car, rummaged in the bag that was hooked over her shoulder, and sighed. 'Well, since you're being Mr Coy, I suppose you better come in.'

Gus avoided looking at Alice as he swallowed the smile that threatened and instead gave a sombre nod. 'If you don't mind.'

'Oh pleeease. Enough of the Mr Coy act, *Mister* Coy. We both know you and Ms Giggly Pants over there can't wait to get inside my brother's dump.'

This time Gus couldn't swallow his grin and as Alice's snort developed into a full-blown guffaw, he splayed his hands before him. 'You got me, Ms McCarthy. We're dying to get inside your brother's gaff.'

With a wave of her hand, she tutted. 'Gem. My name's Gem, OK?' Striding past them towards the gate she sidled through, careful to avoid her pristine white linen trousers from brushing against it. Once inside the small front garden area, she screwed her nose up and wafted her hand toward the garden. 'What a flucking state. So flucking glad I got my mum and sister out of here. The boys a bloody mucky little scrote.'

The first time she used the word flucking, Gus assumed he'd misheard, but on hearing it the second time, he smiled. Gemma McCarthy was a character and with her no-nonsense attitude, he quite liked her. She spun back, almost bumping into him as he squeezed through the gate. 'Hope you're gonna put the flucker away this time. He's worse than my dad ever was.'

Her expression until this point had swung between mild amusement and slight disgust. Now, though, her entire stance changed. With her shoulders tensed, and her brows pulled down, casting veins of wrinkles over her brow, her lips tightened. When she next spoke, the undercurrent of anger in her tone sent a chill up Gus's spine. 'He deserves to rot in jail.'

Her piercing blue ice-cold eyes turned to Gus and held his gaze. 'He made a huge miscalculation when he asked me to help, detective. The biggest one of his flucking life.'

This was one angry woman. Thankfully, her anger wasn't directed at the police, so perhaps, if they were careful, he and Alice could use this to their advantage. Gus nodded and gestured to the door. 'Best if we talk inside, Gemma. Bit more private.'

Gemma started as if she'd just come back to the present and then glanced round at the neighbours and voyeurs who'd gathered on the road near her car. She lifted her index finger and prodded the air towards the lad who'd thrown the half full can earlier and who now thought it safe to return. 'You, turd boy. Look after my wheels and I'll bung you fifty on the way out. One mark on it and I'll dissect you from your balls, got it?'

The lad flushed, thrust his hands deep into his pockets, and nodded. 'Yep, Miss, I'll watch it. You can trust me.'

Rolling her eyes, Gemma swung two fingers between her and the boy in the universal, 'I've got eyes on you', gesture. And said for Gus and Alice's ears only, 'Not as far as I could throw you.'

After watching Goyley being transported to BRI for an X-ray on his nose, the three of them trooped inside the house, which was a far cry from the scummy garden at the front of the house. After wandering through to the living room, flicking on a series of tastefully positioned lamps and closing the curtains, Gemma threw her bag on the ultra-thick cream coloured carpet next to a sumptuous maroon leather armchair and flopped into it. 'Sit.'

Gus walked over to the couch opposite, his eyes drinking in the anomaly that was Razor McCarthy's abode, while Alice let out a massive breath before bouncing onto the couch and positioning a cushion behind her back. 'Wouldn't have had Razor down as a cream carpet and scatter cushions sorta guy, would you, Gus?'

Gemma released a huge snort, her grin wide as she pointed a finger at Alice. 'I like you. You say it like it is.'

Pulling herself forward in her chair, Gemma's eyes moved between the two detectives. 'I'm a busy woman, you know. Got my own business and don't want to waste any more time here than necessary. What do you want to know?'

'Appreciate your time, Gemma. So we'll crack on. Any idea where your brother is?'

'Well, Mr Coy, that's just it. I don't. I don't usually have owt to do with him. We' – she paused as if considering her words – 'Don't get on. He doesn't like that I don't rely on him like my mum and younger sister, and I don't like the way he treats them, so…' She shrugged, and blinked a few times as if remembering past encounters she'd witnessed between her mum and brother. Inhaling, she smiled. 'Where was I? Oh yes. Well, my mum's not well – MS – she's going through a bad spell at the moment, and Daisy, my younger sister, is on holiday. Soooo, when Razor's text came through to my mum, she got in a right state and forwarded it to me and…ta da.' She splayed her hands towards them.

'What did the text say?'

Gemma picked her bag off the floor, placed it on her knee, and rummaged through for her phone. When she found it, she unlocked it, found the relevant text, and held it out for Gus and Alice to read.

Unknown Number: Mum, get yourself to my house and dump all my electronic equipment and my stash before the pigs get there. You better fucking do it, or else. Remember who pays your bills.

'Your brother not much into the warm and cuddly emoji, then?' Alice tilted her head to one side, her tightened lips belying the lightness of her words as she read the text.

'That's a flucking understatement. He's a bully. When I get my hands—'

Before she got distracted by insults to her brother, Gus interrupted. Much as Razor's bullying words to his sick mum disgusted him, Gus latched onto the opportunity this presented – one he suspected they'd be lucky to get again. 'He use a burner phone often to text your mum?'

The sneering scowl on Gemma's face said it all, so Gus continued, 'Is that why you're here? To remove his electronic equipment and his drugs?'

A smile spread over Gemma's lips as she shook her head. 'Actually, no. Contrary to public *or* police opinion, not all of us McCarthy's are bent. Some of us run legitimate businesses and despite my mother's pleas, I've decided that it's time to cut his hold on her. I'm moving her and Daisy out of the area and so, Mr Coy, you could say that today's your lucky day. I only came to grab some of her things.'

She stood and gestured to an open door that led to a dining room. 'Have at it. Take whatever you want. Just make sure my brother, when you catch him, goes away for a long time. I'm done with him terrorising us. Done with worrying about Mum and my sis. He's a bad, violent little flucker, and he needs to be stopped.'

Gus's fingers itched to phone Compo to come over to go through the equipment, but he knew that, although Razor's sister had given permission, that might not stand up in court. 'Thing is, Gemma. Much as I'm dying to see what he's got hidden on his laptop and to confiscate his stash, I'm going to have to wait—'

'For a warrant? No, you don't Mr Coy. My mum's name's on the mortgage for this house. She owns it and, more importantly, she signed this.' After another brief rummage in her bag, Gemma thrust a signed document towards Gus. 'I got my lawyer to prepare this – it's all legal. It shows that this property is owned by my mum and that I can deputise for her. My mum's had enough of living in fear, so she's signed this giving permission for you to search the property. Good job you were here when I arrived. Saved me having to phone you and wait for you to arrive.'

Gus handed the proffered document to Alice, and she took it and moved through to the kitchen. 'Alice is just checking out the legality of this with our legal team. If they OK it, we're good to go.'

As Gemma slumped back into the chair, frowning, Gus realised how much of a strain this was placing on her. Familial relationships were often hard to navigate, but to get to the point where you took on a violent brother with many contacts throughout the region was brave.

'Look, Gemma. You're not on your own now. If you, your mum, and your sister need help, we can offer it. If you're prepared to turn witness against your brother, we can offer a safe house. My boss will agree to it.'

Gemma shook her head. 'No, no. We're fine. If he gets put away, we'll be fine.'

Much as he wanted to believe in the power of the legal system, Gus was unconvinced. The wheels turned slowly and with Razor's contacts and a good lawyer, who knew what might happen in the future? Gus had been in the game for a long time, and he'd learnt over the years that nothing was ever dead certain. Still troubled, Gus wanted to push his offer of help, but Alice bounced into the room, grinning like the proverbial cat with cream. 'We're good to go, Mr Coy. Compo's on his way as are a team of uniforms to help search the premises.'

Since they were on a high, Gus opted to let the 'Mr Coy' thing go…for now, especially as he was so relieved to have an olive branch to offer Nancy. He exchanged a grin with Alice before turning back to Gemma. 'You don't know how thankful we are, Gemma.'

Gemma batted his thanks away with a smile before turning serious. 'You don't know what it's like to grow up with a manipulative psychopath, Mr Coy. It's crap. Really flucking crap. We should have dobbed him in long ago. There's no calculating how much destruction and heartache he's caused, both on this estate and beyond. The folk here have enough of a struggle on their hands without people like him making it worse. We used his dirty money to escape this life. I got an education and now we're in a position to stop him.' She picked up her bag, handed him the house keys, and smiled as she prepared to leave. 'Just catch him, OK?'

'Just a minute, though. Any idea where he'll be? Where he'd hide?'

Before he finished his question, Gemma was shaking her head. 'No idea. Your best bet is to ask one of those two idiots that do his bidding for him – they both hang out on the estate terrorising decent folk. They won't be hard to find. Now I don't suppose you'll let me take any of my mum's stuff right now. Give me a buzz when I'm free to collect her things, yeah?' And with a last nod at Alice, she was off.

Gus took out his phone and requested a couple of uniforms head over to HP's address before turning to Alice. 'Upstairs or down?'

Alice was notoriously reluctant to search kitchens, so it didn't surprise Gus when she skipped past him.

'I bags the upstairs. You can search the kitchen. Oh, and make me a cuppa while you're at it.'

CHAPTER 25

Angel

I study my devoted servants sitting opposite me in the booth in the seedy café halfway up Great Horton Road. I've chosen this meeting spot for precisely that reason. Its seediness serves my purpose. Nobody in here is interested in us – too busy jabbering away in their foreign languages, their mobile phones jammed so tightly to their ears that I suspect they'll need them surgically removed soon if they're not careful. Today, we're discussing the final steps in our therapy, and I want to make sure everyone is on side.

Already, See is getting twitchy. She rolls her left shoulder almost as if she's trying to oust the demon that sits there. I smile. She can't do that. That particular demon is too personal for her. Its words thunder in her ear, taunting her, clawing at the last vestiges of her self-esteem and keeping her committed to the task at hand. She's out of options and I don't have to worry about her.

I turn my attention to Hear. He's always hard to work out – the strong silent type – lots of simmering rage gurgling just beneath the surface. He too has a vested interest in making our project work. However, the coercive messages delivered by the demon on his shoulder are harder to work out. Even now, he remains quiet. He's not distracted by the surrounding noise. Just sips his coffee, his eyes on the table, making it difficult to anticipate his reaction to my proposal.

Speak fills the silence with inconsequential chatter that I find quite draining and annoying, although not as irritating as See appears to find it. The looks she's shooting at Speak would silence most men but Speak is oblivious. He's the only one with no real personal commitment to the programme – apart, from me, that is. Of course, his motivation isn't as pure as mine. I suspect he's simple. My smile deepens and See frowns at me. I know we're not supposed to use that sort of word these days, but what the hell, it's not like I said it aloud. Besides, compared to me, he's definitely lacking in the grey cell area. Everyone's too het up on being woke. Well not me. I wink at See and she lowers her gaze, a slight flush blossoming over her cheeks. Speak's still talking and I nod as if giving him my full attention. He's always indignant at our meetings – full of moral outrage – most of it cribbed from social media platforms, I believe – yet I sense that he perhaps protests too much. I've seen the way he looks at the young lads. Not Claude – but then he's too old to tempt anyone. In fact, I'm not sure how Claude's survived with his guilt all these years. But the younger ones? Hm. I'll monitor that. Speak will not derail my progress by losing hold of his own morals.

It's strange to be here together in everyday clothes. Of course we can't go traipsing around Bradford in our robes and masks, even so, it's off putting to see them in their dowdy unceremonial attire. Nondescript – ordinary people – that's what everyone else sees, but they're deceived because what we're trying to achieve transcends the ordinariness of others' paltry lives. Still, donning our robes is energising – it symbolises the gravitas of our work and it places them as the servants and myself as the master.

Tapping my fingers against the edge of my mug, I think back to the way I recruited each of them. See and Hear were easy. They wore their pain like a gruesome façade, trying to mask it with smiles and not succeeding. Ripe for an intervention, I courted them individually at first and then brought them together. When I realised I might need muscle, I turned my attention on Speak. He was so desperate to join in with the wider group, but nobody felt at ease with him. Not a single one of them did the Christian thing and offered him the hand of friendship. So, I stepped in. With separate meetings in cafés around town, I nurtured all three of them and finally our little off cut was born. It was all down to me and my foresight and the guidance I took from the Lord. Mind you, Speak is a bit of a dark horse. When it came to my attention that he'd breached confidentiality earlier in the year, I'd had a genuine dilemma on my hands. It had taken me a few days to reach a decision regarding his fate. It would have been so easy to cut him loose. To end his life, and the other two would have agreed, but I had to weigh that up against what he brought to the group – the things the rest of us couldn't do. Speak was the muscle of our group and we needed him – we needed him badly, so in effect it was 'decision made'. Besides, in the end it was easy to sort out. Bought one of those onion routing browser things – they call it a TOR. Allows me to surf the dark web incognito, and job done – Speak's indiscretion anonymously covered up.

I clear my throat and place my half-drunk coffee on the table. Despite the background noise, I keep my voice low and the other three lean in so as not to miss my words.

'Tonight will be pivotal in ensuring the success of our venture. We each have to remain strong. Tonight, we will push them until those who lack the commitment to change reveal themselves.'

I study them, satisfied when even Hear meets my eyes and offers a small nod. Tonight will be hard. It will be messy. We must prevail even though it will push us to the edges of our forbearance. We have a duty to do so. I extend my hand and place it palm down in the middle of the table. 'Are you all with me?'

One by one they place their hands on top of mine and with the heartening pressure of three hands over mine, I close my eyes and together we pray for the strength to deliver the sinners from evil.

CHAPTER 26

'Gus, Gus. Quick. You've got to see this.'

Alice's voice rang down Razor McCarthy's stairs, along the hallway and into the kitchen where Gus was piling onto the pristine heavy oak table, block after block of drugs wrapped in plastic that he'd found hidden under the work units. Dropping a wrapped-up block, Gus marched through the hall and took the stairs two at a time, hoping that Alice had found something that would indicate where Razor might have gone. In the distance, the sound of sirens blared, reminding Gus where they were. It was almost possible in Razor's chic dwelling to forget you were on one of the roughest Bradford estates.

'In here, Gus. God, you will not believe this.'

Four doors stood open. It took Gus a moment to realise that Alice's voice was coming from the double bedroom at the back. Gus padded along to the door and poked his head inside. 'What, you…?' His voice trailed off when he saw what Alice was pointing at.

'You ever seen anything like this?'

Gus blinked twice, then shook his head. For now, words escaped him. This was wild – really wild and, if he was honest, unsettling. He stepped inside and did a complete turn to get a panoramic view of the room. 'Bloody hell!'

Alice, bouncing on her toes her eyes brimming with mischief, nudged him. 'Maybe take a few snaps for your personal records. You never know when you might want to redecorate your bedroom.'

Gus snorted. 'Yeah right. Not sure black and purple are my colours and as for that…' He pointed at the king-sized four poster bed which had manacles hanging from its leopard skin headboard and wooden stocks at the foot. His eyes drifted to the range of whips and ball gags displayed on hooks along the top horizontal post, and he cringed. 'Wouldn't want to be on the receiving end of some of those and' – he stepped closer, his eyes drawn to a pulley system – 'as for that…? What do you reckon it's for?'

Alice shrugged. 'No idea, but if I were you, I wouldn't touch anything. Reckon there's bound to be more trace DNA on that bed alone than in your average Travelodge room.'

Gus stepped backwards. 'Eeugh, Al.' Still mesmerised by the fur rugs and erotic paintings on the wall, Gus exhaled. 'Don't suppose you found any sign of where we might find Count Razorslave?'

'Mm?' Alive tapped her finger on her lips. 'Maybe try an S&M club?'

At that point, Gus's phone rang. He checked caller ID then answered, raising an eyebrow in Alice's direction and mouthing, 'Taffy' as he did. 'Yep, you got HP?'

He listened. Then, 'What do you mean, not exactly?'

As he flicked the phone to speaker, Taffy explained.

'The uniforms you requested to pick up HP just phoned in. By the time they arrived, his gaff was on fire. They called it in, and the fire fighters are there but, well – unless he wasn't at home, they say there won't be much left.'

'OK, Taff. Keep me updated. We'll be heading back soon, anyway. How's it going with Goyle?'

'He knows summat, boss. Got that shifty, won't-meet-your-eyes look about him. Fucker's lawyered up though and no commenting all the way down the line. We'll have to release him by this evening, because he had under the quota of drugs on him for us to hold him any longer.'

Gus considered that and then decided. 'Get Nancy to authorise a couple of detectives to follow. He's not too bright, so we might be lucky, and the little tosser might just lead us to Count Razorslave.'

'Count what?'

Gus shook his head. 'Never mind. Just make sure he's in our sights. Let me know when you have more information on the fire. I'm hoping that HP got out, but the sooner we can confirm that the better.'

After hanging up, Gus turned to Alice. 'Well, that explains the sirens a little while ago.'

'Certainly does. You reckon Razor's house cleaning?'

Gus scowled at the sex bed. 'Looks like he is. Little bloody turd that he is. Come on. Let's head back to The Fort. Compo's there now. Maybe he'll have some good news for us.'

CHAPTER 27

Carl Morris was in a business meeting in his offices – a potentially very lucrative business meeting – when he got the notification about Artemy Ivanov's punishment. He shouldn't jeopardise this deal – millions of pounds were in the balance, yet he found he didn't give a damn about that. He hadn't given a damn about anything since the other night when he saw those images on that Slave website. Right now, he couldn't drum up a modicum of interest in this deal. Besides, it wasn't as if he needed the dosh and, after all these years, he reckoned his reputation could stand the knock of his absence at the final push. So, he got to his feet, smiled at the pompous arseholes sitting round the table, files and charts spread before them, and shrugged.

'I'm not feeling it today, gentlemen. We'll postpone. Maybe I'll feel more engaged on a different day.'

His smile widened as he swept from the room, ignoring the cacophony of voices that followed him demanding an explanation. His heart thumped and adrenalin surged through his body as he released a full-throated laugh into the external office space. All around him, the admin staff paused in whatever menial tasks they were doing and gawped at him. Enjoying the energy flooding his veins, he laughed again, enjoying the bemused looks on his employees' faces before, with a flamboyant flourish, he extended one leg, to the front, wafted his arm in the air for good measure and executed a flawless bow, which no doubt any prince would be envious. As he straightened, he winked at the nearest employee – a pert young red head with matching lipstick – and extended his hands before him. 'Ta da…Like magic, your prince issues you with an unscheduled day off. '

From their frowns and shared glances, Carl knew his actions confused them. He wasn't renowned for his sociable nature nor for his generosity. It might be time for things to change. Maybe he should embrace this personality transplant he was currently undergoing. Perhaps being so close to getting payback had mellowed him. He laughed aloud again, aware that his personal assistant, William, was hovering behind him, red faced and nervous and instead of turning to him, he clapped his hands loud enough to make most of the workers jump. Some cast glances towards William, hoping for some guidance on how to deal with this situation, and that amused Carl even more.

'Go on then. I'm giving you the day off. Get your arses out of here. Normality will be resumed tomorrow.' He didn't see William give them the nod, but he sensed it, so he turned to his PA, still grinning. 'You too, William. Take the rest of the day off.'

'But, Carl?' William stepped closer, his face reddening more by the moment, and Carl hoped the man wouldn't have an aneurysm.

Carl shook his head. The businessmen he'd left in the conference room had trailed out, briefcases in hand, power suits immaculate, and hovered with mystified frowns on their supercilious faces. Observing what they no doubt suspected was Morris having a breakdown. This thought amused Carl even more.

'Gentlemen, I'd like to reassure you that I am fine both physically and mentally. I'm just redefining my priorities – perhaps you should all take a leaf out of my book and allocate yourselves some down time. You all look a tad het up and stressed.' He gestured to William, who was now unbuttoning his top button and showing signs of hyperventilating. 'If you want to re-schedule our meeting, speak to William. Now, I, like my very dedicated and hardworking staff am having some well-deserved 'me' time. William, call my driver and then deal with these gentlemen for me.'

An hour later, back in his flat a chilled bottle of Moët and Chandon open on his coffee table, he opened the notification that had prompted his melodramatic exit from the office and pressed on the encrypted link, knowing it was safe to do so. Before pressing play, he studied the still image on his screen. So, this girl, with dyed black hair, a pierced septum, and tattoos sprawling up both arms and appearing onto her neck from under her black crewneck T-shirt was Artemy Ivanov's weak spot. Her hands were cuffed behind her back and a gag bit into the corners of her mouth. Morris could detect the fear that lurked in her eyes and for a moment, he considered if he felt anything for the girl. Pity? Regret? Empathy? He shook his head, a frown troubling his brow. Why did he feel nothing for this petrified girl? Why was this basic human emotion denied to him?

He considered what he'd felt when the bitch had betrayed him– anger – unadulterated rage, a surging gnawing desire for revenge, but had he felt grief for his loss? Sadness because his heart was no longer intact? He thought not. Then he cast his mind back further than that. Had he experienced love before the betrayal? That erratic, heart-fluttering, stomach-tickling emotion? Again, no. That was just the way it was. The way it had always been, but more importantly, the way he preferred it.

He pressed *play* and the laptop screen erupted into a writhing, blood-splattering frenzy of motion. He turned the volume up high and allowed the violence to penetrate him to the core.

CHAPTER 28

Flynn

The atmosphere feels different tonight, and I don't think it's to do with the fact that the sun's been out today. It's summat more than that – but I can't put my finger on what. It's like it's in the air – suffocating – claustrophobic. Like, although it's contained in a bottle for now, it might bust open and all hell will break loose.

Despite the warm day outside, I feel goosebumps pop out on my arms under my hoodie as a shiver judders through my body and I'm not sure if they're caused by the penetrating chill in the air or fear.

A sharp pain in my jaw distracts me and I realise it's because I'm clenching it so tight and I'm grinding my teeth too. The beginnings of a tension headache dart up the side of my face and into my temple. The throb there pulsates so much I raise my fingers and try to massage it away. We're all on edge and it's not in an excited, looking forward to summat, sort of way. No, it's like we're all expecting summat to happen tonight – summat bad. Maybe it's because of what happened the other night. The throb flashes across the top of my head, so I roll my shoulders – this is sooo weird – sooo bad and I'm glad it's my last session. Can't go through this crap again.

Angel's assistants are watching from the front of the line, so I duck my head down so that I don't have to meet anyone's eye. I'm still reeling from what happened to Lucy, and I just can't settle. My one hand, with its purple fingernails, is a constant reminder of what happened to my friend, but I wouldn't have it any other way. This pain, this dull ache that makes me feel like I can't catch my breath, feels good. It means that *she* meant something. That Lucy was important, and I don't want to *ever* forget that. She's the only reason I'm back here tonight. The only reason I haven't just kicked these sickos into touch and submitted my research to the group.

We're all struggling – *all of us*.

Linc's insisted on a daily check in since that bastard murdered Lucy. He looks like crap. All pale and stringy – like he's on summat – but I know he's not. Linc doesn't do shit like that. Like the rest of us he's grieving, but he doesn't rant and vent. Maybe because he's older, he thinks he's got to set the tone for the group. He's been here before. Lucy's not the first of his trans friends he's said goodbye to too soon. When he told us that, we all got that what he didn't say was that Lucy wouldn't be the last, either. It's rocked him to the core that Lucy was murdered. That we saw her being killed and could do fuck all. The last two meetings were sombre affairs. Each of us tried to put into words how we felt, but it was too hard. We were like strangers avoiding eye contact with each other on the screen, keeping our heads dipped – a bit like I'm doing now. It's as if none of us has any energy to interact because all we've got is used to hold it together. Not like we can chat about it with our families, after all.

Suppose I could talk to Carrie, but I just can't. My dad's eyes lit up when he saw the nail polish on my hand. He didn't say owt, but he kept sneaking little peeks at the dinner table and I know he hopes it means I've reconsidered. I feel like a dick for putting him through that – for giving him false hope, but what can I do? A bit of nail varnish shouldn't make him think I'm reconsidering. It's not a damn fad – no matter what *he* thinks.

Fuck!

Why can't folk just let me be me? I'm not harming anyone. All I want is to be happy.

I shuffle forward a bit. It's not Angel at the front collecting our phones. It's See. Fucking stupid names – what do they think they are – superheroes? Saviours of the damn universe? You'd think they'd have been able to come up with something more inventive, wouldn't you? Despite my oversized hoodie and the jumper underneath, I shiver. I haven't been able to get properly warm since Lucy. Doubt I ever will. Mum moaned about me being in the shower for so long this morning. I just wanted to get warm. Besides, when you cry in the shower nobody can hear and if nobody knows I'm in bits, then they won't keep asking questions.

Bailey's in front of me. I can smell his aftershave – Lynx Africa. Wish he wouldn't wear so much of it because it catches in my throat. He's shuffling too, and I sense him looking back down the line. He's looking for Ali but trying to be subtle about it. Poor sod needs to work on that.

I sense someone approach behind me, and a quick glance tells me it's Ali. Can't believe he came back after the other day. *Why would he?* By the end of the session, he could hardly walk – his knees must have been agony. My head was ringing with the damn videos and the sounds and the constant preaching by the end. An urge to grab him by the shoulders and shake him – tell him to run – to run and never come back because these bastards won't stop till they've destroyed us, almost overtakes me, but I swallow it, and instead clench my fists inside my pockets. I want to tell him why I'm here. That tonight's my last night and that I'll be exposing them all online for what they're doing. That he and Bailey should just get the fuck away and not bother what these bastards tell them. That there's nowt wrong with any of us – not a sodding thing. But that would take energy and I'm running on empty.

Instead, as Bailey moves over to the seats, still casting surreptitious glances in Ali's direction, I take my place in front of See and relinquish my phone. Usually, that small act makes my stomach churn as anxiety grips, but today, it's like I'm floating through a strange, non-sticky, cushioning version of candyfloss and nothing feels quite real. I sit next to Ali with Bailey on my other side. Angel hasn't even started the torture – sorry – 'lesson' yet, but Bailey's legs are already going up and down, up and down like a bloody pneumatic drill. I've no idea what a pneumatic drill is, but that's how it looks to me. He's struggling today. His eyes are watery, like he might burst into hysterics at any moment. His fingers are white from clenching the edge of the seat. His nails are all bloodied and bitten right down to the quick, and when he changes his grip, I see marks on his wrists.

Earlier, when I strolled along from the bus stop, I saw him getting out of a car at the end of the road and as he hoisted his bag onto his back and headed towards the building the car waited, its engine still running. By the time I reached the doorway, he'd gone inside and when I turned round, the car roared off. Poor sod was being forced to attend this crap and once more, I realise how lucky I am. My family is great. Although Dad's a bit of a dick sometimes, my mum and sister are brill. I've got my online support group and I've got Carrie.

When the session ends, I'll try to catch up with Bailey before she's whisked off – maybe she could do with a friend.

I subdue a snort. The reason I want to connect with Bailey is nothing to do with me being kind or supportive. It's all to do with Lucy. If I was a half-decent person, I would have reached out to her before now. Not like I couldn't see before how fragile Bailey is. Then, Angel steps forward, arms raised like he thinks he's Jesus Christ, and I have to focus on holding it together.

It all starts off predictably enough with Angel and his sycophants preaching their warped version of righteousness and everything's fine – well, not exactly fine, but OK. I can cope with their crap. I just keep my eyes focussed straight ahead and keep them out of focus as I chant my own little mantra. 'Ignore the haters. Ignore the haters. Ignore the haters.'

Then, something happens. I'm not even sure what. All I know is that I lose my focus and instead of my mantra filling my head, it's Angels booming voice calling us names, using hateful destructive words – poofs, lesbos, perverts. But it's not his words I hear, it's that fucker Nigel's. The bastard who murdered Lucy and, in my mind, I register the fear on her beautiful face and all I can hear is, *You whore. You fucking poofter, whore*…followed by the thuds of his fist thumping into Lucy again and again before his shovel hands…

Then I'm on my feet, striding to the front of the room, my fists clenched, my entire body buzzing with anger as I yell, 'Lies, Lies, Lies. Every word coming from your mouth is a lie. You are the aberration, Angel. Not us. YOU!'

CHAPTER 29

'You gotta see this, boss.' Compo rushed towards Gus and Alice before they'd fully opened the door to the incident room.

One look at Compo told Gus that he'd found something of note. Despite the dark circles, which made his eyes look like dark orbs in his pale face, Compo was bouncing on his feet, like he did when he'd caught a lead and excitement flashed in his eyes. In response, Gus's heart picked up a beat too. They desperately needed something. There had been no sightings of Razor McCarthy. The fire fighters were waiting to declare HP's house safe before they could enter and ascertain whether he'd been a victim of the blaze.

On his release, Arthur Goyle had headed straight back to his home, where two detective constables had the unenviable task of blending into the estate as they tried to keep tabs on any moves Goyle might make.

Gus was convinced that the fire at HP's house and Razor McCarthy's disappearance were related, so he hoped the detectives assigned to trailing Goyle would be up to the job. If anyone could give them a lead on McCarthy's whereabouts, it was Goyle. On the off chance that McCarthy might have accessed his bank accounts, Gus had applied for a warrant to disclose any action on his bank accounts, but that was a long shot. Razor wasn't stupid enough to use any accounts which the police could access. Besides, the likes of Razor

McCarthy didn't rely too much on traditional banking, preferring to keep as much cash as they could in a variety of secure locations around the city or, if Razor had indeed, as Gus expected, branched out into the big leagues, he might have set up an account in an off shore bank. Gus had asked Compo to find out if Razor had set up accounts under the names of his family members, but that had come up clean. Seemed that if he had any UK accounts, he'd created them under a false name.

Now, with Compo bouncing in front of him and leading him back to the bank of screens that lined the computer station he'd set up for himself, a glimmer of hope flickered inside Gus. Maybe Compo had found something to drive their investigation forward.

'I'm running loads of different programmes on the Slave Auction website.' Compo shoved the remnants of a chocolate chip donut in his gob and bent over his keypad, bringing up a variety of flickering lines and statistics on each of his six screens. When he looked at Gus, his grin wide despite the crumbs falling from his lips, Gus could only shake his head. Whatever he was looking at made no sense to him, and Compo should know that by now. 'Come on, Comps. I know you're a geeky genius, but for god's sake just tell me what this all means.'

'Aw, yeah, yeah right, boss. Forgot you didn't get this. I'm running searches to discover as much as I can about the website. You know, keywords searches, frequent user searches, a program to flag up IP addresses with minimal encryptions that I can easily break, and' – he paused and, beaming at Gus, gestured to the screen where a group of five different auctions were revealed – 'a facial recognition programme which matched images logged on our system. Those are the ones that were flagged.'

Eyes narrowed; Gus leant forward as a grin spread across his face.

'Al, you better come here. Comps has just found a link between Razor, Jo Jo, and Zachariah Ibrahim.'

Compo raised his arm, palm outwards and rolling his eyes, Gus indulged him in a high five before turning back to the screen as Alice joined them. The slave identified by Compo's programme was Zac Ibrahim. Gus felt like punching the air himself. It had torn him apart to shelve the investigation into Zac's murder but, despite working their arses off the team couldn't catch a lead that hadn't ended in a dead end. Now, seeing the still of the minute-long clip of Zac Ibrahim sitting bound on a wooden chair, eyes wide and mouth gagged with a piece of fabric, Gus's heart rate sped up. The prospect of seeing the young man he'd only ever known in death as a living being, sent shivers up Gus's spine. This would not be easy. Gus realised that the time stamp on this auction was two days before Zac's body had been discovered. The time stamp on the actual recording showed one day before that.

'Zoom in, Compo. Let's see the background, see if we can establish where Zac is when this footage was filmed.'

Although there was no telling if what they were about to view was consensual or not, Gus doubted that Zac would have agreed to sell it to the highest bidder on a tawdry website on the dark web. This video was incontrovertible evidence of a link between Zac and Razor. This new evidence would allow the team to cast fresh eyes on Zac's murder and made it even more imperative that they find Razor McCarthy. Even if McCarthy was innocent of Zac's murder, he knew more about this footage and could no doubt give them more information.

As Compo zoomed in, Gus craned his neck to get a sense of the room in which the video was recorded. However, the footage was grainy and dark, making it hard to work out anything other than walls cast in shadows.

'I'll play it, boss. Maybe a different clip will shake something loose.'

Gus nodded; his hands clenched into fists by his sides as he waited to see what new information they might ascertain from the recording. 'Go on then, Comps.'

As Compo pressed play, Gus cricked his shoulder and watched the footage, his eyes drinking in as much information while deliberately not allowing his mind to dwell on the pain and fear in the boy's eyes as he struggled against the ties that bound him, unable to yell for help. The clip went on forever and although no actual torture was shown, Gus knew that the sick minds lurking in the darkness of these sordid sites would get off on the fear that rolled off Zac in spades. The desire to punch a wall was strong, but when it ended, Gus contented himself with tightening his fists.

'Again, Comps. Play it on loop a few times so we can focus in on it.'

As Compo set that up, Alice grabbed a chair and sank into it and when Gus glanced at her, he saw his own anger reflected in her tightened jawline. Compo too looked pale and his earlier excitement was replaced by a sombre silence and a shadow of pain lurked in his eyes. It never failed to affect Gus that his team stoically took so much pain into their lives. So much of other people's suffering, so much darkness and evil. Sometimes, he wondered how they coped and then he reminded himself that they didn't always cope. Sometimes they needed time out or professional help to work through the atrocities they witnessed. Sometimes, they were there for each other and that's how they got through. By having each other's backs. Through shouldering the crap together, but mostly by catching the bastards that did these things, so that others didn't have to witness it. So that others could have some sort of resolution to the darkness that had visited them.

On second viewing, Gus noted that the recording was wobbly, like some sort of hand-held device was being used. 'Do you reckon they recorded this on a mobile phone, Comps?'

'Yeah, that's my reckoning, boss. The quality isn't as good as, say, the recording taken via Jo Jo's webcam. I'd say the phone was an older model, but not sure how much that helps us.'

Gus nodded, and they watched the recording of Zac's terror another three times in total before Gus, sickened to the gut and tenser than he'd been for ages, called a halt. 'Any thoughts on this?'

Alice nodded. 'Yeah, I thought the angle was weird. I agree with you and Comps that the recording has been taken from a hand-held device, but I don't think they took it from arm's length.' She demonstrated what she meant by standing and holding out her own phone at arm's length as if she was recording Gus and Compo. 'The angle the video has been taken from is far lower. Maybe at hip or waist level.'

That hadn't occurred to Gus. He'd been too busy focussing on the surroundings to consider the angle, but now she'd drawn their attention to it, Gus realised she was right. 'Sooooo, you reckon this person was either very short, sitting down, or...'

Alice grinned. 'Yeah, I reckon whoever recorded it was doing it surreptitiously, which means…'

Compo punched the air. 'That there were at least two people in the room with Zac.'

Gus nodded. He'd already noted a couple of occasions when a shadow had fallen over Zac, indicating that someone other than the person recording was moving around. He pointed this out to Compo, then added, 'Get the footage to the lab, Comps. Have that new photographic expert enhance it and see if they can capture anything we've missed from the footage. Now, have you been able to pinpoint any more useful information from this?'

'You betya I havey doo doo.'

As Compo cracked open a can of Red Bull, Gus and Alice exchanged amused glances. Compo's excitement combined with too much caffeine often led to weird little phrases, reminiscent of those their expert psychological advisor, Ali Carlton was prone to. However, as long as he got the job done, they were prepared to put up with this mild eccentricity.

'I've isolated the IP address of Lot 05's buyer and the only encryption used was via TOR, which, of course I'm more than capable of cracking. We'll have the address by this evening. I'm also running the other clips that were thrown up to see who bought them. In your absence, I got DCI Chalmers's permission to send uniforms to the addresses of the other four unsuspecting people we identified from the site.'

Gus had almost forgotten that Zac wasn't the only person identified by Compo's programme. 'And who are they?'

'Well, one of them is deceased – you remember that CSI who was murdered last year?'

'Erica?'

'Yes, well, she was one of them. Her clip showed her binge eating piles and piles of ice cream and chocolate and such like before dashing off to purge.' Compo shook his head. 'Poor thing, and then…'

He shook his head again, then sniffed. 'Two were known sex workers and the last one was that poor kid who committed suicide online last year at the instigation of some group on the dark web – bastards. We got that recording taken down, but it does periodically resurface again.'

Gus flopped into a chair next to Alice and exhaled. Today had thrown up a lot of viable leads, and Compo was the one largely responsible for finding them. When it came to budget cuts time, Gus would take great delight in telling the brass about Compo's contribution to the team. No way would he allow them to cut Compo's job. No bloody way!

CHAPTER 30

Angel

What possesses the girl, Flynn, to react that way is beyond me. I'd noticed her heightened colour when she entered but put it down to the extended walk from the bus stop and the chill evening air.

'Lies, lies, lies. Every word coming from your mouth is a lie. *You* are the aberration, Angel. Not us. YOU!'

Flynn's words reverberate around the room and she's on her feet, pacing around, out of control, like the devil within has taken full control of her.

The other attendees look at her as she jerks his arm away from See. She tries to mollify him, to offer succour in his rage and to calm him down. Of course, we expect erratic behaviours. It's in the nature of the work we do. Denial and anger are regular combatants of ours, yet not normally in week six. Or not since Zac, anyway. I signal to Hear who moves across the room, weaving his way through the cross-legged attendees to reach Flynn. Flynn is irrational now. Saliva and tears flying from her face, like a rabid dog needing put down. It disgusts me. Her feral eyes cast around the room and when they land on me, she pulls against See and Hear's grip and tries to reach me, her arms outstretched, her fingers poised to scrape down my face.

'*Torturer*! That's what you are. It's *you* who is the animal. You and your animal friends, not us. *We* are pure. It's you who carries the impurity of hate and vengeance and evil. Not us! We *are* pure!'

As Speak steps in to assist, Flynn rears her head up, snarling, displaying all her satanic perversions as she roils and struggles against us. I pray, but instead of continuing to fight, she slumps between Speak and Hear, her eyes casting round the room and defeated, she whispers to the attendees, 'Get out of here. Don't come back. *He* is evil and *you* are all pure.'

I raise my prayer voice to a thunderous roar and cast my own eyes over the attendees, forcing their attention back to me, demanding their acquiescence. I lash them with tales of sin and punishment and evil as my disciples drag Flynn into the next room. The room with the chair.

CHAPTER 31

'Come on, come on, come on, Goyley, where the fuck are you?' In the fading light of day, Lister Park became quieter as families headed back home for the evening, leaving the basketball courts and play areas deserted. Razor sloughed off up to the bandstand, steering clear of Cartwright Hall where there were CCTV cameras in use. He'd avoided any dodgy looking characters all day, and he had no intention of a minor slip up on his part, landing him in their sights.

He'd been lucky earlier when some kid left his phone on a bench near the duck pond to go and chat to a mate. Razor had taken a calculated risk and pocketed it before ambling further round the lake. He'd reached the other side before the kid had noticed his phone was gone and had asked people nearby if they'd seen it. Razor watched, smiling as the kid got more and more hysterical when he couldn't find it. It hadn't been top of the range. Just a bog-standard Nokia. Still, the boy would be in for a hammering from his parents when he got home. Razor shrugged. He'd survived a childhood of beatings from his old man, so he had no sympathy for the brat who stood bawling like a baby by the café. *Tough luck, kid. That'll teach you to take care of your stuff, won't it? Toughen you up a bit, eh*?

Liberating the phone from its owner had been a godsend. Razor had nabbed it before the screen timed out and he could change the password. Now, using the kid's mobile data, he had access to the internet. The first place he visited was Bradford's *Telegraph and Argos* website. Harbingers of bad news, he expected if anything had kicked off on the Belle Hill Estate, they'd have reported it. The only newsflash remotely relevant to Razor's current predicament was the report of a house fire. Razor grinned. Looked like Goyley had taken care of HP as ordered. So where the hell was he now?

Razor, keeping his shoulders down and avoiding eye contact with anyone he passed, began yet another circuit of the park. This was one fucking awful day and the fact that Goyley hadn't turned up yet concerned him. He needed money urgently, and he needed the bag Goyley would bring if he were to escape Bradford for a while. The stolen phone burnt a hole in his pocket. He could contact Goyley on his personal mobile. He weighed up the risks and benefits of doing that. The number would register as unknown and, as nobody knew Razor had possession of it, there would be a window of opportunity to use it. One call would be OK, surely? Worth the risk? No, no, he wouldn't chance it. He exhaled and climbed the steps to the bandstand. He'd hunker down in here till Goyley turned up and nobody would see him. That was for the best.

He needed a piss, too. Had been holding it in for ages. Didn't want to risk going to the Cartwright Hall café, so he'd just held it in. Now it was getting desperate. He'd have to either piss himself – not an option – or go behind a bush. Thank fuck. The park was quiet now. He didn't want to risk some goodie two shoes mum calling him out for pissing in public.

He dived back down the steps, took a quick glance around him to ensure no one was nearby, didn't enjoy slumming it, and he'd need more cash than his mum or girlfriend had to ensure his enforced down time was spent somewhere nice. He could hang around on the assumption that Goyle was on his way – but what if the guys who were after him had waylaid Goyle? What if the gormless git led them straight to him? This last thought made him pause. If Goyley was compromised in some way, then they could send people to snatch Razor. *Fuck*! Here he was sitting like a damn pigeon waiting to be offed by a kid with a BB gun. *What to do*? *What to do*?

In the end, the only logical option was to use the stolen phone. See if he could speak to Goyley and then, if necessary, dump the Nokia. At least he'd know where Goyley was and, more to the point, if he had his stuff. Action plan decided, Razor returned to the bandstand and rolled a cig. Then, crossing his fingers, he took a deep breath and dialled Goyley's personal phone, muttering a mantra under his breath; *Come on, Goyley. Come on, Goyley.*

As the ringing down the line showed the call had connected to his mate, he heard a corresponding ring from nearby. He almost hung up, but then his face broke into a huge grin as he recognised the *Ghostbusters* theme – Goyle was nearby. Thank fuck!

He jumped to his feet, hung up the call and peered through the dusk, hoping to see his mate approaching. Arm in the air, he waved when he saw Goyle's gambolling figure appear from between two bushes a hundred yards from the bandstand. He placed his fingers between his lips, ready to whistle to attract Goyley's attention, when two figures appeared fifty yards behind his mate.

Goyley, unaware that he was being followed, raised an arm in the air and waved. 'Hey, Raze, I'm here. Got shit loads to tell you, man.'

But Razor had vaulted the side of the bandstand, executed a near perfect landing after his six-foot dive and legged it towards the Emm Lane side of Lister Park, his arms pumping and his heart thumping like there was no tomorrow. Which there wouldn't be if the men following Goyley had owt to do with it. Adrenalin surged through him and, for once, Razor was thankful of his small stature, as it also made him agile. *Fucking Goyle. Fucking stupid bastarding Goyle.*

He'd almost reached the Emm Lane gates and, with the welcome thought of freedom in sight, he risked a glance behind – his two assailants were flagging and the space between them was lengthening with every stride. The gates were padlocked, so he diverted, prepared to vault the wall at the side and disappear into the labyrinth of roads that fed off Emm Lane. He grinned, realising that he'd be able to hide out in a garden or shed, and these two pillocks were too far behind to get a sense of which direction he'd headed in. He placed his hand on the sandstone wall, ready to jump over, when a car screeched to a halt on the road. The driver and passenger doors flung open and two figures got out.

Fuck, fuck, bastard, fuck! Razor spun round panting, sweat dripping into his eyes as he considered what to do next – downhill towards Keighley Road – that was the only sensible choice. His leg muscles cramped. He hadn't run like this in a long time, still he forced them to move as he hobbled along the side of the wall. Behind him he heard angry yells, but he was too focussed on his escape to register the actual words. *Come on, Raze, you can do this. Remember all the medals you got for running at school? Come on*!

The voices behind him faded. *Thank God*! The men in the car couldn't gain entry to the park.

Throat dry, he coughed and a glob of phlegm hoiked up. He spat it on the path and kept moving, his ears straining to hear the padding of feet on the concrete path.

There were none. With his hoodie soaked, Razor saw the entrance at the bottom of the park near the statue of Titus Salt looming ahead and he pushed himself for a final spurt then from the right a figure surged forward, flung itself at Razor, and tackled him to the ground.

'Gottya.'

Razor's cheek grated across the concrete and in a last-ditch attempt he tried to kick his attacker off his legs, but the other man's grip was too tight. Razor had one last chance for escape, so he relaxed his limbs and allowed his body to go slack, waiting for the assailant's grip to loosen so he could kick him in the balls or wriggle away or – anything – just anything to escape.

A low laugh rumbled through the air and instead of loosening, the man's grip tightened. 'Oh, Razor. You'll need to do better than that if you want to get the better of me. I eat scrotes like you for breakfast.'

CHAPTER 32

When word came in that Arthur Goyle was on the move, Gus could hardly believe it. He'd been thinking that Razor had already left the city and that having officers monitoring Goyle's movements was an enormous waste of time and resources. Now, it seemed it had paid off and Gus could breathe a little easier knowing his boss wouldn't be breathing down his neck about budgets and suchlike. He had no time for that. His job was to lock up the bad guys and if that took money, then so be it.

In radio contact with officers Habib and Boardman following Goyle, it soon became apparent that their target was heading towards Bradford nine, which made Gus even happier as that was where he and the rest of his team were situated – in The Fort.

'Goyle's on the 680 bus heading towards Heaton, boss, and we're on his tail. Have to say, he's not exactly a challenging target to follow. He trotted right down Manchester Road as if he'd not a care in the world. You'd think after being hauled in for questioning earlier, the git would have been a bit more cautious.'

Gus snorted. 'Razor McCarthy's always been the brains behind that set up, Boardman. Just keep us in the loop. I've got officers on standby. What's your precise position?'

'The bus is just pulling onto Oak Lane and taking a left along the top of Lister Park. Oh wait. It's slowing down – someone's getting off…it's him. It's Goyle. We'll park up and follow.'

Gus grabbed his jacket and gestured to Taffy and Alice to follow him from the incident room. 'Let's see where…?'

But Gus didn't get to finish his sentence as Habib's voice interrupted. 'He's crossing the road, sir. I think he's heading into the park. Yes, he's slipped between the barriers. He's heading into the park. We're on him.'

Gus nodded at Compo. 'Notify the officers in that area pronto. Al, you and Taffy take a squad car. I'm going on foot' and without waiting for a response, Gus, earpiece in, took off down the stairs and out the front doors of The Fort. He ran this way daily, and it would be quicker for him to jog down than wait to get a car and fight against Friday prayer traffic to reach Lister Park.

'Keep me informed. I want to know your location at all times.'

Gus didn't need to consider his route. The quickest way was down Oak Lane and into the park through the bottom North Park Road entrance. Once in the park, he could head in whatever direction Goyle did.

'He's heading towards the bandstand.'

Gus changed direction and headed that way. 'Shit, there's Razor. I repeat, we have eyes on Razor McCarthy. Shit, the fucker's vaulted out of the bandstand and heading towards Emm Lane.' Gus increased his pace and soon overtook Habib and Boardman. 'Al, get in position at the Emm Lane top exit.'

'Roger that, boss.'

Gus could hear the excitement in Alice's voice and as he sprinted faster, he felt the surge of adrenalin loosening his limbs and making his movements more fluid. He'd catch the little scrote. He could see him ahead. McCarthy's slight build was playing in his favour, but not for long. Not if Gus had anything to do with it. Then through the earphones he heard the car screech to a halt on Emm Lane and Taffy yelling for McCarthy to stop.

Ahead, Gus registered Razor changing direction and heading downhill to the Keighley Road exit. 'Keighley Road exit – get it covered. Now.' Once more changing direction, Gus tanked down towards the top end of the lake. It would only shave off seconds, but seconds were important. Last thing he needed was for McCarthy to exit the park and hide among the residences in Frizinghall or Heaton. Worse still, he could steal into the woods and escape up near Shay Lane or down into Shipley. In the park, he was contained, and Gus was intent on catching him. Gus burst out from the side of the Titus Salt statue at the same time as McCarthy. His lungs protested against his activity, but Gus ignored the discomfort. He had a job to do. Pushing further, he realised McCarthy was so intent on escaping on to the main road that he hadn't seen Gus approach.

After pushing himself a little more, he dived for it. 'Gottya.'

His arms locked round Razor McCarthy's feet, Gus used the prone man's legs to pull himself further up Razor's body until he had a firmer grip round his knees. Razor struggled, trying to loosen Gus's hold on him. Then without warning McCarthy played dead – his body stilled and his limbs loosened. Gus almost laughed aloud. Did the little scrote not realise that he'd done this before? No way would he fall for the 'dead fish' gambit.

Satisfied he had McCarthy where he wanted him, Gus laughed and tightened his grip. 'Oh, Razor. You'll need to do better than that to beat me. I eat scrotes like you for breakfast.'

Within seconds, mobile phone torches illuminated the two men lying on the floor. Taffy stepped forward, handcuffs in hand and read Razor his rights while Alice helped a grinning Gus to his feet. Eyes checking him over for injuries, she returned his grin. 'Not bad for an old git, if you don't mind me saying.'

Still catching his breath, Gus snorted. 'Yeah right, I'd like to see you doing any better, Al.' He bent over, resting his arms on his knees and waited for the inevitable adrenalin slump to kick in. 'Gonna help me to the car, Al. I got a cramp in my calf.'

Rolling her eyes, Alice hoisted his arm around her shoulder and helped him to the squad car, leaving Taffy to escort their prisoner to another car. 'Don't suppose anybody nabbed Goyle, did they?'

Alice grinned as a voice came over the airwaves. 'One Arthur Goyle cuffed and en route to The Fort as we speak, sir.' Gus collapsed into the car, massaging his calf, and sighed. 'Thank fuck for that.'

CHAPTER 33

Flynn

They must have given me something to make me sleep, for when I wake my mouth and throat are parched and my head thumps with a persistent drum, but I'm alone. I'm in the chair, a subdued orange glow from behind my only company. The one they showed us all at the start of week one. Its hard wooden base and legs make my bones ache. My buttocks are numb and when I look down, I see that I've soiled myself, for my jeans are sodden and the distinctive stench of urine invades my nostrils. It's only when I try to stand up I realise that I'm bound to the chair by some sort of leather sash round my middle.

It's at that point that I realise I'm in deep shit and my legs tremble as I try to stretch my arms behind me to loosen the sash that tethers me to the chair. When exhaustion takes over, I slump. A downward glance shows that the chair is screwed into the concrete floor. I realise struggling is futile and hope that someone appears soon so that I can beg my way out of this predicament. With the silence pressing against me, almost suffocating me, I reflect on the stupidity of my earlier actions. How could I have been so stupid? My friends and I had prepared ourselves for the sort of crap being spouted, and none of what Angel said was worse than the reports from my online group. I'd just snapped. Snapped because of his self-righteous crap and because I couldn't bear the way the others looked at him – so eager to please – so eager to sell their true selves down the river and I couldn't stand it anymore. #NotMyCleverestMoment

Now I would have to swallow my pride and beg. Say it was only a momentary blip. That I was scared and confused. Even thinking of the depths of lies I'd have to churn out fills me with pulsing red anger, and I'm not sure I'll be able to do it.

A scratching sound reaches my ears and I realise someone is at the door inserting a key. This is my chance. This is something I have to do. I have to get away and never come back. I know I'll disappoint my online group, but maybe they'll understand. After all, I have six weeks of research to add to the mix. I've done my bit.

The door opens and ghostlike, he floats in flanked by his minions. Their faces are in shadow, and I can't get a read on their intent. I exhale slow and long, preparing myself for my inevitable verbal lashing and prepared to plead for forgiveness. He steps closer and flings off the hood that covers his head, revealing a hard face with sunken cheeks and brooding eyes. 'So? Do you repent?'

Even his words are harsh – lacking in solace filled with undercurrents of rage and as his eyes flash over me, his nose scrunched up against the piss smell, I realise it might not be as easy as I thought to escape his clutches. Still, I try. I bow my head and force a quiver to my voice and say the words I'd practiced earlier.

'I'm sorry. Don't know what I was thinking. I got scared and confused and…'

I jerk my head up and meet his gaze, trying not to flinch as he rakes his eyes over me.

'You're not sorry, Flynn.' His quiet words crawl over me like a snail, leaving a trail of fear behind. 'I see no sign of repentance.'

He raises his arms, and his next words hammer down on my head like a cannon bolt. 'You are the worst of the worst. I have never encountered anyone as depraved and unrepentant as you. There is no cure for what ails you. NONE!'

My leg jiggles like Bailey's did in the other room. Is he still there? Are the other attendees still there? Do they know what's going on? Surely, they'll stop this madness. I flick my eyes to Hear, See, and Speak but their heads are bowed. See's fingers flit across the front of her robe, as if they have a will of their own and I realise that she won't help me.

I am at the mercy of this man who displays no self-control. The smooth cultured manner I've become accustomed to has been replaced by this cold creature.

As I twist and turn on the seat, his hand reaches out and grips my throat. He squeezes, his eyes locked on mine, and all the time he mutters an incoherent prayer as the breath is stolen from my lungs and I descend into oblivion.

CHAPTER 34

Once back at The Fort, Gus took a shower while Taffy and Alice dealt with processing Razor McCarthy and Arthur Goyle. As expected, both lawyered up. Still, Gus hoped that having them both in custody and with the threat of a murder charge for HP's death as well as the drugs they'd found in Razor's house and the illegal distribution of porn, he'd be able to turn them against each other. It only needed one of them to break for the house to tumble down around both of them.

The solicitors would advise against revealing anything incriminating, but in Gus's experience some of these criminals became too arrogant for their own good and wanted to appear ultra-intelligent. That was the strategy Gus hoped to use anyway, and he looked forward to it. Just not tonight. The clock was ticking, and he had a limited window of opportunity to charge them without applying for an extension for further questioning. However, Gus was certain he would be allowed an extension, and he wanted to let them both stew overnight. Plus, he needed to rest – his entire team needed to rest, so he'd interview Razor and Goyle tomorrow.

Just about to leave the incident room after ordering everyone else to do the same, Gus halted in his tracks by Compo's 'Oh Fuck! This is bad.'

Compo rarely swore, so Gus closed his eyes to prepare himself before approaching Compo's workstation. Whatever he'd found must be bad. Compo's eyes were glued to the screen, his hand hovering over his mouse, not touching it. It was like it had rendered him immobile. 'What you got, Comps?'

As if Gus's words had broken some spell or other, Compo shook his head and blinked a few times in quick succession, but rather than answer Gus's question, he appeared to be addressing himself. 'How can this be? We've halted all activity…' His fingers flew across one keyboard and then he swung his chair round and repeated the process on another one. 'Don't understand this. Don't get this at all. Who's doing this?'

Gus laid his hand on Compo's shoulder.

'Comps, what's going on?'

Compo, wide-eyed, pressed a key and then gestured to a screen where an image flickered into focus. It was a paused video of a young girl – a Goth with a pierced septum, purple hair, and a whole load of tattoos. 'You ready for this, boss?'

Gus knew from Compo's flat, almost robotic, tone that he wasn't ready for whatever. He glanced round and saw that Alice and Taffy were also watching the screen. He swallowed, wishing that whatever hell humans did to one another would stop – just for a few days even. Just long enough for him and the team to recharge their batteries. 'Who is she, Comps?'

'It's been posted to the Slave Auction website with this message attached.' He directed their attention to a second screen, which displayed a typed message.

You have to stop the broker. This is what he did to my Irena. He won't stop. You need to stop him. He is getting close. Those two children are in danger. You need to protect them. I can't give you any more. I will be dead too before long. Take this seriously.

'Can you—'

'I'm on it, boss, but…' Gus didn't need to finish his sentence and eyes averted, Compo pointed a finger at the screen with the Goth girl. 'I can't do…' He swallowed, shook his head and stood up. 'Press *play*. I need some air.'

Shocked, the three remaining members of Gus's team watched as Compo left the room, his shoulders slumped, his normal jaunty bounce flat and shuffling.

Taffy was the first to speak. 'Shit, it must be bad.'

Gus exhaled, his jaw tense as he prepared for what he was about to see. 'None of you need to watch. Go to Compo.'

But Alice, chin raised, glared at him, while Taffy just dragged a chair over and sat down. 'Taffy will go to Compo once we've seen it. He'll take care of him, won't you, Taff?'

Taffy gave a single nod, then reached over and pressed *enter* and at once the terrified girl who'd been inanimate seconds before burst to tortuous life on the screen in front of them. By the end of the clip, a tear rolled down Taffy's cheek. It was as if someone had punched the air from Gus's gut. Alice inhaled and pulled a chair up beside Taffy. 'None of us need to see that again. But we need to catch whoever done this and make sense of it. '

As she finished speaking, the door opened, and Compo re-entered the room. Although still pale and still lacking his jaunty walk, his shoulders were back, and he met Gus's eyes without flinching. 'I'm sorry, boss. That was unprofessional of me. Won't happen again.'

Gus shook his head and opened his mouth to speak but realised he couldn't. Couldn't articulate his feelings. He swallowed and tried again. 'Comps, that was awful. Fucking, abysmally awful and you are not unprofessional. What makes all of us excellent at our jobs is the fact that' – he gestured to the screen – 'this sort of crap still affects us. When we become immune to it, when we lose our compassion for the victims, or when we can't empathise with their pain, that's when we become unprofessional and ineffective.'

A pulse throbbed at Compo's temple, but he walked past them and sank back into his chair. 'I'll find out where this came from.'

CHAPTER 35

Carl Morris was on the move. All those years ago, his hands had been tied. No matter what he did, what stones he tried to upend, all he did was to punish those who'd helped him and those who'd failed to foil his plans. First, he'd dealt with Gabe and he'd done that himself – after all, it was personal. By the time he'd finished with his employee – the one he'd trusted with his most precious belongings the man had been unrecognisable. He'd put every drop of pent-up anger into the act of punishment, pummelling the man till he was nothing but a mass of blood, gore, and splintered bones, and still his rage was unabated. Even as he watched his men throw what was left of his long-term employee into the Tyne, his fury simmered beneath his skin like ants trying to escape. Each fiery nip a reminder of what he'd lost – of how she'd duped him.

So, he'd turned his attention elsewhere. The slut hadn't escaped on her own. She'd had help and Morris wouldn't rest till he'd administered his own sort of punishment. Not until he'd got justice. When he'd had that teacher, Ms Roxanne Turner, and her weedy little boyfriend in the seedy boxing school room in Gateshead, he'd been on fire. The coke had done the trick, and he'd felt invincible. Of course he wanted information, so he'd been happy to allow his employees to use their special extraction skills on the whimpering pair, but in the end he had to concede that Iris had been smart – she hadn't revealed her destination to anyone and that meant there were no loose ends for him to follow. So, while his men had taken their time, when Morris had his turn, he ended their lives in a frenzy of pain and horror.

Still, there was one other person complicit in his misery. The little turd who'd covered for his son. The lad who'd covered for Jacob in the school play – Amar. His men had told him to let that one go, but it festered in his gut like maggoty meat, until he could bear the agony no more. Thinking it might look suspicious to draw more attention to the school where a pupil, his mum, his teacher, and his best friend went AWOL, Morris resigned himself to punishing from a distance. Tasking someone with cutting the brake cable on their car had been easy, and when the small local news item covering the tragic road accident that caused the death of a family of four had aired, Morris had expected his pain to subside. But it never did. It had been his constant companion, and even the drugs and alcohol had only taken the edge off. Which is why he bashed hell from his punch bag and threw himself into ever more lucrative, if risky, business deals.

Despite his best efforts, he'd been unable to locate her, but now? Well now, a chance online encounter had brought them closer than ever. He had a real clue, something to work with and Artemy, for all his faults, had come up with the goods and located the website owner. With the skills of his contacts, Morris was closer than he'd ever been to finding her and find her he would. It was a matter of following the breadcrumbs, and this Razor McCarthy character from Bradford had left a string a mile long. His men were persuasive, so Morris knew this McCarthy would send them on the next leg of their journey, furnished with everything the disgusting little bastard knew. He was so close he could almost smell the bitch's perfume.

In fact, the only small stain on the horizon was the fact that Artemy had uploaded the video of his sluttish girlfriend's death to the Slave Auction site and then topped himself. *Bastard*! Still, Morris had no use for him anymore, so his death was no loss to him, for he'd got the information he needed and had sent his contacts to seek out the lay of the land. However, according to Artemy's replacement, they weren't the only ones monitoring the site. For the new hacker's sake, he hoped they could identify those who were on his tail.

Morris smiled and watched the reflections of people walking up and down the train carriage play out in the darkness from outside the train windows.

Bradford, here I come!

SATURDAY

CHAPTER 36

It was the sound of a high-pitched excited cry rather than the sound of his name being called, that alerted Gus to the little girl, face framed by the metal bars of the play area in Lister Park calling for him.

'Mr Gussy, Mr Gussy!'

The sight of Jessie's riotous red curls haloing her cherubic face as her face poked through the gap, the spattering of freckles adorning her small nose stood out, made him overlook the fact that 'Gussy' sounded too much like gusset for his liking. Alice had already enjoyed a few jokes at his expense when she'd heard the little girl's nickname for him. References to knickers, thongs, panties, and suchlike had regaled him for a while every time he entered the major incident room at The Fort.

Still, Jessie was a cute child, and he just didn't have the heart to tell her to call him Gus – besides – Gussy was a sign of her affection for him and he cherished that.

Jogging over, Gus pulled his ear buds out and still jogging on the spot, he cast a surreptitious glance around to make sure the officer he'd attached to Jessie and Jo Jo was nearby. When he identified the officer, he nodded before leaning over the fence and ruffling Jessie's hair. Grinning at Jessie's use of the nickname she'd adopted for him – one Gus's best friend, Mo's kids, also called him – Gus hunkered down. 'Hey, Jessie, you OK?'

Behind Jessie, tall and gangly, not yet grown quite into his body, an uncertain smile on his face, stood Jo Jo. Under cover of listening to Jessie's excited chatter, Gus studied her brother. Jo Jo had been through the mill over the last few days, and Gus wanted to make sure he was coping with the stress. The bags under Jo Jo's eyes and the way he glanced round, as if looking for enemies, told its own story. He was on high alert. The way the boy scrutinised each passer-by prompted Gus to wonder if Jo Jo could identify this anonymous bidder. They'd assumed that the person going to such lengths to locate the siblings was either a trafficker or a random paedophile who'd taken a fancy to the brother and sister. But what if that wasn't the case at all? What if Jo Jo was hiding something from them all? Jo Jo, sensing Gus's scrutiny, looked at him and for a moment a smile flickered at his lips only to fade when he saw the look on Gus's face. His eyes flicked away – down to the ground and then back round the park, continuing their silent appraisal of their surroundings.

'You OK, Jo Jo?'

Jo Jo shrugged. 'Yeah, yeah, fine, you know.' He gestured to Jessie. 'Watching out for my sister, that's all.'

Now it was Gus's turn to frown, for the flush blossoming on Jo Jo's cheeks and the way he shuffled his feet avoiding meeting Gus's eyes seemed to confirm Gus's suspicions. Then a taller, dark-haired boy approached and slung his arm round Jo Jo's shoulders, smiling at Gus. Confidence oozed from him in a way that Gus hoped Jo Jo would soon learn. So, this was Jo Jo's boyfriend? Gus made a mental note to check the boyfriend out, just in case his sudden appearance on the scene was related to recent events, but even as the thought crossed his mind, Gus berated himself. *Do you always have to be so suspicious, Gussyboy*?

Jessie, head nodding faster than a yo yo made Gus's smile widen. 'Jo Jo and Idris brought me down to give Mrs Mulholland a chance to get things ready for my party. It's my birthday today. I'm seven and aaaalllll my friends are coming, in't they, Jo Jo?'

For a moment, the haunted look on Jo Jo's face lifted as he rested a hand on his sister's shoulder, meeting Gus's eyes now. 'It's going to be chaos this afternoon. Ten seven-year-old girls running mad. Eileen's an angel to do this for her. Jess has never had a birthday party before.'

Had Jo Jo ever had a birthday party before? Gus doubted it. He'd seen where the boy had lived before. There had barely been enough cash for the essentials, never mind for a party. It was testament to the boy's love for his sister that there was no trace of jealousy in the way he looked at her and that was one of the reasons that Gus had allowed the party to go ahead as long as the officer remained in situ at all times. Jo Jo had done his best to look after their small family and he deserved the security that living with his new foster parent brought. Jessie made a whinnying sound and tossed her head before dancing and prancing like a pony, she ran towards the slide, her high-pitched voice carrying through the air.

'Watch me on the slide, Mr Gussy. I can do it on my tummy.'

Eyes flicking away, Jo Jo swallowed hard. And it didn't take a genius to work out that his thoughts had drifted to their existence prior to their mum's death. Jill James, Jo Jo's mum, had tried her best to look after her children, but as a single parent with cancer living on one of the worst estates in Bradford, she'd struggled. Gus suspected Jo Jo was struggling with divided loyalties right now.

'Your mum did the best she could for you and Jessie, Jo Jo, and you did too. Between you, you looked after her, got her to school, kept her fed, and kept her clothes clean. It's just the system is broken. You know that, don't you? You and your mum *should* have got more help. *You* should have been treated better.'

Jo Jo nodded, and Gus gave a nod as the other boy – Jo Jo's boyfriend, moved closer and squeezed his arm.

'Your mum – I mean your mam – would be happy to see Jessie settled. She'd be pleased that Jessie was getting a birthday party, that she had friends, that she's with you.'

Jo Jo nodded, but his eyes still carried doubt. That was something Gus recognised. It was survivor's guilt. He'd had it after defending himself against his best friend Gregg a few years ago. He'd been on a psychotic break – didn't know what he was doing, – and had killed his wife and child – Gus's god son, Billy. While trying to defend them, Gus had killed Gregg. Even years later, that crushing weight still landed on his chest out of the blue and he'd be right back there. Then the questions would peck away at his brain like vultures. *Why wasn't I the one to die? Why couldn't I save them? If I'd got there earlier, would they all be alive now?* It didn't go away, but it became less intense and happened less frequently. But Gus also knew that telling Jo Jo this was futile. He had to work that out for himself.

Seeking a distraction, Gus asked a question he'd meant to ask before, but had never quite got round to it. 'Always wondered why you and Jess call your mum 'mam'. It's not so much a Yorkshire word, is it?'

Expecting Jo Jo to shrug and answer with a dismissive, oh my mum was a Geordie or some such,

Gus was unprepared for the way Jo Jo flinched, his shoulders tensed, a pulse throbbing by his temple nor for the hitch in his breath. Gus frowned. *What the hell have I said now*? He was on the point of asking Idris a question just to give Jo Jo the time to calm himself when Jo Jo replied.

'We didn't always live in Bradford.'

Despite his shrug, Jo Jo's smile was forced, and he didn't elaborate, causing Gus to ponder his incomplete response and once more, his earlier thought tugged at his mind. *What was Jo Jo not telling him*? Gus made a mental note to ask Taffy and Compo if they could shed any light on the question.

Jessie ran back over to join them, her curls bouncing and a pout on her lips. 'You didn't watch me, Mr Gussy. I slid right down on my belly.'

'Aw, Jessie. I saw you. I was watching from the corner of my eye, and I saw you slide right down on your front.' As Jessie's pout disappeared to be replaced by an angelic smile, Gus reached into his jogging shorts pocket and retrieved his wallet. 'If I'd known today was your birthday, Jessie, I'd have got you a card and a present. But I didn't, so use this to buy yourself something nice.'

As Jessie's small hand gripped the twenty-pound note, Jo Jo frowned and stepped closer. 'Aw, no, Gus. We can't accept that.'

But Gus shook his head. 'Yes, you can, Jo Jo. We're friends, aren't we? That's what friends do.' He leant over the fence and high fived Jessie. Her flushed face and sparkling eyes made him think that today would be a good day – at least for Jessie. He, on the other hand, was heading into The Fort to interview Razor McCarthy and Arthur Goyle and he could only hope that some new leads had firmed up overnight.

CHAPTER 37

Angel

They're mad at me about last night, but it can't be helped. Speak's the only one who's not bothered by the result. He's buzzing and I suspect his only regret is that he didn't get the chance to record it so he could make a few quid on that appalling website of his.

Thankfully, we'd got rid of the others – told them we were offering Flynn one-to-one counselling because she was clearly at a crucial stage in the process and needed more help than they to relinquish the abhorrent thoughts and desires that took hold of her body and mind.

They seemed glad to go, and, for once, I was happy for them to leave. I hadn't meant to end it with Flynn. Not again and certainly not like that, but her obstinacy angered me more than it should. However, that is my cross to bear – my sin to atone for and in comparison, it is a small misstep to make. Hardly a sin at all, still I take my leadership responsibilities seriously and know that in the face of God, I must remain pure.

See and Hear were less at ease with the unfortunate turn of events. See's poisonous tone might have seared a lesser man, but I'm made of stronger stuff. I can absorb the venom and release it through the blood of my purity. 'You promised no more after Zac. This isn't what we agreed.'

With her brow drawn into a scowl and her lips tight, she resembles how I imagine Judas might have looked at the Last Supper – full of righteous indignation, but no real gumption to take responsibility for his actions. I meet her ferocious eyes with dignified quiet before reminding her of Corinthians 6:9-11 'Don't you realise that those who do wrong will not inherit the Kingdom of God?' I let the words sink in. 'We cleansed her. We cleansed Flynn and now she is with the Lord. She is no longer caught in the throes of sin. Let her rest in peace.'

I turned then to Hear who sobbed over Flynn's body and placed a solid hand on his shoulder. 'Be strong. This was the right thing to do. Flynn was beyond redemption on this earth, but now her soul flies free. She will sit with the angels in heaven.'

I shake my head and dispel the thought of Hear's anguished sobs. The memory of moving her is a blur to me, but I know we did it together. That's what we did last time, too. Now I must concern myself with moving forward. If we're to avoid a repetition of Flynn's behaviour, then we must intensify the program. No more talking therapies. Instead, we must immerse the sinners in rightful behaviours to vanquish their demons. That is my way forward and last night, after we'd prayed for Flynn, we agreed on it.

I position myself between the two full-length mirrors in my bedroom and study my naked body. It bears the scars which symbolise my commitment to and adoration of the Lord and I am proud of them. They are my medals of honour, the proof of my devotion. Anticipation ripples in my stomach before spreading its warming tendrils through my limbs and casting delightful shivers up my spine. As my flaccid penis hardens, I straighten and look into my own fevered eyes.

Saliva gathers in my mouth as I lift my whip and brace myself for its welcome pain. 'Owww.'

Again and again, I raise my hand crossways over my body and drive the leather's healing licks across my back, each one a painful caress, each one leaving a loving welt to remind me of the power of prayer and supplication. With each crack of the whip, my body fills with strength and humility. I am great. I am the Angel. I am God's servant doing his will and stamping out aberrations in this earthly world.

CHAPTER 38

Despite the prospect of spending a sizeable chunk of his day with Razor McCarthy and Arthur Goyle, Gus was still smiling from his chance encounter with Jessie, Jo Jo, and his boyfriend when he entered The Fort. It had eased a little of the dark cloud that hung over him these days. Jessie's excitement over her birthday party, and Jo Jo's cautious yet definite smile, told him the siblings were mending, although he still wondered about Jo Jo's defensive attitude when he asked about the word choice that seemed to place him as initially hailing from further north.

It would be a slow process for the siblings, but Gus was optimistic. His lips quirked as he recollected the shy, almost reticent way Jo Jo had introduced Idris. It was good to see the lad being himself – not consumed by responsibilities to his family. Once away from the estate and the gangs it had allowed him to breathe and flourish. Gus was damned if he'd let anything happen to them. Not knowing the anonymous bidder's identity made the threat to the pair more insidious.

Despite it being a glorious Saturday, Gus couldn't summon up interest in anything much other than the investigation into the Auction Slave website and its link to Zac's murder.

Overnight, everything had taken on a new intensity and his mum's response was to drop by with a variety of unidentifiable and inedible offerings 'to fatten you up'.

Offerings which Gus gifted to Compo, who devoured them with gusto, extolling the skill of Gus's mum's baking, much to the entire team's amazement.

Gus had overheard his mum telling Alice months ago that he was pining for his little boy, when he'd only met Billy once.

Gus had disputed his mum's diagnosis at that point. How could he pine for a son she'd denied him knowledge of for the first few years of his life and had only just met? He'd told Alice, 'You can't pine for something you didn't know you had, can you?' And in his mind that logic held…still…maybe his mum was right. He didn't know and had a hard time pinning it down. The only time he could put a tag on his emotions was when he was pounding pavements, parks, and woods. Only then, in the safety of his own head, with each step pushing him further through the pain, did he acknowledge his rage. It festered in his chest, bubbling with venom. Sometimes, in the silence of the woods, he'd release a roar and in those moments, he felt like a ferocious lion claiming his territory.

He loved Billy. There was no doubt of that. The lad was a joy to be with. He looked so much like Gus – his hair with its golden streaks spiralling through the curls, his smile, and his eyes – blue with their distinctive black ring round the iris – that there was no doubt of his parenthood.

That Sadia had named him Billy was the only point in her favour. She'd chosen the name to commemorate Gus's godson who Gus had failed to save from being killed by his own dad. That pleased him, but it wasn't enough to make him forgive her. How could he? Gus had always wanted children, and Sadia knew that. She broke his heart when she left and that he could understand. She'd been in an awful place at the time, coping with her father's death. But to cut him from her life knowing she was carrying his child. A child he would have given up everything for. No, Gus couldn't forgive her for denying him that. His relationship with Sadia and his parents, who'd known of the lad's existence was, as far as he was concerned, irreparably damaged.

Despite being at pains to connect with his boy, the pressure of distance and lost time had Gus considering a move north. He'd put out feelers with his boss, DCI Chalmers about a transfer north of the border and was sure that his track record and skill set would make him a favourable candidate, yet something stopped him from finalising the transfer application. It wasn't only Nancy's doubts at the wisdom of 'chasing a dream' that had made him pause. It was the fact that he was unsure of Sadia's reaction. Should he move?

At the moment, she was fine with the sporadic visits he'd managed to Livingston and had brought Billy down to see Gus a few times. But he suspected she'd view him moving north as an invasion of her personal space. Hmph, who cares what she thinks? It wasn't only her opinion that was the issue, though. It was what she might do. Would she up sticks and disappear with Billy leaving Gus not knowing where they were, or would she contest visiting rights? She'd hinted that she was looking for a move when she last brought Billy down and that petrified him. Now he knew about his son there was no way he could countenance giving him up. Alice had told him that he needed to put his claim to Billy in more legal terms, but he'd been pussyfooting about not wanting to rock the boat, which ignited his inner rage even more.

Sweat dripping from his forehead, Gus paused in the waiting room to execute a few stretches as he waited for Hardeep, the duty officer to let him in. With his ID tucked at the bottom of his small rucksack, Hardeep knew the drill. However, this morning, Hardeep seemed to be having an argument with the printer and hadn't noticed Gus arrive. As he waited, Gus's eyes drifted round the small waiting area with its flip-up plastic chairs and noticeboards filled with information on various crimes and entreaty's to Dob in a Dealer or to take advantage of Bradford's knife and gun amnesty by dropping off knives and, occasionally, guns, to leave fewer weapons on the street. Not for the first time, Gus thought it wasn't the most welcoming of entrances. He sighed. Humanising the first point of contact with the police appeared to be a minor consideration for those who rarely interacted with the public. For Gus, it was a wasted opportunity. The more people friendly the police station presented as, the more likely relationships with the public would improve and with accusations of misogyny, racism, and homophobia a near daily occurrence – thank God Bradford hadn't shown itself in as bad a light as the Met – still, it was only a small step in building relationships.

As he took in the scuffed floor, dull paintwork, and scratty leaflets, Gus almost didn't notice the woman sitting in the corner. As his eyes passed over her, he paused, frowned, and then backtracked. The woman, in a grey hoodie and leggings, was folded over herself, making her blend into the background. Her shoulders slumped and her arms were wrapped round her waist as she rocked back and forth, causing the flip-up chair to creak with every movement. Gus wondered for a mere second if she was high but dismissed that when the woman lifted her head and glanced his way. Her eyes, though red rimmed were clear, her face and skin spotless and vibrant. She was upset, but it was Hardeep's job to deal with whatever problem the woman had.

Gus stepped towards the door as Hardeep, printouts in hand and a satisfied smile on his face, approached the desk. Before the older officer released the door, something prompted Gus to glance back at the distraught woman. Now that his brain had had time to catch up, Gus was certain he'd seen this woman sitting in the same spot yesterday when he arrived for work. As he studied her, he thought there was something familiar about her.

He stepped through the door, allowing it to swing closed behind him. 'Hi, Hardeep. You always on duty or what? Haven't you got grandkids to spend time with?'

Hardeep was approaching retirement and his plans were to spend half the year in India and half in the UK, so he and his wife wouldn't be expected to child mind his grandchildren. Gus knew the man's protestations were all bluster and suspected that Hardeep would want nothing more than to spend his retirement with his grandkids. But still, you have to keep up appearances, don't you?

'Took them to Chester Zoo yesterday. Cost me a damn fortune. Not sure I'll be able to afford to retire after that trip.'

Hardeep's grin belied his grumpy tone and Gus rested a hand on his shoulder and pretended to glance around to make sure they couldn't be overheard. 'You can't fool me, you old curmudgeon. You love those kids.'

The older man's grin widened as he copied Gus's surreptitious glance and responded in the same quiet tone. 'Sh. Don't you dare let that lot in there' – he pointed to the office staff behind him – 'hear you say that. Ruin my reputation that would.'

Gus moved closer; voice still quiet.

'That woman in the waiting room?'

Hardeep nodded.

187

'She was there yesterday too, wasn't she?'

'Yes, poor soul came in day before yesterday to report her son missing, but it hadn't been twenty-four hours yet and he's eighteen, and not in any at risk categories, so we couldn't progress the report. Poor soul was beside herself, so I settled her down with a cuppa and told her to come back after forty-eight hours.'

'So, it's been three days now? Has she filed a report?'

'Nearly. I took the details and forwarded it to Missing Persons. Someone's coming down shortly.'

Gus studied the woman through the reinforced glass that protected the officers from any prospective violence from the public and wished he didn't feel like he was observing an animal in the zoo. After all, this woman wasn't in her natural habitat. Coming to a police station to report a family member missing was nobody's natural habitat.

The feeling that he knew her still plagued him.

'What's her name, Hardeep? I have a sneaky feeling I've met her before, but I can't quite put my finger on whether it was in a personal or professional capacity.'

'Elizabeth White, I believe. Son's called Bailey. Thing is, she says he left a note saying he was going to his dad's in Huddersfield, but the dad's not seen him. I spoke to him myself. Bloody charmer, that one, I'll tell you. Effing and jeffing like it was going out of fashion and called his ex a fair few choice names an' all. Anyway, upshot was that he thinks she's overreacting and that she should let the lad have a bit of freedom. Said she was babying him and that's more than likely why he's taken off.'

Gus had met a few dads who treated their exes like crap and the narrative was all too familiar – on the one hand framing the mother as irrational, overindulgent, too protective while at the same time having the temerity to also characterise her as a promiscuous nymphomaniac. Of course, the same was often true of the female partners describing their exes and when an investigation necessitated consulting with both parents, it often made the interviews take on the semblance of a tightrope walk.

It made him relieved that despite the huge wedge between him and Sadia, and all the anger he harboured against her for the decisions she made regarding their son, neither of them was in the market of dissing the other and they'd been at great pains, despite their differences, to keep it civil.

Elizabeth, Elizabeth White? Now that name rang a bell. In his mind's eye he visualised first a freckly faced, pony-tailed, confident kid from primary school and then, in a flash, a sultrier, skinnier, young woman from upper school who was always in bother for sassing the teachers and had developed a fiercely competitive spirit from her involvement in any sport the school offered. This woman sitting alone and in pain was as far from either memory as it was possible to be, and it was that image that made Gus cave.

Aware that with Missing Persons involved, this was well outside his remit, Gus couldn't leave her out there and not at least attempt to reassure her.

'I was at school with her. My mate Greg had a crush on her when we were about eight and she gave him short shrift when he sent her a Valentine's card. She was tough as nails then and in upper school too…'

His words trailed off and Hardeep studied the woman. 'Looks like she lost her oomph somewhere along the line, dun't it, lad?'

'Or had it knocked out of her. Whatever—'

'Yeah, yeah, I know. You're a big softie at heart, Gus, lad. You have a quick shower and I'll settle her in one of the nicer interview rooms with a cup of tea.'

Gus grinned at the older officer as he headed for the lifts. 'You keep my secret, Hardeep, and I'll keep yours. No point everybody knowing we're both pushovers, is it?'

Within twenty minutes Gus, hair damp and wearing a crew neck jumper and jeans, was outside the interview room, where Hardeep had put Elizabeth White. Before pushing the door open, he hesitated. Was he stepping over the mark? This wasn't any of his business, and it must have been fifteen years since he'd last set eyes on Lizzie. Besides, it wasn't like he had nothing else to do. Still, the memory of a feisty teenager lingered. He exhaled. It was that contrast between his memory of the vibrant girl she'd once been and the frazzled woman worried stiff about her son that had piqued his interest. He didn't owe her anything, yet somehow, her current predicament was mixed up with childhood memories of one of his best friend's crushing on her and the way she shut him down with humour, but no nastiness.

He knew he couldn't bring Greg back, and he'd never forgive himself for his part in his friend's death. A niggle at the back of his mind told him he couldn't ignore this woman in her hour of need. That by helping her, he'd be, in some small way, making up for what had happened to Greg. If he'd been religious, he might have had fanciful ideas of Greg looking down on him from above with a benevolent smile, but Greg would have laughed at him and shook his head, saying in his slow drawl, '*For a copper, you're a real bloody teddy bear. You need to toughen up, mate*!' The thought made Gus smile and the remains of the smile were still on his lips when he pushed the door open and entered the room.

For a few seconds, Elizabeth stared at him across the table, where she cradled a mug of lukewarm tea in her hands. Her brow furrowed as she tried to place him, and Gus allowed her the chance to work it out on her own as he crossed the room and sat in a chair opposite her. Aware that the room smelt of stale food and Dettol, and that the positioning of plastic chairs at opposite sides of a table wasn't the most conducive set up for a comfortable chat, Gus forced the smile to remain on his face, hoping he didn't look too creepy. It felt that he'd barely smiled over the last few months, except when he was with Billy and now his cheek muscles protested at the effort.

'Long time no see, Lizzie.'

As soon as the words left his mouth, he cursed himself for such a jovial greeting in the circumstances. But Lizzie, recognition finally dawning on her face, broke into a smile that was a faint echo of the one Gus remembered from their youth.

'Well, I'll be damned. It's Gus McGuire. I heard on the grapevine that you were a copper, but I didn't believe it. Always thought you were too sensitive to be a police officer.'

Gus's smile settled into a more natural rut as her words elicited a snort of laughter from him. 'Funnily enough, you're not the only one to think that, but' – he splayed his hands in front of him – 'turns out I'm good at catching the bad guys.'

They sat in comfortable silence for a few seconds before Gus got to the point. 'Sergeant Singh tells me your lad's gone AWOL, that right?'

Lizzie exhaled a long breath and pushed her mug away from her, slopping a little drop of the milky liquid on the tabletop as she did so. Her eyes, which had come alive when she'd recognised Gus, became shadowed, and she licked her cracked lips before continuing. 'I know. Bailey's eighteen. The other officers explained that because he's an adult and left a note, there's nowt they can do.'

She paused and pinched the bridge of her nose between her thumb and forefinger. 'It's just, my Bailey wouldn't go off like that. Not leaving just a note. He just wouldn't do it – you know?'

She stood up and began pacing the room, her arms wrapped tightly round her skinny frame. 'You won't get this, Gus, but this is just like when I was in labour with him. I told the midwife I was ready to push, and the old bat wouldn't listen. "You can't possibly be ready yet, Ms White. You were only 4 cm dilated an hour ago." I kept telling her I was, but still she wouldn't listen and…' She stopped and glared at Gus, her eyes flashing. 'You know what? The old cow was wrong. I was ready to push and five minutes later there he was. My Bailey. All red and wrinkled and bawling like a banshee.'

Her voice hitched in her throat as she raised shaking fingers to cup her mouth as if they would block the anguish that threatened to engulf her.

She slumped back into the chair, head bowed, and in a voice barely loud enough for Gus to hear, said, 'It feels the same now. It feels like I'm back in that maternity unit knowing my baby's head is crowning, yet nobody will listen. I don't care how many *experts*' – she bunny eared *experts*, her tone leaving no doubt what she thought of those experts – 'tell me I'm overacting, or being overprotective or any other of those demeaning tags they give to us mums to justify their protocols, I know my son and he wouldn't go off like that leaving a scrappy note behind. He just wouldn't.'

She rummaged in her bag until she found what she was looking for. 'Here.' She thrust a photo towards Gus.

'That's Bailey. That's my son. He's not some faceless anonymous missing lad. He's my son.'

Gus took the photo and studied it. Bailey had his mother's colouring and facial structure, although his hair was darker. He was grinning into the camera with a Pride flag draped round his shoulders. Gus smiled. 'He looks like you, Lizzie. You must be so proud of him.'

He made to give the photo back, but with tears streaming down her face she batted his hand away. 'Keep it, Gus. Pin it somewhere so you remember to check up on him.'

She wiped her cheeks with the back of her hand and sniffed. Gus rummaged in his pocket for a tissue and on finding one that, although crumpled, was unused, he handed it to her.

'I believe you, Lizzie. It's not my department, you understand? But I'll have a word with DC Shah from Missing Persons. Huda is good at her job, you know? And when I checked, she'd already created and updated a file with all Bailey's details on the system. He's on our radar and she's actioned various investigative points to establish Bailey's last known whereabouts and she's going to interview his dad and his friends.'

Lizzie snorted. 'Good luck with that. His dad's a homophobic, sexist arse. Ricky won't have told your lot, but last time he saw Bailey, he told him to – and I quote – "be a man or fuck off back to bum chum land". He hates that Bailey's gay and says he won't speak to him till he "straightens himself out".'

Gus absorbed the words, wondering how people with those sorts of values could still exist in today's society. What damage could those venomous words have caused a young lad? Gus made a mental note to double check that Huda turned the screws on Bailey's dad. It was worth checking to see if Savage was behind his son's disappearance. He was unconvinced that there was anything concerning about Bailey White's absence, but there was no harm in making sure.

When his phone rang, Gus glanced at it and saw it was Alice, who wouldn't contact him unless it was urgent. She knew he was in the building, so maybe she'd got McCarthy set up for their interview. With a shrug, he stood up and allowed the phone to go to voicemail. 'I'm sorry, but I have to go. That's my detective sergeant and she wouldn't call if it wasn't important. We're in the middle of an active investigation. I just popped in out of courtesy, Lizzie. However, I promise I'll monitor how DC Shah is progressing with locating your son's whereabouts.'

Lizzie seemed less agitated now, having spoken to Gus, and as he handed her his card, she smiled.

'Thanks, Gus. I appreciate your help.'

After accompanying Lizzie White from The Fort with an entreaty to let both him and DC Shah know if Bailey turned up at home, Gus checked the text that Alice had sent after her earlier call had gone to voicemail.

Alice: Cybercrimes taking over McCarthy and Goyle interviews. We've got a suspicious death – teenager – Haworth Rd. Get a move on.

His heart sank when he saw the age of the victim and, relieved that he'd already said his goodbyes to Lizzie before checking the text, Gus sighed. The coincidence of his school friend reporting the disappearance of her teenage son and Gus being called to the scene where a teenage boy had been found wasn't good. He'd hoped that Bailey White would turn up safe and sound, but now that looked much less likely.

As he made his way upstairs to find Alice, Gus couldn't help being annoyed that he wouldn't get his shot at interviewing Razor McCarthy. It was sensible that cybercrimes, with their in-depth technical knowledge, conduct those interviews. Still, he felt his experience with McCarthy might have shaken a few snippets of information loose. Cybercrimes had made it clear that Gus's team's involvement was a mere courtesy because of Compo's involvement in finding the site in the first place, and he knew well that they could have shut his team out completely. It pissed him off to give up his hold on McCarthy after all the work they'd done processing his home, and bringing him in. Still, he'd be able to watch the interview later at his leisure and Compo was being allowed to watch from the observation suite, which guaranteed immediate notification of any salient information.

CHAPTER 39

Jessie had insisted on using the money Gus had given her for her birthday to go on the pedalos on the lake. Jo Jo, still unable to get over not having to scrimp and save had initially resisted, but when he saw her face fall and then Idris had intervened with a quiet, 'It's her birthday money, Jo. Let her enjoy her day.' So he'd conceded. Having spent the last hour with Jessie yelling out directions to them, with he and Idris pedalling for all their might, they now sat on a bench, eating ice cream while Jessie played a game of tig nearby with a little girl she recognised from school.

Idris nudged Jo Jo. 'What's up?'

'God, am I that obvious?' Jo Jo slapped the heel of his hand against his forehead and gave an unconvincing laugh.

'Only to me…' Idris gripped his hand and tilted his head. 'And possibly to that copper we met earlier. He knows there's summat up with you too.'

Shit! The last thing Jo Jo wanted was Gus muscling in and coaxing his secret out of him. Experience told Jo Jo that Gus was very adept at that and Jo Jo couldn't afford to let him succeed this time. There was too much at stake for both him and Jessie.

'He seemed like a good guy. Maybe you should tell him what's on your mind. He'll help you. '

Jo Jo slid across the bench till he was close to Idris. 'I can't. I just can't. It's about my mam. '

Idris sighed. 'Your mam's gone, Jo Jo. Nothing you tell Gus about her can harm her now, can it?'

But Jo Jo wasn't worried about what he knew harming his mum. He was worried that his secret, if it ever came out, would be disastrous for him and Jessie. He just couldn't risk it. But he didn't know what to do. Watching Jessie so carefree in her new birthday clothes emphasised just how much they had to lose. Her smile brought a corresponding one to his own lips.

Today was Jessie's day. They'd enjoy it and then tomorrow he'd think about what he would do. Tomorrow he could make the hard decisions even if it meant he could lose everything. Jessie was the most important person in all this, and Jo Jo would do whatever it took to protect her.

CHAPTER 40

Despite the sun breaking through the late September sky, when Gus and Alice arrived, there was a subdued feel to the crime scene on the B6144 to Haworth. On the drive from The Fort, Gus asked Hissing Sid if they had an ID, but had been told not yet. The only information Sid was prepared to divulge over the phone was that it was a mother with her toddler who'd found the body of a teenage boy who looked to be about sixteen or seventeen years old. To avoid an accident in the car, she'd parked up when her two-year-old needed a wee and headed for some bushes away from the road. The poor souls had got more than they'd bargained for. Sid confided that it looked like a suspicious death because there were fingerprints around the neck indicating the boy had been strangled. The post-mortem would confirm if that was cause of death.

On arrival at the scene, they were cleared to drive through the outer cordon which blocked the road towards Wilsden and Sandy Lane. Alice parked up behind a line of six police and CSI vehicles. This had created single lane traffic, monitored by a uniformed officer at either end of the cordon, and was also drawing unwanted attention from passers-by. Gus suspected it wouldn't be long before the journalists arrived. For a few seconds, he observed the cars slowing down on the opposite side of the road as they tried to glimpse whatever had caused the police activity.

Bloody lookie loos!

With reluctance, he got out of the car and surveyed the scene. Whoever had left the teenage boy there had been wise. This area on the side of the road adjoining the moors had no buildings on it. In addition, this body dump spot was far enough away from both the farms situated nearer to Sandy Lane and the crossroads further towards Haworth, which was flanked by The Flappit pub. Of course, avoiding buildings minimised their risk of being caught on security cameras. Because this side of the road had an abundance of gorse and groups of bushes and trees, it provided ideal cover to hide a body. In normal circumstances, the chances of an early discovery were slim. Whoever had dumped the teenager there had been unlucky that the body had been found so quickly. This would narrow the time of death window and hopefully give Gus's team an advantage when they discovered how long the body had been in its hiding place.

A weight settled in his chest – a little heavier than the one that normally took up residence there when he was called to a child death. Gus was savvy enough to realise that the heaviness was because of his earlier meeting with Lizzie White. If this was her son, it had just become much more personal than usual, and those sorts of investigations always took a harder toll on the body and the mind. The thought that he'd have been better off heading right up to his office instead of involving himself in the business of someone he hadn't seen in fifteen years flitted through his mind. Then he tutted and frowned. *What am I thinking? Don't be such a selfish git, Gus*.

Alice walked round the car and stood beside him, allowing him the moment of respite before they approached the scene. He'd filled her in on his meeting with Lizzie en route, so she was well aware of the implications of this young man's body being found so soon after Lizzie reported her son missing and so close to where Lizzie lived.

'Come on, Gus. No point in standing about like a big wimpy wuss is there?'

Aware that this was her attempt to diffuse the situation, Gus tutted and gave a slow head shake. 'Really? *Wimpy Wuss*? Is that the best you've got?'

With a shrug, Alice marched off, leaving him to trail behind her towards the crime scene tape and the officer who was managing entry to the site. As he walked, he scanned the area. The first officers who'd responded had done a grand job of creating a good outer cordon which extended beyond the edge of the moorland and into the middle of the road and for thirty metres on either side of the scene. Gus suspected that the body would have been transported by vehicle. The likelihood was that the small, indented lay-by would be the most likely place for a vehicle to stop. It stood in a direct line between the road and the bushes behind which the gleaming white of the crime scene tent was visible. The grass verge was damp underfoot and as Gus neared the inner cordon, he spotted an array of small yellow plastic A-frames showing that the CSIs had already found likely forensic evidence.

The CSIs had positioned a few numbered plastic tags in the muddy lay-by. If luck was on their side, this might be where the person, or persons, who'd dumped the lad had parked up. However, all of this was mere conjecture until the pathologist could confirm timings and cause of death.

By the time he reached the tape, Alice was half into her crime scene suit and was hoiking the hood up over her short black hair. As he donned his own protective suit, his eyes were drawn to the tented area within which lay yet another lost life and possibly the son of the old friend he'd comforted not an hour earlier. Like furrowing bloated maggots, some white suited CSIs worked with their noses nearly touching the ground, while others resembled animated snowmen as they scoured the area for clues. It was a familiar scene. Yet like every other, it toyed with Gus's emotions.

The violent loss of a life and particularly a young life was cause for despair, yet underneath that sadness, a frisson of excitement churned. The adrenalin surge, the challenge of slotting the clues together, building a case, and arresting the bad guy was intoxicating.

Ducking under the tape, Gus walked over the predetermined path the CSIs had lined with treads to preserve the scene's integrity and closed in on the crime scene tent. As he did so, an officer he recognised despite his wearing an oversized bunny suit, mask, and hood left the tent and began making his way towards him.

'Hey, boss.'

Gus hadn't needed the *Hey, boss* to recognise Taffy Bhandir. If the lad's bouncing walk wasn't identifier enough his grinning round face beneath the elasticated hood was.

'What you got for us, Taff?'

Almost standing to attention, but refraining from a heel click and salute, Taffy flicked open his tablet and then, having trouble with his nitrile gloves, used his teeth to pull one off so he could operate the machine and cleared his throat. 'Mother and toddler found the body when the little one needed a wazz.'

He met Gus's eyes. 'Potty training you see? Mum didn't want an accident, and' – he shrugged – 'you know what kids are like. When they have to go, they have to go.'

Gus rolled his eyes at Alice who'd now joined them and waved his hand in a get on with it gesture. Taking the hint, Taffy continued, 'Well, she called it in. I've taken her statement and details. She had the good sense to move well away from the bushes. She was shaken but held it together for the little 'un, so I let her go.' He risked a glance at Gus, a small frown playing across his brow as if he wasn't sure he'd done the right thing in letting their star witness go.

'You did right, Taff. She found the body and reported it, so she'll probably have limited information to give us.'

But Taffy winced. He wasn't quite finished. 'The only thing is, she parked in the same place as we reckon the perpetrator parked. We've taken images and treads from her vehicle and one of the uniformed officers backed her car away from any possible remaining treads from other vehicles, but...' Instead of finishing his sentence, he exhaled and rolled his neck creating a series of audible clicks as he tutted.

Eyebrows raised, more at the number of clicks Taffy's neck was producing – *how bloody stiff can one neck be*? – than in dismay at the possible scene contamination. 'So, we've got a mishmash of tread marks on the verge?'

'Precisely.'

Mirroring Taffy's neck roll, Gus added a hand and massaged the back of his own neck as he observed the CSIs working near the verge. 'Well, nowt we can do about that, Taff. If we get something there, then all's good and well. If not' – he tutted – 'then we'll just have to find something else.'

Aware that he was delaying finding out whether the dead boy was Bailey White, Gus pulled in a breath. He stepped towards the bushes where the body still lay. 'What about the lad, Taff? Got an ID yet?'

'Not yet. Sid's just been through the scene with the new pathologist.'

The slight emphasis on the word *new* spoke volumes. Rumour had it that the pathologist now sharing Gus's dad's job was difficult to like. Wanted things done her own way. Not that Gus considered that a bad thing in itself. Particularly if it kept Sid on track. Hissing Sid followed a code of his own – one which had caused many disagreements between him and Gus over the years. While Gus appreciated the need for gallows humour as a coping mechanism, the crime scene manager often took it too far and Gus had called him up on it frequently. There was a fine line between gentle humour to get you through a difficult crime scene and disrespecting the victim and their fate. The latter was one thing Gus would not stand for.

Gus sighed. It looked like he might have to give a visual ID from the photo Lizzie White had given him. His heartbeat peaked at the thought. If this was Lizzie's son, then he'd be the one who told her there was no doubt about that.

Fuck, fuck, fuck, and more fuck! With that in mind, he increased his pace, wanting to get it over with. Sid appeared from behind the bush, waving a sealed evidence bag in one hand.

'Got an ID, Taffy lad. Driving licence in the back pocket.'

The diminutive CSI paused, pulled his face mask down and rewarded Gus with a smile.

'Oh hallo, Gussy boy. Didn't know you'd swooped in yet. Come on then. I'll show you what we've got.'

Heart pounding, Gus wanted nothing more than to rip the evidence bag from Sid's hand and see the ID for himself, but instead he inhaled and followed Sid back round the bushes and into the crime scene tent. As always, despite the warm weather outside, courtesy of heat from the bright lights in a confined space, the tent was roasting. Almost as soon as he entered, sweat broke out across Gus's brow and an all too familiar claustrophobic feeling took hold. As Sid stepped to the side, revealing the teenage boy lying there, Gus's eyes focussed on the way the boy looked crumpled like an empty crisp packet scrunched up and discarded as if he was worthless – less than somehow.

He'd just taken a step nearer, the image of Bailey White printed on his retinas when Sid farted and then followed up with an insincere, 'Oops, sorry.'

Thankfully, he continued before Gus could respond. 'Moving on let me introduce you to Flynn Arnett. Driving licence and image match. He lives in Cottingley. Not registered as missing. Looks like cause of death is manual strangulation. But don't hold me to that. The new' – again with the slight emphasis on *new* – 'pathologist would string me up.'

Even the insidious stench of Sid's fart wasn't enough to stop Gus from inhaling. Alice clutched his arm and squeezed. Almost as soon as his relief that the dead boy wasn't Bailey White hit him, Gus's shoulders tensed. *What the hell am I thinking? This might not be Lizzie's son, but he sure as hell is someone else's*. He moved closer and inspected the bruising around the boy's neck.

Alice stepped forward, and they stood abreast, looking down at Flynn Arnett for long seconds, each making their personal vow to find the person who snuffed out this teenager's life. 'You thinking what I'm thinking, Gus?'

Gus nodded. 'Damn right I am. Zac Ibrahim's cause of death was manual strangulation. Coincidence?'

Although the force of Alice's snort was contained behind her mask, the certainty of her words was not. 'Not a chance in hell.'

'My thoughts precisely. We need to work out what Zach Ibrahim and Flynn Arnett had in common and also try to find a link between them and Razor McCarthy.' He took a moment before straightening. 'You finish off here, Al. I'll contact a Family Liaison Officer to meet me at the parents' house and I'll take Taffy to inform them.'

With a last glance at the dead boy, Gus retraced his steps, gathering Taffy as he left.

The next few hours would be unpleasant for any of those concerned, and there was work to do. It was no accident that Flynn Arnett's body had been dumped there. The lack of CCTV along that stretch of road made it near impossible to get an ID on any vehicle, and that showed Gus that their killer was aware enough to take counter measures to avoid detection.

Although the road was busy enough during the day, in the dead of night, Gus reckoned whoever had placed Flynn's body there would have had a fair chance of going about his or her dark deeds unnoticed. Still, before he got into Taffy's car, Gus directed the uniformed officers to request CCTV footage from the businesses and dwellings on the road from Wednesday onwards. Until they had a confirmed time of death, Gus wanted to err on the side of caution. Later, when he made his statement to the press, he'd ask for information from anyone using that road overnight, but again, that would result in a shed load of *helpful* information that would more than likely elicit no clues. Still, it had to be done. It was all part of due diligence and although it took up many hours of police work, it was necessary.

CHAPTER 41

While Taffy drove, Gus phoned Lizzie White. Reporters would soon catch wind of a body being found, and he didn't want her to panic. The least he could do was reassure her that this dead boy wasn't her son. Although he suspected that knowing someone out here had killed a young lad wouldn't reassure her of Bailey's safety. It certainly didn't reassure him.

The Arnett's house was in a small quiet cul-de-sac in Cottingley. There was nothing out of the ordinary about the street or, indeed, the Arnett house. It was a typical middle-class semi with a neat garden and two cars lined up in the drive outside. But now, he and Taffy were about to shatter the hearts of occupants of this cheery home into a trillion pieces. Their lives would never be the same and Gus hated that he had to deliver such tragic news. Experience told him that families responded to tragic traumatic incidents like these in many ways, and statistics told him that few families came out of it in one piece.

This was the worst job in the world, but it was a necessary one. Gus, accompanied by Taffy, rang the doorbell and waited. His mind was still partly on the crime scene he'd just left and partly on a crime scene he'd visited weeks earlier. What was the common factor between these two murders? The contrast between Zach Ibrahim and Flynn Arnett's lives was vast. However, often, once you turned over a few stones and rummaged about beneath the surface, things would come to light which might show a link – however tenuous.

It had been three hours since Flynn had been discovered. Three hours during which time the Arnett family were unaware of the death of their child. Three hours of blissful ignorance – of normality for the family. Gus exhaled. From now on, this family would have to adjust to a new normality. A normality that didn't include the physical presence of their son, but one that would be forever haunted by his absence. He hoped they would be strong enough to withstand the grief and the pain.

Because they'd found an ID easily enough through finding the lad's provisional driving licence in the wallet discovered tucked into the back pocket of his jeans, Gus had run his name through HOLMES – the police record keeping system. Nothing had flagged up for the boy, indicating that he was unknown to them. Gus had extended the search to Flynn's immediate family and had found a single instance of GBH for the father five years earlier. Although, worth noting, it wasn't necessarily something that might be relevant to this case. Still, Gus would bear it in mind during his interactions with the dad.

When no one answered, the part of Gus that wanted to turn and walk away kicked in. He could come back later. Give the family a few more hours thinking of themselves as a complete family. He could even delegate the responsibility to someone else. But that wouldn't be fair to them and besides, it was his job. He'd seen their son in death, and that made it his responsibility. Besides, it was best to tell them sooner rather than later. Before the press parked outside in this quiet Cottingley cul-de-sac. Before some arse wipe let it slip on the news, or before some well-meaning friend messaged them with condolences.

No matter how much Gus instructed the teams working on the crime scene to respect the privacy of the investigation, there was always somebody for whom the allure of a tax-free hundred quid overrode their professional obligations.

His shoulders tensed as he cast his mind back to the teenage boy's body callously discarded on a less populated area of the B144. Whoever had killed and dumped Flynn was calculated enough to hide his body behind bushes, far enough off the road that it wouldn't be visible from the road by cars driving past.

'Nobody in, boss?'

Taffy's words jolted Gus from his reverie. At 11 on a Saturday morning, two cars were parked in the pristine drive, and the front room curtains were open. 'Nah, Taff, I think someone's home.'

As he spoke, he heard the distinct sound of footsteps approaching and seconds later, a teenage girl with hair dyed bright purple, a nose ring, and skilfully applied eye make-up opened the door. Her eyes raked over them and a light frown danced across her brow as she glared at them in silence, making Gus feel like a specimen under a microscope.

He and Taffy proffered their warrant cards, which the girl studied with as much interest and more distaste than Gus would offer a dog turd. 'I'm DI Gus McGuire and this is DC Talvinder Bhandir. Are your parents home?'

With no discernible change in her disinterest levels, the girl backed away from the door, leaving it ajar in an unspoken invitation and shuffled back along the carpeted hallway, heading towards the kitchen at the end. As she went, she yelled upstairs, 'Mum, Dad, the five-oh are here. Flush the coke and ditch the benzos, eh?'

Despite the seriousness of the situation, Gus's lips twitched. This girl was a card and her sassiness reminded him of his goddaughter, Zarqa.

Seconds later, a frazzled, barefoot woman pulling her dressing gown around her ran downstairs, followed by a taller figure – her partner – tucking his T-shirt into his jeans and frowning at his daughter. 'God's sake, Millie, you shouldn't joke about stuff like that. You'll get us arrested.'

Millie shrugged and continued into the kitchen while the Arnett adults gawped at Gus, their faces holding almost identical frowns. Gus stepped closer, extending his warrant card once more and repeating his earlier introductions. This was the bit he hated. He'd witnessed death notifications where officers had allowed the notification to fade away unfinished, forcing the bereaved relatives to reach their own conclusions. In Gus's opinion, this was a cruel, unprofessional, and insensitive way to inform parents of their loved one's death. He could tell by the way Mrs Arnett's fingers wrung the neck of her dressing gown that she was already expecting bad news and Mr Arnett's flushed cheeks echoed her worry. So Gus got to the point.

'I'm sorry to have to tell you both, but a body, we believe to be your son Flynn, was discovered earlier this morning.'

He waited for a fraction of a second before confirming his previous words. 'Flynn is dead.'

The Arnetts blinked, then exchanged a glance with each other, before Mrs Arnett crumpled before him, falling to her knees, clasping her mouth with her fingers, and shaking her head. Mr Arnett said 'No, No. You're wrong. Flynn's at a sleepover with a mate. He's not…'

Mr Arnett looked from his wife to Gus and back again. His flush hadn't faded and Gus, concerned with his sudden pallor, stepped forward, but the man waved him away. On the point of helping Mrs Arnett to her feet, the daughter, Millie, breathing heavily, her eyes wide and brimming with tears, nudged Taffy out of the way. Her voice when she spoke held only a slight tremor, and Gus once more was fleetingly reminded of Zarqa.

'I got this. Come on, Mum. Let's get you upstairs and dressed, then we'll speak to the officers.'

She glared at her dad. 'Make yourself useful, Dad. Put the kettle on. She'll need it when I bring her back down.'

Like an automated toy whose battery was about to give up, Mr Arnett moved through to the kitchen and hovered near the kettle. He rolled his fingers through his hair and looked out the window as if fascinated by the mown lawn. Taffy edged past him and checked the kettle was full, before flicking it on, while Gus guided the bereaved father to the kitchen table. Once seated, Mr Arnett, head bowed, studied his fingers, his breath coming in rapid rasping shallow gasps that increased in volume with each one.

Hope the Family Liaison Officer gets here soon.

'Try to slow your breathing down, Mr Arnett. Sloooow in, sloooow out.' Gus repeated the mantra he employed when his breathing was in danger of erupting into a full-blown panic attack, but Mr Arnett was oblivious to Gus's instructions. Instead, he jumped to his feet, raised a fist, and punched it straight into the wall, creating a fist shaped dent in the plaster and leaving behind a smear of blood. Then he slumped back onto the chair he'd just vacated and stared at a point just above Gus's right shoulder. Now that Mr Arnett appeared calmer, Gus was happy to leave him be until his wife and daughter returned. No doubt they'd be better equipped to deal with him than Gus was. Still, Gus made a mental note to include the violent outburst in his report about the visit. Although it didn't necessarily indicate anything, the circumstances warranted logging it. Who wouldn't be driven to extreme actions on hearing that their child was dead?

By the time Taffy had deposited a set of five water filled mugs, each with a tea bag floating inside, Mrs Arnett and Millie entered the kitchen. The faint sourness that hung in the air around Mrs Arnett told Gus she'd been sick. He swallowed hard, preparing himself for the tough interview ahead as Millie, with shaking hands, settled her mum on a chair and pushed her tea towards her. With the warm mug cupped in her hands, Mrs Arnett looked straight at Gus, her eyes brimming with unshed tears, yet despite her earlier reactions, she seemed more together now.

However, it was Mr Arnett who spoke. 'You've come here and told us our child is dead.'

'Daughter!' The single word catapulted from Mrs Arnett and hung in the kitchen alongside a silence that was filled with a deeper emotion than just grief.

Gus looked at Mr Arnett, who bowed his head and focussed on his clenched hands, the mug of tea beside him ignored. It seemed that Mr Arnett wasn't about to expand on his wife's outburst, so Gus turned to Mrs Arnett, who with her tears now streaming down her face, had raised one hand to cover her mouth and was moaning as she rocked herself back and forth.

What had she meant? Was she blaming her daughter – Millie – for their son's death? Or had the shock rendered her incoherent? Gus wondered if there was a second daughter whose presence was needed. After tense seconds had ticked by, it was Millie who responded, her

words staccato, her pitch high as she spoke to her mum.
'Flynn is your *son,* Mum. Not your daughter. We've
been through this. So stop being an idiot. Think of what
Flynn wanted for once, eh?'

Exchanging a swift glance with Taffy, Gus realised
that his DC also understood the implications of both
Millie's and her father's words. *Where the hell is the
FLO?*

Millie's words seemed to activate something in Mrs
Arnett, for she jumped to her feet, raking her hands
through her short hair and paced the small room. 'She's
my *daughter*. She's my pretty little girl. No matter what
you lot say, she's my daughter. Not *Flynn*. She's a girl.
My beautiful, wonderful girl. Not a lad. It's just a
phase…she'll come round. I know she will…'

Millie tutted, glaring at her mum, but Mr Arnett
moved to his wife and, wrapped his hands round her
shoulders as she fell back onto the seat, tears streaming
down his cheeks now too.

'Aw, Tess. Flynn wasn't our daughter. Not for a
long time now – maybe even never. Flynn's our son and
we need to find out what happened to him. We need to
be here for him. No more denial. No more hoping he'll
change. You need to accept him for who he is, or you'll
never cope with this.'

Fingers gripping his wife's arms, Graham Arnett
succumbed to his tears while Gus averted his eyes,
conscious of being an awkward bystander in such a
painfully private moment. In different circumstances,
he'd leave them time to process their grief a little – time
to absorb the shock that rattled their entire being, time to
gain strength from each other, but he couldn't. He had a
murderer to find and the unexpected revelation that
Flynn Arnett was transgender opened up further areas of
investigation. His eyes drifted to Millie, who stood

angled away from her parents as if embarrassed by the charged emotions. With her arms folded over her chest, her face was a mask of unreadable emotions. Then his gaze moved to her eyes, and he reconsidered. Her chest heaved and dark anger sizzled in their depths, her unbridled anger further emphasised by her fingers nipping at her arm. Was it grief that prompted these outward responses, or was there something darker at work? He followed the direction of her gaze and judged it landed on her father. Perhaps she was embarrassed by his reaction to her brother's death. Whatever caused Millie's discomfort, combined with Tess Arnett's attitude to her son's transgender status, would have to be explored in more detail – but not now. For now, he needed specific information about where Flynn was expected to be and his friendship groups and, of course, details surrounding his gender identity and responses from the community in which he lived and his school.

Gus was so caught up in his thoughts as he offered the family a semblance of privacy for a moment, that when Mrs Arnett spoke, he hesitated before replying.

Still with her arms around her husband, but with her piercing eyes on Gus, she raised her chin as she asked the inevitable question. 'Was it a hate crime?'

Her voice wobbled a little, but her gaze remained resolute. Gus leant forward, injecting all the sincerity he felt into his tone when he answered. 'It's still early days, Mrs Arnett. Until just now we weren't aware that Flynn was transgender and right now we're following many leads, and of course the possibility that this was a hate crime, will form part of our investigation strategy. However, right now, we need information from you. I know this is hard, but there's crucial information that you can give that will speed up our investigation. A family liaison officer has been assigned, and that officer will be your point of liaison between myself and the wider investigation and your family.'

'How did he die?' It was Millie who asked the question. Her eyes were wide and her words like gun shots.

'We don't know the cause of death for certain yet, Millie. We will conduct a post-mortem to be certain, but…our initial observations indicate Flynn might have been strangled.'

As if Millie's question had opened up the family's need for specific details, Tess Arnett, pulling away from her husband but retaining hold of his hand, added a question of her own. 'Where did you find…' Instead of saying Flynn's name or using a pronoun, Mrs Arnett wafted her hand in the air.

But Mr Arnett interjected in a firm voice. 'She means where did you find *Flynn*? Where was our *son* found?'

As Tess Arnett swallowed and offered a slight nod of agreement, Gus once more looked at the father. 'Flynn was found just off B1644 between Sandy Lane and Haworth, Mr Arnett.'

With a frown, he wafted away his formality. 'My name's Graham.' He blinked a few times as if processing the information and then shook his head as if rejecting Gus's words. 'Flynn had no need to be there. The friend he was having the sleepover with lives nearby. He had no need to be up Sandy Lane.'

Wondering how to frame his reply in the least upsetting way, Gus hesitated, then said. 'We believe his killer moved him to that area. We believe they killed him elsewhere. I know you have questions to ask, but right now, we need to focus on getting the information that can help us. When the FLO comes, he or she will answer all your questions.' He hesitated. 'Later on, a crime scene investigator will come and will need access to Flynn's room. Until then, can you write a list of Flynn's friends and enemies, and can you give us contact details for the friend he was hanging out with last night and when you each last saw him…?'

CHAPTER 42

It had been a disappointment to discover that his one lead – this Razor McCarthy character – was in custody. He hadn't slummed it travelling down to this shit-hole to have the little turd out of reach. Still, Norm, his fixer, had promised that he'd sort it. Before the end of the day, Razor McCarthy had better be in his clutches. The thought that before long he'd know where his feckless wife was had mollified him. Norm had never let him down yet, but all this hanging about was doing his head in.

You couldn't even call the dump a hotel. Fucking Travelodge. Staycation destination for the proles!

What had Norm been thinking?

Morris rubbed his body dry on the rough towel and sat on the bed. Right about now, he should have been ordering room service. Instead, he was stuck in a substandard shit-hole in a substandard city. He wasn't sure why he was surprised. Everyone knew Bradford was a dump and his experience so far had confirmed it.

On arrival at the Interchange the previous night, he'd seen Bradford's great unwashed. The place was a hive of smelly homeless scroungers, begging and clawing at him and even more dodgy lads in hoodies who looked like they might have machetes tucked into their pockets. He'd wanted something to eat but ended up at Nando's – bloody Nando's. He hated that sort of cheap crap, but Norm had insisted. 'Keep under the radar, boss. Keep under the radar.' Suppose it filled a hole.

To keep a low profile, Norm had booked him into this atrocity using a stolen account. Morris exhaled and scratched his belly. Shit, he hoped he hadn't caught bed bugs from the mattress. He jumped to his feet and moved over to sit on the plastic chair, glad that with the towel wrapped round his waist, he could avoid too much contact with it. He supposed he should be grateful for his henchman's foresight. Left to his own devices, he'd have been living it up in The Midland Hotel. Now that was a hotel. It would have room service and a decent damn breakfast on offer too, but of course that wasn't keeping a low profile, was it?

Morris repeated Norm's words under his breath in a singsong, taunting voice – *keep under the radar, boss, keep under the radar* – and rolled his suitcase towards him. He'd opted not to unpack and as per instructions, had packed only casual clothes. His fixer had wanted him to remain in Newcastle, but Morris had been determined to face the little scrote responsible for Slave Auction. He hadn't come this far to allow someone else to sort it out in the end. Jeans and a crew neck would do. Surely Norm would be happy with that. His stomach rumbled and Morris picked up his burner phone, having left his personal one at home. He was starving, and he wanted to know what was going on. Norm should have contacted him before now. What was it about keeping in touch that the man didn't understand?

Morris's Burner: *Update*?

Unknown Burner: Under control. Have organised a better solicitor. He's being processed for release now. Will be in touch!

A slow smile spread across Morris's face and just like that, all thoughts of his rumbling belly dissipated.

He massaged his knuckles, anticipation unfurling like molten lava in his gut. Now he hungered for something completely different.

CHAPTER 43

Angel

I couldn't resist driving that way into Bradford. Just to check. To see the area in the cold light of day, so to speak. Imagine my surprise when instead of the normal flow of traffic, I encounter a police cordon. I hadn't expected Flynn to be found so quickly, but you can never plan for life's vagaries, so I wasn't concerned. Why would I be? There was nothing to connect me to Flynn's death, and I'd been sure to leave no forensic trace on the body.

In some ways, it's exciting to be guided through the single-track flow of traffic by the police. Everyone's edging past, necks craning to catch sight of the white tent just visible behind the bushes. Their imaginations running riot, wondering who lies dead on the moorland, and relieved that it's not one of theirs as they gain a vicarious sense of importance as they store up this sordid, transitory little experience – their brush with death – to entertain their friends with in the pub later on.

These thoughts bring a smile to my lips as, in order to fit in, I too slow down, and I too crane my neck as if fascinated by the horror of what's happening just metres away. Little do they know that I can visualise the scene almost exactly.

A group of pedestrians have gathered on the far side of the cordon and further down, a meandering line of cars is parked. These people have no sense of decency. Of course, some of them are reporters and I can understand that. They're only doing their job after all, but the others? No, I don't get what they're getting from loitering at a serious crime scene, soaking up someone else's misery. As I edge the car forward another two inches, I wonder if I'm employing a double standard here –I mean, I drove past with the express intention of scoping out the area, but in my defence, I didn't realise at the time that Flynn had been found. I didn't intend to ogle and gossip, but rather to protect my interests. So, not the same thing. Not the same thing at all.

The car in front glides forward and, as I follow, I cast a final glance over the loiterers and then brake. The car behind me honks its horn, but I ignore. I'm too focussed on the familiar figure staring at the tent. What the hell is Bailey doing here?

CHAPTER 44

After the Family Liaison Officer arrived, Gus and Taffy headed upstairs to have a look round Flynn's room before the crime scene techs arrived to log and take away Flynn's electrical appliances for analysis.

Being away from the tears and atmosphere downstairs allowed Gus to gain some perspective. The news of Flynn's transgender status opened up possibilities to explore, and Gus was keen to discover more about his online status. Gus would be sure to instruct the lab to forward Flynn's computer to Compo, ASAP. Not that he didn't trust the CSI lab to do a thorough job, it was just that he trusted his geeky DC, John Compton more. Now, though, suited, booted, and gloved, he and Taffy stood just inside Flynn's bedroom with the door shut behind them. Gus always took a moment to absorb the nuance of the room before conducting any sort of search. He believed that allowing the air around the room to settle gave them more of a sense of its occupant. Moving in and searching too quickly could displace the essence of Flynn and might distort their assessment of any clues the room might offer. Unlike some of the rooms Gus had searched previously, there was no evidence of teenage sweaty hormones lingering in the air. Vanilla infiltrated the room and when a swooshing noise broke the silence, Gus noticed a room freshener plugged in by the door.

Whether that was Flynn's choice or his mum's, Gus didn't know, but it made him smile.

The room wasn't a complete mess, nor was it overly tidy. Mucky football boots lay discarded near a laundry basket and hanging over the lip was an equally muddy sleeve. It seemed Flynn played football, and that gelled with the Bradford City scarf hung over the end of his bed and the couple of Bradford City posters on the wall. The room wasn't spacious, but by pushing the single bed along the back wall under the window, Flynn had created more room for himself. Space which was taken up by a desk at the bottom of the bed, with a laptop on top and various schoolbooks scattered nearby alongside A4 lined pads. Judging by the textbooks, Flynn was studying A-levels in RE, psychology, and sport. Along the wall behind the table was a three-shelf bookshelf filed with various fantasy novels from *Lord of the Rings* to Terry Pratchett's *Discworld* series. Underneath the unit was a printed out copy of a school timetable.

A free-standing double wardrobe in pine – an IKEA make – stood opposite the bed, leaving enough space to squeeze past. One door stood half-open, allowing the leg of a pair of jeans to escape. The rest of the floor space was taken up by a bean bag positioned so that Flynn could easily view the wall mounted telly.

Stuck near the top right-hand corner of the mirrored wardrobe door was a peeling rectangular sticker. Gus stepped closer to get a better look and used his fingers to smooth the sticker out so he could view it. It was of a stained-glass archway – like a church window – in various shades of blue with a cross in gold reaching from the top to the bottom of the arch and with the horizontal bar stretching like arms to either side. Underneath, ornately styled once more in the stained-glass effect is a logo:

Manningham

All Saints

C of E Church.

As he ran his fingers over the logo, Gus cast his mind back a few weeks. He'd visited Manningham All Saints Church during the Zac Ibrahim investigation. The church had an organised outreach programme for the homeless and Zac had often attended it for food or to use the village hall shower facilities. Sceptical of coincidences, Gus's pulse quickened at yet another potential link between the two young victims. The vicar had seemed very progressive thinking and the few congregants who had interactions with Zac had seemed harmless enough. Still, that didn't mean a further chat wouldn't throw up additional information. Gus was particularly interested in whether Zac and Flynn had interacted.

'Taff, you seen this?'

Taffy joined him at the mirror and when he saw the logo and registered the significance of it, he ran his fingers through his short hair, making it stand out in peaks like an Asian Oor Wullie. 'Well, well, well. Looks like one of us will be making another trip to Manningham All Saints.'

Nothing else odd stood out to Gus, but he and Taffy would do the necessary swoop round the room looking for early clues and would wait for any information gleaned from Flynn's devices. Gus wanted that information fast, as he was certain it would give him a better starting point than relying on the parents' insights. Experience told Gus that teenagers kept secrets from their parents. Whether Flynn's secrets would be pertinent to the investigation remained to be seen, nonetheless, Gus would go through the motions. He'd already ascertained who Flynn's mobile phone provider was and had instructed Compo, who was coordinating things back at The Fort, to apply for a release of the details from the phone provider. He'd also provided Alice with the list of friends Flynn's parents and sister had provided, and she would coordinate interviews with them. Now, it was a matter of dotting Is and crossing Ts until the results of CCTV, their appeal to the public, and the forensics came in.

Gus gestured for Taffy to go through the lad's desk, while he opted to search the bed area and the wardrobe. Teenagers had a few popular hiding places, and Gus wondered if Flynn had any.

'The mum's reaction was weird, boss, don't you think?'

Gus agreed, but at this stage would not make judgements based on a gut response in a moment of trauma. Nevertheless, he'd tasked the FLO, Sylvia Edwards, to probe a little more into the family dynamics, into how long ago Flynn had transitioned and at what stage of the transition process he was at – although the post mortem would reveal that. Still, he wanted to understand what made this family tick. Sylvia was an experienced FLO who was best placed to assess whether Flynn, being transgender, had caused friction.

'It's hard to say this early on, Taff. We're still getting a feel for things. Try not to let that single moment cloud your judgement. We don't know much yet about this family, or Flynn for that matter.'

He'd also instructed Sylvia to speak with Flynn's sister. If anyone within the family circle knew anything notable that might impact the investigation, he suspected it might be her. She had seemed capable, taking it upon herself to put her grief to the side in order to help her mother. Lifting the pillow, Gus slid his hand into the pillowcase, but found nothing there. A pair of pyjamas lay in a crumpled heap under the pillow, but on further investigation, they too offered no clues. Undaunted, Gus got onto his knees and looked under the bed. It was clear, other than a couple of stray balled-up socks and a few chocolate wrappers.

He turned his attention to the mattress and slid his hand between it and the bed base, stretching his arm in as far as he could reach. He'd almost given up when his fingers touched something hard, wedged right at the top corner of the bed nearest the wall. *Gottya*! Whatever this was, Flynn had pushed far enough under the mattress to avoid anyone finding it by accident. This was the sort of thing he'd hoped to find. Exerting himself a little more, his fingers clasped the item and pull it out from its hiding place. 'Well, well, well, Taff. Looks like our Flynn had a few secrets.'

Taffy turned from flicking through the pages of the textbooks with a grin and moved aside so that Gus could position the A5 hard backed book on the desk. Hoping that this find would give them insight into who might have wanted Flynn Arnett dead, Gus opened the first page. A few paragraphs of neat, legible writing covered the paper. Flynn had chosen a purple pen and his script veered to the right, and despite its neatness, it reminded Gus that Flynn was only seventeen. In silence, he and Taffy read:

I hate this so much, but I know it's necessary. We have to put a stop to this. After everything we've all been through, it's essential work. I promised the group I'd log my experiences in a physical diary and online – we all are – but fuck, it's hard. I know we need to if we're to contribute to the research, but sometimes when I'm in the middle of it, it almost breaks me. It's really hard. Mind you, listening to the others' experiences is even harder.

I sort of thought we'd all encounter the same shit, but we didn't. It's different for each of us, but sometimes I think mine is the worst. Maybe that's because I've had it easier in the first place. Maybe that's as it should be. They've been through so much more than me. It's only right I shoulder the worst of it now. It's like karma or summat.

As Taffy came to the end of the writing, he glanced up at Gus, his brows tugged together in that *little boy lost* look he sometimes wore. Gus's lips twitched. Taffy was barely six or seven years older than Flynn. Close enough in age to the dead boy to remember how hard being a teenager could be. 'What the hell is this, boss? I can't get my head round what he's writing about?'

Gus couldn't either, but the tone of Flynn's writing had Gus wondering how this impacted on his death, for he was almost certain that whatever clandestine activity Flynn and this group of anonymous others to whom he referred were up to, it was linked to the lad's murder. Gus looked at his DC. 'You ready for the next page, Taff?'

Visibly stiffening his spine and squaring his shoulders, Taffy nodded, but his frown remained in place. Still, when he spoke his tone was firm. 'Yep. Let's read on.'

Wondering what the next page would reveal, Gus flicked the page. Although still written in purple, Flynn had highlighted words and sentences in green and yellow. Towards the bottom of the page, the writing got scrattier, as if Flynn was in full flow and desperate to get his words down on paper.

The highlighted words jumped out at Gus; SPEAK, humiliation, ANGEL, disgust, taunts, SEE, torture, HEAR, The Chair.

Leaving those for a moment, Gus's eyes drifted up to the title at the top of the page where Flynn had written *SESSION ONE* in block capitals and underlined it.

It was easy to get invited to the sessions, just like the group told me it would be. It was like they were desperate to recruit another one of us to their sick fucking cause. Don't know how I hid my anger. Besides the attendees – that's what they call us – there are four of them. Fucking tossers only gone and given themselves code names like they're some tossing Marvel character or summat. Really? Fucking ANGEL, he's the boss. The others SPEAK, HEAR, and SEE follow his every lead, nodding and agreeing with every warped word that he spouts.

Angel's the worst. He seems to revel in TAUNTING and HUMILIATING us. Threatening us. Calls us FREAKS. It's sick – totally fucking sick. None of them hit us, but maybe it would be easier if they did, because listening to the audio therapies and watching the visual therapies makes me want to curl up and die. Maybe that's what they want. Maybe if we don't change, they will really hurt us. Maybe it won't just be words they hit us with, maybe…

The group told me to get photos if I could, but we're not allowed phones. They locked all electrical devices in what he calls The Faraday Box – but it's not a damn Faraday Box. It's a small metal safe. But that was my first impression of Angel – that he thinks he's all that. That he's cleverer than he is and that's what makes him dangerous, if you ask me.

So Angel. He sounds old – middle aged? Older than my dad – forties, fifties – hell, I don't know? They wear hoods. But he's built. Maybe six feet tall – six two, maybe. He's muscly and I reckon he spends some time at the gym.

I kept my trap shut this time. Didn't want to stand out too much, it being my first session and all that. Wanted to blend in.

A rap at the door makes both Taffy and Gus jump, and as the door opens, Taffy steps in front of his boss, allowing Gus to close the book and push it under one of Flynn's textbooks.

'Mum says do you want tea or summat?' Millie's eyes are red and they rake round the room as she delivers her message, as if looking for her brother or maybe trying to capture the last scrap of his essence.

Gus's heart went out to the girl. How will she cope with this? She's already shown that she'll put her mum first, but she needs time to process her own grief. Time with no responsibility. 'Thanks, Millie, but we're OK.' Her gaze rests on her brother's bed for a moment and then, exhaling, she turns to leave.

'Millie?' Gus's tone made her pause, and she turned towards him, her hand resting on the handle. 'Does Flynn go to church?'

With a frown, Millie nodded. 'Yes, he does. We all do. Manningham All Saints. They've been great with…' She wafted her hand in the air. 'You know, all Flynn's stuff?'

Still smiling, Gus nodded, and the girl turned to leave, drawing the door closed behind her, but not before Gus saw the tears gather in her eyes.

After retrieving the book, Gus put it into an evidence bag and with a final glance round Flynn Arnett's room, he sighed. 'Come on, Taffy. Let's get this back to The Fort. I want every single page copied and printed before we send it to forensics for processing. While I say my goodbyes to the Arnett's, contact CSI and tell them to go through this room asap. Then send them up to his school to go through his locker.'

Gus was relieved that Flynn didn't attend City Academy. Although Patti, his ex-girlfriend, no longer worked there, he had too many bad memories of the place. Flynn's school was Swain High, and its head teacher was about to have her weekend off interrupted with devastating news about one of her pupils.

CHAPTER 45

Gus took a moment to consider everything they've learnt today while Alice and Taffy set up the incident board. He liked to have a solid visual of ongoing investigations and hoped that the board would illuminate likely connections and threads linking Flynn and Zac's murders. They also needed to find out the significance of the Slave Auction website to Zac's death. Compo had already run a check to ascertain if Flynn Arnett appeared on the site and had drawn a blank. What that meant was open to discussion. The presence of Zac, Jo Jo, and Jessie's images on the website was significant and had to be pursued. Although Flynn's absence from the site weakened the link between it and the murders, they had to explore the possibility that the website was a significant part of this investigation.

That both Flynn and Zac used the church; Flynn for worship and pastoral care and Zac as part of their homelessness outreach work, was worth pursuing. Them both having had interactions with people at Manningham All Saints Church elevated the importance of the congregants and employees of the church.

All these ifs, buts, and possibilities made focussing difficult. His head felt filled with cotton wool and a persistent throb pummelled his temple. His inability to get a proper handle on everything spread tension across his shoulders and up his neck. Were his personal feelings about the Zac Ibrahim investigation and his failure to find his killer clouding his judgement? Yes, the links were there, but was he placing undue importance on them? Cupping a drink in his hands, Gus studied the crime board as it developed and saw that, although he hadn't directed them to, Taffy and Alice had drawn the same conclusions he had regarding the links and had included further interviews at the church in their action plan.

Pleased that his team was on the same page, Gus stood up and paced the room as he considered another aspect that could provide a more tangible link between the boys – their cause of death. Although there was no official confirmation of Flynn's yet, Gus had recognised the bruising round his neck at the crime scene earlier and was confident that when the PM results came in, they would confirm COD as manual strangulation. Because the two deaths seemed to share a similar modus operandi, Gus wished that, for consistency, it was the same pathologist also conducting the PM on Flynn Arnott, but his dad was on job share. Not that he doubted the new pathologist's abilities. *Hell no!* His dad would never allow a substandard pathologist to share his labs, so the quality of Flynn's PM was not in doubt. It was more the small insights Dr McGuire offered and the way he offered educated opinions that might help expedite an investigation, subject, of course, to scientific confirmation. Few pathologists did that and Gus worried that Dr Horne would be unwilling to hypothesise. However, that was a separate issue. Taffy was heading off to the post-mortem shortly, and they'd made a list of questions they needed to ask - Cause of death, time of death, and her thoughts on similarities and differences between the two bodies.

Alice cleared her throat and, holding a marker, hand poised to add something to the white board, she looked at Gus. 'What do you reckon, then, Gus?'

It was only when he registered her impatient eye roll that he realised she'd asked him a question. 'Sorry, Al. Miles away. What'd you say?'

'Just wondered if I should add *sexuality* or *sexual identity* or *gender* or something like that to the board. I mean Zac was gay and Flynn was transgender?' Her voice faded as she let her hand drop away from the board.

Gus considered her suggestion and then shrugged. The thought had crossed his mind that perhaps Zac's sexuality and Flynn's gender identity had played into their deaths. It was another possible, but unconfirmed, link between the two boys and it couldn't be ignored. These investigations were inundated with bloody unsubstantiated possibilities, and it was so damn frustrating.

With a pile of printouts in hand, Taffy paused. 'Flynn's mum didn't seem too happy with his transgender status, did he? And' – Taffy pursed his lips, like he'd sucked on a lemon – 'both lads were at the church. Definitely worth pursuing. Maybe they were friends. Maybe they knew each other, maybe…'

Gus set his mug on a nearby desk, slopping some coffee over the surface. 'That's just it. Maybe, maybe, maybe. That's these two investigations to a bloody T. Full of maybe's and severely lacking in certainty.'

He glowered at the board and then nodded to Alice. 'Write it on. We're going to explore every possibility because I'm damned if the killer of another teenage boy is going to go unpunished on my watch.'

Taffy handed a copy of the printouts to Gus and Alice. 'These are the copies of Flynn's diary. I've skipped through it, but it's going to take time to read it all.'

Gus flicked through the pages. Now he was reading Flynn's words in black and white and without the multi-coloured highlights, they seemed even more sinister. The rainbow colours had softened them somehow, but now every one of Flynn's emotions was laid bare, with no distractions to detract from the enormity of his words. There were so many questions surrounding the content and the people referred to in it, but Gus was certain of one thing. The people Flynn wrote about were real and Gus was convinced that they were connected to Flynn's death.

As he flicked the pages over, a name caught his eye. *Bailey*! For a moment, he wondered why that name tugged at his memory, and then it hit him. Lizzie White's lad was called Bailey. Was the Bailey mentioned in Flynn's diary – the one made to watch another lad sit on cold slabs for hours while audio therapy was conducted – Lizzie's son? Mention of two Baileys in the course of a few hours was another uncorroborated possibly coincidental strand that in Gus's mind seemed an unlikely coincidence – another one. The memory of Bailey's smiling face in the photo his mum had shown him earlier sent a shiver up Gus's spine. Bailey's continued absence made it even more imperative that they locate these people – this Angel, See, Hear, and Speak. He fired off a quick text to Lizzie in case Bailey had returned unscathed, but her quick reply in the negative dashed that slim hope.

The more the coincidences piled up, the more certain Gus was that they were anything but coincidences. They needed more information – they needed to discover Flynn Arnett's secrets, and that required action, not sitting around navel gazing and trying to slot symmetrical pieces into an asymmetrical investigation. He jumped up, keen to get the ball rolling. 'Taffy, you got the list of questions and Zac's PM report?'

When Taffy nodded, Gus gave an abrupt nod. 'Right, get yourself over there and let me know when you have something to report. Alice and I will work on an immediate action plan while the uniforms are checking CCTV and the lab's processing their findings from the crime scene. We need to be proactive on this. If Zac and Flynn's deaths are linked, we've lost weeks of investigation time. We'll text you your instructions for after the PM. Looks like we'll be pulling in some overtime hours on this one.'

The faint but thrumming sound of 'All Along the Watchtower' alerted Gus to the fact that Compo had taken off his headphones and was waving his arms in the air to attract Gus's attention. 'Got a hit on Flynn's online support group from his laptop. Just FaceTimed the group admin – a lad called Lincoln – Linc for short. He'd no idea about Flynn's death. Poor lad lost it for a while, but then pulled it together. The group members – four of them – are situated all over the country, so difficult to interview face-to-face unless we send local police to each of them. He said Flynn's the second member they've lost in the past week and the group will be devastated. Poor kid's happy to arrange a Zoom meeting for this evening with the four remaining members. That OK?'

That was more than OK. At last it seemed they were edging forward and Gus hoped meeting Flynn's support group would fill in some gaps. An online meeting was the next best thing to seeing them in person and Gus was keen to get answers. 'Yes, that's great, but you said they'd lost two members in the last week? Is that another coincidence to add to our growing list?'

With a chocolate chip muffin in one hand and a can of pop in the other, Compo shook his head. 'Don't think so. Linc gave me the details. Seems the group was at their regular weekly online meeting when Lucy was beaten to death by her abusive partner right in front of them. Linc reported her location to emergency services, but they got there too late. He gave me the crime number and I've confirmed it with Birmingham Police. Her death though tragic, doesn't seem related to Flynn's.' Compo took a bite of his cake and chewed. 'These kids get a hell of a lot of abuse, don't they?'

Gus looked at the crime scene photos of Zac and Flynn that hung on their crime board. Both boys wore wide smiles, their eyes alive with laughter, and Gus wondered just how much pain that laughter hid. 'More than any kid should have to endure.'

It took an enormous effort to drag his eyes away from the victims, but he rolled his shoulders to release the tension building across his neck and upper back and turned to Alice. With Taffy gone and Compo immersed in dissecting the rest of Flynn's electrical stuff, Alice and Gus considered their next moves. 'I reckon we split up, Al. You interview Flynn's best friend, this Carrie girl, while I go back to the church.'

Before leaving, Gus checked in with Jo Jo's foster mum, Eileen to make sure all was well with them. Although their focus was divided between their ongoing murder investigation, Gus wanted to make sure Jo Jo and Jessie were safe. Even with McCarthy in custody, Gus couldn't be sure the two kids were safe and he was glad his boss had okayed having an officer allocated to protect them. At the very least, it allowed him to focus on catching Flynn Arnett's killer.

CHAPTER 46

Flynn's friend Carrie Jenkins was a wreck when Alice arrived at her house to interview her. Her cheeks showed evidence of mascara rubbed away and her eyes were bloodshot. As she stood beside her mother in the doorway, her fingers clenched and unclenched as if the girl was seeking a way to keep a tenuous hold of reality. Her swollen eyes blinked as if the light from outdoors was too bright for her, but Alice suspected it was more a reaction to the prospect of facing the outside world without her friend Flynn in it.

'Carrie's had a shock, detective. She's in no state to be interviewed. Surely it can wait till she's had a chance to process what's happened.' Mrs Jenkins's fingers clutched her collar as she stood ready to fight her daughter's corner for her. 'She and Flynn were inseparable you know. It's all been…' Her voice trailed away as she placed her arm round Carrie's shoulder and pulled her close to her own body in a tight hug as if she'd never again let her daughter out of her sight.

Carrie struggled to detach herself from her mum and from somewhere summoned up a sad half smile for Alice. 'I'm not an invalid, Mum. I want to help. I want to speak to the officer about Flynn. It's all I can do now.'

Understanding the older woman's concern for her daughter, Alice smiled at her. 'I promise, Mrs Jenkins, I'll be as sensitive as I can with Carrie and if it's too much for her, we'll stop. I wouldn't even ask her to speak with me right now if it wasn't important.'

With a sigh, Mrs Jenkins stepped back and ushered Alice into the house. 'OK, but I'm not…'

Before she could finish the sentence, which Alice was sure would end with insistence that she be present, Carrie grabbed her mum's hand and squeezed tight. 'Look, Mum. I know you want to be there, but I want to tell DS Cooper stuff about Flynn – secrets and stuff – and if it's only me and her, it won't seem like a betrayal.' When her mother looked set to protests, Carrie tightened her grip and tacked on a heartfelt, 'Pleeease, Mum.'

'OK, Carr, but' – she met Alice's eye – 'fifteen minutes tops, OK? Then I'm coming in.'

Alice returned the mother's gaze, offering a silent promise to take care of the grieving girl during the interview. As she followed Carrie upstairs to her bedroom, Alice marvelled at how strong the young woman was. She'd just lost her best friend in tragic circumstances yet, here she was still determined to help in whatever way she could. Carrie's earlier reference to *secrets* had piqued Alice's curiosity, and she hoped that whatever Carrie was about to divulge would shed some light on Flynn's diary.

Recently, Alice had been in Gus's goddaughter, Zarqa's room. Although the two girls had very different interests, the rooms had the same signs of girls trying to work out who they were, from the posters on the wall to what they displayed on their dressing tables. Unlike Zarqa, Carrie appeared to be a girly girl, with cosmetics and creams littered all over a dressing table with a mirror attached, which was framed by pink butterfly fairy lights with matching feathers alternating with the bulbs.

Carrie plopped herself on her bed and indicated that Alice could take the cushioned seat. Alice looked around, taking her time so the girl could adjust to a strange adult's presence in her domain, then smiled. 'Cool room.'

Carrie's laugh was cut short as she bunched her fist and shoved it on her mouth. Alice waited, allowing the girl time to recover.

'Flynn hated it. He hated anything girly. He always did. Right from the first time I met him when he was five, he told me he was a boy.' She looked at Alice, her eyes flashing, her words firm and challenging. 'And he was. No matter what anybody said, he was a boy.'

For a moment she picked at her duvet, head bowed before continuing.

'His dad was cool with it – well after the initial shock like. It was his mum who couldn't get her head round it. Kept buying him dresses and stuff. Couldn't hack it when he started binding his boobs and that. But Mr Arnett – he was all right.'

'It must have been hard for him. He was lucky to have such a good friend as you, Carrie.'

Carrie nodded, her eyes glazed over for a moment, she smiled. 'Yes. He was lucky to have me as his friend, but you know what? I was damn lucky to have him as mine.'

Again, Alice allowed the silence to lengthen. She sensed Carrie didn't need prompting and that she would reveal whatever she had to reveal in her own time. Outside, the sound of an ambulance siren passing by, the deep thrum of a quad bike racing round the streets of Carrie's estate, and kids' voices as they jostled with each other on the pavement outside, filtered into the room. Life going on regardless of the tragedy impacting Carrie and Flynn's family in a nearby street.

'He made me promise, you know?' Carrie waited till Alice nodded to show she understood the importance of a promise between friends. 'Told his mum he was staying here on Friday night but he was going to that bloody therapy. I told him not to, and he promised that Friday would be the last time. He was going to come here afterwards, but he never arrived.' Frantic fingers plucking at the duvet, Carrie's voice lowered till it was so quiet Alice had to lean closer to hear her words. 'I thought he'd gone home. When he hadn't arrived by midnight, I didn't even text to check. I should've fucking texted to check he was OK. Then, maybe—'

'No, Carrie. No. We suspect Flynn died earlier in the evening. You're not responsible for Flynn's death. The *only* person responsible is whoever took his life.'

Carrie sniffed and nodded. 'Yeah, well. If you're looking for suspects, there's an entire school full of the haters at Swain High. But…' Carrie grabbed one of the cuddly toys that sat across her pillow and hugged it close to her chest. 'Though I doubt any of them would follow through on that. I reckon it's more likely to be that therapy group.'

'You've mentioned a therapy group twice now, Carrie, but Flynn's family didn't mention he was in therapy.'

'No, well, they didn't know about it, did they? It was a secret. It was something he did for that online support group he was involved with. They got him doing it and recording it all. I didn't really get it. I thought it were dodgy, but Flynn insisted on going. He got so angry about the stuff they did at that group.'

This *was* intriguing. If Alice understood what Carrie was saying, Flynn was a member of two separate groups: an online support groups and another one that he attended in person.

'So Flynn was in two groups?'

'Yep. The support group with other trans teens and this fucking mad shit Pure Life group that was all about stopping folk being gay or trans or bi or whatever.'

'You're saying that Flynn went to two groups – one that supported his trans status and one set to destroy it?' Alice couldn't get her head round that. It seemed such a strange contrary thing to do. Did Flynn have doubts about his gender identity?

'Well, like he wasn't ever going to be a girl again. Not Flynn. He were a lad. Always been a lad. This online group, they really helped him. There aren't many trans folk and even less trans kids, so they were a lifeline for Flynn, you know?' She pushed her hair out of her eyes. 'But some of them had been through crap compared to Flynn – I mean real crap – physical abuse, rape, homelessness, the lot, so they were like, I don't know – political or summat. He was secretive about it.'

This information had opened up many possibilities. Alice hadn't heard of Pure Life but maybe Compo could unearth information on them. 'Where did this Pure Life group meet, Carrie?'

A tear rolled down her cheek. 'No idea. He wouldn't tell me. Thought I'd tell his mum or summat. They met in secret though and Flynn said it was in a right dump of a place.'

Alice considered this. Maybe if they contacted Flynn's mobile provider, they'd be able to identify where these meetings were held. Before continuing, she fired off a text to Compo asking him to sort that. 'Was he keeping a diary or anything like that?'

'No idea, but it wouldn't surprise me, like, Flynn documents his transition and experiences and that on an anonymous blog called *Trans R Us*. Don't think even his parents know he does that. He keeps his identity private for obvious reasons – haters ain't afraid to hate what they don't understand.'

Alice's heart went out to the Flynn that, after all his efforts to be true to himself, would never grow up to be the man he wanted to be. What a waste of a life.

'So, this online group…'

CHAPTER 47

It broke Jo Jo's heart to leave Jessie and his foster mum. Despite feeling disloyal to his mum for even thinking it, he admitted to himself that these last few months had been bliss. His sister was happy, thriving even, and Jo Jo didn't have to worry about whether he could afford the leccy or if Jessie's uniform was clean or if they had anything to eat in the fridge. Most importantly, though, he didn't have to do that sex crap online any more. That was his biggest relief. He'd got rid of his sex toys and if he never saw baby lotion again, then it would be too soon. He'd hated what he was doing. The thought of those dirty old men yanking themselves off, grunting and groaning sickened him. Even thinking about it made his heart speed up and brought a tear to his eyes.

But everything had changed. Soon as he'd seen those images on the Slave Auction site, his heart had plummeted to his feet. Then he'd seen the messages and the huge bid, and he'd known that everything his mum had worked so hard to avoid had finally caught up with him. Gus and the others thought they could protect him. The thing was, they didn't know who they would have to protect him from. They didn't know what was at stake for him and Jessie. That's why he was doing this. For Jessie. He'd end it all once and for all, for Jessie. It was the only way, because he couldn't risk that bastard taking Jessie away from Eileen.

If he got his hands on her, she'd have no life and his mum's sacrifice would be in vain. So, Jo Jo would do the only thing he could.

He'd agonised over the note, wishing he'd the time to do more for Jessie. To write notes for every birthday that he'd miss from now on. A special note for when she graduated or passed her driving test or got married or had her first kid. All those things he wouldn't be there for. But he'd left it too late. He'd left a brief note for Idris telling him how happy he'd made him, and one for Zarqa, telling her how much her friendship meant to him and how sorry he was that it had to end like this. Then he'd tidied his room, placed the notes on top of his pillow, and taken all his savings and his favourite drone and placed them on Jessie's bed. He checked once more that the machete he'd bought from the shop in town was still there, then slung his backpack over his shoulder. It was time to go.

He'd make it easy for him to find him – really easy, for Jo Jo knew that by now, the dad he hadn't set eyes on in six years – the dad he hated with every part of him – would have traced him to Belle Hill Estate. And Jo Jo was prepared to wait till he turned up.

Now he knew that Razor McCarthy was behind the Slave Auction site, he could kill two birds with one stone. He would gladly wait because as soon as he appeared, then Jo Jo would end this once and for all.

CHAPTER 48

Gus pulled up outside Manningham All Saints Church and observed the building. Although it was a traditional sandstone church, being in the heart of Manningham where the Muslim community was in the majority made it an anomaly. Its grounds were well tended and, although the stained-glass windows were covered in some sort of Perspex covering, presumably against the risk of vandals breaking them, it looked in good nick.

Next to the church stood a modern, one-storey concrete building with cladding that served as the church hall. And from his position, Gus had a clear view through the large windows of people milling about inside the main hall. From his previous interviews here during Zac Ibrahim's murder investigation, Gus knew that the church community offered an extensive outreach programme designed to help the homeless, families in need, and teenagers. The Reverend Anne Summerscale was both charismatic and energetic in her commitment to improving the Manningham community, and she was one of those Christians who looked beyond your faith to the person beneath. Her outreach work helped anyone regardless of their faith and so Gus was unsurprised to see men in prayer hats leaving the building with kids swinging from one arm and a bag of food from the other. Life in Manningham could be hard and local businesses supplied the All Saint's food bank with donations.

He got out and walked up the meandering cobbled path leading to the church doors and then veered onto the newer more recently laid paving stones that brought him to the entrance to the church hall, where he had arranged to meet the vicar. Inside the small hallway, a series of doors fed into other rooms; a shower area, toilets, a kitchen, a main hall, and a door locked by a keypad, which led to the administration annex. Gus took the door into the large hall that today appeared to function as a food bank with tables piled high with food lining one side and another row opposite piled with folded clothes and toys sorted by age. Volunteers staffed each table and at the kitchen hatch, hot and cold drinks and sandwiches were served.

Tall with red hair and a ready laugh, Reverend Summerscale drew his eye as soon as he entered the room. With a careless wave, she extricated herself from a conversation with a tall man who, clasping her hand in his, appeared to be flirting with the vicar. Gus smiled, noting that Reverend Summerscale appeared to be enjoying the attention as she inclined her head closer to the man and whispered something. Behind her, the vicar's husband, Graham, with his arms piled high with cereal boxes, watched them. Unable to interpret the look on Graham's face, Gus frowned. He'd had the sense previously that Graham Summerscale lived life in his wife's shadow and had wondered at the time if he harboured resentment about it. As Anne pulled her hand free and patted the man on the arm, Graham moved away, leaving Gus unsure if he'd misinterpreted the man's expression. As Anne walked towards Gus through the crowds, she shook adult hands, ruffled children's hair, and smiled at everyone she met, and all at once Gus felt like he was the grumpiest person alive in comparison. The man she'd been in conversation with joined Graham at the cereal table and as he handed a box to an elderly woman pulling a trolley bag behind her, his eyes met Gus's and he nodded. It was only then that Gus realised he recognised him from the previous round of interviews. He'd been one of the vicar's staunchest advocates but couldn't contribute any insights into Zac's death as he'd never interacted with the boy.

But then Gus noticed another familiar figure, and his brow morphed into a frown. Zac Ibrahim's brother, Nazir, was sitting at a table near the fire exit. The table was filled with fliers and leaflets, and opposite Nasir sat a wizened old man in a prayer hat. Nazir, in suit and tie leant across the table nodding as the old man spoke. Gus wished he'd shown the same compassion for his dead brother as he did for his constituents. During the investigation, Gus's dealings with Nazir had been volatile and demoralising. Recently elected as a councillor for the local area, Gus had found it difficult to pin the man down and when he did, the callousness he displayed regarding his brother's murder sickened him. He was the de facto spokesperson for the Ibrahims, and he excluded Gus from the home. No amount of persuasive talk could budge the family to offer any information in Zac's murder. Almost as if Gus's glare had seared the man, Nazir raised his head and his eyes found Gus's. The smile faded from his lips as he raised his chin towards Gus in silent challenge. Gus held his gaze until the vicar approached, then raised his own chin in response before turning to greet her with a smile.

'Hello, hello, DI McGuire. No offence, but I hoped we wouldn't meet again for a long time.' Her ready smile and Irish lilt brought a corresponding smile to Gus's lips, and he felt less grumpy and less weighed down. 'I'd hoped the same, vicar. I'd hoped the same.'

'Anne, please. Vicar makes me sound like some old fuddy duddy doddering old male vicar from the nineties, whereas I like to consider myself more of a cross between a Geraldine Granger of the 2020s and Banksy, offering a voice for the people. Fanciful, no?'

Gus's grin widened as he shook his head. Anne had that effect on people. 'Not fanciful at all. However—'

'Ah yes.' She raised her hand to beckon a familiar-looking woman to join them and then guided Gus towards the small annex where she had her office. 'This will be about Flynn. Poor boy. Poor family. I dropped in earlier and they're besides themselves. Not surprising, is it?'

When the older woman joined them, Anne smiled and placed a hand on her shoulder and squeezed. The friendly gesture seemed forced, as if the two women didn't really get on, but kept up a front.

'You remember Ada, don't you, Detective McGuire? She's my right-hand woman and' – she looked around, a small furrow appearing across the bridge of her nose – 'her husband, Claude, is my right-hand man. Where is he, Ada?'

With her hands constantly moving – adjusting and readjusting her cardigan, patting the bun on the top of her head, clutching at her blouse – Ada gave the impression of being full of nerves. Gus had been fooled last time by her timid appearance and was amazed when he'd witnessed the diminutive woman single-handedly split up a fight between two homeless men double her size over a pair of trainers. So it did not surprise him when her reply filled the air and startled a couple entering the building. 'No idea where he is. Probably cadging some tea, if you ask me.'

But at that point, Claude lumbered into the entranceway from the toilets, rubbing his hands down the leg of his corduroy trousers to dry them. When he saw them, his face split into a reserved smile as he joined the group. Gus wondered if the man had been ill, for his clothes hung off his hunched frame and his hair although thinning looked patchy. While the vicar greeted him warmly, Ada glowered at him, her expression similar to the one his own mother used when his dad had committed some minor misdemeanour and, with an inward smile, he wondered what the hapless Claude had done to deserve his wife's wrath. Ada typed in the code to allow them access to the staff annex, while Anne brought the older man up to date.

DI McGuire is here about Flynn Arnett's murder.'

As he walked towards the door, Claude stumbled and had to grab the frame to prevent himself toppling straight onto the floor. Unable to forgive whatever annoyance her husband was responsible for, Ada tutted. 'For *goodness*' sake, Claude. Lift your damn feet. We've no time to take you down to A&E if you crack your head open.'

Claude glared at his wife and then averted his gaze – no match for the titan to whom he was married, as he replied like a sulky toddler. 'Maybe you'd rather I cracked my head open and died, Ada.'

Gus almost chortled at the absurdity of the petulant statement and was glad when Anne stepped forward and placed a hand on Claude's arm. 'Come on, you two. I know this is hard, but we're *all* grieving Flynn's loss. We need to be strong though, don't we?'

Claude's lip trembled and Ada averted her gaze before nodding. 'Yes, you're right. Even though the poor girl – I mean boy – was mixed up in his head, he didn't deserve this.'

The vicar rolled her eyes and exasperation tinged her response. '*Ada*. We've spoken about this before. We need to respect Flynn and his family's wishes on the matter. His parents accepted who he was, so who are we to doubt him?'

But Ada seemed determined to have the last word. 'Graham might have accepted Flynn's nonsense, but Tess didn't. Broke her heart to see her little girl dress and act like that.'

'For heaven's sake, Ada. The boy's dead.' Claude's words, though quiet and unthreatening, made Ada pause. Hand raised to her lip, she nodded.

'Yes, you're right it's tragic. Poor lamb.'

Once in the small office space, the four of them sat on plastic seats which they'd pulled into a circle. Gus still pondered the reactions of the adults he now shared a room with to Flynn's trans status. Of course, not everyone would be supportive of Flynn's family's decision to support the boy, but what intrigued Gus was the corroboration that Flynn's father hadn't been on board with it. Had he been so distraught over Flynn's gender identity that he would kill his own son? And, if so, how did that tie into Zac Ibrahim's death?

With that in mind, Gus had a thought. 'If you give me just a moment, I need to message someone.' He took out his phone and texted the Arnett's FLO, Sylvia Edwards, requesting that she ask if anyone in the family was acquainted with Zac Ibrahim.

Job done, Gus put his phone away and smiled. 'I've only got a few questions at the moment, so I won't take up much of your time. Tell me a little about Flynn and his family. Were they close? How did the strain of his transition affect them?'

Claude, head bowed focussed on his hands which were linked in his lap, while Ada's eyes drifted with apparent concentration to the trees swaying outside the window. After a few seconds of silence, Gus exhaled and raised an eyebrow at Anne.

'I suppose I better start,' she said glancing at the other two. 'I've been here eight years and in all that time, Flynn has struggled with his gender identity.'

'No, he didn't.' Claude didn't raise his head, yet his words were firm. 'The lad didn't struggle with it. He were always quite definite about who he was – what he was?'

Gus focussed on Claude, hoping the older man's demeanour would illuminate how he felt about Flynn's gender identity, but Claude didn't flinch. His shoulders remained loose, yet his eyes remained downcast.

Gus's phone buzzed. It was a text from the Arnett's FLO. *Sorry no. No one in the family recognises the name*. Gus slipped his phone away and looked at Anne.

'Actually…' The vicar tapped her fingers against her lip. 'That's quite true, Claude. Very perceptive of you. Flynn didn't struggle with his identity. He was always sure of who he was. It was everyone else who struggled, yet.' Her lips twitched. 'He refused to budge on the matter. He was a boy – end of.'

'But it was hard for her mum and dad.' A deep red flush stained Ada's cheeks as she straightened in her chair, her fingers caressing the gold crucifix encircling her neck. 'What a thing to put his parents through. They went through hell and back again.'

It was Claude who replied, and again he focussed on his hands, avoiding eye contact. 'I suspect it was just as hard for the lad. He got a lot of abuse, you know? Lost his friends – even some of the congregation taunted him. And at school? Well, that must've been intolerable. But the lad didn't falter, did he? He bore it. He bore the burden right up till the moment he died.'

Claude's words hung in the air, heavy and anguished as he fumbled in his pocket for a tissue before blowing his nose.

When Ada responded, Gus flinched as her words bounced off the walls and back into the middle of their circle. 'And look where that got her. Death and pain. At least she's at peace now.'

'*He*, Ada, *he*. But you're right, *he* is at peace now and Claude?' Anne waited till the man lifted his head and looked at her. 'You don't know what happened at his death.' Anne leant over and patted his knee. 'None of us do. We can't torment ourselves with thoughts of what might have beens, or admonish ourselves for actions taken or not taken in the past. All we can do is improve on past versions of ourselves as we move forwards on our life's journey.'

For a moment Gus considered how Anne's works reflected on him, then he shook his head. It all felt too practised, too pious, too convincing. An excuse to let someone off the hook for past deeds? But then he was a grumpy old bugger, wasn't he? He cleared his throat and moved the interview on. 'I wondered if Flynn knew Zac Ibrahim? You know the homeless boy who the church worked with as part of your outreach project?'

'Oh, Zac. Of course.' Anne frowned. 'Are you thinking the two boys' deaths are linked?'

Anne's use of the word *deaths* rather than *murders* irked Gus. 'Deaths' sanitised what had happened to the boys and murder wasn't something that should be made more palatable by labelling it as something less visceral. Somehow, he smiled.

'They were murdered, Anne. They didn't just die. Their lives were wilfully extinguished, and we should remember that. In answer to your question, though, we're still investigating and exploring all avenues, that's all.'

Gus wasn't sure if he imagined the flash of anger in Anne's eyes. However, when she responded there was no trace of annoyance in her tone. 'Of course, you're right. It's important not to minimise their murders. However, I'm afraid I don't know the answer to your question. They may have met, but I have no knowledge that they did. Ada, Claude?'

The older couple exchanged a quick glance and then shook their heads. Gus wondered if there had been a warning note in the slight emphasis Anne used when she said their names. Perhaps she wanted to distance her church from the murders, and Gus couldn't blame her. Nobody wanted the good work being carried out here to be tainted – unless, of course, there was a reason for it to be so. Gus's mind flickered back to the extracts in Flynn's diary. They had a definite religious fervour feel to them and where were you more likely to find religious fervour than in a religious establishment? Definitely worth bearing in mind. Thoughts of the diary shook loose a thought. 'Last question. Does Bailey White use your facilities or worship here?'

The three exchanged glances, as if waiting for someone else to take the lead. As expected, it was Anne who filled the gap. 'Bailey? Bailey? I'm not su—'

'The only Bailey around here is that Ricky's lad, and it's Savage. Not White, so you're out of luck, Officer McGuire.' Claude interrupted.

Gus would have corrected his use of 'officer' but was thrown by the change in Claude's tone. It was almost as if, now they were nearing the end of the interview, the older man was desperate to escape. This was in direct contrast to his subdued, somewhat flat demeanour throughout. It took Gus a moment to compose himself, and it was with a disconnected feeling that Gus thanked them and took his leave. He felt that his visit to the church had unearthed something. He just had no idea what. Once settled back in his car, he hesitated before belting up and, staring through the windscreen, he reflected on his visit. There had been a series of strange vibes, but perhaps that was due to a church community grieving one of their own. Still, from the moment he'd entered the church hall, he'd felt out of sorts – discombobulated – that's what his dad would call it. The strange interaction between the vicar and the grey-haired man, whose name he had yet to remember followed by the equally peculiar expression on Anne's husband's face. And that was before he even considered the weird meeting, as they sat like a coven of witches around a cauldron in the annex. Overall, he supposed that although he had learnt nothing of substance, he had confirmed Flynn's mother's anguish at her child's gender dysphoria and eliminated a link between Bailey White and the church.

Gus pulled his seat belt over and had just clicked it in place when Compo rang. 'Hey, Compo. I'm on my way back. You got something for me?'

'Bad news, boss, I'm afraid. Razor McCarthy lawyered up – some smooth git from out of town and they've bailed him.'

Gus slammed his fist on the steering wheel. 'You got to be kidding me. They've bailed him?'

''Fraid so. Processing him as we speak. But, Gus, that's not all.'

The worry in Compo's voice made its way over the ether and wound itself round Gus's gut, squeezing tight. Gus inhaled once, then again. 'Go on, Comps.'

'It's Jo Jo. He's gone AWOL, and he's left a note.'

Not bothering to hang up, Gus threw his phone onto the passenger seat, engaged the clutch and yelled so Compo could hear. 'I'm on my way. Get Alice and Taffy back here. Oh, and make sure you get a couple of plainclothes officers tailing that scrote McCarthy. Last thing we need is for him to get his hands on Jo Jo. That little bastard would happily sell him to some unscrupulous bastard for the right price.'

CHAPTER 49

Razor didn't know where the hell the posh, sleek lawyer came from, but it worried him. He doubted either of his sisters or his mum would fork out good money in his defence. Besides, he hadn't told them the pigs had nabbed him. Wouldn't do to get them involved in his business.

He asked the man – Mr Forbes-Jameson – who was footing the bill, but the snooty bastard looked at him as if he'd farted and studied a sheet of paper with typing on it. 'You understand your bail conditions, Mr McCarthy? You need to stay at your registered address in Belle Hill Estate – number 33 Wycliffe Terrace. Is that correct?'

Razor, pissed off that the git was acting all superior, nodded and slumped in the plastic chair, his leg slung over the opposite knee. 'M' not fucking thick, you get me?'

For long seconds, Mr Forbes-Jameson regarded him, a sneer on his pasty face. 'Well, you're certainly *fucking* thick enough to land up in here, aren't you?'

The snooty git's posh voice swearing almost brought a grin to Razor's lips. Almost, but not quite, for underneath his bravado something nasty squirmed in Razor's gut. The strange warning he'd received had unsettled him enough to up sticks and run. Then the Five-o had nabbed him and Goyley and now this. Something wun't right and Razor wasn't sure how to extricate himself from this situation. He'd expected to be in the wind by now, instead here he was in the police station with a solicitor he couldn't afford getting him released back to his home address. Razor wasn't dumb enough not to realise that he'd be a sitting target there. So while he put on a front to the big posh geezer, his mind churned over workable solutions to his problem.

Razor had mates on the estate. Mates who owed him favours and if he could just survive long enough to contact them, he'd be all right. They'd protect him – after all, they were Razor's personal army, weren't they? Still, the niggling wouldn't go. Whoever was after him had money – more than Razor – and deep down, he knew his mates were all fair-weather ones. The mere hint of a few extra quid bunged their way, and a snort of the hard stuff, would be enough to make them guide his enemies straight to his front door.

For a nano-second he considered kicking off. That might make them keep him inside. Maybe he could land a punch on old FJ there. But underneath his well-cut suit was muscle and Razor wasn't that big, or that much of a fighter. Maybe he could kick the fat officer outside the door in the nuts. That might work. But again, the old git was fucking massive. No, best to take his chances outside. He could duck and dive, pull in some favours. He'd be all right. Wouldn't he?

CHAPTER 50

Eileen Mulholland sat on one of the soft couches in the child friendly interview room. Jessie was curled up on a beanbag in the opposite corner, tablet in hand and earphones in watching some flashing animated series. Every so often a giggle would escape the little girl's lips, but when Gus entered with Compo and Alice, all they got in acknowledgment was a wave of her hand and a huge grin. Gus was glad of that. It was better that Jessie was occupied so they could talk about her brother without distressing her.

'How long has he been gone, Eileen?' Gus sat opposite her and tried to instil some calm into the situation even though a persistent throb pulsed at his temple and his throat felt clogged up with emotions he couldn't afford to dissect right then.

'Not sure. You know we had Jessie's birthday party today? Well, it finished around two and Jo Jo was there till then. Afterwards, he and Idris helped me tidy up and then I shooed the pair of them out of the house.' She smiled at the memory. 'They'd been on Jessie duty all day – took her to the park to give me space to set up for the party and then helped when Jessie's friends arrived. Maybe if I'd kept them at home?' She closed her eyes, arms wrapped tight round her torso as if to warm up her chilled body. Despair and guilt rolled off her and Gus knew that if anything happened to Jo Jo, she wouldn't forgive herself. 'I last saw him about 3ish.'

He shook his head. 'No, Eileen. From what I've heard, Jo Jo's note shows he planned this. This isn't on you. Something else is going on. Did you check in with Idris?'

'Yes. He's not seen him since about four. Said Jo Jo wanted some down time. Said he might drop in on Zarqa – but he wasn't with her either. I checked.' She hesitated. 'I didn't tell them he was missing or about the note.'

'That's good. Best not get anyone worried until we know more. Could I see the note?'

Eileen nodded at a piece of folded paper lying on the small coffee table to her side, and Gus picked it up. Compo had already seen it, so it was only Alice who craned over his shoulder to read it.

Dear Eileen, Gus, Compo, Alice, and Taffy,

I'm sorry, but I have to do this – for Jessie's sake. I'm not who you think I am. I don't want Jessie to suffer for something me and my mum did six years ago. Deep down, I knew he'd find us in the end and now he has there's only one thing I can do to make everything all right.

You've all been so good to me and I'm really sorry to disappoint you yet again. Don't try to find me. This will all be over soon, and Jess will be safe.

Please tell Jessie I love her

Love Jo Jo

'What the hell does all that mean?' Alice bit her lip and exhaled, her breath warm against Gus's ear. 'What the feck is he up to? What's he going to do?'

Compo, who'd been pacing the room as the others talked, his fists clenching and unclenching, his face screwed up in a snarl of anxiety, paused. 'It's bloody obvious what he's gonna do, Al? He's gonna either top himself or he's gonna sort it out. It's what we're gonna do about it all that's important now.'

Silenced by the venom directed at her, Gus looked first at Alice, then at Compo. The colour drained from Alice's face as if paled, as if Compo's words had sliced through her. Compo pulled off his beanie hat and was raking his fingers through his hair, oblivious to the hurt he'd caused. Gus leant over and squeezed Alice's arm and was reassured when she shrugged and smiled and whispered. 'It's OK, Gus. I know it's the stress talking.'

Gus stood up, walked over to Compo, and guided him over to sit down beside Eileen. 'We're going to find him, Comps. That's what we're going to do. But we need to work out a few things first. Are you up for that?'

Compo blinked twice in rapid succession and as his shoulders slumped, he looked at Alice. 'Sorry, Al, I was a dick.'

Alice batted his words away with a small wave. 'No probs, Comps. It's upsetting. But let's discuss the note. Who the hell is this mysterious man? Why is Jo Jo so scared of him and what the hell did Jo Jo and his mum do six years ago?'

That was precisely what Gus wanted to know. 'Six years ago, Jo Jo would have been 11 years old. What could he and his mum have done to make him suspect a man was after him now?'

A groan filled the room – low and visceral, like an animal in pain. Three pairs of eyes turned to Compo. 'It's that Slave Auction stuff. I'm sure of it. Jo Jo was upset that he and Jessie were being auctioned off, but something about the anonymous punter petrified him. I thought at the time it was for Jessie's sake, but maybe…' Compo's words trailed away as he used the back of his hand to wipe his tears away.

'Look, I'll put a BOLO out on Jo Jo and have some uniforms go round Belle Hill Estate, Lister Park, the city centre, and anywhere else you can think of where he might be,' Gus said, referring to the police code for 'be on the lookout' for.

'I'll go out looking too, boss.' Compo jumped to his feet, ready to head straight off.

But Gus shook his head.

'No, Comps, I need you here. We still have an active murder investigation on our hands, and I need your skills here. However, you can also do what you're good at and find out more about Jo Jo and his mum and what happened in the past to make him go off like this now.'

CHAPTER 51

Razor had no choice but to return to the estate. He made the two guys following him as soon as he left The Fort. Straight up, they were Five-o – couldn't be anything else with their white shirts poking from out the top of their cool 'down with the homies' hoodies. In some ways, that was reassuring. It made him feel less alone. Who'd have thought Razor McCarthy would welcome police scrutiny? But, right now, he did, for he was certain that the plods weren't the only ones with beads on him. At least the Five-o weren't out to off him.

He'd considered taking a taxi – he normally used Elvis taxis, but even that seemed risky – confined space and all that. So, instead he walked toward the bus stop on Duckworth Lane, figuring safety in numbers and all that, still he knew that whoever was after him had better resources than the pigs and he doubted that crowded public spaces would be a deterrent. For a moment, he regretted ordering Goyley to put out the hit on HP. Then he laughed out loud, causing the old dear walking down the hill to glare at him. No, HP would have been worse than useless. Too fucking reliant on the white stuff to help Razor in his current situation. No, it was better that he was on a slab somewhere. If Razor survived this, he'd be glad that HP wasn't there to drag his outfit down.

It was the word 'IF' flashing in ten-foot figures in his mind that scared him. Razor wasn't used to feeling scared. He'd always been the shark among the minnows.

Now, the sharks were bigger than he was and he felt smaller than a fucking minnow.

He got on the bus and, sensing his new besties following him, he swung upstairs and ousted the two brats that were hogging the back seat with a glare and the threat of a slap round the ear if they didn't budge. Scowling, and cussing under their breath, they skulked down a few seats, trying to keep their swag, though there was only a smelly old tramp to see them. From here, Razor could monitor who got on and off the bus.

By the time they arrived at the Interchange, Razor's knee was bouncing up and down. Never had a bus trip been so fraught with anxiety. Sweat soaked through the T-shirt he wore under his hoodie, and he longed to change out of these stinking clothes. As he headed downstairs, relief flooded him when his two besties followed him from the bus and loitered nearby when he stood at the Belle Hill stop. He'd been tempted to grab a taxi, but who the hell knew if he could trust the driver or not. If they could pay for a swanky lawyer, they could bribe a taxi driver.

When he arrived in the estate, hoodie pulled down over his head, he felt like a million eyes were on him. As he slouched through the back streets to his house, every bush, every tree, every parked car made him break out in a cold sweat. The back streets were quieter than the main ones and as he turned into the alley behind his house, he wondered if his decision to take a low-profile route had been wise. He had many friends on the estate and normally nobody would even look out of turn at the big Razor McCarthy. But things had changed, and he knew that his rival, Hammerhead, would do anything to oust him from power. On balance, he'd had no choice. Until he recouped, reassessed his position, Razor McCarthy couldn't trust anyone. Oh, how he wished Goyley had been released, too. At least he wouldn't be alone then.

The air was chilly, and a slight breeze had picked up as he sent a furtive glance around him before he slipped into his back garden. Crime scene tape, courtesy of the police from earlier, fluttered against the back door. All he had to do was get inside and he'd be safe – well, safer.

Inside, he could triple lock the doors and hunker down. His breath came in fast gasps as he approached. He sensed that once the pigs had seen he was heading home that they'd dipped back – probably to avoid being clocked – dicks hadn't realised he'd already clocked them. *Idiots*!

Keys in hand and every sense alert to any threats, he approached the door. All good so far. He inserted the key in the lock, turned it, and was pushing the door open when he felt a prod at his back.

'Get inside, McCarthy. Now.'

CHAPTER 52

That weird song 'Writing on the Wall' kept playing out in his head. Sometimes it even drowned out everything else, and he clung to it as if a melody with a few words thrown in could offer him a lifeline. He'd known the writing was on the wall for him as soon as he'd seen her face this afternoon when he'd dared to defend the boy. She'd snapped. Had enough of him and more than that, she'd realised that no matter how hard they tried, how many therapies he endured – he'd never change. He'd always be a disappointment to her – a scandal waiting to happen. So, he hadn't resisted when she'd bade him come with her. He owed her that much. Despite his peccadilloes, she'd been loyal to him over the years and now he was prepared to free himself. He was tired. Too tired to go on. Too tired to live and she deserved to be rid of him – although she and her cronies deserved to rot in hell for the other things they'd done.

By now he was used to the fabric bag over his head, although he couldn't be certain of how long he'd been sitting here in the chair, arms cuffed to the arms, ankles shackled to the wooden chair legs. The air was fetid with waste product – his waste product. With each breath he took, the fabric sucked into his mouth and against his nose, the fabric moist and claggy against his sweating skin. Had he expected things to be any different? He thought not. This was his penance for the choices he'd made. For all the illicit, sordid things he'd done over his fifty-plus years on God's own earth. Each successive sin had accumulated the ball of guilt that squeezed his belly, making it almost impossible to eat or even to drink.

He'd thought the ulcers, the fainting fits, the hair loss as his anorexia became more pronounced was his punishment. Through the mask he laughed; a dry painful scrape regurgitating up his throat and emerging from his mouth like a creaking door hanging half off its hinges. He should have known better. He should have realised that a guilt-ridden, self-inflicted end would not appease those who needed to be the vengeful perpetrators of his punishment. It was only right after all. His actions had caused suffering beyond measure to those he had vowed to protect, to those he was duty bound to care for.

His current predicament was almost a relief. The need for pretence had long gone. All that remained was a weary sense of inevitability and acceptance of his fate. He'd done wrong. In fact, he'd done wrong many times – too many times to count, too many times for the average person to remember yet, he remembered every occasion with a combination of stomach-clenching disgust, heart-thumping gratitude, and a twitching frisson of joy in his groin.

Over the bag, headphones rested against his ears, offering no escape from the desultory tones that admonished him. Their vile words making him flinch as if each one was a whip stripping the flesh from his bony back, then soothed him with promises of being saved, each of those words a healing, cleansing balm across the whip scars of the previous ones. The words went on and on and on. Different voices delivering the same message. Sometimes the whip words lasted for eternities, followed by the soothing caresses stolen away after mere seconds of solace. Sometimes the soft murmurs and promises of redemption and forgiveness lulled him into a blanket of down, nurturing and, when he felt his head nodding, his eyes closing and the comfort of sleep embracing him, the whip words would return, louder and harsher than before. He couldn't think. Could no longer formulate the protests that had left his dry lips so easily at the start. Fragments of images flitted through his mind, yet none offered a cohesive narrative to guide him. His body was dying, but worse than that, so was his mind. Although on some level he understood that he'd brought this upon himself, he had no real wish for it to stop. If his dark world became silent, then he'd be left with his own thoughts – his guilt for every betrayal he'd committed, and that was too much for him to bear.

When they took the bag from his head and forced him to open his eyes, he flinched. His head was heavy on his neck and lolled to the side, but even through his closed lids, yellow and white light scalded his eyes. The freezing water hitting his tepid skin jolted him and his eyes opened, only to be stabbed with light too hot to bear. His tongue tried to lap up the remnants of water on his skin, but the whip words began again. This time, they came from the man. A large angel in white robes, arms raised before him, with a halo of light behind him, and this time they expected him to reply.

'What is your decision? Do you renounce your sins?'

But he couldn't respond. He had lost his grasp on reality and even if he had not, his throat was too dry to utter a sound and his neck too weak to offer a response.

With a single nod, the angel made the final judgement and as the knife entered his heart, the end was nigh.

CHAPTER 53

Carl Morris roamed around Razor McCarthy's home feeling puzzled. From his drive through the less than salubrious estate, and the dubious external appearance of the house, he'd expected the inside to be equally run down and had dreaded spending time in an unclean hovel. However, although the inside was too gaudy for his tastes, the level of cleanliness had surprised him. None of McCarthy's possessions would find their way in his own home. Still, the awful little scrote clearly had a desire for better things. His possessions betrayed his hidden wealth. Before Morris finished with Razor McCarthy, he'd know all about his wealth, as well as the information he'd come for. With a smile, he ran a finger along the edge of McCarthy's gross torture bed. He would apply his own brand of torture here. This time, though, there would be no safe words for McCarthy.

Before Norm's call, Morris had been on the verge of throwing something at the poxy TV and screaming out the window of the Travelodge. Norm's, '*He's out and we've got eyes on him. Forbes-Jameson did his job. Time for us to prepare*', filled him with adrenalin like a shot of heroin to his bloodstream. The end was in sight.

Now pacing through the cramped house, in the darkness of the curtained windows, Morris could barely contain himself. It wouldn't be long now. Not long until Razor gave him the information he needed. The information that had eluded him for six long fucking years. It was only a waiting game now.

'Boss, he's here.'

The hissed whisper drifted upstairs, and Morris's heart flipped. This was it. McCarthy was here and things were about to get soooo much better. The next few hours would be the most enjoyable he'd had in a long, long time. After a couple of deep breaths to calm himself, he moved from the main bedroom and downstairs to where Norm waited at the kitchen table, a nine-millimetre pistol aimed at the back door. Morris could hear scrapings as the first of the three locks was unlocked.

Then the door was pushed open and Morris, his smile wide, stepped forward, taking care not to stand in the way of Norm's aim.

Razor's eyes widened when he saw the duo waiting in his kitchen. 'Aw fuck.'

For a moment, Morris, mouth agape, could only stare. Not at Razor, but at the figure standing behind him.

'Fuck's sake, shoot.' Razor's tone was high-pitched and desperate – a man petrified and out of control.

But the person who'd forced Razor at gunpoint into his home groaned deep in his throat and dropped the length of copper piping he'd pretended was a gun.

With a laugh, Morris stepped forward. 'Well, well, well, if it isn't little Jacob all grown up now. How's your mum?'

Jo Jo glared at Morris. 'Fuck off.'

CHAPTER 54

The trio kneels before me and their similarity to the Wise Monkey statue in my study doesn't escape me. In this instance, though, there is nothing learnt about these monkeys. The first looks up at me. Hear's hands cup his chin, fingers covering his ears as if anticipating the dressing down they believe they are due to receive. While the second, See has bowed her head, hand across their brow, eyes closed as if it is possible to unsee what lies behind them – the result of their failure. Number three, Speak's eyes, holding an indecipherable message, are latched on mine, while both hands cover his mouth as if to prevent any errant words from escaping those treacherous lips. Number three is the monkey to be wary of. The one who will bite my hand off and betray me if I'm not careful. However, I am careful – very careful. Besides, I have my other monkeys and they are too cowed to rebel against their organ grinder.

I'm not sure what to say, so I turn my back on them and begin pacing the room, buying time. When See had approached me, requesting a special meeting – assistance because she felt we were all in danger, I acquiesced. Little did I envisage what might happen. I'd taken my eye off the ball while focussed on that he/she Flynn and hadn't realised the real danger in our midst. Now we had a problem. One I'm sure we can solve, but a problem, nonetheless.

This type of – shall we say – accident has only happened twice before. I dealt with them effectively then, so there's no reason I can't do so again. If only more time had elapsed between them. If only the police weren't investigating links between the previous two. What will they make of this one? I do a mental checklist of our actions the last time; number one cleaned up the realignment studio while two and three wrapped the body in heavy duty cling film and transported it in the group vehicle to the dump spot.

I pause and, still not addressing them, sit down at the table and consider the next moves. Whatever I decide next is critical. One mistake and everything we've worked for over the past few months will come tumbling down and I can't allow that to happen. Our work is too important, and, in such a libertine climate, it lies on us to offer the true and just moral compass for our flock. This is only the start. Our preachings are effective and many have graduated and gone on to lead fruitful and sin free lives. Even those from other faiths have approached us with their brethren to offer our teachings and realign their warped and sinful behaviour. It is for this reason that I can't stumble at this hurdle. Not when there are so many more souls to redeem.

I run my fingers over the smooth amber contours of my ring and study the way the light catches specks of fiery orange, giving it life in the same way as our teachings have given life back to the transgressors.

I consider my options. The previous accident was so dissimilar to this one and that's an excellent thing. The difference in age, sex, experience of the previous accidents will make it difficult for the police to link them. Of course, where we dispose of our current accident is a delicate matter. We can't use the same spot – to do so would invite trouble. Instead, I smile. I have just the spot. A road with few cameras, and little footfall in the middle of the night. In that sense, it is similar to the previous spot.

As I exhale, my monkeys fidget. Their knees must ache from their time spent in contact with the uncarpeted floor. I flick my hand at them, allowing them to stand, and watch as they shake off the stiffness in their limbs. As if sensing that my judgement will be forthcoming, they watch each other from the corner of their eyes. Perhaps willing one of their friends to break the silence first. I approach them, meeting their gazes, enjoying the frisson of power at their fidgeting and the way their eyes avert when mine seeks them out. I am in control, and they are aware of that. They rely on me, and I am prepared to take on the yoke of leadership. After all, I am not the first of our kind to do so. No doubt I won't be the last. I walk around them, and they turn, their lips quivering, fingers fiddling with their robes, as I look down upon our dear departed brother lying on the stone floor before the custom-built chair we use only for the most resistant of our sinners. In his nakedness he looks serene – free of sin. Our previous sinner didn't make it out of the chair, either. However, the marks found on her body differed from these. Even then, I knew we hadn't made our last sacrifice. Even then, I realised more sinners would make the ultimate payment. That's why I thought ahead. That's why I plan, and that is why I am in charge.

I offer a prayer for his soul, knowing that our work with him has guaranteed him a place in heaven with our Lord. 'May Christ, who was crucified for you, bring you freedom and peace as you enter his kingdom at last, free from the sins of your body.'

Words like these mean nothing to me. I use them as a tool to draw the others to me. My trio of monkeys repeat the prayer in subdued voices and when they're done, I turn and smile at them, slapping my hand on Speak's shoulder. 'Our spiritual work with this brother is complete. Still, we have to take care of his earthly body. Here's the plan…'

And as I reveal the plan, my monkeys relax. Their shoulders lose their tension, their faces become less taut – still, Hear is less calm, less relieved. His eyes twitch between us and I know he might yet be my kryptonite.

As they get set to go about their jobs, I call See to me and, with whispered words, set her an additional task. One I can see she is reluctant to do, but her loyalty knows no bounds and by the time I've finished instructing her, her lips have stopped trembling and she understands the importance of the task she has been given. She grips my hand and raises it to her lips.

'Angel, I will do this task in God's name to the best of my ability.'

CHAPTER 55

Jo Jo's heart pounded in his chest as if it was going to explode out of it. As soon as he'd seen the two men waiting in Razor's kitchen, he realised he'd made a grave error of judgment. He'd thought Razor McCarthy would lead him to Carl Morris, not the other way around. Now he was in deep shit. When he'd got the text from Compo warning him of Razor's imminent release, he'd thought he could get ahead of the game. Find Morris and do what he and his mum should have done years ago. Kill him.

Not that he was in any way certain he could take an actual real human life, but, for Jessie's sake, he must. No way could he let Carl Morris claim her as his daughter. No way could he allow Morris to bring Jessie up. The man was a psychopath. Jo Jo had seen the things he'd done to his mum, and he would never allow that to happen – not to Jessie. That's why they'd run in the first place. Six years living on Belle Hill Estate had been better than six minutes living with Carl Morris.

He'd fucked up. Fucked up big time. Nobody knew where he was. Nobody would ride in on a stallion and rescue him. Not even Gus could help him this time. They'd never in a million years guess he was at Razor's gaff, and he'd dumped his phone. Fuck, why had he dumped his phone?

'No hugs for your old man, Jacob?'

'Jacob? Nah, mate, you got the wrong kid here. His name's Jo Jo.' Razor, keen to ingratiate himself to

273

Morris, grinned as he spoke, arms outstretched as if could sort this huge mistake out. He didn't know Carl Morris, though.

Morris looked at him, a smile and Razor smiled back. Jo Jo could have told him that the smile wasn't a good sign, but he was past caring about Razor and his crap. Even though Jo Jo had been expecting it, he still flinched when Morris's fist whammed into Razor's gut, sending him flying backwards to crash against the sink unit. Razor retched and as he slid down the unit to sprawl onto the floor, a thin trickle of bile trailed from his mouth.

'Where's your sister, Jacob? Where's little Gracie? And your mam? Where's she? Whoring it up in some Bradford crack den?'

Jo Jo had split seconds to decide what to do. Razor clutched his belly and tried to mouth something, but he was still too winded to talk. Jo Jo had to make sure Razor couldn't tell Morris anything about his sister or his mam.

He turned to Morris, his lips quivering, ignored the bruiser who sat statue still and emotionless with the gun trained on him. 'Don't hurt Razor any more. Just don't. He's done nothing wrong. Let him go. Please don't hurt him. I'm begging you.'

Morris studied Jo Jo for ages, making the boy wonder if this man – his biological dad – had seen through him. Had he laid it on too thick? A glance at Razor's widened eyes, as he struggled for breath, told him he'd seen through Jo Jo's ploy. But Morris seemed too wrapped up in his own self-importance to make rational decisions.

Eyes fixed on Jo Jo, Morris stepped over and gripped Razor by the collar before dragging him to his feet. 'Please don't hurt him.' He mimicked Jo Jo's previous tone and then slammed Razor's head onto the sink. 'I'm begging you.'

Razor's eyes rolled back in their sockets and Morris dropped him unconscious back onto the floor. That the bigger man hadn't intervened reassured Jo Jo that Morris called all the shots and, therefore, was vulnerable to mental manipulation if only Jo Jo could pull it off.

Eyes wide, Jo Jo felt his belly lurch as the enormity of what he'd instigated hit him. If Razor died, then Jo Jo had, in effect, killed him. Gulping in huge breaths of air, Jo Jo attempted to settle his nerves, but his heart was hammering too hard and waves of dizziness rolled over him, blurring his vison. If he submitted to the dizziness and allowed it to engulf him, he wouldn't have to answer questions from Morris and maybe, just maybe, he could buy himself some ti…

The thought remained half-formed as he slunk to the floor in a heap at his dad's feet.

CHAPTER 56

The quartet of teens Zoomed into Gus's incident room were subdued. Gus couldn't blame them for, over the course of a week, these kids had witnessed their friend being beaten to death online and then heard of Flynn Arnett's murder.

All the four teens on the screen at the front of the room were transgender. This group, according to Linc, the self-appointed team leader, had been a lifesaver for them. Much as he sympathised with their plight, Gus's focus was on getting any information that might relate to Flynn Arnett's murder.

'I know this has been a tough week for you and the last thing I want to do is make it any harder. However, if we're to find Flynn's killer, I need any help you can give.'

Linc was the first to speak. 'It's my fault he's dead. It was my stupid, stupid idea for us to take some power back.'

'No, it wasn't, Linc.' Bev's voice carried a gentle Scottish lilt. 'We all agreed to it. All of us.'

Davy butted in. 'Yeah, we all did. We'd had enough of being the victims. We all wanted to be proactive. Fuck, Linc, you can't take everything on your own shoulders.'

Gus waited for a moment to give Anita the chance to jump in, but although she nodded her agreement, the slender girl, hunched over her laptop remained silent.

'So, what were you all doing and could it relate to Flynn's murder?'

'None of us are old enough to vote and yet decisions are being made about us by people who don't understand what it's like to be us. So, we logged our experiences. We were going to take our evidence to Stonewall or somewhere like that. We wanted people to realise how we were treated. The struggles we faced before they judge us. Some guy from his church approached Flynn and asked if he wanted to be 'cured'.'

Linc spat the last word out and Gus flinched. *Shit, that was crap*.

'He recruited a group of 'sinners' – you know, gays, trans, and that and was doing conversion therapy. Flynn was logging it. He'd been to about six sessions. '

So, that's what the diary was about. Flynn's sessions of conversion therapy. Gus had read it through prior to this meeting and was disgusted by the abuse Flynn had catalogued. What sickened him most was how the group leaders elevated themselves to an almost godly stature. This was crucial to the investigation and although the diary did not indicate where this group met or the identity of the group leader's, Gus now had confirmation that Flynn had been recruited from his church. Of course, that didn't mean the church was actively involved or supportive of this sort of stuff – in fact. Anne Summerscale had always seemed very liberal. One of her kids was gay, and she supported him. However, it offered a pool of potential suspects. Gus saw another visit to the church on the horizon. 'Did he share the identities of anyone involved in this group – either the leaders or the attendees?'

But Linc shook his head. 'I've been wracking my brains, detective, and no. Flynn didn't give us any names. The only thing he said was that the building where they met was freezing cold and quite a distance from where he lived.'

Gus and Alice continued to ask questions of the group, but gained no more information. After expressing his thanks for their time and promising to keep them informed of the progress, Gus hung up.

'Right? Where are we with Jo Jo? Still no sightings?'

Compo shook his head. Although it had only been a few hours since they'd received Jo Jo's note, Compo looked to have shrunk. His eyes held a glazed look that hinted tears were never far away. Taffy had returned from Flynn's PM and now looked as drained and worried as everyone else.

'So, what do we have? Update on the Flynn investigation first and then Jo Jo.'

Taffy stood up. 'The PM confirmed cause of death was manual strangulation. It's unlikely we'll get fingerprints from the skin either, although Dr Horne says she'll try. Dr McGuire tried with Zac's body and was unsuccessful, if you remember. The bruising around Flynn's wrists and ankles is consistent with that found round Zac's. That's the only thing this PM threw up which links the two.'

'Uniforms have been monitoring CCTV at the Sandy Lane and Flappit pub junctions, but nothing concrete yet. The hotline hasn't thrown up any legitimate leads, so it looks like we're back to the church tomorrow morning. Luckily, it's a Sunday, so we'll be able to interview most of them in church, which should save time.'

Gus paused. Frustration and worry about Jo Jo had given him a headache and forced inactivity made him feel antsy. After the briefing, he'd jog back home and try for an early night. 'We've had no luck locating Jo Jo either. He's not been seen anywhere, and he's not at his old house in Bell Hill Estate. Compo, have you had any luck finding out what happened six years ago?'

'All records of Jo Jo's family started when they arrived in Bradford six years ago. I couldn't trace them back before the time they arrived here, which, like previous cases we've worked on, indicates—'

'They were in witness protection?' Gus bit his lip as he considered the likelihood of that. How could Jo Jo's family have been under witness protection, yet living the way they were? But more to the point, it was unlikely that the National Crime Agency would admit or refute their involvement in the family's relocation to Bradford six years ago, unless…

While Alice grumbled on about the gross negligence of the witness protection scheme, Taffy scratched the back of his neck as if that might bring some reality to the situation. Gus caught Compo's eye. He couldn't believe what he was about to ask the lad to do. Under any other circumstances, he wouldn't. But this was Jo Jo and Jessie. They'd already rescued those kids once and National Crime Agency or not, Gus was damned if he would let them fall through the cracks. 'Compo. You need to take some downtime. You need to get away from the office and veg out doing computer stuff.'

For a second, Compo glowered at Gus, his cheeks flushed as he looked set to argue.

'Compo. I mean it. We don't need you here. You're better off at home for now. Where you can do whatever you like in peace and quiet. Understand?'

Silence reigned in the room as everyone registered what Gus was asking Compo to do.

'You mean…?'

But Gus broke across Compo's words. 'Yes, I mean you need to go home. You need some downtime. Maybe

Taffy will look in on you later, but you should go. Go now.'

Without another word, Compo began gathering up his things and when he had everything he needed, he turned to Gus. 'Don't worry about me, boss. I've got everything I need at home.'

Heart thumping, Gus nodded. What he was asking Compo to do was a gross misconduct offence. Should they be discovered, Gus wouldn't let Compo take the blame. 'I've got your back, Comps. From here on in, you're acting under my orders, OK?'

A smile flickered across Compo's lips. 'Well then, I better be careful.'

After Compo left, Gus slumped into a chair and looked at his colleagues. Of course should things go wrong, he'd protect them too, but he was aware he'd crossed a line tonight and he didn't know what they would think about it, but although both looked as wan and drained as he felt, they approached him with strained smiles on their faces.

Alice hugged him – something she never did in the workspace, and for a second, Gus allowed himself to absorb the warmth of her embrace. 'There was nothing else you could've done, Gus.'

Taffy, gaze averted, shuffled his feet. 'This is Jo Jo we're talking about, boss. Jo Jo and Jessie. We're in this together. Compo will come up with something. I know he will.'

SUNDAY

CHAPTER 57

DI Gus McGuire hesitated, observing the new crime scene activity from the comfort of his car. He'd slept badly. Thoughts of what might be happening to Jo Jo churning round his mind. Now, with this new body to consider, the prospect of viewing another dead teen curdled his gut. What if this body was Jo Jo's…or Bailey White's? He reversed into a tight spot on the opposite side of Glen Road near Bracken Hall House between two police cars. In the lay-by opposite, a blue Mondeo was parked at an angle and officers had incorporated it into their ad hoc crime scene. Other vehicles, mostly police and CSI vans, were dotted along the narrow road blocking movement. The wavering blue and white police tape securing the outer cordon stretched along Glen Road a few hundred yards on either side of Bracken Hall House but on the opposite side of the road, before creating an enclosed three-sided area. The fourth side securing the scene was the sharp drop to the glen. Within the confines of the inner cordon, bunny-suited figures went about their business around the white tent, while the 'igloo' protected the body from external conditions and preserved any forensic evidence in the immediate vicinity of the body.

It was early, with the light grey streaks of daylight barely making an impression on the Shipley Glen crags. Huge flat stones spanning the heath overlooking Loadpit Beck and with death defying drops and offering stunning views, weather permitting, of course. The area was full of nooks and crannies, perfect for dumping a body. Gus had been called to crime scenes here before, but none for a while. It was a popular spot for teenagers to congregate under cover of darkness and, again, he considered the likelihood of finding a dead teenager at the scene.

Gus shuddered as the memory prompted him to consider all the victims he'd encountered over the years. For the vast majority of them he'd gained justice, but the toll of mopping up after the barbaric actions of humanity's darker inhabitants, year after year, sometimes left him despondent. He wasn't quite ready for whatever scene waited for him. This was particularly so because this mind was still with Flynn, Zac, Bailey, and Jo Jo. His entire body was taut with frustration, making it hard to focus. He hated having to tell Flynn Arnett's parents they still had arrested no one for their son's murder. He hated the pounding dread that pierced his heart every time he thought about Jo Jo. For the first time in a long time, it was as if everything was slipping through his fingers. He didn't know where to turn and the thought of having to tell another parent – possibly Lizzie White – that their child was dead left an acid taste in his throat.

Gus had no details of the body found this morning other than a snippy message left on his phone from DCI Nancy Chalmers while he'd been jogging. '*Dead body. Get your arse over to Shipley Glen, pronto.*'

Gus tried to reconcile the hope that this body might offer a valuable clue, with his dread of finding Bailey White or Jo Jo in the igloo. Surely Sid would have told him if it was Jo Jo. Perhaps the deaths were unrelated. Maybe there were two murderers roaming the streets of Bradford. Shit, that didn't bear thinking about either.

He rummaged in the glove compartment before finding a stray can of Irn Bru. In the absence of coffee, this would have to do. Might not be the best drink for first thing in the morning, but he needed a jump start. After a couple of long swallows, he crushed the can, waited for the sugar rush to hit, then cranked open the car door. The frigid morning air nipped at his face as he pulled up his collar against its frosty tendrils and marched over to the officer who staffed the outer cordon.

'Hey, Jonesy, how bad is it?' Gus reached for the pad to sign himself in as he waited for a response from the experienced sergeant.

'Not right good, Gus. Not right good.' As he retrieved the log from Gus, he pointed first to the box of cellophane wrapped bunny suits by his feet and then at the car just behind him, before lowering his voice. 'The lass in that car found him. Poor thing's near hysterical with the shock, but her boyfriend's on his way. Pregnant, she is. Poor thing only stopped because of the morning sickness, like. Got out of the car and wandered off the road to be sick.' He pursed his lips and shook his head. 'Poor lass got more than she bargained for.'

Jonesy was still shaking his head when Gus, now bunny-suited up, slapped him on the back and ducked under the crime scene tape. As he walked over the treads placed by the CSIs to preserve the scene while allowing a pathway to the tent, Gus ducked under the inner cordon tape, nodded at the officer he didn't recognise there and had almost reached the tent when DS Alice Cooper, hood pulled tight round her face emerged. Her face lit up when she saw Gus. 'Took your time, didn't you?'

Alice had arrived at the scene before him and, ignoring her taunt, Gus moved closer. 'Well? What have we got?'

All traces of her previous humour left Alice's face as she recounted their findings so far. 'Male, in his sixties, naked, emaciated, marks around wrist and ankles – shackles of some description. Cause of death undetermined.'

Hmm! Not another teen victim, so probably unrelated to their ongoing case. He'd hand it over to another team after the initial necessities were complete.

'Who's the pathologist on call?' There had been a time when Gus would have dreaded hearing his father, Dr Fergus McGuire's, name, but today he would welcome his dad's familiar brusqueness.

Alice gave an almost indiscernible shrug and her lips drooped downward. Gus understood. 'It's my dad's job share colleague, isn't it? It's Dr Horne?'

With a sigh, Alice nodded. 'Yep…and she's already at the scene…well, in a manner of speaking…'

Gus frowned, but Alice gestured towards the crime scene tent and after opening the flap and peering inside, he understood what she meant. Hissing Sid, the crime scene manager, was kneeling beside the body, obscuring it from Gus's view. His tablet was trained on the victim's upper torso. 'We all right to come in, Sid?'

A voice Gus recognised echoed tinnily nearby. 'Who's entering my crime scene, Sidney?'

Gus glanced around the tent, but there was only he, Alice, Sid, and a busy CSI inside. Puzzled, he waited till Hissing Sid, cheeks flushed, lips tight, turned towards him. 'It's DI Gus McGuire and DS Alice Cooper. Would you like to speak to them?'

Sid turned his tablet so they could see Dr Horne. Even without her green scrubs and the hair net that almost, but not quite, encapsulated her hair, Gus would have recognised her. Dr Amanda Horne, the pathologist who now shared his father's job. Gus had been surprised when his dad announced his intention to cut down on his hours, but he'd also been relieved. His father wasn't getting any younger and, although he tried to cover it up, Gus had noticed how he struggled with crime scenes, and had been concerned with his father's overall health for a long time.

However, since Dr Horne had started work three months ago, Gus had yet to meet the pathologist in person. Her work philosophy was different from his dad's and in the few investigations where she'd been the pathologist, she'd declined to attend the scene, preferring to do an 'audit' via the CSI manager's tablet. That wasn't particularly a problem, however, what Gus had taken objection to was that she'd declared the pathologist's attendance as 'obsolete, unnecessary, and a criminal waste of time as the CSI managers were more than capable of logging the crime scene' and had compounded this by saying that those pathologists who '*indulged their superiority by pitching up at the scene should retire tout de suite as they clearly weren't au fait with cutting edge practice.*'

Apart from the annoying Frenchisms, dropped in every couple of sentences, Gus had been outraged by her audacity and had taken her statements as a direct criticism of his father. Sid had initially been enamoured by the new pathologist, viewing her stance as a validation of the critical importance of his role as CSI manager. This had been short-lived, however, when Dr Horne insisted on a step-by-step walk through via video link of the crime scene and the body in situ led by the CSI manager. Her sharp instructions to '*zoom in there*' followed by acerbic comments regarding his ability to fully allow her visibility because of lighting deficiency or some other obstacle made her soon become a thorn in Sid's side.

If Gus didn't feel so sorry for the CSI, he would have smirked at Sid's glum expression. Instead, he put on his politest voice and kept his tone mild. 'The crime scene is Sid's responsibility and until he's satisfied that all forensic evidence has been collected, logged, and transported to the lab, we're here because he has allowed us access. Oh, but you're not actually here, are you?'

The smile faded from Dr Horne's lips and Gus, ignoring Alice's muffled snort and Sid's grin, continued, 'When Sid has finished here, he'll hand the scene over to me as Senior Investigation Officer. I don't consider this guided tour via video link a valuable use of his time. The first hours after a murder are crucial and we need this scene processed tout suite.'

As he uttered the French word, Gus's eyebrow twitched, eliciting a louder snort from Alice and a wider grin from Sid. 'So, if you want to view the scene, Dr Horne, I suggest you either get down here, or wait until the team upload their findings to the joint folders.'

'How dare you? This is a valuable part of—'

Gus shut her down. 'Look, images and recordings will be available to you soon. In the meantime, it looks like you have another PM to do, so, for now, let us get on with our job.' He smiled. 'I look forward to meeting you in person as my father speaks very highly of you.'

A frown danced across the pathologist's brow, as if she was trying to interpret a hidden meaning in Gus's last words. Then, with a sigh, she pulled off her hairnet, releasing a cascade of grey curls that reached down to her shoulders. 'I've been overly demanding, haven't I? It's my major flaw. I'm so desperate to live up to your father's sizeable footsteps that I've been trying to reach a compromise between his very hands-on approach and my own less than hands on approach and I'm afraid all I've done is alienate people.'

She shook her head '*C'est la vie*! I'll back off and hopefully we can reach an amicable working relationship, DI McGuire. Sidney, I'm sorry if I've caused you hassle. Let me know when to expect the body and I'll study the scene from the recordings and photographic evidence before commencing the PM.' With no more ado, she gave a wave, and the screen went blank.

'Thank God for that.' Sid exhaled and looked at Gus. 'I owe you one, McGuire.'

Gus winked. 'I'll hold you to that.'

He and Hissing Sid had a chequered relationship. The CSI manager had, over the years, got into the habit of intentionally releasing noxious farts at crime scenes. Gus realised that this habit had most likely arisen from an attempt to lighten the darkness of dealing with violent death and while some levity could be cathartic, Sid's farting was a catharsis too far. However, the fragile bridge they'd managed to gulf after the murder of one of Sid's colleagues earlier in the year was strengthening and Gus's intervention on Sid's behalf was another building block in their relationship. 'So, let me have a look at our victim and then you can talk me through your observations so far. I take it we've no ID?'

Sid stood back from the body, allowing Gus access. 'None yet. We've sent off his images to Missing Persons, so maybe that will give us a name.'

But Gus was already shaking his head. 'No need. I can identify him. He's Claude Douglas. I spoke with him and his wife at Manningham All Saint's Church yesterday afternoon.'

While his previous hope that this murder would not be related to Flynn's disappearance, Gus studied the body. Whatever had led to Claude's death, Gus was sure it had something to do with Zac and Flynn's murderers.

Two boys with a link to Manningham All Saints could be coincidence. Three deaths linked to the religious establishment could not.

Claude lay naked on his back, his hands resting on his stomach, his nakedness making his skeletal frame more pronounced. The man was skinny to the point of malnutrition, which reminded Gus of Zac Ibrahim. He too had been undernourished, but of course that was hardly surprising considering Zac had been homeless.

Taking his time, Gus started as he always did at the feet and worked his way upwards. His bare feet showed signs of neglect. His toenails were over long and the soles of his feet were filthy, as if he'd been walking around barefoot and hadn't bathed since. However, the absence of cuts and scrapes indicated that he'd not walked to his current resting place. Both ankles were chafed and bruised with clear marks indicating he had been shackled before his death, which again was consistent with marks found on both Zac Ibrahim and Flynn Arnett's bodies. 'Any ideas what could have made those restraints marks, Sid? And do they seem consistent with those found on Flynn?'

Sid moved in and pointed. 'You can see they're quite wide – a couple of inches at least. I'd say metal shackles, but who knows what kind? Interestingly, I spotted some scratches on his calves and I think, when her highness does the PM, she'll find splinters in there – probably wood, but that'll be up to her to determine. I'm going to bag his feet and lower legs as soon as you're done.'

That was interesting. Although cause of death wasn't determined yet, the use of restraints and the location of the man's naked body in the middle of nowhere showed suspicious death and more than likely murder. Gus knew that bagging the extremities helped preserve possible forensic evidence, and he had high hopes that they'd find some this time, giving them a tangible lead. Gus's gaze moved upwards. He flinched when he registered how emaciated the man was. He hadn't noticed how thin Claude was when he'd met him the other day. Had he been ill? The way his bones pushed against his skin was heartbreaking.

Gus moved up to his lower torso, where the man's hands lay over his lower abdomen. Again, there were marks around his wrists, but unlike the ones on his ankles these were thinner and had dug into the flesh more. *Cable ties*? His hairless chest and concave belly told the same story as his skinny legs – this man was seriously underweight. Gus's gaze continued upwards until it rested on Claude's face. His eyes were shut, his mouth agape as if releasing his final breath. Sunken cheeks and wrinkled neck again told the story of lack of nutrition and Gus wondered why Claude was so emaciated – did he have an illness? That would be for the PM and medical records to determine. Moving closer, Gus bent over the body, studying the neck. 'Look, Sid, Al. Do you see faint marks around his neck, or am I seeing things?'

Both Sid and Alice leant forward and focussed on the area Gus pointed at.

'Well, I'll be damned.' Sid edged even closer. 'I missed that, but you're right. Something, maybe a thin cord, has been tied round his neck. Not too tightly, by the looks of it, but it's definitely there. Her Highness will find out if there're any fibres to help us.'

Gus stood up, took a last look at the victim. Were the fine wrinkles across Claude's brow the result of worry or age? Grey hair sprouted in two unruly tufts from either side of his head, once more prompting Gus to compare it to his dad's hair. Claude had a wife and friends, and Gus was determined to find out who had discarded him like this in death. He turned to Sid. 'Your team found anything else worth mentioning?'

'Nothing conclusive. A few tyre tracks, your usual myriad of rubbish – used condoms, weed bags, empty cans, etc. We'll bag it all up, but…' He shrugged.

Gus understood Sid's reaction. Other than a dead body and the prospect of finding useful information like cause of death at the PM, there wasn't much to go on. He marched from the tent, glad to feel the cold air against his skin after the claustrophobic heat inside.

'Right, Al, CCTV? Check out Bracken Hall – they must have cameras. Maybe they'll have caught something. Also, see if any of the houses near the Shipley Glen Tram have CCTV. Maybe we'll be lucky and whoever dumped our victim here came up that way.'

Alice rolled her eyes. 'Yeah, because we're always so lucky, Gus. Yeah, whoever dumped the old boy will have left a trail of crumbs leading right to his door.'

Alice had a point, but they had to try. This was a nightmare. Three dead bodies – some consistencies in cause of death, but other inconsistencies like the thin cord-like imprint on Claude's neck puzzled Gus. Regardless of that, the overriding link between the victims and All Saints was huge. Gus turned to the Mondeo where the pregnant woman sat in the driver's seat, head bowed and a bottle of water hanging from her hand. 'I don't suppose she'll be able to tell us much, but have a uniformed officer take her statement and then make sure she's escorted home. I don't want her driving until she's calm.'

'I've already done that, Gus. Just waiting for her boyfriend to turn up. I've issued instructions for him to be allowed through the traffic cordon when he gets here.'

As if on cue, three figures appeared at the far end of the outer cordon – two of them were journalists. Alice tutted. 'Bloody parasites have arrived, Gus. How the hell did they find out?'

Gus shook his head. They'd nothing to tell the press and inevitably, a press presence would develop at some point. His thoughts remained with the old man lying cold in the igloo. What series of events had led to his death and subsequent presence here on Shipley Glen? Although nothing like Gus's old man in terms of age or constitution, Gus couldn't help wondering about Ada, Claude's wife, who was unaware of his passing. Had she missed him overnight? Was she waiting for him to phone or turn up unharmed? Perhaps she was blissfully asleep unaware that her husband was even absent from the house. Death was always a sad and depressing thing to encounter. Unexplained death multiplied that effect by a trillion and the death of an unidentified person amplified it even more. He'd done everything he could at the crime scene and now he needed to get back to The Fort and attempt to draw an investigative strategy together.

CHAPTER 58

Jo Jo came round to discover that they'd moved him from the kitchen, and he was now lying on a thick carpet with a duvet thrown over him. He took a moment to ground himself in his current reality. He'd planned to force McCarthy to divulge Carl Morris's whereabouts and then had intended to kill him. Instead, he was imprisoned in Razor's house with the psychopath that was his dad. Rather than give him a modicum of respect, Jo Jo decided to call him Morris from here on in. That man had never been a father to him, and he would not give him that status now. Gus had been more of a dad to Jo Jo in the short time he'd known him than Morris had for the first 11 years of Jo Jo's life. But now, with his plans destroyed, things couldn't be worse if they tried. So, what was he going to do?

Rather than divulge that he'd come round, Jo Jo kept his eyes closed and remained still as he tried to work out who else was in the room with him. Sporadic groans of pain reached his ears, intermingled with the faint rustling of fabric and the faint creak of bed springs and from that, Jo Jo deduced that Razor was in the room too – probably on the bed. That puzzled him. Why would his dad have given Razor the bed and confined his son to the floor? Perhaps Jo Jo had misinterpreted Morris's motives. Maybe he wasn't interested in resurrecting his warped idea of happy families. Maybe he wanted to take revenge on his kids. It was then Jo Jo remembered that Morris didn't realise his ex-wife was dead. That was the only slight advantage Jo Jo had. Well, that and the knife that was wrapped up in a hoodie in his backpack. If only Morris hadn't checked the backpack and if only it was nearby, Jo Jo might still have some hope.

With only Razor's moans breaking the silence, Jo Jo thought it was safe to open his eyes. Greyish light filled the bedroom and street lights shone through a gap in the curtains. It wasn't quite dawn yet. Jo Jo pulled the duvet closer round him and waited to see if his movements had been noticed. So far, so good. There was nobody here except Razor. Jo Jo pulled himself up till he was leaning against the wall under the window and studied the tableau before him. What the fuck was that?

Razor's king-sized bed dominated the room, but it wasn't its size that shocked Jo Jo. It was the sight of the shackles, whips, and sex toys that decorated the hooks along the bed. His gaze moved to the figure lying retrained on top of the mattress. Spread-eagled on the bed, cuffed to each of the four bed posts, blood covered Razor McCarthy. His face was swollen and despite the groans, Jo Jo wasn't sure he was properly conscious. That explained why McCarthy got the bed, at least. Jo Jo was relieved that they hadn't shackled him.

His eyes wandered round the rest of the room with its garish but plush décor – being a drug dealer paid well – until they landed on a leopard skin fur chair. On top sat his backpack. Jo Jo strained his ears for movement outside Razor's bizarre S&M room. When he heard none, he edged over to the backpack and opened it, relieved that his hoodie was rolled up inside, just as he'd left it. Morris clearly underestimated the extent of his son's hatred for him. Moving as fast as he could, Jo Jo removed the machete from the depths of the hoodie, pushed it down the waistband of his jeans, replaced the backpack how he'd found it, and moved back to his position in front of the radiator. He heard someone on the stairs and lying back down, he closed his eyes and waited.

CHAPTER 59

'Ada…? Ada, are you all right?' Gus's words seemed to wash over Claude's wife who, fingers clenched in her lap, gazed into the distance as if she'd blocked out Gus and Alice's presence in her cosy little cottage.

Moments earlier, when they'd rang her doorbell in the predawn light, Gus had expected that she'd be asleep. But Ada, fully dressed, had answered the door almost immediately – almost as if she'd been expecting them. She hadn't invited them inside, instead she'd drifted down the hallway and into the chic living room, leaving them to follow. Only a single lamp sat on a delicate octagonal table beside the chair in which Ada now sat, lit the space, and Gus was tempted to flood the room with light from the main bulb and thrust the curtains open to welcome in the morning light. Instead, he sat opposite her on the chair that presumably was where Claude sat and leant forward, meeting her expectant gaze.

'Ada, I have some bad news for you. Earlier on today, we found Claude's body on Shipley Glen. He's been murdered.'

Ada offered a single nod of acknowledgment and from that moment on had sat, statue still, with her gaze averted. Gus and Alice exchanged worried glances. This was odd. Gus had delivered many death notices over the years, but never had he encountered complete silence. What was wrong with her? He didn't want to leap to any conclusions because, as he well knew, grief and traumatic shock affected people differently and a bereaved relative's atypical reaction when learning of a loved one's death wasn't necessarily an indicator of guilt or innocence. Gus had witnessed loved ones who disintegrated on hearing the news, only to later be found guilty of the murder. The reverse was also true. Yet Ada's reaction was concerning. The fact that she'd been up and dressed so early again didn't mean anything sinister, but until Gus could interview her, he couldn't progress the investigation.

'Ada, shall I call Reverend Summerscale to sit with you?'

Still Ada remained silent and so very, very still. Again, Alice and Gus exchanged glances. Alice stepped forward and crouched by her, her hand closing over the older woman's clenched fingers. 'Ada, dear. What can we do for you? You've had a shock and you shouldn't be alone. DI McGuire is asking if we should call the vicar. Would you like that?'

A flicker of a smile flitted over Ada's lips and in the shadowy lighting from the lamp it resembled a sneer. Ada snatched her fingers away from Alice, ignoring her as her gaze lasered on Gus.

'I think we need to go to the police station, DI McGuire.'

Alice stood up and backed away from Ada, allowing an intimate bubble to form around her and Gus. Skin prickling, Gus nodded. Whatever was going on here, Ada had information. Sensing her fragility, Gus was careful not to disrupt the tenuous bond they shared. 'And why would you think that, Ada?'

'I loved Claude, you know? For years, I loved him, and in his own way, he loved me too. But...' She looked down at her hands and ran her finger over her wedding ring. 'I wasn't really what he wanted and bless him, he was too weak to withstand all the temptations thrown at him.'

She exhaled, a waft of coffee breath hitting Gus as he edged forward, keen to hear every word she said. Over Ada's shoulder, Alice had her phone out and was no doubt recording Ada's words. They wouldn't be admissible as evidence, because Gus hadn't cautioned her. However, Gus sensed that breaking the intimacy of their current situation might make her clam up for good. He was prepared to take that risk if it meant gaining valuable insights.

'He was so handsome. Everyone thought he was such a catch. All my friends were jealous. But none of them knew the heartache and lies that lay beneath our marriage. He shamed me, detective. He shamed me and he shamed himself. He committed base sins. Each time he promised it would be the last. Each time he swore on the Bible that it would be the last…but it never was. It never was.'

She twisted the gold band on her finger and then wrenched it off, tossing it onto the occasional table with more despair than anger in her actions. Then, as it landed, she turned to Gus. 'He wasn't normal, you see. Not like a real man. Not normal at al. All he wanted was to be normal. So in the end I could stand no more and neither could he. He wasn't eating and when he did, he purged straight afterwards. He was in hell – especially after Zac. What happened with Zac tipped him right over the edge. That's why he agreed to the therapy.'

Fuck! *Zac*? *Therapy*? Everything was adding up, and it was time to formalise things. However, before Gus could caution Ada, she stood up, smiled at Gus, and said, 'Shall we go? I'll tell you everything at the station. My solicitor is meeting us there. It's time to end this.'

CHAPTER 60

At The Fort, while Ada Douglas spoke with her solicitor, Gus caught up with his team. Alice organised the CCTV and witness trawls by the uniformed officers, and Taffy kept up to date with findings from the crime scene on Shipley Glen. The incident room buzzed with invigorating excitement. Despite operating on adrenalin and coffee, Gus, for the first time since Flynn and Zac's investigations converged, felt like they were on the cusp of a breakthrough. Although concerned by the absence of reported sightings of Jo Jo, Gus was relieved that neither had there been any reported suicides. He'd be lying if he said a shiver of dread hadn't pulsed through him when he got the call out earlier. His first thoughts had been of Jo Jo and then of Bailey White. He wasn't sure his team would survive if anything happened to Jo Jo, and he sure as hell didn't know how Jessie would be affected. He was desperate to know if Compo's 'homework' had elicited any tangible information, so he phoned him.

'Comps, you got anything?'

The faint thrum of whatever music Compo was listening to filtered down the phone and Gus imagined Compo's headphones lying on his workstation amid discarded food wrappers, half full energy drink cans, and a sea of crumbs. Anxiety plagued him. His chest was tight. Each breath an effort, as if he was drowning. Every time he thought about what he'd asked Compo to do –

the extremity of the breach he'd requested – a wave of dizziness washed over him. Gus didn't like breaking the rules, but he had no choice. He had to do whatever it took to save Jo Jo and if he had the skills, he'd do it himself and leave Comps out of the equation. Compo, in stark contrast to how he'd been when he left the Fort seemed, if not exactly chipper, then certainly in better spirits.

'Hey, boss. Was just about to call you. I, em…well, like, you know, I got in.'

Now that Compo had succeeded, the enormity of what he'd asked Jo Jo to do hit Gus. He exhaled through his cotton wool chest, trying to slow his heart rate. He hoped whatever Compo had discovered would help Jo Jo. Even if it was impossible to reconcile what he'd asked Compo to do it with his conscience, he could justify it in terms of saving a life. 'Go on.'

Against a background of tapping keys, Compo shared what he'd found. 'The National Crime Agency gave Jo Jo's mum, Jo Jo, and Jessie new identities six years ago. Jo Jo's mum provided the NCA with incontrovertible digital and written evidence of her husband's criminal empire. They changed their names from Iris, Jacob, and Gracie Morris. Iris's husband was Carl Morris, an Irish criminal who built his way up the ranks in Newcastle by intimidation and brutality. He's a financial mastermind with an extensive network. Unfortunately, even with the intel provided by Iris, nothing stuck. Witnesses disappeared or changed their stories. The jurists were compromised and, in the end, despite a massive trial, Carl Morris was found not guilty.'

Compo paused, then under his breath muttered, 'Bastard.' He paused and swallowed. 'He's a real thug, boss. We need to get to Jo Jo before he does.'

Gus agreed, but so far nothing Compo told them gave him any leads. He assumed that Carl Morris was the identity of the anonymous bidder on the Slave Auction site. Reading between the lines, Gus thought it likely that Morris had come across Jo Jo and Jessie's lots on the site and recognised Jo Jo as his son. Why the hell hadn't Jo Jo trusted them enough to confide in them? Jo Jo had been 11 when his mum escaped Morris. Old enough to know what his dad was like. The lad was bright and would have worked out who would invest huge amounts of money into locating him and Jessie.

As an appalling thought occurred to him, Gus slammed his palm against the wall. Jo Jo wasn't running away from Morris. He didn't plan on taking his own life either. Jo Jo was behaving true to form. He was going to do what he always did – put Jessie before everything else. 'Compo, Jo Jo's going after Morris. You need to locate Morris before Jo Jo does.'

Before he hung up, Compo's, 'shit', followed by a flurry of keyboard sounds, reached Gus. He smiled. Compo was on the case.

Ada Douglas's solicitor poked his head out the door and gestured for Gus to come in. Straight backed, hands linked on the table in front of her, Ada smiled. She could have been about to entertain a welcome visitor to her own home, rather than be interviewed about a series of murders, including that of her husband.

Once Gus had done the introductions for the purpose of the tape, and repeated Ada's caution, her solicitor – a tall man who dwarfed his client and who had the annoying habit of looking at Gus over the top of his spectacles, making Gus feel like he was in his old head teacher's office took over.

'My client, Ada Evaline Douglas has agreed to provide a written statement after which if you insist on questioning her, she will offer a no comment interview. I will read the statement forthwith.'

Gus had suspected that the presence of Ada's solicitor would change the dynamics of their interaction and, although irritated, he was interested to hear whatever information Ada was prepared to offer. This was the start of the process, and there was plenty of time to delve deeper into Ada's story. So he leant back and ignored Ada. 'Please continue, Mr Baxter.'

The older man cleared his throat, lifted sheets of paper in both hands, and wafted them rather as if he was about to read an article from a broadsheet. '*I, Ada Evaline Douglas, confirm the veracity of the following statement.*

'In October of last year, I was approached and asked to help formulate and lead a very specific educational therapy group called Pure Life. I agreed and with one other similarly minded person and my husband Claude, I joined the group which was led by Angel. I took on the persona of See, Claude was Hear, and the other educationalist became Speak. The aim of the group was to assist confused youth and help guide them away from their abhorrent sexual deviancy and into the light. We met once or twice a week in one of the old Mills where Angel had secured an area which secured us privacy to conduct our educational programmes.'

Educational programme? Gus's gut clenched and any sympathy he had harboured for the elderly woman dissipated among thoughts of the horrors those young people had suffered at the hands of Ada Douglas and her compatriots.

'We employed various therapies to assist our young recruits, many of whom we became acquainted with from our work at Manningham All Saint's Church, and the therapies, although extreme, were successful to a large degree.'

Baxter paused in his recitation and loosened his tie a little before taking a sip of water. Like Gus, Baxter appeared disgusted by this sanitised description of what could only be called conversion therapy.

'In February of this year, I became aware that one of the Pure Life attendees – a young homeless boy by the name of Zac Ibrahim – had drawn the attention of my weak-willed husband, Claude Douglas. The pair indulged in illicit and depraved sexual acts for an unknown period. Unfortunately, the vagrant, Ibrahim, not content with assistance from the church's outreach programme, blackmailed Claude. I was unaware of this until March when Claude arrived home in the middle of the night, dishevelled and upset. He took me to the mill where he'd been meeting Zac unbeknownst to Angel or the others. Unfortunately, Zac had attacked him, and my husband had no option but to detain him in The Chair – a tool we used to reinforce our commitment to clean living – where Zac accidentally met his death.'

Gus stared at her. How could Ada justify in her own mind what she'd written? Zac Ibrahim had been strangled, and that was not accidental. Even after Claude's death, Ada was still protecting him.

Again, Baxter cleared his throat. His eyes met Gus's and for a moment, the solicitor's professional mask slipped. Gus wanted to interrupt, to fire questions at Ada, but he had to remain silent till the end of the statement.

'Unable to decide on a satisfactory course of action, Claude and I consulted with Angel and Hear. They believed Zac had found redemption in death and should be removed to a place where he would be found speedily.'

Gus's previous resolve to remain silent vanished.

'*Redemption in death*? Your husband murdered that boy and then you and your sanctimonious cronies dumped him like a pile of rubbish by a skip? How is *that* not sinful? How is *that* not perverted?' He got up, raking his fingers through his hair, his breath coming in anguished pants, and leant his knuckles on the table towering over Ada. '*You're* the sick ones, not Zac. *Your* husband took advantage of a homeless kid who was under *your* care. *Your* husband killed him.'

She smiled her weird half smile. 'We did the Lord's work, Inspector. We did the Lord's work.'

Gus slumped back into his chair, shaking his head and with a gesture towards Baxter he said. 'Go on. Get this over with.'

'Oh yes, of course. Now where was I...*found speedily*...Em...here we go.

'At that point, we recruited Flynn Arnott to replace Zac. That girl was more confused than the others. Her perversions required additional strategies to rectify. Unfortunately, Flynn soon demonstrated her incompatibility with the group and became a disruptive influence over the others. It was with regret that in order to maintain the integrity of the group, Angel, in his infinite wisdom—'

'He's not the fucking Dalai Lama, is he?' The words burst unbidden from Gus. As the solicitor spoke, a flaming ball of rage had gathered in Gus's chest. Sweat soaked his shirt and red dots flashed in front of his eyes. He wanted to crash his hands down on the table and wipe the self-righteous smirk from Ada's face – make her flinch. Make her suffer even one iota of the terror Flynn and Zac had suffered. The woman behind her mild persona was a monster!

'Inspector McGuire, please.' Baxter's voice broke on the *please*. 'Let's just get this over with, shall we?'

He was right. Prolonging this travesty of a statement served no purpose. Gus took a deep breath, clenched his fists by his thighs and nodded for Baxter to continue.

'It was with regret that in order to maintain the integrity of the group, Angel, in his infinite wisdom, opted for a more permanent punishment. The girl would never give up her perverted opinions, despite the strain it put on her family and so, with regret, Angel dispatched her and after affirmative prayers to ensure she'd take her place with God as a woman, we laid her to rest on moorland off Haworth Road.'

The fireball in Gus's chest ballooned, starving him of oxygen and crushing his heart. This was a child she was talking about. A child with so much talent, a brilliant future ahead of him, and she was justifying 'despatching' him on the fucking moor?

'Claude, at this point, became quite unmanageable and so desperate measures were required. Right until the end, Claude agreed with our decision. He knew he could not live the rest of his life as a real man, and it shamed him. This was best for him – best for all of us. So we despatched him, relieving him of the arduous burden of a lifetime of sins and reunited him with the purity of heterosexuality. We freed him.'

Baxter placed his pad on the table and exhaled as he looked at Gus. 'That's it.'

As the enormity of the confession he'd just heard swept through him like a tsunami of sordidness, Gus closed his eyes. There were so many questions raised. Who are Angel and Speak? What other teenagers had suffered at the hands of these people? The time for diplomacy and pussyfooting around was over.

'I want to know who Angel and Speak are. I need their names now.'

305

Ada shook her head and tutted. 'Dear, dear, dear, Inspector. You don't listen, do you? That' – she pointed to the statement lying on the table – 'is all you're getting from me. So, in answer to your question: no comment.'

Gus rose and gestured to the uniformed officer standing by the door. 'Arrest her for conspiracy to murder for now, but' – Gus looked at Baxter – 'expect a significant number of additional charges to follow.'

Without another glance at Ada, Gus left. He had two delusional killers to catch, Jo Jo to locate, and a psychopathic career criminal to find. Ada Douglas could wait.

CHAPTER 61

Alice had observed the interview from the observation suite and now joined Gus in the corridor outside the interview room. She gripped his arm and squeezed. 'That was bloody intense, Gus. Who the hell are these characters Angel and Speak?'

Filled with nervous energy, Gus strode along the corridor, leaving Alice to scurry along behind him. 'Don't know yet, but we will, don't you worry. We will. We need to scrutinise every male with links to Manningham All Saints Church. Those two characters have got to be involved in some capacity with the church, whether it's a religious, pastoral, or community based one. We need to find them before they decide to skip town. Get a team of CSIs and officers on standby. Our first stop is to locate the mill she told us about and get ourselves over there pronto. With any luck, this bloody Angel and his buddy Speak will be cowering there and we can nab them. If not, at least we'll get some forensic evidence to tie the bastards to the murders when we catch them.'

'Already sorted. They're on standby and awaiting notification of a confirmed location.'

Adrenalin surging through him, Gus arrived at the incident room just as Taffy burst through the door, almost banging straight into him. 'Boss, I was looking for you. Razor McCarthy was released to his home address last night, but today he missed his check in time as required by his bail conditions. The officers who've been observing him say the lights in his house have been going on and off all night. It seems like he's there, so why didn't he turn up for his sign in?'

Gus spun on his heel. That was ominous. Why would Razor McCarthy flout his bail conditions if he was at home? Then it hit Gus and all thoughts of heading to Priestley Mill faded. Carl Morris wanted to find his son and daughter and McCarthy could direct him to them.

'Shit. Carl Morris. I bet Carl Morris has got him. Come on. I hope we're not too late. Keep those CSIs on standby to process a possible scene at McCarthy's house and redirect the uniforms to Belle Hill Estate. We'll need them. We'll have to rely on a skeleton team and Compo to find the mill that Pure Life group used.'

As Gus dashed from the room, Alice on his heels, he cursed himself for not considering that perhaps Jo Jo would have gone to Razor's house, for although it wasn't confirmed yet, Gus was convinced Jo Jo would have seen Razor as a way to reach Morris. With adrenalin surging through him, Gus pounded down the stairs. 'You drive, Al, and make it fast.'

CHAPTER 62

Harsh light from the landing flooded the bedroom as the door was thrust open so hard it banged against the wall. Jo Jo screwed his eyes shut, then relaxed them and, aiming for a more natural sleep pose, he slowed his breathing down, fighting against the panic that engulfed him as he heard cushioned footsteps approach. He wanted to buy some more time. Wanted to lull Morris and his crony into a false sense of security if they believed him to be still out of it.

A waft of stale sweat, combined with the lingering scent of some upmarket perfume spray, assailed his nostrils as someone – probably Morris – crouched beside him. 'Jacob, Jacob. You awake?'

Skin crawling, Jo Jo focussed on maintaining the charade of sleep when in reality all he wanted to do was to plunge his machete into Morris's jugular. But now wasn't the right time. Before he freed the machete from his jeans, Morris and his thug would be on him, and that would be the end. He had to wait and if that meant sacrificing Razor, then so be it. After all, he owed the gangster nothing.

Satisfied that Jo Jo was still out cold, Morris got up and seconds later Jo Jo heard the distinct sound of a leather whip lashing flesh followed by an oomph that could only have come from Razor and a snort of glee that Jo Jo assumed as belonging to Morris's henchman. Straining to listen, Jo Jo tried to work out the positions of the two men in the room. If they were both near the bed and focussed on Razor, then he had a faint chance if he was very careful and moved slowly to pull the knife from his jeans and conceal it under the duvet.

Cautiously, Jo Jo moved his head to give him a view of the bed, then paused, waiting to see if his movement had been noted. When the whipping, snorting, and 'oomphing' continued, Jo Jo risked half-opening his eyes. Both men towered over Razor, the henchman further back, and Morris within lashing distance of Razor's supine body. Both men's backs were to Jo Jo. Reaching down beneath the cover, Jo Jo edged the machete from his waistband, checking to ensure the men were still otherwise occupied.

When he had the machete free, he edged it under his body so the blade was concealed, but the handle accessible. All he had to do was judge the best time to mount his attack. Jo Jo appreciated it was a long shot. So much could go wrong, but as far as Jo Jo was concerned, if he could kill Morris, Jessie would be safe, and that was enough for him. He didn't much care what happened to him as long as his sister could stay with Eileen and have birthday parties every single year.

As Morris's pounding continued and Razor's oomphs became quieter and less frequent until they were no more, Jo Jo felt sweat pool under him and soak into the carpet. What sort of animal was Morris? How could he inflict this suffering on another human being? Jo Jo had to bite his lip to stop himself from yelling out in protest. The desire to cover his ears was almost overwhelming and the strain of holding his body so still sent sharp piercing arrows up his limbs.

Finally, with the air tinged with coppery blood smells and evacuated bowels, Morris, a hysterical laugh filling the air, slumped onto the carpet. 'Get me a beer, Norm. I deserve it.'

Jo Jo's breath caught in his throat as the door slammed closed and the sound of retreating footsteps going downstairs entered the room. Now that he had Morris alone, the horror of what he had to do gripped his chest and squeezed hard. *Come on Jo Jo. You can do this*!

'I know you're awake, Jacob. Did you enjoy the performance?'

Morris's words sent ice-cold shivers up Jo Jo's spine. This had all been for his benefit? Morris had tortured the life out of Razor to put on a show. A wave of nausea caught in Jo Jo's throat, but he swallowed it back as his fingers edged towards the machete handle. This was his chance to do the world a favour. To rid it of a monster. But his limbs felt foreign and heavy, as if they were pinned to the sumptuous carpet, and it took all his inner strength to respond.

'Jo Jo. My name's Jo Jo'

Still panting, Morris barked out a laugh as he got to his feet. Jo Jo making no pretence of sleep, watched as he approached him, swinging the whip casually in his hand and sending droplets of blood over the cream carpet.

'Don't be like that, son.'

Hands slick with sweat, Jo Jo, still lying down, held Morris's gaze as he surreptitiously wiped one hand down the leg of his jeans before grabbing the handle of the machete again. Just another few steps and Morris would be close enough. All Jo Jo had to do was make him hunker down, and he'd be able to drive the knife into his neck. With a sneer, Jo Jo pursed his lips. 'I'm not your son.'

One step closer and Morris dropped to one knee beside Jo Jo. He reached out a hand as if to caress Jo Jo's cheek and in one fluid movement Jo Jo whipped the machete out, threw off the duvet, reared upwards, and with all the force he could muster drove it towards Morris. For a second, Morris's eyes widened and then he held up his arm to deflect the blow, but Jo Jo, one step ahead, screamed at the top of his lungs and rolled away. Then, yelling even louder, with an upper thrust, he plunged the knife into Morris's belly, only vaguely aware of steps pounding upstairs and into the room.

CHAPTER 63

The scream was visceral, sending lightning shivers up Gus's spine. He dived towards the house and using the key Razor's sister had provided, Gus, sweat breaking out across his forehead, unlocked the front door and wrenched it open as another shriek splintered the air. *Upstairs. It's from upstairs.* Taking the stairs two at a time, using the banister to propel him upwards more quickly, Gus reached the landing as the screech faded to be replaced by gasping sobs. Razor's room. *It's coming from Razor's room.*

Footsteps thundered up the stairs behind him, but Gus didn't care. He had to find Jo Jo. A hand landed on his shoulder, firm fingers almost piercing his skin as they spun him round, a guttural grunt accompanying the effort. Gus didn't hesitate as he crashed his forehead into his assailant's nose. Blood spurted out and landing on the carpet as the hulking brute of a man flinched and cupped his nose, releasing his grip on Gus. It wasn't Morris, but Gus had no time for more because the tortured sobs were increasing in volume behind him. So, he stepped back, raised a leg, and kicked the man square in the chest. As the man crashed backwards down the stairs, his body thumping and banging against the treads and wall as he landed. Gus spun round again and headed to the closed door of Razor's weird bedroom, not sure who he would find alive inside.

As the door hammered against the wall, Gus flicked on a light, illuminating the strangest scene he'd ever encountered. Images flicked past him as if on fast forward. An immobile and bloody lump chained to the bed, a pool of blood on the carpet, and Jo Jo, machete in hand, blood covering his T-shirt as he knelt before a man whose sneering grin taunted the boy.

A surge of rage propelled Gus forward and Carl Morris's sneering smile widened as he clutched his belly, blood oozing between his fingers. Gus could have helped the man. He could have applied pressure to the wound, he could have taken out his phone and called emergency services, he could have offered some platitudes to make Morris's transition into death easier. He did none of those things. Instead, he went over, took the machete from Jo Jo's hand and dropped it to the floor before engulfing him in a hug that absorbed his anguished sobs.

'It's over, Jo Jo. It's over. You're safe now, and so is Jessie. It's over.'

At his words, Jo Jo slumped against him, his hiccupping sobs lessening as Gus lowered him to the ground. From downstairs came the sounds of the cavalry's arrival and Gus, unable to even yell out to them, continued to hold Jo Jo close to him, breathing in the boy's life and uncaring of anything else. He closed his eyes and for long moments allowed relief to cocoon him.

'And what was wrong with our original plan? The one where you wait till Taff and I made a distraction at the back door?'

Gus opened one eye to find Alice standing over him, hands on hips and dark eyes flashing.

'Oh hey, Al. You found Morris's thug at the bottom of the stairs, didn't you?'

Alice glowered at him and swatted his head.

'Find the thug at the bottom of the stairs did you, Al? Clean up my mess will you, Al? Phone for an ambulance will you, Al? Arrest all the bad guys will you, Al.' She kicked him on the shin and added 'Meanwhile, I'll just loll about doing nowt.'

'Ow, watch it.' Gus paused. 'You have phoned the ambulance, haven't you?'

'Course I've phoned the damn ambulance and the CSIs and Nancy.' She ran her fingers through her short, spiky hair. 'You were supposed to wait, Gus. That's what we agreed. You were supposed to damn well wait till Taffy and I created the distraction at the back'

Jo Jo pulled himself away from Gus and blinked up at Alice. 'Wow, you're angry, Al.'

Alice rolled her eyes and crouched beside Jo Jo. 'I'm not angry – not with you anyway, Jo Jo. It's that pillock I'm cross with. Diving in all *Die Hard*, when, let's face it he's no Bruce Willis, is he?'

Jo Jo snorted, and Gus smiled, pleased to see some of the fear leave his eyes. Alice was good at that – deflecting tension, making things seem less serious.

'You OK, Jo Jo. You hurt?'

'Nope, I'm not hurt. But Razor's dead, and you need to arrest me for killing him.' He gestured to where Morris lay, eyes closed and silent.

Paramedics rushed into the room and while one attended to Razor, the other knelt beside Morris and having heard Jo Jo's words, she smiled at him. 'You're in luck, kid. He's not dead yet.'

Later, after Gus – with a sizeable bruise on his forehead from head butting Norm – and Jo Jo were checked over, he took Jo Jo to one side. 'Look, Jo Jo. We'll need to question you and you'll need a solicitor, but…' He looked at him, making sure the boy understood what he was telling him. 'It seems clear to me that Morris abducted you and Razor and that you acted in self-defence. You understand me?'

Jo Jo returned Gus's serious look. Eyes shining with tears, he nodded. 'Got it, Gus.'

Gus sighed. Jo Jo had no need to confess his plans to kill Carl Morris. In the end, he'd acted in self-defence, and that was all he needed to say. This was the week for bending rules, thought Gus as he nodded for Taffy to take Jo Jo down to The Fort.

'Let Compo and Jessie see him, Taffy. Cybercrimes can wait a little longer to interview him.'

Because of Gus's team's relationship with Jo Jo, the Slave Auction website cyber team investigation would liaise with Witness Protection and the Morris task force team would interview Jo Jo. With the murder of Russian citizens, the nature of the Slave Auction site, and Carl Morris's wider dealings, the case had taken on an international agenda which would take years to untangle.

Gus was glad that Carl Morris was no longer a threat to Jo Jo and Jessie. They would dismantle his network with methodical precision, which would result in the arrests and imprisonment of many of Morris's colleagues. Already, Morris's thug, Norm, was spouting forth all sorts of information in the hope of a more lenient sentence. His leads had already resulted in the team being able to round up a range of international hackers, bounty hunters, and hired assassins and key players in counterfeiting, trafficking, fraud, and other major crimes. All in all, a good haul. However, the cherry on the cake for Gus had been when he heard Morris's injuries, although severe were not life threatening. Morris would spend the rest of his life in a maximum-security prison, but more importantly, Jo Jo wouldn't have to carry the burden of having taken his father's life.

Exhausted but relieved, Gus turned his attention to the investigation he was responsible for. 'Come on, Al. We've got a mill to find.'

Alice glowered at him. 'You look more ready for bed than working.' She glared at him, hands on hips. 'You know what, though? When we find the mill, you better not go all gung-ho. We play this one by the book. This Angel and Hear might be inside and if they've got wind that we've got See in custody, they'll be desperate.'

Gus, prodding the bump on his head, sighed. 'You know what, Al. I've barely got the energy to get into the car, so if any gung-ho action is required, it's on you, OK?'

Monday

CHAPTER 64

The only thing keeping Gus going after the events of the previous day was anxiety, nervous energy, and caffeine. Compo had pulled out all the tricks and between his IT skills and the dedication of officers on the ground, they'd finally eliminated many potential mills that could have been used by the Pure Life group and Compo was convinced that this one – Priestley Mill – was the most likely of the remaining possibilities.

Gus had been in his fair share of Yorkshire mills and many had been renovated and now stood statuesque in testament to their former glory. Lister's Mill, opposite the Fort, was a business complex with state-of-the-art accommodation above, while Salt's Mill in Saltaire hosted small businesses, an art gallery, and restaurant. Priestley Mill, however, hadn't received this treatment.

At first sight, the words dark, gloomy, and forlorn sprung to mind. Only the proliferation of weeds that engulfed it supported the ramshackle fence surrounding the mill. While other deserted mills carried a sinister, threatening aura, Priestley Mill was pitiful in comparison – like the mill everyone forgot – the orphan of Bradford's textile industry – the first to fall into decline and the first to be ignored in favour of its more regal siblings. It was probably because the mill was largely ignored that made it appeal to Pure Life. Even the homeless and rough sleepers usually gave it a wide berth. From Ada's interview, they knew that inside the mill, towards the rear, Angel had secured a room which they used for their repellent conversion therapies.

As he and Alice kicked their heels, the firearms unit, in full protective armour, entered the building from the front and rear. Gus had no desire to repeat his performance at Razor McCarthy's house and the after-effects of the adrenalin rush were taking its toll on him. His limbs were heavy, and nausea made him careful how he moved his head. He suspected he might have given himself a mild concussion by head butting Norm, but it had been worth it. Alice handed him a can of Irn Bru and although it was warm, Gus was grateful and after downing it in almost one go he felt energised, if still a little dizzy.

The firearms unit was in the building two minutes when the *all clear* came through. Gus wondered what that meant. Had they been mistaken? Was this not the place Pure Life met? He, Alice, and the team of CSIs entered the mill. Disappointed that Angel and Hear appeared not to be in the building, Gus was optimistic that inside the padlocked room described by Ada, they'd find clues to their identity. Inside, the air was damp and filled with a melting pot of disharmonious odours that Gus elected not to break down into their component parts. He trudged through the meandering hollow, echoey rooms until, tucked away right at the back of the mill, two looming figures appeared through the shadows, indicating they'd reached the room.

The firearms unit leader stepped forward, his Scouse accent breaking through the hushed silence as Gus stared at the padlocked door. 'Thought we'd wait for you before cracking open the padlock.'

On tenterhooks, Gus gave an abrupt nod. 'Appreciated, mate.'

The other silent officer stepped forward, crowbar in hand, and broke the padlock. 'Easy peasy, boss.' He flexed his sizeable muscles and winked at Alice.

But neither Gus nor Alice was interested in small talk. Now the door was open, Gus and the CSI team donned their protective suits and, together with the crime scene manager, stepped forward. She held her hand up to Gus's chest. 'Uh, huh. No way, DI McGuire. Don't care what liberties you take with Sid, but you won't be taking them with me. You wait here till we're ready, OK?'

There was nothing Gus could do about that. She was right. He couldn't go blundering through her crime scene. Too much was at stake. He needed the identities of the two killers who were still at large and he needed to ensure the correct protocols were in place to ensure none of the evidence was compromised. One thing Gus wanted above all else was to ensure that Zac and Flynn's killers went down for a long, long time. When he nodded, her stern expression softened.

'Let my team in and you and your sergeant can stand by the door. I'll yell if we find anything that will point to the identity or current whereabouts of your killers.'

'Thanks. I owe you one.'

She pulled her mask up and entered, gesturing for the other three CSIs to follow. 'Doing my job, McGuire, just doing my…' Two steps into the darkened room, she stopped. 'Holy fuck…'

At her words, Gus's heart flipped a beat. On tiptoes, he attempted to peer over the CSIs' shoulders, but could see nothing. The desire to elbow his way past them was strong, yet Gus knew the protocols and instead took a step back as the CSI manager barked out orders inside.

'Skirt the room, till you're within a few feet of it, placing treads as you go.'

What the hell was 'it'? Gus exchanged a look with Alice, who shrugged in response. Neither of them could hazard a guess.

'We need lights set up pronto and' – she raised her voice – 'McGuire? If I were you, I'd get a pathologist down here. This is a scene they'll want to see first-hand.'

Alice rummaged to find her phone. 'I got it, Gus.'

'And paramedics,' the voice from inside the room continued. 'We got a live one too.'

CHAPTER 65

The paramedics rolled the barely conscious boy past Gus. They'd hooked him up to a drip and his breathing sounded laboured. 'How's he doing?'

'We need to get a move on. Will know more later.'

Gus exhaled, wishing they'd been quicker to arrive at the mill. If they'd come here first, Jo Jo would be dead. Gus tried to thrust that thought aside. Now, as he looked down at the lad, whose eyes flickered but remained closed, he said, 'Hold up. Let me see him.'

The paramedics frowned and shook their heads. 'We need to get him to the BRI.'

Gus's phone rung – *Compo! Drat, not now*! He dismissed the call and rummaged in his pocket as he jogged beside the paramedics. His phone rang again. *God's sake, Comps give me a break.* Again, he ignored it. At last, he found what he was looking for and held it up as the ambulance crew raised the trolley into the vehicle. 'Is that him? Is he the lad in this photo?'

The younger paramedic scrutinised the photo and then nodded. 'Yep, that's him. You got his name?'

'Yep, Bailey White. I'll notify his mum and get her to meet you at the hospital.'

Again, his phone buzzed and again he dismissed it. Compo could wait two seconds.

'Right, you do that, but we need to get off.'

Gus took out his phone to give Lizzie White the news that they'd found her son and alive…for now. Then he frowned as once more his phone rang. Compo was persistent. 'Hey, Comps, this better be good.'

'It is, boss. It soooo is. You know I put out a trace on the IP address that uploaded Zac Ibrahim's image to the Slave Auction site?'

'Yeah, I do, but speed it up, Comps. I've got to make another important call.'

'Aw, right, sorry.'

Gus ignored Compo's dejected tone. He didn't have time to let the geek have his moment in the spotlight. He needed to phone Lizzie White and then get back to the crime scene.

'Well, I got a hit. The PC that uploaded that file belongs to a Ricky Savage and I've got a Bradford address for him.'

That name seemed familiar, but he couldn't place it. However, Compo was still talking. 'Thing is, this guy's in the system. A GBH a couple of years ago and a few domestic abuse house calls over the past ten years, buuuut…'

The excitement in Compo's tone made Gus visualise him, dancing in his computer chair. 'Go on, Comps.'

'He's noted as next of kin on an active missing person's report.'

Before Compo finished his sentence, the pieces fell into place. 'Ricky Savage is Bailey White's dad, isn't he?'

The dejected tone was back. 'How did you know that?'

'Because I've just seen Bailey White being loaded onto an ambulance en route to the BRI. Get an officer down to the hospital pronto. I want that kid put in protective custody. The only person to get near him is his mum, Lizzie White, OK? I'll phone her now. In the meantime, get a photo of Ricky Savage over to me, Comps. We found a dead one in the mill too, and it might be him.'

As he called Lizzie, Alice watched the ambulance drive off and when he was done, they turned as one to walk back into the mill.

'Well, at least that's good news.' Kicking a stone with more ferocity than her words required, Alice exhaled. 'You ever wonder how long you can do this job, Gus? I mean, it takes its toll, doesn't it? And it's like a conveyor belt. No sooner have we got a sicko packed off to prison than another even sicker one jumps on.'

She had a point. They lived in a world of darkness where good people got hurt. Sometimes they made deals with the devil just to get justice. Sometimes – rarely, but sometimes, it all got too fucking much for them to handle. When no reassuring words came to mind, he rested his hand on her shoulder and squeezed. Sometimes all they had was each other.

'Angus, Angus. Could you guide me to the unfortunate deceased?'

Alice's lips twitched at Gus's, 'Bloody hell, not my damn dad.' And Gus grinned at her. They'd make it through another day and they'd be OK. 'Over here, Dad. And, just to be clear, I'm not so sure this one's an 'unfortunate' deceased. This one might have got what he deserved.'

Fergus McGuire frowned, and his eyes raked over first his son and then Alice, before, with a gentle nod, he smiled. 'This has been a tough one, Angus, but Bradford should be glad you two are on the case.'

As the trio walked through the dank building, sticking to the sides of the concrete paths where, regardless of the dark, shoots of greenery still strove to reach the light. In some ways, that's what he and his team did. They strove to escape the darkness and bring more light to the world. In the chaos after they'd found Bailey White, Gus had yet to set eyes on the dead body or indeed set foot in the room used by Pure Life. Preserving the crime scene had become secondary to preserving life. Thus, although the CSIs would continue to gather forensic evidence, the crime scene wasn't the pristine one they'd banished him from earlier. He and Alice changed into their bunny suits while his dad donned one of the XXXXL ones and stepped inside, adhering to the metal plates placed by the CSIs.

While they whipped Dr McGuire off to study the body in situ, Gus took a moment to observe the room. As with old mill buildings, the room was cavernous with high ceilings. A row of small windows high up along the external wall was the only source of natural light, but as Gus scanned the walls, he saw spotlights had been fixed to the two front corners and were directed towards a line of six chairs that faced a raised dais. The CSIs had dotted yellow crime scene identification markers around the chairs, indicating a preponderance of forensic evidence. The crime scene manager approached. 'We identified the deceased through fingerprints. He's…'

'Ricky Savage?'

The CSI frowned. 'How the hell did you know that?'

It seemed like they'd uncovered the identity of either Hear or Angel. One down, one still to find. 'Long story. Tell me what else you've found.'

'Luminol shows blood trace around those chairs and in a couple of areas closer to the raised platform. Not enough to be life threatening, but interesting when you add in the torture chair in the sealed of room to the right. We're also getting a lot of prints from those chairs.'

Gus looked at the CSI who was working on obtaining fingerprints from the chairs. 'He's lifting them from under the chair?'

'Yeah, that's what it looks like. The mobile print scanner has already found matches on the seats to Flynn Arnett, Zac Ibrahim, and Bailey White – all three prints were discovered on the underside of the chairs, which suggests—'

'These lads were sitting in the chairs and gripping the edges.'

'Bullseye. We also matched prints on the chair backs' – she made a gripping movement with her fingers – 'as if they'd been lifted by the back. Those matched Ada Douglas, her husband Claude Douglas, and our dead man, Ricky Savage.' Her eyes twinkled as if ready for a *ta da* moment. 'Of course, there are other prints which don't correspond to anyone in the system. It'll be your job to locate them…'

That Savage's prints were on the rear of the chairs rather than the seat again pointed to him being either Angel or Hear. All that remained was to discover who killed him.

The CSI was still talking when Gus got his phone out and dialled Compo. 'Comps, you identified who uploaded Zac's clip to the site? Have you had any luck discovering who bought that auction lot?'

'Yes – just working on it…' His voice faded away and then 'Bloody jeepsters, Gus. You won't believe who bought it…'

CHAPTER 66

Zac Ibrahim's dad opened the door to Gus's hammering. 'Where is he, Mr Ibrahim? Where is Nasir?'

Behind him, Mr Ibrahim's wife hovered, her eyes wide and her fingers plucking at the ends of her dupatta. Mr Ibrahim, lips curled, raised his chin. 'Why should I tell you?'

Gus had no time to play games. After Compo's earlier revelation that Nasir Ibrahim had bought the auction lot of his brother's death from the Slave Auction site, things had become a lot clearer. Nasir's antipathy towards the officers investigating his brother's death, his involvement with Manningham All Saints Church outreach projects, his active anti-gay sentiments, his involvement in campaigns against schools supporting LGBTQ+ inclusive curriculums – all of it made him a homophobe and a hateful brother – but did it also make him a murderer? 'Because if you don't, you'll end up in a cell on obstruction charges. Where is your son?'

Colour suffused the older man's cheeks as he crossed his arms over his chest. 'Arrest me then. Go on. Do it. Let's see what my community will think of you arresting an old man dying of cancer for protecting the only son he has left.'

Shit. The old bugger had pulled out a trump card. Gus stabbed a finger at him, his own cheeks flaming red now too. 'If one other person dies because of your inaction, Mr Ibrahim, cancer or no cancer, I will charge you with obstruction.'

Without waiting for a response, Gus spun on his heel and marched back the way he'd come, only to be halted by a soft voice calling his name.

'DI McGuire, please…'

He turned and saw Mrs Ibrahim, scarf pulled over her hair, standing in front of her husband on the doorstep. Her eyes seemed fevered to Gus – hot and anxious, but looking beyond that, he saw determination. 'I've lost one son, Detective. I won't lose another, and I certainly won't lose my husband. Nasir rents the house next door.' She inclined her head to the adjoining terraced house. 'I think he's at home.'

Then she turned, linked her arm through her husband's and helped him back indoors. Two frail old people united in grief, weighed down by regret and tortured by what was about to happen. Gus studied with interest the house that Nasir Ibrahim rented. Why was Ibrahim – a man with a decent disposable income at hand – renting a house next door to his parents while registered as living with them? The house was like any other three-bedroomed terraced home in the street. It shared a wall with his parent's' house while an alleyway separated it from his neighbours on the far side, allowing both parties access to the rear of their homes.

Gus raised his eyes at Alice, who nodded and began directing the uniformed officers who had accompanied them to move to the rear, while she and Gus approached the front door. The small patch of lawn at the front had been cut and there were signs that someone had been weeding the small flowerbeds to the side. Blinds shielded the front window, making it impossible to see if anyone was in the living room or not. The two front-facing upstairs bedrooms were also curtained. Gus hesitated on the doorstep, listening for any noises inside. When he heard none, he hammered on the door. No responses and no movement, so he poked open the letter box and peered along the hallway to the open kitchen door at the end.

'What do you reckon, Al?'

Alice shrugged. 'We need to get in, but God knows how long a warrant will take – especially on a Sunday.'

Gus exhaled and considered. This investigation had forced him to take actions he would never have before. He'd ordered one of his officers to break the law. He'd coached a suspect to be creative with the truth, so what harm could one more rule break make?

'I smell…'

But Alice was already shaking her head. 'Oh no you don't. No more, Gus. No damn more of this. We can't just go around breaking rules because it's expedient.'

Her cheeks were flushed, and she stamped her foot to emphasise her point. Gus was torn. Above everyone else, he valued Alice's professional opinion, but…

'Detective McGuire?' The same soft voice from earlier interrupted his thoughts. Mrs Ibrahim stood, a tear rolling down her cheek, her eyes filled with a depth of sadness Gus had never witnessed before. 'Here. It's the key. You need to stop this before anyone else dies.'

Gus took the key. 'You're very brave, Mrs Ibrahim.'

She shook her head. 'If I was brave, Detective McGuire, I'd still have two sons.' And with that, she turned and made her weary way back indoors, closing the door behind her with a final snap.

'Happy?' Gus spat the word at Alice, still hurt by her earlier admonishment.

'As Larry…now let's do this.'

Gus gestured to the two officers waiting by the gate. 'When we're in, you open the back door and clear the downstairs. DS Cooper and myself will clear upstairs, OK?'

The key turned in the lock and, with a sense of déjà vu, Gus pushed the door open. Unlike Razor's house with its lush carpets, this property had bare floorboards which the door skimmed over, eliciting a loud scraping sound. Once inside, he and Alice paused, allowing the house to settle around them. A faint moan floated downstairs, followed by a mumbled voice. Gus gestured to Alice and began creeping upstairs, Alice behind, his ears straining to identify the location of the voice. At the top landing, he turned towards the bedroom at the back of the house. The door was closed, yet the sound of low mumbles, followed by moans and interspersed by a strange slapping sound was clear. Edging closer, Taser in hand, Gus reached out, flicked the handle, and kicked the door open to one of the strangest sights he'd ever seen. A naked Nasir Ibrahim stood facing the back wall where an enormous mirror hung, with a whip in one hand. Bloody welts covered his back and as he caught sight of Gus and Alice's reflections, his smile widened. Raising his hand, he brought the whip down sharply over the opposite shoulder. When it hit his skin, droplets of blood flew through the air, and both Alice and Gus flinched in harmony.

'Put it down, Nasir. Put the whip down.'

Nasir turned and, arms stretched to the side, erection hard, he dropped it, like a rapper dropping a mic and stared them out – daring them to avert their eyes. Gus moved forward and kicked the whip away, but catching him off balance, Ibrahim shoved him backwards into Alice, who landed on her backside. As he darted downstairs, he grabbed a short dressing gown from a hook on the door.

'Aw! Noooo.' Gus spun on his heel, jumped over the still sprawling Alice and dashed after Ibrahim. Did the idiot think he could escape dressed in only a bloody dressing gown that barely covered his arse, never mind his erection?

Taking the last three steps in one almighty jump, Gus was just in time to see the tail of Ibrahim's robe disappear through the front door, his hairy legs pumping as fast as they could. Gus landed on the mat, sprinted forwards and out the door, and eager not to turn the chase into a fiasco that would reach the front pages of the *T&A*, he dived through the air and landed on the fleeing man's back, sending him crashing to the floor, where he provided cushioning for Gus's landing. Winded, the two lay for a moment, both breathing hard and when Gus looked up, he saw two smirking uniformed officers, cuffs in hand and Nasir Ibrahim's parents peering over the fence behind them.

Struggling to his feet, Gus scowled. 'Arrest him and get him down to The Fort.'

Still panting, he walked away. Then, reconsidering, he turned. 'And get him covered up.'

As the officers dragged Ibrahim to his feet, he sneered at Gus. 'No matter what you do to me, I will be found innocent in the eyes of God – in the eyes of Allah. I have done God's work.'

Gus's stomach muscles tightened, and his fists clenched as he studied him. Had that maniacal look always been in his eyes? Had it been there when he'd interviewed him about his brother's death? Had he missed something?

Alice appeared at his side, her fingers plucking at his sleeve. 'Don't do this to yourself, Gus. You couldn't have known what he was like – what he was capable of. None of us did. Not one of us.'

Logically, he accepted what Alice said, but still his mind flashed back to Zac Ibrahim's body on the slab in his dad's post-mortem suite and although he accepted that he couldn't have saved Zac, he couldn't squash the feeling that he'd failed Flynn Arnett and the others. He'd interviewed Nasir Ibrahim and Claude and Ada Douglas and hadn't seen the insanity lurking behind their eyes. If he had, they could have saved lives. Instead of replying, Gus nodded and marched back into the house. 'Get the CSIs here. I want this wrapped up as tight as a racoon's scrotum. This lot are all going down.'

CHAPTER 67

With the CSIs processing Nasir Ibrahim's house, Gus took his time absorbing the incriminating evidence Ibrahim had left behind. Still reeling from the extent of Ibrahim's delusions and the union of disturbed minds that had led to so many deaths and so much anguish, Gus refused to balk as he studied the images that covered the walls of Ibrahim's bedroom. Seeing photos of Claude, Zac, Flynn, and others shackled to the sturdy wooden chair they'd found in Priestley Mill was chilling. In other images the victims knelt, heads bowed, before hooded figures dressed in robes that reminded Gus of the Ku Klux Klan.

The strange, ritualistic set up of mirrors, positioned to allow Ibrahim to observe himself from the front and the back during acts of self-flagellation, with candles and the photographic shrine, sapped Gus's energy.

How could the human mind splinter so badly? So definitively that it lost all sense of reality? He had no doubt that insanity drove Ibrahim's actions but trying to understand how others could be so readily absorbed into his fanatical obsession was beyond Gus. The contradictions between Ibrahim's zealous commitment to eradicating what he considered to be fleshly deviance and his own self-flagellation, with its distinct sexual gratification, baffled Gus. What went on in the man's mind to allow him to justify his own carnal impulses yet condemn others to Draconian therapies and ultimately

334

death. That Nasir Ibrahim was the mysterious Angel mentioned in Flynn's diary and referred to by Ada was not in doubt.

As he watched the CSIs bag Ibrahim's sheets for forensic analysis, Gus exhaled. His shoulders, weighed down with sadness, ached. His head throbbed and deep in his chest lurked a festering boil that needed lancing. The only way to do that was to wind up the investigation and tie the evidence so tightly it couldn't be severed. He needed to do that for the victims. He had to do that for their families, and he also needed to do that for himself and the team. They'd caught those responsible, and now their job was to make sure they remained incarcerated.

CHAPTER 68

Hordes of hooded people, cat-o'-nine-tails in their hands, descended on him, forcing him to run. Their leering eyes threatening behind their masks and with every expert flick of their wrists, a crack rent the malevolent night air. No matter how fast he moved, their slow insistent progress kept them at his heels, like silent hounds salivating before pouncing. Ahead, an ornate four-poster bed loomed, spotlighted by flickering candles encircling it as if in some sordid welcome to death. The sheets were blood speckled and from each corner, thick metal shackles with inch long spikes trailed. Around the bed, cold blue figures shimmered, their feet not quite touching the ground, their faces unsmiling as they beckoned him closer – Zac Ibrahim, Flynn Arnett, Claude Douglas, Razor McCarthy, Jo Jo's mum – each one condemning him to his deserved fate.

He tried to change direction, but wherever he looked, the whip-wielding, hooded figures descended on him, their voices a low magnetic chant, their eyes piercing him as sharply as their whips would. The chants got louder to the accompanying backtrack of whip cracks and laughter. Rats skittered nearby and his limbs became heavier as if he was scrambling through setting concrete, each step and effort. And all the while his heart hammered in his chest, his lungs on fire. As they got closer – within arm's reach now – their snatching, gripping fingers scraped his arms, his legs, and icy fear stopped his heart…dead…

Gus woke up, his chest heaving, panicky flutters making him strain to catch breath. Perspiration drenched his jumper and his legs wobbled when he tried to move them. For a nano-second his startled eyes strained to make out his surroundings and as he recognised the familiar incident room, with his team dotted around working at various desks, his breathing eased. His taut chest loosened, and the palpitations stopped. Just a nightmare. He was safe. He was at work.

Gus grabbed his water bottle and devoured its contents as he tried to put the nightmare behind him and gear himself up for the work ahead. His head throbbed and wafts of dried sweat drifted to his nostrils. He was drained. There was nothing left in the tank and as that realisation hit, he pulled open his desk drawer and ran his fingers over the printed copy of his application to Police Scotland. Should he just send it? Would being closer to Billy ease the pain that resided in his chest? He wasn't foolish enough to believe that Scotland would have fewer murders, or that they'd take less of a toll on him. However, being close to his son was becoming as important to him as breathing. He closed the drawer. Before he made any final decisions, he had work to do – an investigation to wrap up and victims and their families to avenge. What Angel, AKA Nasir Ibrahim had instigated had far-reaching consequences. It was Gus's job to make sure that the investigation was airtight, and that's what he'd do.

Gus watched his team working. Alice, pale and with many more frown lines, as well as deeper, unseen scars, than she'd had when they'd first met years ago. She was still lively and energetic, but her spark shone dimmer and less frequently.

Taffy, the newest team member was enthusiastic, dedicated and would move up the ranks swiftly, yet today, battering his keyboard, his shoulders slumped, and his smile was nowhere to be seen – this case had added another nick to the lad's heart.

Compo too was subdued. He'd discarded his beanie hat on the floor near his rucksack. No music for him today as he trawled through evidence log after evidence log ensuring that all the evidence for both the Carl Morris case and the Pure Life cases were airtight.

Yes, they'd caught Angel and had foiled Carl Morris's attempts to reclaim Jo Jo and Jessie, but nobody felt like celebrating, because each of them had lost a little bit of their soul and that was the real toll of the job. Gus considered how he'd feel if he upped sticks and left – moved away. They weren't only his team; they were his best friends too, and they'd shared so much. Then, of course, there was Mo and his family and his mum and dad and Nancy. They could survive without him. The real question was: *could he survive without them*?

He stood up, moved to the front, and stopped before the incident boards. 'Hey, guys! Let's just catch up on where we are with everything. I know cybercrimes have taken over the Morris/McCarthy investigation, but we've got a vested interest in it and Compo here has been dividing his time between that investigation and our murder investigation into the Pure Life group. So Compo, over to you.'

Compo swung his chair round until he faced the others and cleared his throat. A tomato-coloured flush bloomed across his cheeks as he prepared to address his colleagues. 'At present, Carl Morris is in the BRI, but should make a full recovery. The evidence provided by his henchman, Norman Robertson, ties Morris to historic crimes in Newcastle namely, the murder of people who helped Jo Jo's family escape; Jo Jo's school friend – Amar Farooqi, his teacher Roxanne Turner, and the bodyguard, Gabe McPherson, employed by Morris to restrict her movements. Further evidence ties Morris to the murder of the Russian hacker known only as Irena. Her distraught boyfriend Artemy Ivanov has struck a deal with Interpol and will provide evidence of Morris's interest in the Slave Auction site. Jo Jo's testimony regarding the systematic beating which resulted in the death of Razor McCarthy will put him behind bars for a long time. Robertson also backs up Jo Jo's account of what happened at McCarthy's house. Other charges of incarceration, stalking, and historic murder charges. Carl Morris won't see the light of day again.'

Although this was excellent news, the team remained subdued. Would Morris's incarceration make up for all the harm he'd done? All the lives he'd destroyed? The pain he'd caused? Gus doubted it. Morris's legacy would taint many lives for a long time, but at least he could do no more physical harm to innocent people. Would it have been better if Jo Jo had killed him? Gus shuddered at the thought. Taking someone's life had devastating consequences and Jo Jo had enough to deal with without having to bear that load, too.

'Sooooo,' Taffy hand in the air, bounced in his seat like a kid at school desperate to be heard. 'Who was the brains behind the Slave Auction site? No way Razor McCarthy was smart enough to carry that one off.'

Compo exchanged a glance with Gus. 'No, Taff, that was – you know? That bloody…' Compo exhaled, blowing his cheeks out like puffer fish so Gus came to his rescue.

'As expected, that was Zodiac, Taff. The site's been active since before we ever caught wind of Zodiac's activities. Cybercrimes have their work cut out identifying all those victims.'

Taffy groaned. 'Aw, no. Please don't say we're gonna do more interviews...Not with Zodiac?'

'No. No more Zodiac interviews. That's not happening.' As soon as Zodiac's involvement of the crime had been confirmed, Gus absolved his team from any involvement in the information-gathering process. His team had suffered too much during Zodiac, Pisces, and Leo's reign of horror, and he wouldn't subject them to that again. 'So, moving onto the Angel, Hear, See, and Speak investigation. Alice, you want to update?'

Alice's scowl was ferocious as she jumped to her feet and headed to the front of the room. 'Hate these bloody sickos with their stupid damn names. It's like they're either hiding behind them or getting off by elevating themselves above the rest of us. Bloody *Angel* indeed.'

Although her outrage failed to hide the deep-seated despair that kept her pacing at night, keeping Gus awake, it lightened the tension in the incident room. And they needed that. Pulling herself to her full height, Alice began.

'We're awaiting a psych evaluation for Nasir Ibrahim.' Her expressive shrug showed which way she expected that would go. 'Ada Douglas AKA See is also being evaluated.' She pursed her lips. 'We should prepare for them both to be diagnosed insane. But, hey ho, at least the fuckers are off the streets, eh?'

Despite her flippant words, Gus knew that, like the rest of them Alice's thoughts lay with the victims' families. How were they supposed to get closure when their relatives' killers were locked up in some cushy psychiatric unit? First Zodiac. Now Angel and See would evade a trial for their crimes, and that didn't seem fair. Who would be held accountable?

'As for the other two from that little band of torturers, well they're both dead. The motivation appears to be their belief that conversion therapy would cleanse the world of – in Ada Douglas's words – aberrant behaviour. Nasir Ibrahim contacted them through his involvement in outreach work at Manningham All Saints Church and recruited the three of them to his cause.'

'Bastard! Bastard!' Taffy's words ricocheted around the room as he jumped to his feet. 'What the hell? That bastard wasn't lacking in the perversion department, was he? Can't believe he put his own brother through that warped therapy.'

Gus placed a hand on Taffy's arm and squeezed. 'One thing we learnt from Ibrahim's ravings when we brought him in was that Zac wanted to reconnect with his brother. That's why he went along with the group. He wanted to be part of the family again. He was easy pickings for someone as manipulative as Nasir Ibrahim.'

Alice cleared her throat. 'Yes, well, that didn't work out well for him, did it?' She dragged a chair over and sat down. 'Ada and Claude Douglas had their own problems. Claude was gay and was conflicted about his sexuality for decades. Ada saw Angel and his conversion therapy to cleanse her husband once and for all.'

'Well, that backfired, didn't it?' Compo's interjection was unexpected, but accurate.

'Yep, you got that right, Comps. Seems Claude became attracted to Zac and met him privately. In some sort of sex encounter gone wrong, Claude killed Zac and, like he did every time, he contacted his wife to help clear up his mess. Of course, the rest of the team were happy to help. At this point, they recruited Flynn Arnett, not realising he had his own agenda. Flynn wanted to expose

Pure Life and was documenting every warped and deranged thing the group did.'

'So, did they find out about Flynn's real agenda?'

Alice looked at Taffy. 'We can't corroborate that. Neither Nasir nor Douglas have confirmed that. But whatever happened, Flynn ended up dead at their hands. However, we've spoken to Bailey White who has been and is recovering well at home, and he's provided us with valuable information. What we now know that Nasir Ibrahim killed Ricky Savage, AKA Speak. Bailey White is Savage's son. He forced Bailey to join Pure Life and forced him to stay away from his mum. Hence, the missing person's report filed by Lizzie White. Bailey was living at his dad's and attending the group. However, after seeing his friend Ali tortured by Angel followed by Flynn's disappearance from the next meeting, Bailey tried to extricate himself from the group. When Flynn's body was found, Bailey didn't know what to do. He didn't want to involve his mum because of his dad's violent nature, so he slept rough for a few days. Finally, he decided he'd threaten to expose the group if Savage didn't let him leave. He met up with Savage and Nasir Ibrahim in Priestley Mill and according to him, Angel "went all psycho with a whip and a knife". The only reason Bailey is alive is because he played dead.'

Gus had visited Lizzie White at the BRI and although Bailey was still in a fragile state, he would recover physically, however it would be a long journey for him mentally. When he'd arrived, Gus had been surprised to see a boy called Ali holding Bailey's hand and Jo Jo and Idris sitting beside him. That Bailey would have support from his school friends was good. This little group of four could help each other heal and in addition, Ali's corroborating statement about the Pure Life group's activities added weight to their case.

'So, what was Ricky Savage's reasons for joining the group?'

'I'll take this, Al.' Gus turned to Compo. 'According to his ex-wife, Savage was a homophobe and couldn't bear for his boy to be gay. Alongside this, Savage had a history of violence – so maybe it was a combination of his homophobia and his violent nature that enticed him to join. Maybe he got off on all the power. Wearing a hood and all the rest of it.'

Alice chimed in. 'So, to round things off, we suspect that Claude Douglas was having second thoughts about the group. Gus, you said he seemed to be upset about Flynn's death when you spoke with him the other day.'

'Yeah, that's right. He seemed deflated – combative with Ada and sad about Flynn's death. That combined with the post-mortem report which showed Claude had anorexia and the recent self-harm scars to his thighs and wrists supports the theory that he may have become a liability to the group. One which Ada and Angel couldn't allow to live. Ada knew Claude was dead before we arrived at her house. She was ready for us. I think she finally found living a lie to be too much for her.'

CHAPTER 69

Angel

They think they've caught me. That this is the end of Pure Life. What they don't understand is that a man like me – an Angel like me – can find monkeys anywhere. It doesn't matter where they put me, I'll thrive. I'll find soulmates, I'll find like-minded people and I'll also seek out those who live aberrant lifestyles.

I watch them. They don't know what to think of me. My smile disconcerts them. My scarred body perturbs them. They don't understand the release that pain offers to the tortured soul. They may have taken my whips, they may keep me locked up, but they can never – NEVER – stop me from my bloodletting. Killing Speak taught me that spilling my own blood wasn't the only way to be emancipated. So, now I look forward to my time on sabbatical. That's what I consider my incarceration to be – a sabbatical during which time, I will study and perfect new methods to punish the unworthy, the impure. New methods to alleviate my internal pain and I will be reborn!

Pure Life *will* be revived, for I am the Angel. The Angle of Death. The Angel of Mercy. The Angel of Vengeance and I *will* prevail!

CHAPTER 70

With the warm sun on his back, Bingo by his heels, and no work to think of, the tensions of the past few weeks faded. Yes, he carried the mental scars of the investigation his team had just closed and yes, he could have hoped for better results, but for now, he was content that the bad guys were either dead or locked up. That was a win.

'Come on, Bingo. I can see the gang up by the bandstand. It's picnic time.'

Although looking forward to this downtime, Gus had a secret to share and who knew how they'd take it? In a few minutes, he'd find out. As he neared the group, he paused, drinking in the image of his extended family sprawled in small groups on picnic blankets. Alice, Mo, and Compo were laying out the food and drinks. *Not sure having Compo on that particular job is a great idea.* The kids: Jo Jo, Jessie, Idris, Zarqa, Bailey, and the rest of Mo's brood sat to the side, eyes glued to their phones, effectively blocking out the adult activity around them. Taffy was walking down the hill towards them, his hand clasped round that of a tall woman in a sundress. *At last, we get to meet Taffy's girlfriend*!

With Bingo excitedly erupting into the middle of the picnic, Gus raised his voice.

'Hi, guys, before we get started on the food…' He looked at Compo who flushed and replaced the samosa he'd just snatched from a plate piled with them. 'I've got an announcement to make.'

He glanced round at the group. Each of them his friend, each of them an important part of his life, and he felt a tingle at the back of his throat. *Shit! Not now. No damn crying!* The lump in his throat felt too big to dislodge. He swallowed. Then swallowed again. This was hard. So damn hard. He cleared his throat.

'There's no easy way to say this. No way to sugar-coat it, so I'm just going to spit it out. I've asked for a transfer to Police Scotland and yesterday my application was accepted.'

The tableau before him floated in front of his eyes, each of his friend's faces hovering in slow motion before him. Alice's horrified frown, the tears rolling down Compo's cheek, Mo's angry glare, Taffy's mouth formed into a perfect O.

Then his phone rang. Thankful for the distraction, he answered.

'What? Stop, Mum. Breathe. What's wrong?'

Heart thundering, a spear pierced his heart, and he slumped. A groan left his lips. In that split second, that one phone call had changed his life forever. He took off running, yelling at the others. 'It's my dad. Look after Bingo for me!'

Acknowledgements

Unjust Bias means a lot to me and it was at times difficult to write, but I felt it was also a very necessary novel to write.

In the 80s as a student, I was an active campaigner for Gay rights, particularly in the weight of the AIDS epidemic and with the subsequent introduction of the draconian Clause 28 legislation.

I had assumed that forty years later, I wouldn't have to be concerned with LGBTQ+ equality, but it seems I was wrong.

Once more a marginalized community is being used as a ping pong ball for politicians to wrangle over and it saddens me to witness the hate and regressive attitudes that appear to becoming increasingly prevalent with the Trans debate.

Whilst, I'm unlikely to go on demos or protests nowadays, I will still champion LGBTQ+ rights wherever possible and my writing is one of the ways in which I can do it. As Baroness Lola Young once tweeted: *'writing novels as a form of activism! Part of a long tradition of lit/art engaging with difficult problems, raising awareness. Once you know, you can't claim ignorance'*

I like to think that crime fiction as a genre takes that on board by addressing such issues.

I want to thank all those members of the LGBTQ+ community and their supporters who are committed to change, despite the sometimes, intemperate attitudes they sometimes face and who through their activism, make this world a better place for my grandchildren and great grandchildren to live.

347

I also want to thank my amazing family who are brilliantly supportive when I get in the zone and who get me out of my many technical 'fankles'

Cherie Foxley my amazing cover designer deserves huge thanks for putting up with my demands and producing such a fantastic cover as do my Amazing BETA readers, Carrie Wakelin and Maureen Webb whose attention to detail always improves the book and of course my lovely, supportive ARC readers who keep my spirits high deserve many thanks.

If you enjoyed UNJUST BIAS, please consider leaving a short review.

Here's till next time

Best Wishes

Liz Mistry

If you want to connect with Liz, you can do so on:

Twitter: @LizMistryAuthor

Facebook: LizMistryBooks

Amazon: https://amzn.to/2xhdOgG

Website : https://www.lizmistry.com/

MORE BOOKS BY LIZ MISTRY

DI GUS MCGUIRE SERIES:

UNQUIET SOULS
UNCOILED LIES
UNTAINTED BLOOD
UNCOMMON CRUELTY
UNSPOKEN TRUTHS
UNSEEN EVIL
UNBOUND TIES
UNJUST BIAS

DS NIKKI PAREKH SERIES:

LAST REQUEST
BROKEN SILENCE
DARK MEMORIES
BLOOD GAMES
DYING BREATH

Printed in Great Britain
by Amazon

86258309R00203